A SENSE OF ANCIENT GODS

A SENSE OF ANCIENT GODS

Anthony Pacitto

Wine Jar Press

Wine Jar Press

Typeset by Palimpsest Book Production Ltd, Falkirk, Stirlingshire

paperback ISBN 978-1-9998838-2-9
ebook ISBN 978-1-9998838-1-2

www.winejarpress.com

For Anna Chiara

Ce vaje, ma nen ciùfele.

(Ciociaro Dialect)

I don't care a straw who publishes me and who doesn't, nor where nor how, nor when nor why. I'll contrive, if I can, to get enough money to live on. But I don't take myself seriously, except between 8.00 and 10.00 a.m., and at the stroke of midnight . . . The Mediterranean is glittering blue today.

D. H. Lawrence

SUISSE
OSTERREICH
MAGYAR.
SLOVENIJA
Udine
Trieste
HRVATSKA
Milano
Brescia
Verona
Venezia
FRANCE
Torino
Parma
Genova
Bologna
Ravenna
BOSNA I HERZ.
San Remo
M.
Florence
Terni
Rome
Picinisco
Cassino
Bari
Sassari
Naples
Taranto
Capri
Lecce
Cagliari
Palermo
Messina
Taormina
Catania
ALG.
100 km
TUNISIA
60 mi
© d-maps.com

Historical and Literary References.

People, Places, Events, Texts, Myth, Topics.

Compton Mackenzie, (Sir). (1883-1972) 8, 139
Scottish writer, biographer, raconteur and baronet, he met and befriended Lawrence in 1914. He invited Lawrence to Capri where he had a house, the Villa Solitaria. After the war, Lawrence took him up on his offer, and Mackenzie found him a little apartment to stay in. They very much enjoyed each other's company, unusual for Lawrence, and he and Frieda spent many happy evenings at Villa Solitaria, singing folksongs and passing the hours.

Gabriele D'Annunzio, (1863-1938) 8, 65
Writer, poet, playwright, orator, womaniser, patriot, adventurer, famous for his many trysts, affairs, conquests and relationships—the first with the actress Eleonora Duse. D'Annunzio is now best remembered for almost single-handedly dragging Italy into the First World War, whipping up the crowds in Milan and Rome with his mesmerising patriotic oratory.

At the outbreak of hostilities he immediately enlisted, joining the aviators regiment and living up to his reputation with daring missions against the Austrians which included leading a squadron over Vienna, not to bomb it, but to drop leaflets. He never ceased to stir the Italian spirit, not just by his example, but by touring the front lines, rallying the troops, especially in Italy's darkest hour after the defeat at Caporetto in 1917.

Lawrence read him in the Italian.

Fiume, 8

After the Italian victory of 1918, D'Annunzio couldn't give it all up, and he soon found another patriotic cause to throw himself into. Fiume, a mainly Italian city on the Adriatic coast in what is now Croatia, had been promised to Italy as part of The Treaty of London to bring Italy into the war on the Allied side. But at Versailles it was not delivered, mainly due to President Wilson's objection. D'Annunzio denounced Versailles as a betrayal, marched into Fiume at the head of a rabble army of ex-combatants and seized the disputed city, setting himself up as de facto governor, or Duce. Here he remained for fifteen months until eventually forced out by the regular army. The disputants reached a compromise, the city was granted special international status — The Free State of Fiume — which lasted till the Second World War.

Isadora Duncan, (1877-1927) 11

Born in California, moved to Europe, became probably the most famous female dancer of the era—dance as sacred art. She would step around, barefoot, dressed in a short Greek tunic, arms swept back, adopting seductive dramatic poses.

Katherine Mansfield, (1888-1923) 11, 319

Short story writer, born in New Zealand, but came to live in England to write. In 1911 she started a long intermittent relationship with journalist and critic John Middleton Murry. They were perhaps Lawrence and Frieda's closest friends for a time, and when Lawrence and Frieda went to live in Cornwall, they took the next door cottage. It was supposed to be a sort of idyll, but Katherine, very nervous and highly-strung, soon hated it, and they left again. Katherine died of TB in France in 1923.

Lady Ottoline Morrel, (1873-1938) 12

Literary hostess, socialite, garden designer. At their London home, 44 Bedford Sq., and their country house, Garsington Manor, Oxford, she and her husband Philip kept open house for writers, artists, free thinkers, pacifists — Virginia Woolf, Yeats, Augustus John, Strachey, and many others, Lawrence among them. Her naturally aristocratic manner and comportment however made her perfect material for literary caricature — Mrs Bidlake in Huxley's *Point Counter Point*, Hermione Roddice in Lawrence's *Women in Love,* and others. She threatened to sue Lawrence for libel over it.

Norman Douglas, (1868-1952) 12, 128

Novelist and travel writer. After a brush with the law, he escaped England in 1916, spending most of the rest of his life in Italy—Naples, Capri, and Florence. His novel *South Wind,* 1917, was a thinly disguised account of the goings-on on the Isle of Capri. Lawrence spent about three weeks in company with him and Maurice Magnus in Florence in Nov-Dec 1919. Douglas makes an appearance as the boozy Argyle in Lawrence's 1922 novel *Aaron's Rod.*

Martin Secker, (1882-1978) 13, 114

After the banning of Lawrence's novel *The Rainbow* in 1915 for obscenity, no-one was prepared to risk publishing the sequel, *Women in Love.* Finally, London publisher Martin Secker agreed to take it on. He eventually succeeded, and became Lawrence's full time English publisher. In 1920 he brought out Lawrence's first post-war novel, **The Lost Girl.**

Maurice Magnus, (1876-1920) 13, 129, 281

American by birth, lived most of his adult life in Europe, he even spent some time in the Foreign Legion. Theatre man and would-be writer, he had for a while been Isadora Duncan's agent. A slightly pudgy little man . . . *who stuck out his front rather tubbily, like a bird, and his legs seemed to perch behind him, as a bird's do.* (D.H.L.). Appearance was everything to him, and despite his circumstances, (he was nearly always in financial difficulty, leaving hotel bills unpaid and living on hand-outs), he spared no expense perfuming and pampering himself and staying at the best hotels. He must always make an impression, this was his motto. Lawrence came on Magnus at the Hotel Balestri in Florence on the same occasion with Norman Douglas in November 1919 . . . *a European American named Maurice Magnus, who eyed Lawrence in that shrewd and impertinent way of the world of actor-managers: cosmopolitan, knocking shabbily around the world.* (Harry T. Moore). He soon latched on to the English writer, turning up at various other stages in Lawrence's journey south through Italy, [Monte Cassino, Taormina], and usually managing to extract a few pounds from the already impecunious Lawrence, much to Frieda's annoyance.

Dissatisfied with Capri, in spring 1920 Lawrence sets out to look for somewhere else for them to live. The result is a little villa, Fontana Vecchia, in Taormina, Sicily. They love it, it is everything they want, and Lawrence settles again to writing, when, one morning, they hear footsteps on the outside stairs and terrace, and there is Magnus.

Frieda is not pleased. Magnus hangs about in Taormina, badgering Lawrence and trying to get him involved in his schemes. Lawrence and Frieda decide to take a trip to Malta for a week. They board the boat in Syracuse, and there is Magnus again on an upper deck chatting to the captain. To their relief, Magnus decides to stay on Malta, but a few months later his financial problems finally overwhelm him, and he takes his own life.

Magnus had pestered Lawrence to try and find a publisher for his memoirs of the Foreign Legion—really just a pile of old papers and not well written. After his death, out of a sense of remorse, Lawrence managed to persuade Secker to publish them as *Memoirs of the Foreign Legion,* but only if Lawrence himself would write an Introduction. Lawrence obliged, but the lengthy piece, which was none too complimentary of Magnus, soon became the subject of a famous epistolary spat between Lawrence and Norman Douglas.

In **The Lost Girl**, (1920), Magnus appears as Mr May, an American theatre man who latches on to Alvina's father in his final and greatest doomed business enterprise—setting up a theatre for the townsfolk of Woodhouse, [Eastwood]. At the time Lawrence was completing the novel, spring 1920, Magnus was alive and well and happily residing in a villa in Taormina, just down the road from the Lawrences.

Frederick Leighton, (Sir, later Lord) (1830-1896) 15, 68
Painter and sculptor—historical, biblical, classical subject matter. President of The Royal Academy. His sculpture, *Athlete Wrestling with Python*, now in the Royal Academy, was considered a new renaissance in British art, (the model was Angelo Colarossi from Picinisco. Orazio Cervi also modelled for him). Some of his best known works are the huge frescoes in Room 107, V&A.

Rosalind Baynes, (1891-1972) 17, 127
Daughter of William Hamo Thornycroft. When she met and became friends with Lawrence in 1919 she was married to Jungian psychologist Godwin Baynes. But the marriage was on the point of breaking down. In the summer of 1919, Lawrence and Frieda spent several weeks as her guests at her cottage in Pangbourne. It was through Rosalind that Lawrence found his way to Orazio's villa in Picinisco.

In late summer 1920, with Frieda gone to Germany, it appears that Lawrence and Rosalind might have had a brief affair at the Villa Canovaia, Fiesole, in the hills overlooking Florence, which Rosalind had rented and where Lawrence joined her. Several of the finest poems to appear in his collection, *Birds, Beasts, and Flowers*, were written there, *Pomegranate, Fig,* and others, all full of the suggestion of the female body and female secrets.

William Hamo Thornycroft, (1850-1925) 17, 68
Sculptor, Royal Academician, many public commissions including *Oliver Cromwell* outside Palace of Westminster. Two of his most

famous works were the bronzes, *The Mower*, [now in Tate Britain], and *The Sower*, [now in Kew Gardens], both modelled by Orazio Cervi. His daughter Rosalind Baynes became a friend of D. H. Lawrence.

Monte Cassino, 20, 87
Benedictine Monastery founded by St. Benedict himself in 529AD. Perched high on the crown of a hill at 520 metres, overlooking the city of Cassino, it was central to the regeneration of Europe after the so-called Dark Ages. In its fifteen hundred year history, it has been destroyed four times, once by the Lombards, once by the Saracens, once by earthquake, and finally in 1944 by Allied bombing.

Atina, 40
Small town overlooking the Valley of Comino. In **The Lost Girl**, (1920), Lawrence gives a vivid description of arriving there at night on their way to Picinisco. [In the novel, Atina is Ossona, Picinisco is Pescocalascio]. Atina is mentioned in Virgil's **The Aeneid**—Atina Potens.

Horace, (Quintus Horatius Flaccus) (65 B.C—8 B.C.) 59, 137
Roman lyric poet, most famous Work, *The Odes*. He was gifted a nice country estate in the Sabine Hills by Maecanas, [patron of the arts and ally of Emperor Augustus], where he liked nothing better than growing vines and making fine wine. He is best known for his famous phrase, *Carpe Diem*—Seize the Day.

Samnites, 61, 87
Ancient Italic people, a confederation of Oscan speaking tribes that occupied the mountainous central and southern regions of the Italian peninsula. Between 343-290BC they fought three wars with Rome, often coming close to final victory, like the famous victory of The Caudine Forks when they forced the Roman army to pass under a yoke in sign of submission, a

shame which Rome never forgave. But Rome was relentless, finally subjugating the Samnite tribes in 290BC with a series of crushing victories, including the battle of Cominium, later described by historian Livy.

Livy, (Titus Livius), (59 B.C.-17 B.C.) 61, 88
Roman Historian. Wrote *The History of Rome*, [from the foundation to Augustus].

Cominium, Battle. 62, 150
Cominium was a Samnite city supposedly sited near the present day town of Alvito in the Valley of Comino, near Picinisco. It was destroyed by the Roman consul Spurius Carvillius Maximus in 293BC. (Livy, History of Rome).

Picinisco, 63, 81
Small village in the foothills of the mountains of what is now The National Park of Abruzzo. The last three chapters of Lawrence's novel, **The Lost Girl,** (1920), are set there. In the novel it is called Pescocalascio.

Ver Sacrum, [Sacred Spring]. 63, 141
Ancient religious practice performed by various Italic tribes including the Samnites. At times of grave danger or threat, a vow was made to the god Mars, (Mamers in Oscan), that all the animals and children born the following spring would be 'sacrificed' to him. The children however were not killed, they became the sacrati—the holy ones, but when they came of age they were delivered up to him. They were led blindfold to the edge of their territory and left there to await the god, who would appear in the form of an animal, often a woodpecker, (picus), and guide them to lands new.

Giustino Ferri, (1856-1913) 65
Born in Picinisco, Italian novelist and journalist, friend of

Pirandello, D'Annunzio and other literary figures who used to gather at the Caffè Bussi in Rome. His most famous novel is *La Camminante*, (1908), a story of love and loss set in a fictional Picinisco.

Luigi Pirandello, (1867-1932) Sicily. 65
Dramatist, novelist, poet.

The Rainbow, 82
Lawrence's novel, ***The Rainbow, (1915),*** initially the story of **Tom Brangwen**, a Derbyshire farmer who falls in love with and marries **Anna Lensky**, an upper-class Polish woman fallen on hard times, (thinly disguised versions of Lawrence and Frieda). It was condemned for obscenity.

Zennor, Cornwall, 85
In December 1915, Lawrence and Frieda moved to the tiny village of Zennor near St. Ives in Cornwall to escape London and the clamour of war, and also to live cheaply. They found a little place, Tregerthen Cottage, at a rent of £5 p.a., which they furnished themselves from the market in St. Ives. At first they loved it, and the Cornish/Celtic landscape and people. But it wasn't to last. Here, Lawrence started work on ***Women in Love***, really a rewrite and development of the second part of ***The Rainbow***. But Lawrence, as he had done from the outbreak, continued talking openly against the war, and of course Frieda was German. In late summer 1917 they came under suspicion of sending signals to German u-boats off the coast, (the laundry line and curtains and Frieda's white scarf being the supposed means of communication). But they would not tone down their anti-war rhetoric or change their ways—in the evenings they would often sing German folksongs, just like they had always done. In October 1917 the police raided their cottage, and despite no evidence being found, they were given three days to leave Cornwall.

Karl von Marbahr, 96
After being presented at court in the 1890s, Frieda returned to Metz to the life of dress balls and social occasions. Her first beau was a young officer cadet, Lt. Karl Marbahr. She might even have married him, but her mother disapproved and sent her away to Berlin to forget him.

Franziska zu Reventlow, Countess (1871-1918) 97
Writer, artist, translator, rebel. Always controversial, she believed that sexual freedom and the abolition of marriage were the way to achieve social equality with men. She lived in Munich for many years where she knew Frieda.

Jugend, 97
Satirical anti-religious art magazine started in 1896 in Munich. Many famous Art Nouveau contributors. The term jugendstil comes from it.

Simplicissimus, 97
Famous café, bar, and cabaret in the Bohemian district of Munich.

Café Stefanie, 97
Munich café frequented by many famous artists, Kurt Eisner and Paul Klee among them.

Filippo Tommaso Marinetti, (1876-1944) 135, 184
Poet and Futurist, he is best known as the author of *The Futurist Manifesto*, 1908: '*Art can be nothing but violence, cruelty and injustice.*' This quote, from the Manifesto, embodied his vision for a new Italy — the destruction of the old order in favour of a new industrialised society which would express itself in militarism and patriotism, sweep away the old decadence and purify the nation through the outpouring of its blood. At the outbreak of war he immediately joined up, was badly wounded on the Isonzo, recovered, and returned to take part in the final victory at Vittorio Veneto.

Pappus, Bucco, Maccus, Dossenus, 172, 203

Characters from *The Atellan Fables*—improvised farces performed on the public street in antiquity, originally in the Oscan language, and named after the Oscan town of Atella, (modern Campania region). The masked farces were later imported to Rome where they became extremely popular. The Romans though wanted things done properly, and so the farces became scripted, often by famous writers—Ovid, Pliny and the occasional emperor. But the tradition never quite died, and is now considered to be the origin of the Italian Commedia dell'Arte, which in turn had a profound influence on European theatre, from Shakespeare to the English Punch and Judy show.

Eastwood, Nottingham, 192, 244

Lawrence's hometown.

Anna Brangwen (Anna Victrix), Will Brangwen, 268
The Rainbow and **Women in Love,**

Anna Brangwen is the daughter of Anna Lensky, and stepdaughter to Tom Brangwen. She marries a cousin, Will Brangwen, and thus starts the narrative of the second generation of the family saga. In his early passion for Anna, the young Will likes to call her Anna Victrix.

Ursula and **Gudrun,** (**Brangwen**), 269

Ursula and Gudrun are the daughters of Anna and Tom Brangwen. They are first seen as children in *The Rainbow* then as grown women in *Women in Love*, Ursula, a teacher, Gudrun an artist. It is around these two young women and their relationships that the narrative of the second novel unfolds, Ursula with **Gerald Crich**, a rich handsome mine owner, and Gudrun with **Rupert Birkin**, an intellectual, ending with the death of Gerald in the famous closing scene when, broken by Ursula's rejection of him, he walks out into the snow-covered Tyrolese mountains and gives up.

Fontana Vecchia, Taormina, Sicily. 309
After their stay in Picinisco, Frieda and Lawrence spent two months on Capri, but again it wasn't what they wanted and Lawrence set off exploring once more. He headed south to Sicily and found Fontana Vecchia, a lovely old villa on the outskirts of Taormina. He and Frieda moved in there in early spring 1920, and stayed for two years. It was one of the happiest and most productive periods of his life, a place blessed. Here he wrote his first post-war novel, **The Lost Girl,** 1920. Other works followed.

Siculi, 310
Ancient Italic tribe from whom the name **Sicily** derives.

Chapter One

"I, FRIEDA LAWRENCE . . ." INTO THE ICY DARKNESS SHE whispered her little credo, not quite a prayer, she didn't pray, she believed in herself.

A low snow-lit moon cut sharp and electric across the gaunt bare room, she could feel it on her skin, like the night they had arrived. Here, in this fierce white mountain-jagged lair — harsh, crude, unforgiving — yes right here something had happened, a sort of redemption.

Endings and beginnings, beginnings and endings, pack the few belongings, make a wish, hope that the next place will be the one they are searching for—this the rhythm of their life for so long now. Time to test that faith once more. But there would be those who would say — Look, no place will have them, they are permanent exiles. She tossed her head defiantly — Let them think what they liked, she cared not. What did they know of life? She had made her choice. It was a price worth paying.

From somewhere outside, a high-pitched jabber of oaths and animal calls broke the ice-shimmering silence — a little half-man in cape and hat tugging and pushing at the stubborn ass, a slap on its rump, a stunted bray, another slap, the reluctant tread of snow-muffled hoofs, man and beast trudging away, timeless moonlit creatures them both.

She dug herself down under the blankets for a final warm, pressing her body up close to his.

"Lorenzo, it is time."

His eyelids flickered, breath still deep in sleep, the rise and gentle fall, the long pause, as if it had stopped for good, then the memory of life once more. She watched him for a few more moments, then, with a little roar of self-courage, she threw off the blankets and sprang from the bed into the silvery dark, growling like a little lion, fighting off the clawing cold, throwing on her clothes, pinning, buttoning, bending, pushing last strewn items into the case.

Then, of a sudden, she stopped quite still, eyes half closed. Somewhere back in the half-awake night on the edge of dreams she had heard that tapping again, not imagined, but real, she was sure, the sound of a beak on the black iced window.

She crossed the room and peered out at the crystal-still landscape, warm breath on frosted glass.

"I did hear you didn't I?" she whispered. "You were there. It wasn't a dream."

She tapped the pane with her fingernail—tap tap tap, little rapid tappings, just like the ones she had heard. Then she started to scratch something on the whitened glass, the image of a bird, a woodpecker with a sharp beak, a dot for an eye to give it sight.

"There, now you can see we are leaving. Spread your wings for us too, like you have always done for your sacred ones."

She turned back into the room, lit a candle on the dresser, carried it across to the bed and stood looking down at the sleeping man. She put a hand on his shoulder and rocked gently.

"No, I can't bear it. It's too cold. I'm staying," moaned the red-bearded voice on the pillow.

"Then I'm leaving you," spake the hovering candle flame.

"So be it," the voice rasped. "Go forth out of the land of Egypt riding on a donkey. Come back for me when it's springtime."

How had he heard her unspoken thoughts—metaphors of exile? But he had. It didn't surprise her. Should she tell him about the woodpecker? No, better not—not right now. Yet it was he who had beckoned it, he whose imagination had conjured it—the little mountain god of myth who gathered his sacred ones, his sacrati, and guided them to lands new.

Such a place — an Italy before Italy — and he had heard its voice, and it had found its way down inside him. Yes, all this they would take with them, the great pagan twilights of the valleys, the snow-capped mountain peaks, the lonely little villa with its two front doors, future and past, old Orazio sunk in his self-inflicted exile, simple Giovanni lost in a world that only he could see . . . even the donkey . . .

She sat down on the bed and ran her fingers through his soft red-brown hair.

"Capri," she whispered, "Capri . . . The beautiful deep blue of the Mediterranean . . . Just think . . ."

Chapter Two

So this was it, the final farewell to that other world. He gazed down through the scribble of snow-still trees to where they were making ready to leave, wisps of smoke from his cheroot drifting in the blue-white predawn air. The lane was too icy and rutted to get the donkey and cart up as far as the house, and it had snowed again. Heaven knows how they would reach the road, and there was the torrent to cross, but there was no telling his stubborn little brother.

He shrugged. He should have gone down there with them, to embrace, to help them up, just to be present—they were his guests. But no, they had wanted their last view of him to be up there in front of his villa, all wood-smoke and white mountains, a man of two worlds in a place of two worlds — and when he had a set of oils to hand, the Englishman had said, he'd paint the scene from memory and send it to him, a picture in oils to add to the picture in words that the frail man with the fiery beard was already painting in his mind.

He stamped his feet up and down to stop the numbness creeping into them.

". . . But you will live forever," the Englishman had proclaimed that time. He was always confounding Orazio with his riddles.

"A bronze statue is not a living thing," the old model had replied.

"Not so Orazio, for every time someone looks at your likeness, life will flicker inside, you will live again, and just think, you will be eternally young."

He wriggled his toes—maybe he was turning to bronze again there and then, and it didn't feel very life-giving or rejuvenating, quite the opposite. He stamped his feet harder and felt under his shirt for the little Madonna medal that hung round his neck.

Down by the cart, the Englishman turned to look back up the hill, and catching sight of the dancing necromancer, started stamping his own feet in playful sympathy. He shouted something, but the thin icy air made him cough, and his words were lost. He climbed up onto the cart and tried again.

"Carpe diem Orazio," he called out, this time to better effect. Orazio responded with a flourish of his hat. "Mille grazie Sir Horace," the Englishman called again, standing upright now on the rig and facing back up the hill, waving his arms in exaggerated arcs, swaying slightly, breath blowing, waving and warming himself at the same time, until a hand reached up and pulled him down onto the seat next to her, frightened he would topple over. She threw the heavy old black cape around his shoulders, mother-like, the cape Orazio had given him when he first arrived, an Englishman in his worn tweed jacket, not expecting the icy mountain cold, almost not caring, threadbare of soul, gaunt and creased by the grinding adversity of those war years, febrile blue eyes staring out on the world.

Orazio finished his hopping. A first glint of morning sun shot silver across the valley. He shaded his eyes, watching the proceedings, the swarthy awkward figure of his brother heaving the case onto the back of the cart, the woman pinning her hat into her thick fair hair, the man's red beard bobbing up and down in response to some unheard words.

The little man finished checking the harness, climbed up onto the front of the cart, nodded to himself, gave a flick of the reins and one of his animal cries . . . "Brrr . . . Brrr." But the donkey just stood there, stolid, stationary, nodding its head up and down and looking back over its shoulder with large stubborn eyes.

Orazio cursed — would he have to trudge down there and pull the obstinate beast forward? Giovanni filled his lungs and gave out another yowl, whipping more fiercely at the reins, and this time the animal lunged forward, jolting the unprepared passengers backwards. The cart rolled away down the hill, sliding and swaying, the passengers holding onto each other and waving, Orazio waving back—a last glimpse, a last turn of heads, and then they were gone.

He stood for a few moments gazing into the emptiness, then shrugged his shoulders, turned, and walked back into the house, stamping the snow from his feet and muttering to himself . . . "Capri will suit them better . . . yes of course, of course it will." But he wished it hadn't been so. Maybe they would get stuck in the snow and have to come back! No, they were gone—quiet again his life, quiet like before they had come, quiet now forever.

He poured himself the last of the coffee. On the kitchen table there was a folded note.

Caro Orazio,

What a time we have had with you, unlike any other place we have been, full of strange things and delights and surprises. We are the better for it. You have restored us. Frieda too says that your noble little villa will remain with her forever. Of all the places we have stayed in our lives dear Orazio — and they are many — only with you have we felt such ease in a spiritual way, a little edge of heaven. One day we should come back — a springtime return perhaps when the snows have melted and we can see all those wonders you have described, fields of mountain gentian, a flower I so love, the sweet scented yellow broom — ginestra — such a lovely word in Italian, the plant of our old English kings, Plantagenet. I will keep the cape with gratitude and in memory of you. I would not have managed without it. When we get to Capri we are going to finish embroi dering it—also with your initials.

Thank you with all our heart,
Lorenzo and Frieda.

He read it again — 'in memory of you' — yes, there it was, the truth. There would be no more visits, not from them, not from Rosalind, not from any other of the English wanderers who drifted up and down the Italian peninsula in search of sun, escape and inspiration, this he knew, whatever they said. No, this would be the first and last time, there would be no more visits from any of them, it was written in those eyes, deep blue eyes that could not lie.

He sighed and nodded. Then a faint distant smile started to creep over his old face. They were gone, indeed, and they would never return, but nor would they ever really leave, they would be present now always, here in his lonely little villa, and on long winter nights as he sat by the fire he would close his eyes and see them there, talking all their talk, playing all their games, teasing each other, teasing him, sitting in silent annoyance with one another, waiting to see who would be the first to surrender. It had been theatre, all of it. It had filled his house and his hearth and his heart.

They had tried to stay on, had tried to make the best of the icy conditions despite his chest, but in the end the lure had been too much for them, the deep blue Mediterranean sea warmth, the scent of citrus, the play of light, the play of words, writers and artists and all the rest—the English set.

Orazio knew how it would be, he had lived among them in London, knew how they loved places like Capri—little colonies of English society with a few foreigners thrown in for added colour. Whenever the topic had come up they would talk excitedly of all the people they knew who would be there, a certain Compton Mackenzie and others. Orazio didn't really know who they were, or only vaguely, but he listened, and nodded. Yes he knew how it would be, a sort of travelling English house party in the sun— ideas, books, catching up on the gossip, and probably generating some of their own. Capri had a certain reputation, had had ever since the Emperor Tiberius had built himself a villa there, and where he had spent his last years indulging himself in his favourite sybaritic sports, and running the empire on the side.

But there had been times when even the thought of Capri hadn't been enough to keep their spirits high. The post-war world was in turmoil, bolshevism in Russia, empires being carved up, the old order swept away, and here in Italy the streets being fought over, D'Annunzio still strutting and speechifying, banging the drum, marching on Fiume — and talk of the war and its aftermath would whip them into a choking tormented fury, the terrible human waste, the injustices they themselves had suffered. It would excite the Englishman to the point of inflaming his airways, and Frieda would try and calm him. But since her visit to Germany — the condition she had found her poor mother in, half starved, the whole country being punished, made to carry the burden of guilt — she had few reserves left herself, and like this they would spin down together into the abyss, clutching at each other for salvation but hardly succeeding.

Orazio folded the note, put it behind a copper pot on the mantelpiece, and knelt slowly down in front of the open hearth, the weight of time suddenly heavy on his old body, as if it had given up the last vestiges of its distant youth that very morning. He piled twigs on the glowing ash, reached for the long iron tube on its stand, and blew down it till the embers glowed and little tongues of flame crackled into life. Outside the door, the pig gruntled—the smell of smoke, the rattle of its cauldron being hung over the fire, a mess of vegetables for its breakfast. Intelligent pig. Pig first, Orazio second—his guests had joked.

He swept his hand over the table brushing the crumbs and crusts to the edge and dropping them into the pot. They had breakfasted off the last of the bread and cheese, and he had made up a parcel from the leftovers of the Christmas festivity the previous day, dried figs and apricots, polenta bread and slices of prosciutto, all wrapped in a cloth and with a bottle of his misty white wine tucked in for good measure. It would keep them going on the journey—the bus to Cassino, train to Naples, and then the ferry over to Capri.

He looked round at his grimy old kitchen, the smeared windows, the smoke backing from the fire, and just for a moment he wished he could have gone with them. Frieda had even suggested it. But what good would it have been? He shook his head—no, he knew what lay before him now.

Chapter Three

AND SO IT WAS, PIG HAD VANQUISHED. HE LIFTED THE steaming cauldron off the hook and carried it outside—snorts of excitement, snout already hunting expectantly in the empty trough. He poured the mushy mixture in and stood back, muttering unnecessary words of encouragement, the pig grunting and snorting in reply.

He lit the half-smoked cheroot stub in the corner of his mouth and wandered out onto the snow-covered clearing between the slender bare trees, peering down at the crust-white surface, dipping the toe of his shoe here and there into the little divots and depressions, pushing the fresh snow aside—and there, just visible still, the frozen imprints of bare dancing feet. It had been after that first snowfall, all of them sitting in the kitchen, Lorenzo musing to himself and scribbling down thoughts, Orazio dozing, Frieda absently placing nuts and corn husks and pieces of the new cutlery into patterns on the table, when, of a sudden, she jumped to her feet, kicked off her shoes, and skipped out of the room.

She flung open the front door and ran out into the fresh snow, dancing and leaping, dress billowing, bare arms red and spinning, fair hair flying, prancing and jumping and pirouetting, falling to the ground, scooping up handfuls of snow and rubbing it over her legs and arms and face, jumping up again, ululating like a wolf, spinning like a Sufi, till she fell dizzied and laughing into the white powder.

Back in the kitchen, despite the great commotion and whooping and influx of icy air, the writer went on writing into a notebook. He put down his pen, looked across at his host, then over towards the door. Orazio had stayed at his post. He knew English phlegm, had learnt it in the best of circles. He returned the look, then, with a simultaneous raise of their eyebrows they stood up and ambled to the open door to watch the spectacle.

"She is a socialist Orazio," the Englishman whispered with mock confidentiality.

"I thought she was a German," the Italian whispered back.

The Englishman laughed, and coughed a little, and the German socialist redoubled her efforts, thinking they were laughing with approval at her performance, her athletic frame contorting itself into ever more figural shapes, classical, sculptural, balancing on one leg, head and body thrust forward, arms spread back like wings.

"Who am I? Who am I? Guess who I am," she sang out to her audience.

"Isadora Duncan," Lorenzo shouted back, cupping a hand to his mouth.

"No no . . . mythological . . . classical," she sang again, her voice thick and throaty with her efforts and the remains of her wolf calls.

"She is classical," Lorenzo insisted.

"Yes but no . . . real classical."

"Katherine Mansfield then," the red beard grinned and shouted.

"Don't be ridiculous."

"Diana the Huntress."

"No no . . ." the shaking statue could hold it no longer and fell to the ground, rolling about in helpless laughter, ". . . better than that."

"You are right Orazio," the Englishman whispered from behind his hand, "she is both a German and a socialist. Dangerous. Perhaps we should lock her out."

Orazio raised an eyebrow.

"We give up. Who are you?" Lorenzo called across to the half-buried classical statue in the cotton dress that was rising from the snow and brushing itself down.

"Ottoline Morrell . . . Couldn't you see it?"

"But that's preposterous. She's not mythological."

"I know, I know, but it just turned into her somehow, it just became her. She took me over. It started out as the goddess Athena."

"I think Medusa would have been closer for Ottoline. No I shouldn't say that. Poor Ottoline."

Sometimes in the evenings they would put on little theatrical performances, or charades, or imitate one or other of their friends or acquaintances — artists, literary figures, politicians — and Orazio had to join in, or be the audience and guess who they were, and he would search around in his ragbag memory, dig up the name of some personality or other and would invariably be wrong by a country mile, to the great amusement of the performers, who, inspired by his hopeless guesses, would redouble their efforts.

"Who's this Orazio, who's this..?"

And Orazio would plunge in again, happy that his ignorance was making them happy . . . "King Edward . . . Lord Kitchener . . . Oscar Wilde," and there would follow howls of helpless laughter.

"No no, it's Ezra Pound . . . It's W. B. Yeats . . . It's Norman Douglas," and imitation would follow imitation — famous friends of theirs, or some well-known figure but almost certainly not known by poor old Orazio, or just vaguely, and the more outrageous his answers the better, and they would ascribe the idiosyncrasies of one to the other, so that Ezra Pound became a sort of Lord Kitchener wearing an earring, and then they couldn't speak anymore for the hilarity of it all.

". . . Talking of Norman Douglas," Frieda suddenly asked between a passage of laughter, "did his friend Magnus ever give you back that money you lent him in Florence?"

Lorenzo made a face.

"So," she said very germanically, "and how much have we left to live on?"

"I don't know . . . about five pounds." He gave a shrug. "It'll work out. Maybe the good and saintly Secker will send me an advance soon."

To Orazio it felt as if he had woken suddenly from a long slumber — company, jollity, in that so English a way — and he smiled and nodded and shook his head, and took out a handkerchief and blew his nose. England — he had lived there for many years, in London, had mixed with society in a diluted sort of way, on the edges, obliquely, and he had learned his English there, the nice measured tones that marked him out, managing to lose the heavy Italian accent. He had been an artist's model, frequented fine houses in London and the country. They had liked him somehow, liked his looks, his manner, both of which he cultivated and used to good effect, becoming a sort of exotic houseguest come valet come mysterious confidante, a shadowy figure from the artistic demi-monde, a breed much favoured in certain bohemian and new socialist circles.

It was a long way from his other existence, the remnants of which he kept locked away in a trunk at his lodgings in Il Quartiere, as the Italian district of Clerkenwell was known—the outlandish costumes of the remote mountain valleys on the edge of the wild Abruzzo from where he had come. It had a name this place, just about — La Ciociaria — not a geographical name, more a condition, an old way of being that expressed itself in the style of dress, notably the sheep-skin leggings with leather thongs that the men wore round their calves. But there was much more, all manner of dazzling attire, conical hats with ribbons, colourful brass-buttoned waistcoats, bandannas, gold earrings, swirling capes. Add to this the shrill of their wild ancient flutes and bagpipes, their long dark locks and sultry looks, and behold, there was every northerner's romantic idea of the bucolic figures that inhabit classical landscapes—amorous fauns cavorting with woodland nymphs. And in their finery they had turned the heads of half the capitals of Europe. It had been the means of their good fortune. Artists grabbed them off the street eager to paint them, the women with pitchers of water balanced on their heads, or scything corn, or carrying baskets of grapes, the men, jewelled and daggered, swaggering and dangerous, or dancing to the wild percuss of the tambourine.

For Orazio too it had brought good fortune and an introduction to artists' studios and serious modelling. He watched and learned, shed his old skin, and by and by became another, a gentleman, or sometimes a gentleman's gentleman, ambiguous. He travelled in fine company to France, to Nice, to country houses for shoots or just social occasions, talked with important people, at times no-one quite sure who he was, but if he was there then he must have been invited. But sometimes, in the night, he would wake in a sweat, dreaming that all he had to wear was his mountain costume and that he would have to come down to breakfast dressed as a brigand. He flitted like a shadow through the drawing rooms of Bloomsbury, chameleon-like, model, guest, aide, garnering curious uncertain glances from the women, but also from the men. There were murmurings, whispers, but it didn't matter to him, not a bit, for he loved them, loved them all, and they knew it. But back in Clerkenwell in the Italian quarter they had another opinion—he was too good for them, his fine dress and manners somehow disdainful, superior.

The pig finished at its trough, nosed around for anything it might have missed, gave a sort of nod with its flappy ears, and trotted off to its wooden sty. Orazio sucked at his cheroot. It had gone out. The sky was growing heavy. Just then a thick slab of snow slid from the roof and landed with a thud behind him. He turned and looked up at the house, and in the darkening light he thought he saw a woman's face at the balcony window. He sighed. He knew what had come to visit — no, not visit, what was always there, just out of sight, sitting quietly in the grey corner shadows.

Before the villa was built, up here had been just the old stone cottages where he had lived as a boy, he and his brother and sisters. His father had died when he was very small and somehow his mother had managed. But all they had was land, just enough to scrape a living. Out there, in the world beyond the valley, a great event was taking place. The Risorgimento. But what was it? There was talk of course, what little he could make of it— unification, a patria, a king. But unification with whom, and who was this king? The only real effect that anyone round here could feel was that they were getting poorer. Poverty brings on manhood much faster than it would otherwise, and so, still hardly more than a boy, he followed the great exodus out, walking across Europe, working as he went, sleeping in the open, just like all the others.

In London things went well for him, the years passed, now a young gentleman, pockets jingling with gold sovereigns, he decided to make his first visit home to see his aging mother. But he hadn't been back long when a sort of raptus took him, a youthful vainglory. He would build himself a house befitting his new station, an Italian villa with an English heart and an English wooden staircase, and he would hang pictures and photos of the London great with whom he had come into contact—Frederick Leighton and the like. He could see it all.

Perched on the brow of the hill away from the tawdry little hamlet of his fellow villagers, the villa started to rise. A few months passed, almost a year, a sort of spell descending on him, when one morning he opened his eyes and saw reality.

With a promise to his mother that he would return soon, he hurried back to his beloved London. But there was another soul to whom he had made the same promise, whose face hovered over him sometimes in dreams, quiet, patient, accepting, the way he had last seen her, the way she looked back at him now from the window.

Once back in London though he became forgetful of his words, and London had a great variety of ways to help with forgetfulness. He had never meant to break his promises, he just kept putting them off—next year, always next year, until one day unexpected news arrived. There was no need to go back now.

More years passed, the villa episode becoming just an occasional fitful nighttime memory. But then his looks began to fade, and with them his commissions. In Il Quartiere there were knowing glances and nods. And so it was that one grey London morning he found himself sitting in a second class carriage on the boat train from Victoria, staring out the window into the grey river mist of a city oblivious to his departure.

To ease his soul he told himself that it would just be a quick visit. He would spend a little time there, see how he felt, and if he didn't like it, he would sell the villa and go back to London— yes, that would almost certainly be the outcome. He was still pondering this when fate stepped in. On 28th June, 1914, Archduke Franz Ferdinand of Austria was cut down by the bullet of a Serbian nationalist, and soon after, Orazio found himself marooned at the other end of a Europe riven by war. It was as if a great mountain boulder had rolled down to bar the way between himself and that other world.

The war came and went, he managed to sell up most of his London belongings and have the rest shipped out. Now, here he was, the quondam Englishman, reclusive, alone, nobody to see him slowly fading, the last embers of his London existence gone cold forever, just the photos on the stairs to remind him, when one morning a letter with an English postmark arrived.

He perched it on the mantelpiece, contemplating it for a while, then he took his best bone-handled kitchen knife and slit it open. It was from Rosalind Baynes, the daughter of the sculptor William Hamo Thornycroft for whom he had modelled, most notably the two great bronzes, The Sower, an idealised rustic casting seed from his satchel, and The Mower, a countryman with a scythe—both executed just before Rosalind was born.

He had struck up a sort of friendly acquaintance with Thornycroft, and he would go round sometimes to his house in Kensington, and Hamo — he hadn't been knighted then — would make sketches, test ideas, or they would just talk, and the young Rosalind would come in with tea, and Orazio would tell her tales all about his wild mountain home, of eagles soaring, wolves howling, bears prowling, and cruel-eyed brigands with flashing knives and deadly muskets.

He had last seen Rosalind at her father's house in Kensington not long before he had left, she, no longer the child who used to sit and listen wide-eyed to his stories but a young woman on the verge of marriage. And as he was leaving she had said to him — You know Orazio, I still remember all the stories, the wild snow-capped mountains, the mysterious valleys, crystal nights full of shooting stars, and how you used to say that when I was older you would take me there. She laughed. One day I shall hold you to your promise Orazio, don't think I won't.

He picked up the letter, read it, put it down, picked it up, read it again — Dear Orazio, Sometimes things we say in jest take on a life of their own . . . marriage problems . . . need to escape . . . is that invitation still open? I would like to come and stay for a while with my three daughters or maybe even come and live there somewhere, somehow.

Rosalind . . . Rosalind with three daughters . . . come and stay here! He looked around him at his shabby dwelling, at the untidy bachelor world it had become—no, worse, more a farm-yard barn. Yes, outside it had a certain grandeur, but that was outside, inside it was rude, basic, cold, barely furnished, and full of farm stuff—and as if in response to his thoughts, the donkey tethered to the doorpost gave a long withering bray, the pig snorted, and the chickens took fright and ran up the corridor.

To the Rosalind he had entertained as a child he had given full rein to his stories, making it a place of legend and myth, and in a way it was, but there was another reality too, this was a harsh remote mountain world, not a nice little Thames-side town west of London.

For several days he pondered, torn between the pleasure of contact with a world he thought had gone forever and the inevitable exposé of the onetime London man of fashion. He wrote back, not to Rosalind, but to her father, Thornycroft — and of course he would be honoured and delighted to receive Rosalind and the children, but he wondered whether his poor house would meet their needs and the standards of comfort they were used to, remote and simple as it was. He decided to dress it up as some sort of monastic life choice, a renunciation, but that then ran the risk of making it sound all the more interesting to someone like Rosalind.

The exchange of letters took place in the summer. The war had been over just six months. In the autumn there was a reply, but not from Thornycroft. It was from a friend of Rosalind's, a writer by the name of Lawrence — and he wrote that he was just about to set off for his first visit back to Italy since the war, that he had recently been a guest of Rosalind's at her home in Pangbourne and that she had regaled him with descriptions and tales of the wild mountains of the Abruzzi—and it all sounded just too wonderful. He was waiting for a new passport to be issued, but as soon as it was ready he would leave, and he hoped to be in Italy before year end. Could he perhaps come by and stay for a short while? Rosalind would follow later. Orazio wrote back, accepting.

In November another letter arrived, this time with an Italian postmark. It was from the English writer again, and he wrote that he was staying in Florence for a few days with friends at the Hotel Balestri, then it was on down to Rome . . . and then dear Orazio, we hope to arrive about 12th December, myself and my wife Frieda. I will mail you when I am more certain. Could you meet us at Cassino station? I should be much obliged, it seems your place is quite difficult to get to.

Orazio rolled up the letter and tapped it against his forehead. So not quite the forgotten man after all.

Chapter Four

THE BUS, STUFFY WITH PEASANTRY, WOUND ITS WAY DOWN the mountain road. Orazio had dressed in a suit which had been tailored for his youthful London figure. It was a little tight under the arms and his shirt collar chafed at his thickening neck. Despite the discomfort he had felt it his duty to meet his guests in decent order, but his fellow passengers were less impressed, looking him up and down with that peasant scorn. He stared out the window. Below, a flat grey mist covered the wide valley plain, only the ancient abbey of Monte Cassino was still visible, floating serenely high above, as if held aloft by a fanfare of angels in some medieval fresco.

He had left instructions with old Maria to go into the house and light a fire towards evening, otherwise it would be as cold as the tomb by the time they got back. He hoped she remembered, sometimes she liked to sip the wine a little too much.

The train from Rome was not due till the afternoon, and it was always late. It was cold, with that damp misty cold of the low-lying town, a warming brandy or two wouldn't go amiss. Several restorative bars later he swayed benignly towards the station, when, to his dismay, he saw streams of passengers already spilling out to where the buses and carriages were lined up just outside. He hurried himself along, pushing through the crowd, cursing under his breath. He had wanted to be there on the platform when the train pulled in, wanted to cut a dignified figure—English punctuality for his English visitors. He knew the reputation Italians had for their bad timekeeping, and now the train had betrayed him by being on time.

The throng of passengers and porters surged and shoved and shouted around him. Puffing and red-faced with self-annoyance, he pushed through the melee and onto the platform, searching up and down. They weren't there. He made his way back outside to where the porters were hoisting cases onto horse-drawn carriages or in through the windows of crowded buses, to the oaths and maledictions of the already squashed-in passengers. Not there either. Ever more desperate, he climbed onto a wagon piled with cases to get a better view around, receiving a volley of abuse in Neapolitan from one of the porters. Cursing his luck and beginning to wonder if perhaps they had not taken this train after all, he caught a glimpse of something through a bus window, a red beard.

"Why, how have I missed you?" he pronounced in his best brandy-modulated English as he swayed towards them down the aisle of the crowded omnibus.

"Orazio!" the Englishman exclaimed. His voice was high and quavering. He seemed agitated, his face flushed and angry-looking. On his knee was a large case which he was hugging to himself with unnecessary force, as if it might escape. By his side, his fairish hatted companion whispered something softly in his ear and stroked his shoulder soothingly like a child. She looked up at Orazio with a little apologetic smile. Orazio stared for a second, gave a little nod and made an uncertain half-smile back.

"How have I missed you?" he continued, "please forgive me, the station is so . . ." But the Englishman did not let him finish.

"I have had my pocket picked Orazio . . . right here on the platform . . . my wallet stolen from my pocket . . ." His voice was high, his face red and creased almost as if he would cry. He swallowed hard. "Curse them!"

"O Signore!" Orazio threw his hands in the air, flushing with brandy and confusion, searching for words that would not come.

"Curse them," the Englishman repeated, his voice now a bitter whisper. He took a deep breath and brought himself back under control.

Orazio stood rooted to the spot. He put a hand up to his hat then lowered it again, a hundred thoughts crowding in on him, fighting into his brain. Why hadn't he been there? He should have been on the platform.

"But Orazio, today a rare thing happened," an odd sickly grin spread over the Englishman's face, ". . . a rare thing indeed. The jury acquitted me. Divine intervention. Who'd have believed it?"

Orazio stared at him.

"Yes, I was set free," he patted his chest, ". . . found not guilty, given a complete discharge."

His fair companion gave him a little nudge in the ribs. He winced slightly, nodded, and replaced the sickly grin with something more readable.

"By good fortune, a gentleman who had travelled with us from Rome saw the vile act being performed and came to my rescue. I was spared. The gods spared me for once." He subsided, the misadventure aired and overcome, at least for the moment.

Orazio's hand finally made it to his hat. He raised it in polite greeting, mainly to the lady, wiping his brow at the same time. "Thank God indeed Signor Lawrence . . . Signor David. I should have been there. It is my fault. But who was this gentleman?"

"Like I said, he was a fellow passenger. He had just picked up his case and was walking away when quite by chance he looked back and saw what was happening. I had no idea. He came back over and took the thief by the arm and made him restore my wallet . . . Vile little criminals. There were two of them, one distracted me while the other went into my pocket."

Orazio stood, still uncertain how to proceed, muttering something not quite audible but which seemed to have the names of various saints attached.

"How can I apologise? It is so sometimes. Foreigners are fair game for them. They give us a bad name."

"It is alright Orazio," Frieda spoke for the first time, "no need for apologies. It is very kind of you to come and meet us." She smiled reassuringly.

". . . And the man who saved us is from your village too," the Englishman seemed to have recomposed himself, "an Anglo like you. He had travelled down a couple of days ago from England. We shared a compartment from Rome."

"From London? Then perhaps I know him."

"Not from London . . . from the northeast."

"Ah."

"He said he didn't know you either."

The bus gave a sudden lurch forward, unbalancing the already unsteady Orazio. He grabbed at a seat and pushed himself in between a couple of stout unyielding peasant women. Smelling his brandy breath the women crossed their heavy arms in disgust. Then the older of the two in black widow's weeds started muttering about the vileness of the male species and their horrible vices. Orazio tried to free his arms and straighten his jacket, brushing himself down and paying no notice, but this only raised the woman's ire still further, till she had worked herself into a nice little frenzy, pinching and slapping at her arms and face — they shouldn't let drunks onto the bus . . . and hadn't it been the demon drink that had taken her Luigi?

Orazio looked over to where his guests were seated, hoping they wouldn't hear, wouldn't turn round—after the station episode they would wonder what sort of asylum they had come to. But the woman wasn't finished. "Povera me, Povera me," she kept repeating, slapping still at her face, punishing herself for her bitter life—mules were better off. Women were cursed. Toil and childbirth, that's all they were good for, all they were put on this Earth for, while men were useless drunkards. She made a sign of the cross, managing at the same time to land a heavy penitential elbow in Orazio's ribs.

Captive and condemned, he stared through the steamy window. They were out of the town now and speeding across the wide valley plain past straggles of country folk returning from the market or the fields, women with that slow caryatid gait, balancing big wicker baskets or large tied parcels on their heads.

With a rumble and a roar the bus changed gear and started the climb back up the pass, swinging precariously into the bends of the narrowing defile, dusk shadows already settling. The Englishman's free hand gripped at the seat in front as he peered out into the darkening world, the steep rocky hillsides closing in on either side. Orazio was too far back to be able to talk with his guests but he could just hear their conversation.

"Is it too much to ask . . . an end to this malediction, an end to this persecution? . . . But no, on and on it goes, pursuing us like some insatiable beast of the abyss. Why, Frieda, why?"

Orazio played with his hat, still angry with himself.

But the Englishman hadn't finished, ". . . And now here I am . . . come all this way, only to be violated again . . . vile hands on my person, vile hands interfering with me." His head fell forward onto the case in a sort of despair. "A malign force is following us. There is no escape."

His companion stroked his arm. "No Lorenzo. Things are going to change. I can feel it. You know I am always right about these things," her voice was soothing. "Please try not to think like that. I promise you those times are over, they are finished those years . . . and we were saved were we not! You see. It is a good omen."

But he wouldn't be soothed.

"I am soiled. I am made unclean," his voice was rasping. "Am I to be violated like this forever . . . other people's hands touching me, like those military doctors when they examined me, vile sacrilegious hands! Grade three. That's what I was. Grade three. That's what I am." He gave an ironic chuckle. "I should have asked those pickpockets to grade me too while they were at it, see what their diagnosis was, whether there had been any deterioration. What do you think eh Frieda?"

She stroked the knuckles of his clenched fist.

". . . Steal my dignity . . . Steal my money. It's all the same. Here help yourself." A bitter convulsion shook him. "Curse my soul. How do I stop it? I want never to be touched again."

"Not even by me?" She put a hand to his shoulder, teasing the material of his jacket, picking at it. She brushed her fingers through his hair and whispered something in his ear. "Anyway, there was nothing in your wallet. Just think, what an unlucky pair of pickpockets to choose you!" In spite of himself he gave a sort of coughing choking laugh.

The old omnibus continued its torturing ascent up the ever-narrowing pass road, swinging from side to side round impossible bends, the mountain flanks spurred with rocky outcrops and thick with oak woods, a last golden crepuscular light fading high above.

With a grunt of relief the bus crested the top of the pass, headed on a mile or two, rolled into a little mountain town and came to a stop. This was as far as it went. There was a great squeezing crush for the exit door. The foreign couple found themselves being carried out by a molten mass of bodies and bags while trying to hang on to their unwieldy case. Orazio, caught up somewhere behind, tried to get to them to help, but it was no good, and he felt again a surge of helpless annoyance.

The couple waited till Orazio too was disgorged. After the fuggy warmth of the bus, the air was sharp and icy. They were in a sort of open square with a crossroad at its centre, on one side, a narrow columned arcade, the entrance to what looked like a small convent, and next to it a church façade, on the other side a steep slope leading up to a tall arch, here and there old palazzi that had known better times.

Orazio could see their startlement as they looked about them, men in tall conical hats and long black capes, cord trousers to the knees, calves wrapped in sheepskin and bound by criss-cross leather thongs, on their feet some sort of pointed sandals curling up at the toe, the women with blouses and shawls, hair wrapped in coloured scarves, dark eyed, and with something of the hex in them, more threatening than the men. And they would come up and stare long and hard at the foreigners, and grunt and walk off. And then there was the language, almost unintelligible, nothing like the Italian they were used to. They had already heard it in the bus.

Beyond the village they could sense rather than see the presence of a darkening valley. High in the distance, snow-capped mountain peaks blazed magenta pink in the last rays of a molten sun now lost to view below the circling heights. It felt as if they had crossed an invisible frontier into an undiscovered land.

Somewhere, Orazio's brother was waiting for them with a donkey and cart to take them the last leg. But first things first, they would need fortifying. Orazio led them across the square and through a dark doorway into a cavern-like tavern. A fire glowed in the hearth. In the orange half-light, huddles of shadowy murmuring men in conical hats and cloaks stood around drinking, a scrawny cat basked on the earthen floor, a coven of old biddies in long grey weeds and shawls sat near the fire. It was like a scene from one of Goya's Black Paintings, the Englishman thought. Finally, one of the old biddies heaved herself to her feet and gave Orazio a nod of recognition. He rattled off something in dialect to her, they caught her name—Grazia. He pointed at the case— they would leave it here while they went about some business in the town.

The old biddy said nothing, already rinsing out glasses and saucers in a bowl of grimy water. She picked up the coffeepot from where it sat steaming in the hearth embers, poured the hot black liquid into glasses not very carefully, heaped in a spoon of sugar, splashed in a measure of rum so that it all spilled over into the saucers, handed the potions to the new arrivals, wiped her hands down her greasy dress and bent to stroke the cat. They drank down the gritty liquid with a grimace, but the rum warmed.

Back outside Orazio stood looking up and down, a wrinkle of irritation creasing the corner of his mouth.

"I shall buy some provisions," he said, "but where is that brother of mine?"

They wandered up the wide paved slope through the tall stone arch and along a narrow cobbled alley, and always the same stares, and nearly always the women, and they would plant themselves in the path of the foreigners, strong mountain women, unmoving, unsmiling. Some of them, recognising Orazio, would stop and make remarks in their thick dialect, curious, but Orazio pushed on by, brushing off their intrusions. In the butcher's he ordered some thick slices of steak from a strange-looking cut. Frieda thought it might be horse. In the bread shop, the aproned baker was busy pushing a long wooden pallet in and out through the mouth of a glowing oven. Large crusty oval loaves were deposited expertly onto a floury table top. They watched him, happy to stand there in the orangey warmth. He put down the pallet, wiped his hands on his apron, and wrapped a cooled-down loaf in brown paper.

"I will buy some butter," Orazio said cheerfully back on the street, "I know you will like butter on your bread . . . also do I." But in the shop there was no butter.

They made their way back down to the square, still no sign of the brother. No butter and no brother. Orazio's face darkened. He gave a final look around, then marched back to Grazia's tavern, fetched out the case, and to a litany of saints' names, guided his trailing guests to where a horse and cart stood in the dim light of a lantern. There was a rapid exchange in dialect, the driver reluctant to take them because of the dark late hour. Orazio dug in his pocket and handed over a coin, then another. They climbed up onto the cart, the foreign couple at the back, Orazio at the front, the big case stowed behind, and off they set at a crack down the narrow hill road, the driver's nocturnal fears magically vanquished by the extra coin.

The road cut down the side of a steep hillside. The couple huddled together for warmth. In the stuttering lantern light, large yellowish rocks loomed past, above them black bare winter woods, ahead just blind darkness. They rattled along down the hill road, the driver cracking his whip and crying out in high-pitched animal calls, some sort of wild fury on him, till finally they reached the bottom of the hill and he slackened off, the demon exorcised. They were in a wide open valley, the road now straight and flat, in the distance, mountain peaks spectral white, overhead a scintilla of stars.

"Isn't it wonderful? I think it's wonderful," she squeezed his arm.

They passed some dark dwellings with fires lit outside, silhouette figures moving slowly around as if performing some sort of ritual.

"What are they doing?" Frieda whispered. Lorenzo gave a little shrug. She huddled up closer to him. "Have we left the world? This is like nowhere I have been before."

"Look up there," he pointed up into the brilliance of the moon-less night, "Orion."

The cart rolled on through a small hamlet and on again, until the driver pulled at the reins and they came to a stop in front of a low stone building. Orazio turned round, his face shadowed and furrowed in the yellow light.

"This is as far as we can go with the cart. I hope my brother is here with the donkey . . . or perhaps I should say I hope the donkey is here with my brother."

They climbed down. Through a lighted doorway they could see dark figures moving. A woman came out. Frieda braced herself for more brazen peasant interrogation, but the woman smiled and offered her hand in greeting.

"Good evening. You must be real cold. Come inside and get warm." She spoke with an American accent, a youngish woman, good-looking and matter-of-fact in that busy American way. She helped them down with the case, then turned to Orazio.

"Giovanni is here . . . trouble with the rig . . . axle I guess."

"This is my sister's daughter, Claretta," Orazio said, taking the young woman by the arm and leading the travellers inside. A wood fire threw elongated shadows of hatted men against the rough walls. At a table, a group of them sat intent on a game of cards that seemed to entail banging your fist onto the table top, grabbing the cards, and shouting at your opponents in elated murderous triumph. The points were counted out, and a carafe of wine ordered, the losers paying, and then the trouble began, the winners deciding who could drink and who couldn't, all calculated to anger the losers and various other sundry participants who had joined in, till tempers flared, and fists thumped onto the table again. They were too immersed in their belligerent opera to take much notice of the strangers, thumping and dealing, draining glasses of wine, slapping their lips, taunting the losers.

"Take no notice, they are just playing," the young woman said in her reassuring American accent. She put a chair by the fire for Frieda to sit. It was like some place of wonders in a dream where animal characters dressed in strange clothes spin you riddles. There was a short parley between uncle and niece, a mixture of dialect, Edwardian English and Brooklyn American. Then the young woman came over — would they be more comfortable staying here the night rather than continuing on foot through the icy black night? Frieda cast a look around — more comfortable here . . ! It was a kind thought but they had come this far and they would like to reach their destination this evening.

From out of the shadows a little hatted man appeared, his cape held high against his face. He hauled the case outside and loaded it onto the back of a donkey.

"That is Giovanni," Orazio said, "he is a good boy, but not very . . . not very . . . How shall I say? You will see."

After the warmth of the inn, the cold soon numbed. The road was ice hard. Frieda wondered if they had made the right decision. Giovanni, the brother, walked a little way ahead, just his white sheepskin leggings visible in the dark. Orazio walked with his guests, holding aloft the lantern, saying little, but Frieda could sense a sort of nervousness.

"Not far now," he said, and he moved on up to check the donkey, pulling at the ropes but succeeding only in making the precarious load slip sideways. The loaf of bread fell on the ground. Orazio spoke words to his brother. The little man was silent. Frieda ran up behind and picked up the loaf.

"Manna from heaven. I'm starving."

She dug her fingers into the hard crust, tore off a chunk, gave it to her companion, then broke off another piece for herself. They walked along in a sort of numb silence, chewing the bread, breathing in the great expanse of stars and the circling glowing mountain presence. They were neither of them much dressed for the cold but were managing to keep each other warm, or at least less cold, the strangeness of it all helping to distract them.

She rubbed his shoulders and back. From somewhere close by they could hear the sound of fast-running water. Orazio stopped. A steep path led off the road down through some trees and undergrowth. He held up the lantern and led the way down, stopping a couple of times to offer Frieda his arm to balance against. Giovanni came down last, hauling back on the donkey to keep it from running away with him and the precious load.

"What do you think, will we make it to Bethlehem this evening?" Frieda whispered, squeezing her companion's arm.

"No room at the inn," he whispered back, "but fear not, I will find you somewhere to stay, even if it is only a stable."

And now they had the fast frothing waters in front of them, a wide rock-strewn mountain torrent with little sandy islets.

Orazio lifted the lantern again. "It's not as bad as it looks." He started to pick his way across, hopping from one sandy mound to the next. He turned and beckoned them follow, almost losing his hat in the hissing spray, snatching it back at the last minute. They followed him over, icy air grabbing at their ankles.

Somewhere in the middle Frieda turned and looked back the way they had come, a faint smile playing on her lips. She could just see the newspaper headlines—Lawrence Lost! English writer missing! The lost writer stepped up next to her with an enquiring look, but she shook her head and hopped on again.

There was one last obstacle, a stream too wide to jump over, a precarious looking wooden plank lying across it. Orazio looked at his guests.

"This is the last, the very last, I promise you, then we are arrived."

He stepped quickly across, the plank springing slightly under his weight. They followed him one at a time. Giovanni meanwhile had wandered further downstream, trying to coax the reluctant ass to wade across, goading and prodding it, emitting strange animal sounds and fierce whistles, but the beast just stood there, dipping its head up and down, sniffing at the water, the load on its back sliding precariously, and at every forward yank of the lead the beast pulled further back.

Orazio watched, muttering under his breath. With a shake of his head he crossed back over the stream, directing a hail of unintelligible dialect at brother and donkey as he went. Giovanni tugged and threatened and emitted his animal calls and yowls. Orazio herded them along the bank to try again. Not here. And on they moved again only to be met with the same ritual refusal, till the little stubborn beast, having made its point, chose its spot and plunged into the water.

"Bestia maledetta!" Orazio had hurried back across the stream to his waiting guests. "Why were such animals made?"

"He was worried about our case," Frieda said, trying to lighten their host's humour.

From the riverbed there was a scramble up a steep rocky track, over a misty meadow, and there, just visible through a dark of winter trees were a couple of rough stone cottages, and beyond them the outline of a little house, different, separate, alone.

Orazio hurried on ahead up to the door of the house. He stood there looking around him, muttering to himself, the lantern swaying in his hand. The travellers walked the last weary steps up behind him and waited.

"They have done nothing I asked," he said at last, "no fire made or anything."

He seemed uncertain what to do. He went around the side of the house, leaving them standing there, then appeared again a few moments later. Finally, he lifted the latch and pushed the door open. Inside was a sort of cobbled hallway with arched ceiling, farm implements leaning against the wall, baskets of beans and maize cobs on the floor. There was a wooden panelled staircase, and beyond that a corridor and unknown darkness—this much they could make out in the lantern light.

Orazio stood there muttering and shaking his head. Then, with a little shrug, he opened a dark door and led them through into a cavern-like kitchen, their long lantern-lit shadows loping after them across the bare smoke-yellow walls. On a wooden table were more piles of corn and beans and chestnuts. There were a couple of chairs, a wooden chest, all just basic, a cupboard which would be for food maybe, a wall shelf, almost bare, just one or two dusty glasses and cups, cutlery, hardly any, some plates, mostly enamel, not very many. Two small windows were recessed in the thick walls. Underneath one was a small table with newspapers and household tools strewn on it. In front of the fireplace stood a long grimy leather bench, but in the hearth there was no welcoming fire.

Frieda looked round benignly, Lawrence less so. Orazio put down the lantern, lit a lamp and some half-burnt candles stuck to saucers, then disappeared outside again. Frieda smiled weakly. Lawrence was silent. Orazio came back in carrying bundles of kindling and logs and shaking his head. He dropped them with a thump into the great hearth, then, still muttering in Italian, knelt down and set to piling the bundles of faggots and twigs in the thick bed of ash, and quite soon a roar of flames crackled up. He heaved himself to his feet, ran his hand through his long grey-black hair, and raised his eyes despairingly to heaven.

"I have asked Maria to come and make preparations for your arrival . . . light the fire and suchlike. You can see she has done nothing of the sort. I am sorry you have arrived to this. You can rely on no-one here."

The Englishman nodded tiredly.

"But what a wonderful place," Frieda said, imbuing her voice with as much energy as she could muster, looking around her, smiling with exaggerated enthusiasm. When the fire had built up a bed of glowing ash, Orazio sliced the steaks and set to frying them over the embers. All the cooking was done there in the hearth, pots and pans hung under the chimney, and there was a large cauldron on a chain.

They had heard Giovanni come into the hall with the case, but then he had disappeared. The couple sat down on the leather settle, rubbing their hands at the fire, too tired to explore and not a little apprehensive as to what might await them up the stairs. The steaks ready, various hands got the plates down and whatever other implements they could find. They made some space for themselves among the corn cobs and piles of beans on the table, Frieda commenting the while on how charming it all was, the rustic simplicity—just the way they liked it. Orazio slowly thawed, making odd grunts of shy acceptance, his body sagging a little with tiredness and relief. The steaks were surprisingly good, and they ate them with large corners of the crusty loaf. Orazio shunned the table for some reason and ate his on his knee.

They were warm and fed and pleasantly tired. The two men said little, but Frieda kept the conversation going with descriptions of places she had stayed long ago, places in Germany, wood cabins in forests, old hunting lodges on the estates of fellow German nobility, and comparing Orazio's little villa favourably with that distant brass-buttoned Teutonic world.

"This is such fun! Don't you think so? I'm so looking forward to exploring." She prodded the Englishman's arm, looking for him to join in or make some comment, but he just nodded.

Orazio put a pot of coffee on the embers, went out of the kitchen for a minute, and came back with some large pears in a basket — a local variety which conserved well, he told them, easing into his role of informative host. There were also some walnuts from his own tree outside, and under his arm he carried a dusty bottle of white wine. The coffee pot steamed. He poured a cup each and they settled in front of the fire, cracking nuts, sipping the sedimenty wine, and watching the glowing embers.

The front door creaked open and the little figure of the brother came silently into the room carrying a steaming black pot, some sort of vegetable broth. He settled himself somehow in the corner by the hearth, put the pot on his lap with some newspaper underneath, dug a spoon in, blew on it, and slurped it noisily down. Orazio shot him a look and barked something in dialect. The little man stared down at his dinner, the spoon hovering hungrily over the bowl. He looked across at his brother for a moment, then passed the spoon and bowl over to him. Orazio made a sort of resigned face at his guests, took a spoonful or two of the pottage with deliberate quietness, nodded, and passed the bowl back.

"I must humour him sometimes. He means well."

Giovanni skimmed up a spoonful, stared at it, daring it to make a noise, and sipped it as quietly as he could, but his hunger was too great and he was soon attacking it again with frantic slurping mouthfuls, almost biting the spoon off its handle. It was the first time they had been able to see the brother in the light and without the cape muffled round his face, although he still wore his tall conical hat. He was of a different species, short, squab, with a flattish face, simple and shy, but with strangely blue eyes.

With a slap of the lips he finished his bowl of pottage and put it on the floor. He sat with awkward quietness for a while, then squatted down in front of the fire and started to pile handfuls of twigs on the embers. He picked up the long iron tube, poked it into the stack of wood and blew, a weird intensity lighting his eyes. Flames soon roared up. He blew. The chimney rattled with the heat. He blew. The guests slid their chairs backwards. The kettle hanging on its chain started to steam. He blew.

"Basta! Basta!" Orazio called at him, but he seemed fire deaf, his senses tuned only to the raging flames. Orazio got up and pulled him gently away, then hooked the boiling kettle off the chain with a poker and slid it onto the floor. At least they would have hot water to wash with, Frieda was thinking.

Giovanni stared at the flames, then looked around the room as if offering this gift to them all. Satisfied, he picked up his bowl and left. The furnace slowly subsided, the little of conversation too. Orazio roused himself.

"I am forgetting myself. I must show you your room."

Candle in hand, he led them up the narrow wooden stair, Frieda carrying the kettle of hot water. Giovanni had already delivered their case onto the landing. The bedroom was bigger than they had expected, but spare, a wooden bed with headboard, marble-topped dresser, washbasin on a stand, a wardrobe, small table and a couple of chairs. The plaster walls were a rough yellowish white, the stone floor grey with little coloured speckles. But it was cold, so cold.

Orazio lit a candle on the dresser, made a sort of timidly welcoming nod, and wished them good-night. They closed the door after him and stood a minute staring at each other. Frieda took a deep breath, raised her eyebrows in a sort of coaxing smile, stepped up close to him and rubbed him vigorously up and down for a minute. She tugged at his clothes, pulling them over his head, and hurrying off her own clothes at the same time. The hot water on arms and face gave them some warmth and relief, and it was so good to wash a little after the journey.

He rolled into the bed with a shudder, burying himself under the blankets. The mattress rustled, it was stuffed with maize sheaths, and he felt like some sort of woodland creature settling into its lair.

Frieda blew out the candle, the room suddenly electric with the risen moon. She went to the window, pulled open the balcony door and stepped out — brilliant lantern-silver peaks lit the night, winter-thin trees pointed long silhouette fingers over hills and fields, pockets of pearl-white mist hung in the valley depths, from somewhere below, the torrent soughed its freezing whisper — and she forgot the icy cold, forgot the day, forgot the man calling to her, and threw back her head in a sort of voluptuous surrender.

She came back in, closed the window and ran to the bed, rustling up next to him, shivering and clinging. In the night she awoke, whiteness in her eyes, a sudden terror on her, a feeling of being alone . . . lost . . .

Chapter Five

———•———

MORNING LIGHT IN THE ROOM, MEMORY BLANK, DREAM emotions lingering, an owl hooting, white mountain peaks hovering. She reached behind her for the reassuring salt-sweet warmth of his sleeping body. But instead of turning and drawing up close to him as she would normally have, she was up and out of bed, throwing on her clothes, a new post-war post-England version of herself taking the floor—energetic, active, capable, wifely, ready to get her hands dirty. It was going to be a new start. He would see.

Downstairs, the old model pottering around at his usual slow morning routine was suddenly and cruelly swept aside by this new tyrant of cleanliness. Was this how it was going to be? He rather hoped so—a woman in the house! She set to, buckets of warm water, soap, scrub, sweep—face flushed, arms bare, thick fairish hair tied in a bright red scarf. Orazio followed her round with a peculiar male helplessness, apologising for the state of his poor home, holding things in her wake like a bemused scarecrow.

The new Frieda. She smiled to herself, observed herself being another. It was almost like one of their charades. She could just see him following her around, imitating her waddle, bending over, sticking his backside out the way she did, like a Cornish fishwife, that's what he used to say—and she laughed as she pictured it all.

He was so good at imitations. Where was he damn him? Why wasn't he down? He was missing the performance.

Housework. From the beginning it was always he who had done it, he who had cooked, he who was economical, tidy, scrupulous, who mended and made do—all virtues of necessity from his working-class childhood, though not what you would expect from a miner's son. But then he wasn't a miner's son, he was his mother's son, kept clear of all that uncouthness and grime, a nice little boy who picked flowers, a sensitive little boy who had become a sensitive man.

It was thanks to his instinctive economies, the careful make-do mother in him, that they had managed to survive at all over these last lean years. At first he had been acquiescent to her ways, the bliss of their new life together more than enough to compensate for those little omissions on her part, and anyway, he enjoyed domestic chores, they came naturally to him—and she, poor ignorant noblesse, she knew no better.

But this state of bliss was not to last. Circumstances changed— the war, his open opposition to it . . . unpatriotic, and she a German, accusations of spying, expelled from Cornwall, the constant money worries, the condemning of his book. Then there were her children—and his already thin nerves started to shred. She was wasteful, idle, careless, never lifting a finger in the house, always him scrubbing and cleaning and cooking . . . There she is, Madame Bovary, lounging about reading romantic novels, dropping her clothes wherever she takes them off . . . and next thing they'd be on the floor, both of them, wrestling, slapping, hitting, flushed and furious. They would fight in front of people, in front of friends, it didn't matter. He would scream at her, humiliate her, make her scrub the floor, and she would cry and sob and shout terrible things back at him.

From the most wonderful woman in the world, she had become the most terrible, a sloven, a weight round his neck . . . I could walk out on her now, leave her, and I wouldn't care a damn. That's what she means to me. I would be free—he had said this to a friend. Why doesn't he leave her! Why doesn't she leave him!—this the refrain from all around.

When, in October, she had made her first visit back to Germany since war end, he had refused to go with her, and it had seemed to some that the moment had arrived. But they didn't understand, how could they? War between them had become like the weather—the clash and heat of conflict, hit out and be hit, a beautiful electrical storm, a climax, and then peace—ah, and such peace it was, the peace that followed.

She had left Germany and made her way south to Florence, as arranged, and now here they were. But where were they? And where was he—damn him? She wiped her brow, twisted strands of her unruly hair back under her scarf, and set to again, the female Hercules cleaning out the stables of King Augeas, while King Augeas looked on with a sort of benign bemusement, a half-smoked cheroot in the corner of his mouth.

Still no sign. She huffed around and clanked her bucket, knocked her broom noisily against the wooden stair, spoke loudly to Orazio about the journey, about things they had seen, in Florence, in Rome, at every opportunity bringing in the name of the absent one, hoping he would be tempted to come down, even if just to contradict her. He liked to contradict her.

She stopped, leaned on her broom, and looked around her, enjoying the moment—yes, now she too could be numbered among the righteous. But even as she thought it she knew it wouldn't last. She knew herself too well.

Maria — the old woman who should have come and made the fire for their arrival the night before — suddenly appeared. She stood in the doorway, elfin, a wisp of a creature, the skin of her face tight and polished, cheekbones fixed in a staring half-grin, eyes bulging, blue cotton headscarf tied tight, gold earrings, dirty yellowish shawl hanging down over a long grey pleated skirt.

She flitted in, throwing devilish glances at Orazio, but stretching her grin even tighter at Frieda, and watching her curiously, following the foreign woman around with little darting movements, nodding and cackling and making approving noises, as if to say — that's the way we women do it — but offering little in the way of assistance other than just the odd shriek of unintelligible advice in dialect, or the occasional sortie at stray chickens that had wandered in, chasing them out, stamping and shooing, and ending with a strange self-congratulatory gurgle.

There was an exchange in dialect with Orazio, she in a high-pitched half-scream, by the sound of it indignantly repelling any reproof for the night before, her eyes shining defiantly, and looking to Frieda for some sort of natural female alliance in the matter. Orazio gave a long hopeless sigh of surrender, while she continued in her rapid dialect, chasing down her broken adversary, like a dog that goes on barking in triumph after seeing off its foe. After half an hour of nodding and screeching, she threw her shawl round her shoulders up to the eyes, and with a final run at the chickens, flitted back out and was gone.

Orazio took a deep breath and straightened his weary shoulders. "What am I to do Signora Frieda? He shook his head, slowly, grimly. "You can see why so many leave."

Frieda thought about this a minute, but let it pass. And so the great epic of cleaning continued, and as they busied around, Orazio answered questions — Giovanni, the little brother, lived over in the huddle of stone buildings that had been the family home, where Orazio too had lived as a boy. There were no shops down in the hamlet. Mostly the people lived off the land, and for everything else it meant a long steep walk up through the woods to the village proper, some two miles away, or a visit to the market in the little town they had come through the night before, where the bus had stopped—Atina.

Frieda listened, half listened, wondering whether to go upstairs with a cup of tea or something to rouse the sleeping absentee. At the far end of the mysterious dark corridor of the night before stood another double door. Orazio unbolted it. It was quite grand, set in a stone arch, the initials O. C., and the date 1889 carved into the keystone. It could easily have been the front door. From here there was a view down through a stand of winter-thin trees and across a meadow to a straggle of old stone cottages—the hamlet itself.

On either side of the ambiguous entrance were two nice sized rooms which could have been other living rooms. In the larger one to the left stood a great stone vat for making wine, an old wooden winepress, bottles, demijohns, tubes, and other equipment, all rather jumbled and disordered. Orazio muttered something about tidying it up, but with one thing and another he hadn't had time, and that anyway his vines were not very productive any more. There were some old ones from his mother's time but they were nearing their end. He was hoping to have a decent harvest the following year from new ones he had grafted onto old rootstock, mostly a white grape variety local to the area, called Maturano, an ancient vitis grown there since Roman times. He would employ a man from the village to help him, and they would share the harvest half and half—la mezzadria as it was known, the old country method of payment. The room on the other side of the corridor which backed onto the kitchen was just another repository, baskets of produce, fruits, nuts, potatoes, pumpkins and the like. The only real living room was the kitchen itself, enough it seemed for Orazio.

They came back down the corridor, and there he was, standing in the hallway looking thoughtfully up at the vaulted ceiling. He went on looking for a minute, oblivious, then turned to where they were standing. She wiped the back of her hand across her damp forehead, hoping for a comment, even something humorous, but he said nothing, not a word, just gave a little nod and wandered outside.

It was good to arrive by night and then wake to a new place, especially a place such as this and on a morning such as this. He breathed in deep. Peppery-sweet wood smoke drifted on the sharp clear air. He gazed around him, a brilliance of blue sky and white mountain peaks drawing his eye upwards, lifting his spirit, cleansing him of the toxic black vapours that had darkened his soul and his lungs over these last years, dispelling the gloom of the night before.

The little villa stood on a shoulder of land abutting onto a rocky hillside, meadows and pastures sloping away either side, here and there lone trees, or little sleeping lines of them, hornbeam, acacia, slender Mediterranean oak with shrivelled brown leaves—smaller than its northern cousin. To the side of the house, and almost touching it, stood a mature walnut, and next to it a persimmon—one last lone orange-yellow fruit hanging meditatively from a bare branch.

He started to climb the hill. It was steep and rocky, and a bit icy. Further up were the beginnings of woods, bare and thin now. At the first trees he turned and looked back down at the little villa — Orazio's Folly, whisperings of Palladio, a certain hauteur, aloof, equivocal, out of place, not really belonging. He rubbed his red beard, ruddier still now against the frost whiteness—he knew about not belonging.

Chapter Six

FRIEDA THOUGHT SHE HAD DONE A GOOD JOB, BUT WHEN she looked around, apart from the smell of soap, everything seemed much as before. She sat for a while by the fire, a little bit glum, waiting for the wanderer to return. Orazio made her tea and told her stories about himself, about his London life. But the wanderer didn't return.

She ran upstairs and washed off the grime of her labours, while Orazio made up a little package of food for her. She came down, put on her coat, and hurried out in the direction she'd seen him go. After the smoky kitchen, her eyes watered a little in the new brightness. There was still a thin smear of snow from a recent fall, just enough to catch a footprint or two heading up the steep rocky scarp. She followed them up, and soon found herself in open woods, pockets of snow in hollows around the roots of trees, but no more footprints. It didn't matter, she could sense him.

The climb had made her hot. She stopped and took off her coat, pausing to look about her. She hadn't really arrived yet, last night had been just about getting here, about darkness, about tiredness, and this morning, the ballo in maschera — the great masked kitchen ball — had left her no time to really think about where she was. She needed her compass, she needed him. She wandered, letting her senses lead her.

He was sitting against the trunk of a tree in the sunshine, gazing across the valleys in that inward looking way of his. She stood over him for a while, following the direction of his gaze. He said nothing. She didn't mind. She knew this sort of mood. It was just him. He stared out, blue and distant and fixed. She opened the leather bag that hung from her shoulder.

"Look, I've brought you some bread and some sheep's cheese." She tore a chunk of bread from the crusty loaf, broke off a piece of the cheese and held them both out to him, smiling her bright new hausfrau smile, looking into his face, trying to engage him. "Breakfast is served."

He stretched out a hand, allowing her to deposit the goods into it. She reached into the bag and took out a bottle of warm milky coffee and poured some into a glass. It had gone frothy from the jolting climb. She balanced it on the ground next to him and stood back with an indulgent smile — her little boy — a look that sometimes would please him, fill him with tenderness for her, and at other times, for no particular reason, irritate him. Today was a tenderness day. He held out his empty palm again. She ripped another piece of bread off and handed it to him. He picked up the coffee and dipped the bread in.

"What a lovely warm spot you've found . . . and a nice bed of moss . . . nicer than our bed." She sat down next to him, pushed her untidy fairish hair from her face, leaned back against the tree and closed her eyes, shivering slightly in the wintery rays.

"What are you thinking?" she asked after a while.

He finished his mouthful. "Not much. Just taking it all in."

In other new places they had been, he might, in the space of a day or two already have discovered the names of the locals, their habits, their backgrounds, their affairs, their enmities, the gossip, customs, peculiarities—things which should have remained hidden from outsiders, not so to him. Every little wisp of mood, expression, inflection of thought and speech, he would take in and take note of, something almost mediumistic. It was the well-spring of his writing. But of late, even that instinct seemed to have faded from him, as if the gods had deserted him.

"And what do you see?" she asked sleepily.

"I am not sure . . . the sun shines, the mountains circle, the valleys whisper something old. All is peaceful. It lulls you. But it is hiding something."

"I like being lulled."

"Look down there," he pointed away to the meadow behind the villa, winter scrubby trees, patchworks of snow and frosted grass, all still and white and empty, ". . . do you see them . . ."

She rested her head on his arm, looking down along it, screwing up her eyes. ". . . the two white oxen, the wooden yoke holding them, the man leaning into the heavy shafts to keep them straight, the black earth turning?"

She looked down at the empty meadow, shading her eyes. "You look so beautiful when you plough, shirt sleeves rolled up, brawny arms guiding the great iron blades . . . my handsome peasant man." She sniffed at him. "Come close, I love the smell of your sweat . . . the smell of your body. Later I will wash you down, but first let's . . ." And he let her.

"Mmm, you are all sweat and sweetness and earth, I don't think I shall wash you after all, just have you like this."

"With the cow shit too!" He reddened a little under her assault.

"Sweet cow shit . . . better than coal dust . . ." Her hands wandered down under his clothes into his shirt, her nose sniffing at him like a dog on a trail. He squirmed away with a little high-pitched giggle, trying to protect himself.

"Brawny, am I brawny? Aye, I suppose I am . . . Earth strength . . . And where have you been lass while I've been out doing man's work?"

She pulled her hands from his clothes and held them up close to her face, sniffing them, making big eyes. "I've been up here in the oak woods, gathering the acorns for the pig. You don't know I am here, but I love sitting in the sun and watching you."

"I always know when you are watching me, however far away you are."

She stroked his arms, squeezing the new-found muscles. She put the bottle away and the empty glass, shaking the drops out first.

"Let's explore a little. Show me what you've found. I know you've found something."

She got to her feet and reached down a hand. He took it, and let himself be roused up. The woods, all yellow-green lichen and slanting sunlight, drew them further in, and as they wandered, images of another time and another place came to her, those heaven days when the world was new, those first days together . . .

"What is it?" he asked after a while.

"Nothing."

He glanced at her.

Those first days . . . the days the world had turned upside down . . . she was leaving her husband, leaving her children, leaving her old life, her old self, security, comfort, certainty, respectability, leaving all of that for a penniless writer, and this a coalminer's son.

They had slipped out of England, made their way to her family home at Metz, partly to escape, and partly to somehow let her family know the news, she, still hardly able to believe it herself, wondering how it was that he had walked into her life—weak, strong, reddish, searching, unsure of his path, younger than she, a man, but something of not just a man.

"Are you mad?" her father had said when she told him. "Where is he?"

"He's staying up the road in a hotel."

Incomprehension . . . not really anger so much as the extraordinary folly of it all, and maybe a little dose of false morality.

"You have left all that to travel around like a barmaid." These were her father's words. But she didn't care. She had something she had never had before, something that must have been waiting inside her, waiting to be released, and now it had been, and she was free . . . she was vogelfrei.

The English miner's son and the old Prussian Baron smoked a cigarette together, stared at each other for a while, and that was it, the deed was done. A friend of her sister offered them a little rustic house in the Bavarian village of Icking to stay in—the brilliance of the Alpine peaks above, the freezing misty waters of the Isar below. It was a sort of rapture. She was in a state of bliss from the moment every morning when he brought her breakfast in bed with the fresh milk the neighbour had left at the doorstep, and on the tray a bunch of wild flowers he had already been out in the woods to gather. Meanwhile, he was putting the finishing touches to his new novel — other lives lived and loved and left — his own, to be called Sons and Lovers.

"What is it?" he asked again, "and don't say nothing."

"Does it remind you of anything, this place?" she waited, he waited, ". . . the little chalet house in the Isatarl . . . Does it remind you? It does me. All we need is some black bread."

She smiled to herself, remembering how much he liked the schwarzbrot. Simple things that were whole had such richness for him. She had had to learn a whole new vocabulary of life. "If it was springtime, we could look for wild strawberries."

Everything had been new, the world, nature, life. It was her country and yet she was seeing it for the first time, seeing it through his eyes. But he didn't just see, it was more than that, a tiny flower might bring him to a state almost of altered consciousness, like the time he had come across a mountain gentian for the first time, deep and blue — and he had knelt down by it as if he would tend to it, as if it were whispering to him of its soul — he and the little flower, he and she, all of creation. And he gave himself to her in that same way, entirely, deeply, held nothing back. She had no idea such a state could exist, that two people could come together in such a way. Till that moment her life had been perfect, lacking nothing, perfect children, considerate husband, nice comfortable middleclass English existence. What more could she want? It was everything and it was nothing.

She took his arm. "It is like the morning when we set out for Italy that first time . . . you remember . . . It has the same smell, the same light somehow . . ."

He looked down at the ground, looked away. She touched the side of his face, her fingers playing over his eyes, like a blind person, trying to see what he was seeing, but wanting him to see what she was seeing. "Be with me. I know you can. I want that back, and so do you."

They had walked along the valley of the Isar, up through the hills, through the great woods of beech and into the mountains, rucksacks on their backs, a few shillings in their pockets, all the money they had in the world, a little spirit lamp to cook with . . . Oh God, everything in a rucksack, no idea where the next night would find them, where they would sleep, haylofts — she had always wanted to sleep in a hayloft — and in the mountains the rough wooden crosses hung with those peasant Christs that he would write so beautifully about later, and journey's end, Italy, land of dreams, and by her side, this man, this being, her being.

He didn't look at her, he didn't need to, he could feel her thoughts, face aglow, life force welling up. He loved her for that. But it had been so long he thought it almost lost.

They walked on through the crunching ice-snapping woods, his face hidden, looking away and up at the trees. All that had happened since, the last years, the war, the battle with the courts, the battles with her, his chest, the lack of money—it had made him wary of promise, of hope. She heard his silence, heard his fear, but she wanted that other thing back. She would hope enough for both of them.

"You know what we should do while we are here, we should go for a long walk . . . up into the mountains, with rucksacks, rededicate ourselves, reset the clock, start again. You do believe in that don't you?"

He said nothing. They came out into a clearing, before them a great secular beech, around its base clumps of saplings like many fingered hands reaching up. It was the mother tree, the regenerator, the one the woodcutters leave, the old that holds the new.

There was a sudden intake of breath. "Did you know it was here? Did you bring me here?" She stared, her voice hardly more than a whisper. "Oh God." She looked at him, her lips trembling. "Die Buche . . . Isatarl . . . the beech woods. I knew I could feel it. Lorenzo, it is here for us. We are starting again . . ."

She ran forward and lay herself against the tree, her hands wandering over it, whispering words in German and letting herself slide slowly down its lovely smooth bark till she was sitting on the protruding roots. She beckoned him. He came. She pulled him down next to her.

"It is a sign, isn't it! Oh it is."

He didn't reply, just felt with his hand the shape the roots made as if he was looking for something, pushing his foot underneath them. She watched him a minute. "Do you want to take root too?" Her tone had a little inflection. Why couldn't he respond? She got up and looked down at him. He sat hunched over his bony knees, picking at the ground, at the icy twigs. She breathed a long deep breath, her breast shuddering a little, wanting so much that her feeling was true—Come with me. Don't hold back. It is waiting for us. The world is waiting for us.

She walked slowly round the tree, running her hand over the shiny bark just like she had over him. On the other side she sat down and leaned back against it. He heard a match strike, and the smoke from a cigarette drifted round. High above something caught his eye, it was moving along a branch with little furtive watchful hops, a large black squirrel with pointed ears. He watched, fascinated, he had never seen a black squirrel before. He wanted to call out to her but didn't want it to take fright, but just at that moment she called to him.

"Are you there?"

"Ssh."

"No I won't shush."

The squirrel skipped away in little bounds and leaps.

"A black squirrel," he said almost to himself in wonder.

"What did you say?"

"Nothing."

"Yes you did . . . something about an axis."

This he liked. This was too good. "Yes, that's exactly what I said . . . Axis."

"Well go on . . . What about it?"

"I said this tree is an axis, it is the axis mundi."

A puff of thoughtful smoke drifted from the other side.

"Do you think so . . . really?"

"Yes, and it is your tree."

This she liked. He could almost hear her smiling.

"Tell me more." It was the voice of a little girl wanting another bedtime story.

He waited for a while. He liked to bring that little girl out of her.

"Please tell me . . ."

He waited a little longer.

"Please . . ."

He took a long deep breath so that she could hear it. "The axis mundi dissolves all opposites."

Another puff of smoke. "Are we opposites then?"

He didn't answer, just let the question drift with the smoke.

"But you always said that was a good thing, being opposite."

"I didn't say we were opposites."

"I don't understand."

He patted the trunk. "Do you know, I did come up here earlier, and this tree wasn't here." He paused—the storyteller's pause, letting the listener take it in. "You called and it came . . . It came here to find us, all the way from the Isatarl . . ."

There was a long silence. He knew that silence—Frieda, eyes half closed, sinking into a reverie. Suddenly she let out a terrified scream, jumped away, rolled over, grabbed at her leg. Something had bitten her, some creature had risen up out of the snow and leaves and sunk its teeth into her thigh. She kicked out blindly at the attacker before she could see what it was, before she could see the hand, his hand. He had crawled round the axis mundi and sunk his nails into the flesh of her leg.

"I will kill you . . . Yes I will . . . One day I will. It is certain." Her voice was almost tearful with shock.

"That would make a change." He pulled her over to him. "You see what happens if you are opposite, you can't see what's coming."

She subsided into his embrace. He reached down for her feet, pulled them onto his lap and eased off her shoes — he was going to massage her feet to make up for his horrible act, she liked having her feet massaged, she would forgive him this time. But he was in full spate now.

"My shoes! Lorenzo!" He had thrown them away into the trees. "What are you doing, you mad man!" Then she remembered. It was another tale from the Isatarl, part of her early education, the time a heel of her shoe had broken while they were out walking, and so she had taken them both off and thrown them into the river—that's what you do with shoes that are no good anymore. He was shocked — someone had made those shoes, given their honest labour and time, hours, days, measuring, crafting — those shoes had a value beyond just the economic, they should be treated with respect, mended, cared for, and she, without a thought, just goes and throws them into the river for the crime of causing inconvenience to her noble extremities. She had a lot to learn.

The shoe episode had become part of their folklore. She wiggled her bare feet happily — the Isatar narrative was taking effect — absolution, hers for her omissions, his for all those times he had reduced her to tears, and maybe even an acknowledgement of her epic labours this morning, and the picnic breakfast. Throw away your shoes if you like, you are only being yourself after all, the person that made me whole—this is what it meant. It was his way. He wasn't going to say it outright. She smiled inside. It had only taken seven years. It was a good start.

But it wasn't just shoes that he conserved, he was a hoarder of people, their characters, habits, foibles, and just like shoes, they too could be reused, mended, given new laces, new lines of dialogue. It seemed to Frieda sometimes that they had two existences, one temporal and one fictional, and she wasn't always sure which was which, not after she read his accounts.

He looked at her from under his eyebrows, then reached slowly down and started to peel off her green stockings, cupped each bare foot sacredly, as if praying over it, then placed it carefully and ceremoniously back down again. She lay back and watched, the cold didn't matter. Now he took her hands, rubbed them in his, and started to twist off the rings she always liked to wear. He lifted a foot, selected a suitable toe and placed the ring on it, then the same with the other foot, finishing with the placing of the wedding ring.

"In the presence of the Axis Mundi, I hereby pronounce these feet united for as long as they both shall live." He held up one foot. "This is you." He held up the other foot. "This is me." He held them up together, "and we are one." He took her to him, but just as she let herself soften to him, he plunged one of her feet into a hollow of crystal-hard snow and held it in.

"Now I will really kill you." She slapped at his arms and he rolled away laughing.

"Toujours doucement ma petite Frieda . . . .Toujours doucement." She had told him how the nuns at her convent school used to try and calm her when she got out of control.

"Non . . . Jamais . . . I want to fight. I am growing weak. Our battles keep us strong. I don't want peacefulness, it is bad for me, bad for us." She pummelled him some more. He let her. She stopped suddenly. "Wait, one of the rings has come off. Where is it?" She scrabbled around on her knees in the leaves and roots, scooping up the snow. "Now look what you have done."

"That is a punishment," he pronounced.

"Ha, no it isn't." She dug out the ring and held it tight in her fist.

"Maybe it was supposed to come off, maybe the tree is demanding it. Then it will bless us, and every beech tree everywhere will know us, will be our guardian spirit."

She sat back against the trunk, smiling her blissful smile that made her mouth dimple at the corners.

"Die Buche," she whispered again, holding the ring tight, eyes squeezed closed. She dug down under a root into the snow and earth, plunged the ring into it and covered it over.

"Now it is done." She flopped back onto the ground, a little ecstatic smile on her face. "You are a conjuror. I will call you Lorenzo the Magnificent."

"And you are a child." He liked it when she responded so.

"I am older than you."

"It is not a matter of older. You are a child. You will always be a child no matter how old you become."

She pouted and made big supplicating childlike eyes at him. Suddenly his face drained, and an old anguished look returned. "Which ring did you bury? Not the wedding ring."

"Yes." She watched his face tighten, a wisp of wanton cruelty rising in her—if he wanted her a child then he would get her as one.

"No, don't be silly," she relented quickly, "it was just a cheap little thing I picked up in Baden on the way down. Do you think I would just throw away my wedding ring?"

He subsided. But the danger signals were there. It was all still just under the surface. She watched him. She didn't want to break the spell, didn't want to lose the special moment.

"This would be a good place to write if it was warmer, here under the tree with your notebook."

He scuffed the ground with his hand.

"Write what? There is nothing . . . and if I do write again they will just burn it on the bonfire of their ignorance."

She hugged her legs to herself and rested her head against her knees. From high above little pieces of cracked shell dropped to the ground next to them.

Chapter Seven

THE MOUNTAINS SLOPES WERE BLUISH-PURPLE AND BRINY, just the peaks burned golden, lit by a sun still hidden. Peasants streamed along the valley road, all in their costume, the women in their long coloured skirts, the men with capes and hats, pushing carts, leading livestock, milling along, and in among them a donkey and cart, a driver with long greyish hair falling from under his hat, and two passengers, foreigners, a man with a red beard hunched under a cape, a woman with brownish fair hair holding her hat down, all of them on their way to market.

They left the cart at the place where they had taken the rig on the night of their arrival. Frieda detached herself from the men. She wanted to wander a little, observe, feel the place for herself. From a vantage point up by the arch, she watched the two men as they threaded through the piled stalls, eager vendors grabbing at the red-bearded Englishman, Orazio almost a foreigner himself in his grey coat and homburg.

Nearby where she was standing, a pile of brushwood blazed, groups of men warming themselves, talking loudly and gesticulating, the dialect quite impenetrable and a little threatening. She looked back down, squinting her eyes into the low early sun. She couldn't see the two men any more, lost in the crowd. Something squeezed inside her, and just for a moment she imagined herself alone in the middle of all this otherness, making the best of it—the foreign woman.

She scanned anxiously through the throng, then felt the tightness relax as she caught sight of her two cavalieri talking to some hatted denizens and eyeing a couple of old wooden armchairs. She hurried down to meet them — the flushed fair foreign woman — but mostly the people were too busy with their own affairs to give her a second look. Lorenzo caught sight of her making her way through the crowd, her quick nervous step telling him what she was thinking. He held up a handful of cutlery, waving them at her, under his arm some rush mats. Orazio was packing a few porcelain plates in some paper and arranging for the two wooden chairs to be carried to the cart. A successful sortie. It called for coffee at Grazia's dark den, another gritty rum-laced infusion, then they headed home, leaving the armchairs at the inn for Giovanni to collect later with the donkey.

They hadn't been back long when the elfin Maria suddenly appeared, flitting in through the door, cackling still, as if she hadn't quite finished from the day before and had thought of a parting remark to floor old Orazio. Then she quieted and stood around watching, muttering to herself, curious. She wanted to see how these strangers carried on, and it was obvious she had taken a liking to Frieda and felt that they enjoyed some sort of hidden female alliance.

She had brought a bowl of tomato sauce as an offering to get past Orazio, she knew he was still displeased with her. She darted here and there, gold earrings glinting on her unwashed ears, busying herself as if she was part of the household but not doing anything in particular. Orazio unwrapped the new cutlery and plates. Maria gave a little hiss, put a hand to her mouth and stared at the new objects as if they were some sort of royal treasure, then she gave Orazio an odd squinting look.

"She is a witch," he said behind his hand, not that she could understand. But she knew he was saying something about her and brushed deliberately past him, bumping him as she went. She grinned at Frieda—we women know.

She took up position in front of the hearth, banging pots around, preparing pasta with her sauce, her quick movements seeming to speed time, or perhaps it was just that Orazio slowed it, and the meal was ready in minutes somehow.

She picked up a new plate, rubbed a finger and thumb thoughtfully over the smooth white porcelain, then ladled out the short thick pasta. When they were all served, she stood back and watched them as they ate, muttering and nodding, eyes shining peculiarly, ladling out more as soon as they had finished—gabbling away. She didn't eat any herself, too busy getting her fill of the foreigners. She sliced some pears and dropped them into glasses, topping them up with Orazio's cloudy wine. When she was sure the diners had had their fill, she snatched the empty plates away and dropped them into the wooden washing-up tub, eyeing them again curiously. She rubbed her hands down her black dress, picked up the glasses with the pears and wine, and plonked them emphatically in front of the guests, as if to say—now this is something special. She stood back again, pleased with herself, and poked a finger into her scrawny cheek, twisting it a few times — a gesture, Orazio explained, that meant something was delicious. Then, just as she had come, she was gone, clucking and muttering away happily to herself.

"Witch!" Orazio threw after her as the door shut. He sighed with resignation, tore a crust off the loaf as if performing some rite of exorcism and dipped it into the sauce for another taste.

Giovanni appeared with the chairs and lumbered them into the kitchen to much general approval. They had arms, and a sort of leather cushioning like the settle. Lorenzo lowered himself into one, shut his eyes and pretended to fall asleep. Giovanni though was preoccupied.

"He says it's going to snow," Orazio translated, and it wasn't long before they heard the little man crossing behind the house, leading the two giant white oxen from the field back into the stable. Light flakes floated past the window, quickly thickening, the outside world obliterated in a silence of whiteness.

The couple went and stood at the open door, stretching out their hands to feel the little ice crystals. Orazio put some chestnuts into an old pan with holes gouged in the bottom and slid it into the embers. A sense of cosy isolation descended on the room. Frieda went upstairs and came back down with needles and threads which they had brought with them. Then, with a sort of apologetic smile at Orazio, they spread the black cape he had given them on their knees and started embroidering it, not quite what the old model had had in mind for it, but he was pleased they had found something to pass the time, the days could be long here, especially when the weather closed in, like now.

"You must call me Lorenzo," the bearded embroiderer announced, drawing a thread through the thick material.

Orazio knew Frieda always called him that, but he didn't know whether he should, so he had continued with David, or Signor David, and with Frieda he tried Madam Frieda, or Signora Frieda, or just trailed off without a name.

"I was italianised a long time ago, during our first visit to Italy up at Lake Garda, and now it has stuck . . . Lorenzo . . . better than Bert anyway. It was Frieda who christened me." He turned to her. "It was you wasn't it my little songbird. She is good at names."

She looked at him curiously—songbird, what was all this? He smiled at her archly.

"It is her name for me and she holds the copyright, but an Italian has the automatic right to use it without breaking the law . . . Isn't that right?" He gave her another little pecking look.

Orazio shuffled the chestnuts, picked up a burning twig, flicked the heavy mat of grey-black hair away from his face, and lit the ubiquitous half-smoked cheroot in the corner of his mouth. In the short time they had been there he was coming to know their ways a little. Unusually for the English, they didn't hide themselves behind semblance and smiles, quite the opposite, they spoke and behaved almost as if there was no-one else present, sometimes goading or confronting each other, sometimes giving themselves over to open displays of affection. One thing was certain though, you never knew what was coming next, and yet it had a pattern to it, a process they needed to go through. No, they weren't like the English he knew.

"What are you thinking Orazio?" Lorenzo asked airily after a while, still concentrating on the tapestry.

"Ha!" the old model exclaimed, as if he had the answer just there on his tongue. But nothing else came. He had a sudden uncanny feeling that this man could read his mind.

"Come, you can do better than that, a Roman poet like you. Sing to us of the depths of the human soul . . . Sing us one of your odes."

Frieda gave him a little jab with her needle.

"I was thinking . . ." said the model . . .

"Yes?"

". . . I was thinking . . . err . . . about days gone by . . . about youth and love . . ." He gave a sort of grin and rubbed his chin, surprised at his own reply.

". . . while writing an ode to wine I should hope. Your namesake loved his wine . . . Quintus Horatius Flaccus. You know, I think we are on to something here, he too retired to his estate in the country just like you . . . solitary . . . cultivating his grapes . . . making wine. So there you are . . . Orazio and Horace, two millennia, one man."

Orazio smiled uncertainly — an ode to wine? — not his he was thinking. Lorenzo though had downed his first historical calyx and was heading up the Via Appia in search of another wayside taverna.

"Rome. Now how did that happen? Just a city with a river running through it and a high mighty rock in the middle . . .

a bit like Nottingham really." He paused and smiled. "The rest of Italy nicely settled, Celts in the north, Etruscans in the centre, the Greeks further south. Harmony reigned, well maybe the odd skirmish, but peace, mostly, certainly no thoughts of empire building, but up there on their Capitol, the descendants of Aeneas are watching."

Orazio puffed at his little gnarled cigar, rings of smoke drifting around the kitchen.

"What are those horrid little things?" Lorenzo asked, waving his hand at the offending grey mist.

"These?" The old model took the knobbly little cigar out of his mouth and held it up. "These are Toscanelli. Would you like to try one?"

Lorenzo regarded his host for a minute. He was coming to like him.

"Yes," he replied chirpily, "one should try everything don't you think?"

Orazio pulled himself to his feet, reached for the packet on the mantelpiece, flipped it open, and offered one to his guest. Lorenzo took it, held it up like Orazio had done, rolled it under his nose and sniffed appreciatively at the hard bitter skin, aware of Frieda's gaze, playing to it.

"Pass me holy fire from the Vestal flame good Quintus Horatius."

"Lorenzo!" She shot him a sharp little look.

"Great Zeus, what was that? . . . A warning thunder bolt! Oh well, perhaps another time. We'll just enjoy yours for now." He gave Frieda a playful smirk and passed the cheroot back to Orazio.

Silence and cigar smoke settled again over the room for a few minutes. Needles worked. Orazio raked the embers and put some more logs on.

"Now Orazio, I want to know . . . Are you a Roman? Are you Italian even? In fact is this Italy?"

Orazio knew these sort of conversations, how they could

suddenly brew out of nowhere, sitting room conversations with brandy and cigars.

"Ha!" he offered again.

Lorenzo pursed his lips, watching his victim attentively for a few moments.

"Orazio, if I didn't know better, I'd say you were a Japanese. You are becoming more and more monosyllabic. You really must get out more."

Frieda prodded him again with her needle.

Orazio gazed into the fire. Silence fell again, but just when he thought he would be spared, the Englishman called him back.

"Now Orazio, I've been meaning to ask, what language is it you speak around here? It doesn't sound much like Italian, not any Italian I've ever heard." Orazio stared. "It feels to me," the Englishman continued, "almost as if this is another country. I can sense something in these mountains, a strong identity, but not like anything I have met before."

Orazio cleared his throat, sat himself forward in his chair, opened his mouth, but then closed it again.

"Go on . . ."

"Well . . ." he hesitated, "I am not learned, but it is known that once these mountains were the home of an ancient people called the Samnites. They fought a long war with Rome . . ."

". . . and lost."

"Everyone lost against Rome . . . But they almost won, so it is said. You have heard of the Caudine Forks..?"

Lorenzo looked up, his interest suddenly stirred. "The Caudine Forks? Was that near here? Of course . . . Livy . . . The Samnite Wars . . . The Roman army made to pass under the yoke in sign of submission. We could learn from history, except we have gone backwards." He nodded to himself. "So that is it, dear Orazio, you are a Samnite, and if I am not mistaken, so was your famous namesake Horace. I knew I could feel something. Nowhere better than mountains for preserving identity." He paused for a minute. "But the mountains here are different from the ones around Garda.

Up there, they were still thinking about themselves, and I felt I could fall down a hole any moment . . ."

"Fall down a hole?" Frieda burst out laughing, "like Alice in Wonderland?"

Lorenzo shot her a look.

"I have never met a Samnite before. What a fine thing to be."

"I know," Frieda waved her needle in the air, "we could sew something onto the cape, a Samnite name or a symbol. What can you give us Orazio . . . some bit of local history?"

He raised his greying eyebrows. "I am not good at these things . . . I don't think I can . . ."

"Yes you can," Lorenzo interrupted, "you know it even if you think you don't. It's in your blood."

"Well . . ." He paused a minute. "They say that . . ." The listeners sat, needles poised, willing him on. "They say there was a Samnite city here in the valley, then there was this great battle, and the Romans destroyed it."

"Now that is interesting," Lorenzo said enthusiastically. "What was it called? Are there any remains?"

"It was called Cominium, but I don't think there are any remains, just the name of the valley . . . Comino Valley."

"Oh but no Orazio," Frieda stroked the surface of the cape, "we can't put a defeat on here. Isn't there some other symbol or something?"

Orazio rubbed his bristly chin. "I remember when I was a little boy the priest told us a story, an old legend about how the village got its name."

"Oh yes, tell us, tell us," she said excitedly.

Orazio was settling into his new role. He sat himself back in his chair and cleared his throat.

"It is said that the name of the village comes from the Latin word picus, which means woodpecker . . ."

"But I love woodpeckers," Frieda interrupted in a girlish excited voice, "when I was little, whenever I heard one I would try and count the pecks."

Lorenzo hid a half smile behind his hand.

Orazio composed himself again and continued with his history lesson: "Picus. In Italian the word is picchio, and of course the name of the village is Picinisco. So you see . . ."

"Was it a place where woodpeckers were heard a lot?"

Now it was Frieda's turn to muffle a chuckle.

"Don't be silly. How can we know that? Do you think there was a tribe of English ornithologists with binoculars wandering around here at the time?"

"I have a book somewhere." Orazio got up, shuffled out of the room, and came back a few minutes later carrying several.

"I must refresh my poor old memory." He opened a large leather bound book and thumbed through the pages. "Yes, here it is." He read the page to himself. "So . . . yes . . . the woodpecker was a bird sacred to the god Mars, and the god would appear as a woodpecker sometimes. It was part of an ancient religious right called Ver Sacrum, which means Sacred Spring. It was a thing they did . . . what is the word again . . . like you say in court?"

"An oath."

"Yes, no, like that . . . A vow. They took a vow, and all the children born in this special year were given to the god, they became his sacred ones, his sacrati . . ." he traced his finger along some lines of the page, ". . . and then when they reached a certain age, about fifteen, they were taken from their homes and left in the hills, then the god would appear in the shape of the woodpecker and lead them to new lands. There!" He looked up, pleased with his intervention.

But this is fascinating." Lorenzo peered over Orazio's shoulder at the book. "What was the vow taken for, some propitiation I wager."

Orazio passed him the book. "Here, it can explain it all much better than I. It is a history of the area written by a priest sometime last century, a very learned man. It is a rare copy. You read Italian Signor Lorenzo."

"How strange," Frieda said, distracted, "there was an Austrian Art Magazine called Ver Sacrum. I wonder if they got the name from this? They must have done."

Lorenzo ignored her, still smarting a little from her Alice in Wonderland remark. He sat for a while reading relevant paragraphs. "I was right. When there were disasters, wars and famines and the like, the children born that year were offered to the god to appease him, and when they came of age, the god, whose name was Mamers, appeared in the shape of a woodpecker to claim his sacrati and lead them to pastures new. Oh this is splendid . . . almost biblical. And so that is how the village got its name, a sort of Woodpecker Hill. Sounds like an address in Hampstead." He grinned boyishly from under his lowered eyelashes, ". . . And thus it was that a young sacrato by the name of Orazio was delivered up to the woodpecker god who guided him far away to a new home in a new land across the seas."

Orazio looked up, a wry smile on his face.

"I never thought of it so . . . except I landed on Saffron Hill in Clerkenwell . . . not as nice as Hampstead."

Lorenzo clapped the old sacrato on the shoulder, and the old sacrato got up and went to fetch a bottle of his sacred white wine, and they set about toasting the woodpecker god.

Lorenzo held out his glass for a second splash.

"But Orazio, I am bothered. If you were taken to London by the god, why then did you return? Is that not breaking the vow?"

The old model shrugged and looked away, muttering something to himself, something about the malocchio, the bad eye — and he made a sign with his fingers, the horns of the devil, surreptitiously, thinking they hadn't seen, but Frieda saw, and imitated him, trying it out for size. She had seen them do it in the market too.

"There are some here who follow the old religion still. Giovanni knows who they are. Sometimes he disappears for days, like a cat. There is an old man who lives in the mountains. He is a charcoal burner. His name is Mamerkis, like the old god. He even looks like a woodpecker . . . a nose like a beak." He made a beak shape with his hand on his own nose. "We call him Mamo for short."

Lorenzo clapped his hands with delight.

"A real live Samnite. There you see," he said excitedly, turning to Frieda, "the old gods live . . . Sangue . . . It is in the blood," and he got up and did a little war dance round the room. "May the old ways never die."

Orazio smiled, happy he had been able to introduce novelty for his intellectual guests, though not quite sure how blood came into it. He had never imagined that one day his humble kitchen would echo to the sound of decent conversation—English conversation. He sipped his wine. It tasted like champagne.

Frieda was saying something about ways of knowing, about blood and knowledge and consciousness, ". . . Do you follow Orazio?" she asked.

"Of course he follows, he is a man of the blood, all Italians are. That is why we are drawn back here always. They live in their bodies, in their blood, not in their minds."

"My body . . . Hah . . ." Orazio opened his mouth then closed it again.

Lorenzo looked at him, wondering whether to test him further on his body outburst, but deciding they had extracted enough from their poor old host for the present.

"Orazio, you sound more like a jackdaw than a woodpecker."

The old model gave a timid smile. He missed English humour. "I nearly forgot." He picked up the other books he had brought in." This is a copy of Livy where you will read about Cominium, and this other is a novel by a writer from here, born in the village . . . Giustino Ferri. I thought you might be interested. He was a friend of Pirandello and of D'Annunzio, quite well known here in Italy." He passed the books to Lorenzo.

"This is indeed a place of wonders. What else will it reveal?"

Lorenzo read the novel title: "La Camminante. That means the wayfarer I think, but a female one." He looked at the cover thoughtfully.

"You know," Orazio went on, gaining in confidence, "he was a very superstitious man, Ferri. He had a terrible fear of the number thirteen, and do you know what happened Signor David? He died suddenly on 13th March, 1913, at 13.00."

"Sounds like another Samnite curse." The Englishman made the sign of the horns. "Perhaps we better go and see this old charcoal burner."

"What is the novel about?" Frieda asked.

"It is a love story, Madam Frieda, with a sad ending."

"Not a sad ending!" Lorenzo put a hand to his heart.

"Indeed yes . . . ahimè," Orazio hadn't quite caught Lorenzo's smirking tone.

"What happens?" Frieda asked.

"Read it and find out," Lorenzo interrupted again, a little twang of amused exasperation in his voice.

"I will tell the Signora. A young woman is found unconscious in the road just outside the village. No-one knows who she is. She is taken in by this old writer who lives with his sister . . . Signor Ferri himself in disguise . . ."

"Funny how writers do that." Lorenzo sipped his wine.

"And then?" Frieda asked, leaning forward to look at the cover.

"And then, they nurse her back to health. She turns into a beautiful educated young woman. The writer and the girl fall in love. But it cannot be, and one morning she is gone, never to be seen again."

"I think Puccini could set that to music." Lorenzo got to his feet and started to conduct the invisible orchestra.

Orazio poured more wine. Frieda reached over, took the book and read the first page.

"Listen to this . . . the opening paragraph . . . two men are sitting at a kitchen table, sipping wine, talking . . . and one of them is looking at the other with benevola malizia. It could be us. It could be this very moment . . ."

"It could be La Boheme," the conductor proclaimed from his rostrum, "but which one of us will you fall in love with Mimi? With me I think . . . I have more malizia . . ."

Chapter Eight

THE SNOW FELL, AND KEPT FALLING, THROUGH THE DAY and into the evening, hushing the already silent world, filling it with an exquisite sense of isolation. Frieda took a brass container filled with embers from the kitchen hearth and made up a fire in the little fireplace in their bedroom.

Orazio slept in a room across the landing. She presumed he had vacated his room for them, because when she had put her head round the door, which he always left open, even at night, there was no bed, and no furniture to speak of. He slept on what looked like a pile of old clothes and blankets, and the room was full of cases and accumulations from his London life. There was another room whose door was permanently locked, also a small closet, and out on the landing a sort of wide space with a lovely French window, where, she imagined, it would be a pleasure just to sit and while the time, or read or paint when the weather was good.

"A man of parts our Orazio. Which is the real one do you think? He's still handsome in a way, and you can see what he must have been like . . . what they saw in him, Thornycroft and Leighton and the others. He's like a sort of Dorian Gray character don't you think . . . all that London life . . . mixing in circles . . . touched by the gods . . ."

"He's not wicked," Frieda interrupted defensively.

Lorenzo shot her an amused look. He liked how she misunderstood him sometimes.

"There's something about beauty," he continued, "more than mind or logic or cleverness. It is peerless. Do you think there might be a young version of Orazio still wandering about London?"

From across the landing, Orazio would hear snatches of conversations. Lorenzo's voice was quite high, especially when animated, which was often, while Frieda's voice was deeper, throatier. Sometimes he heard his name mentioned. He didn't mind, in fact he quite liked it. It made him feel like a living being again. But sometimes too he would doze off, then wake with a start, hear voices murmuring, and think there were ghosts in the house. He had a fear of spirits.

Frieda opened the balcony door and stepped out. She lit a cigarette.

"It's stopped snowing. What wonder! Oh, I love it like this, so quiet, so still . . . another world."

"Don't smoke."

"Since when did it bother you? It won't come in. Look I'll blow it outwards."

". . . And close the window. If you're going to let the weather in we might as well go and sit outside and freeze to death. My chest. Do you want to kill me . . . and the fire is almost out."

The window clicked closed, irritated stockinged feet thumped across the cold stone floor, logs fell heavily into the fireplace. Silence.

"I'm going to call this bed Bertrand," he announced with exaggerated jollity, trying to smooth over his little outburst.

"Why?" Her voice rasped, not quite ready to accept.

"Because it Russells so much."

He watched her boyishly. She glared back.

"I knew you two were friends, but I didn't know you slept together." Now it was her turn to smirk, but before he could answer she deviated off. "Weren't there rumours about Leighton . . . you know . . . ?"

"No, I don't know." He shot her a glance. "As for Orazio, if that's what you mean, I think he likes the frauleins, especially German ones."

"Frau if you please. I am a married woman."

"Married eh? Who to?" He paused, wondering how far to go. "I've seen him looking at you."

"That means nothing. All men look."

"All men look! . . . All men look!" he said, his voice rising menacingly. "What have I told you on this matter? You are leading him on . . . just like the others. You have had your last chance . . . all your socialist ways . . . I've warned you . . ."

"No, no, it is not so." She looked across at him, searching in his face pleadingly. "It is all in your imagination."

"So, I have decided," he clenched his jaw, "tomorrow I am leaving . . . going away and leaving you here . . . you and your devilish Italian . . . then you can cook up whatever it is you are cooking up and stew in it as far I'm concerned."

There was a little choking sob. "And where will you go?"

"You have lost the right to know." His voice was stern and authoritarian.

"Don't leave me. Whatever anyone says, I love only you, believe me, only you."

"I cannot believe you. I have received a letter. It is here in my bureau. I know everything."

"It is false. Whatever it says, it is all just malice and envy. I beg you."

"This is my final word. I have decided. I have been in touch with my old regiment . . ."

"No no, not that."

"Yes, the Hussars. Next week I will be with my old comrades at the front. I care not for my life anymore."

"And will you write to me?"

"Don't you understand, I said I'm leaving you."

"I will send you socks."

There was the sound of muffled laughter from the bed clothes.

"Will you knit them yourself?" came a quavering voice, struggling for seriousness.

"And chocolate . . . I will send you chocolate." There was a deep sighing pause. "Will you ever come back?"

"Never," he said, with renewed cold control. There was another pause. "Never more than once that is."

"And that once will be forever!" She said, her voice all of a tremble.

"Forever! And then we will go and live in a place that has forever in it."

"Where is forever?"

"America."

"Why America?"

"Because forever is a future place. Europe is the past, marbley white and crumbling . . . like Italy . . . a mausoleum. Forever is light, unphysical, intangible, full of air and brightness."

Across the landing, slow sleepful breathing—Orazio had missed the end of the melodrama. But underneath the spontaneity and play, there was something more. The war years had produced crises, and there had been moments when she thought she had lost him, when he ignored her, like that episode in Cornwall when he spent more time with their neighbour than with her—a young man. Hussars! He didn't realise what he had said, but she did. But male companion or female, that wasn't the point, it was the someone else. And what did she feel? Abandon? Certainly, sometimes. But at other times she couldn't have cared, she had been glad even, and ideas had entered her head too, not of leaving exactly, but of finding some intimacy elsewhere, openly or secretly, it didn't matter. Acting out little scenes like this somehow informed her what she felt, if she still loved him, how much, whether they were coming closer together or heading further apart again, what point in the cycle they were at. It was, she guessed, the same for him.

He was propped up on his pillow leafing through the books that Orazio had lent him.

"What to do Frieda? Is it any good here?"

She knelt on the bed and wrapped him in an embrace.

"Not now," he said, keeping a hand on a page, "you're knocking the books on the floor." He put his head in his hands. "God, what has happened to me? I am dry. I have dried up. I can't write, and now my life urges are drying up too."

She curled up next to him. "I have a feeling about this place."

"How? Here we are, snowed up, and here am I, sinking into a slough of hebetude."

"Something will come."

He sighed. "Look at that big empty wall over there."

"What about it?"

"It's crying out for a picture. Maybe I'll ask Orazio if he minds if I splash a mural on it, liven it up a bit. I'm sure he won't, and he's bound to have some paints or something."

"Why would he have such things here?"

"I don't know . . . I just know he has." He put the books down on the floor by the bed and turned to her.

Chapter Nine

An unearthly heathen caterwaul burst on the silent early morning mist.

"What on earth..!"

They tumbled out of bed, dragging the heavy blankets with them, hopped barefoot across the cold stone floor, and pressed their faces to the glass, shivering. Frieda pulled at the balcony door. It was stuck shut with the cold. She pulled again. It flew open, letting in a blast of freezing air. She leaned out over the iron balcony railing, Lorenzo huddled up behind her, staying just inside. Below, two caped sheep-skinned natives, tall hats with red ribbons, long wild hair spilling over dark beards, were bellowing and blowing their instruments — the white animal-skin of a bagpipe, and a long pan-like flute — cheeks bulging, fingers flying, wild and frantic, clawing at the freezing air, ancient, primitive, yowling.

They stood in the knee-deep snow, an occasional glance from under the brims of their hats up to the balcony. Then the flute player stopped, opened his lungs, and a fierce high screaming sound issued forth as to burst the arteries, repetitive, relentless, the awful sound of a soul fighting to wake from a dream, naked of anything civilised, insistent, unforgiving, while the bagpipe droned on like a dying angel. Abrupt silence. The singer snatched off his hat with a flourish, threw a final glance up at the audience, and then they were gone, plunging away through the snow.

"What was that!" Frieda said, closing the window, but behind her, a libidinous satyr was dancing and cavorting round the room, planting goat-horn fingers on his head, and making large lustful eyes at the half naked naiad, who now fell in with him, following him round, pulling his imaginary tail and clawing at his skin, animal with abandon.

Orazio had been up since dawn, had made the fire, and was busy clearing snow from the front door, kept company by the inquisitive pig, Pasqualina, who watched attentively the swinging shovel, hoping to see bits of food fly off the end of it, and snorting in disappointment at every meteor of inedible snow. The ass watched with big eyes this invasion of its favourite spot by the door, and the chickens scuttled up and down the corridor with fright and cold.

"They will come every day now till Christmas," Orazio told them when they came down. A big pot of black coffee was simmering on the embers of the nicely glowing fire. There was creamy milk, a crusty loaf, and a choice of honey or black liver sausage. Orazio, still complaining about the lack of butter, spread honey on his bread, and stuck slices of sausage on top of that. A look of horror from the visitors, but then they tried it themselves and found it curiously good.

"That was not any Christmas canticle that I have ever heard." Lorenzo took a sip of his coffee. "The voice of the mountains, Orpheus gone mad, tangling with forces, returning from the underworld. Follow me if you dare. Don't look back." He sliced another piece of liver sausage.

"Like I said, they will come every day. Listen, you can just hear them down the hill at the other houses." They listened. Orazio couldn't make up his mind whether they liked it or not, you had to dig into their words sometimes to get to the meaning, especially Lorenzo.

"It is a religious offering. Sometimes we give them a glass of wine or something."

"What religion? Not the Christian one." Lorenzo made the shape of two horns on top of his head.

"It is an ancient tradition of these valleys. I zampognari di natale . . . that is what they are called. At this time of year they go far and wide, they play in the cities, in Roma and Milano. They are famous all over Italy . . ."

"Not those two . . ."

". . . even on the streets of London I have seen them, and artists love to paint them."

"Ha! Was that how you started Orazio. Can you play?" The Englishman spread some honey on his bread and stuck little slices of liver sausage to it as if he was designing a collage. "Italy, the land of music, of Monteverdi, of Vivaldi . . ." he took a bite of his edible masterpiece, ". . . that, dear Orazio, was not music. It was anti-music. I would go so far as to say that that was not even of human composition, it was the voice of the wild things, of the mountains themselves. I am beginning to think those skins they all wear are their real skins."

Frieda made an admonitory frown at him.

"Forgive him Orazio, he gets carried away. You should see what they look like in his home town."

Orazio shrugged and made a gesture with his hands heavenwards. "You are surely right Signor Lorenzo. But what can we do?"

Frieda carried her bread and coffee to the door, opened it, and stood on the threshold looking out at the white ice world, desolate little spirals of snow gusting up and down in the whipping wind. They must somehow get out. He would get testy if he was cooped up. She closed the door and went back across to the fire to warm herself . . . Lorenzo was talking about his idea for a mural on the bedroom wall, and asking whether there were any paints.

"Don't worry about it Orazio," she said, "he can find other things to do."

Lorenzo gave her a sharp look. Why did she have to put in her penneth worth always?

"Somewhere I have a box of materials that Leighton gave me . . . it was just after he crucified me." Orazio wiped his mouth and reached for his cheroot.

"What do you mean?" Frieda looked at him with a sort of disbelieving uncertainty.

"My dear Orazio, do you still have the stigmata?" A glimmer of a smile played on Lorenzo's face.

"What do you mean crucified?" Frieda asked again, still unsure.

Orazio was enjoying his moment. "He had his ways, the maestro, just like all the great Renaissance artists."

"I don't think we can put him in that category," Lorenzo said with emphatic disdain. "He might have had his ways, but as for his art . . ."

Finally, Orazio conceded. "I will tell you. It was for a painting of the crucifixion he was doing, he tied me to a cross and I had to stay strung up for hours. None of the other models would do it. When I went home in the evenings I could hardly walk." Orazio hung his arms down and staggered around the kitchen to illustrate his condition, knocking against the chairs. "I think he liked to give his models pain, especially me. I was not his favourite, he liked his models more fleshy. Well, he promised me extra money so I did it . . . Damn you Cervi, he said to me, you've got to stay there till I've finished, you devil." Orazio smiled, and nodded to himself ruefully. "Then one time, I thought the devil had really come for us . . . he had just finished tying me to the cross, when he lost his balance and fell backward, pulling me with him. There we both lay, he underneath, me and the cross on top. He could not move, I could not move. There we were, two blasphemers. He had to shout for help to free us."

Frieda stared, not sure whether it was funny or not.

". . . So when it was finally finished, he was good to his word and paid me extra. Then he gave me a box of paints, and with his wicked smile he said: 'Here, you poor Christ, your blood must be solid by now, try some of the thinners in your veins.'"

Frieda was still undecided, and Lorenzo's compliant amusement was annoying her for some reason.

"My dear Orazio, fear not, I won't require you to sit for me, and I don't think I shall paint a crucifixion, I don't want to be taken just yet by some angel of retribution happening by, but I would like to leave a mural for you."

"Are you leaving already?" Their plans were always under discussion. They were like a couple of grasshoppers.

"Lorenzo left the enquiry unanswered. "Are there any brushes in the box?"

"I don't know. I don't think I've ever opened it."

"If not we can always use some animal fur or bristle, or some tufts of noble German hair," he tugged at Frieda's thick mane. She let him pull but she didn't smile.

Orazio hurried out of the kitchen, and came back shortly carrying a nicely hinged large wooden box with a London art suppliers name on it.

"You said mural yes? Then you are in luck. In here you will find paints that my torturer used for his murals at the Victoria & Albert in Kensington."

"But Orazio," Lorenzo said taking the box, "you are a genius." He opened it. "Look here," he unfolded a printed booklet, "it says The Gambier Parry Process for Spirit Fresco."

Inside the box was a jumble of materials, all sorts of mixtures and coloured powders and oils, bottles of spirit, washes and turpentines, even some fine quality paper rolled up, and in the booklet, instructions on how to mix them, how to apply the special wash to the wall . . . warm up the ingredients, dip the brush into the oil of spike . . .

"God bless you Orazio, and your cruel friend Leighton. Paints. I am so happy. I should forget about writing." He rummaged in the box. Then he looked up. "But tell me this. The human body is art . . . Good, we agree. All the great artists paint the human body . . . Good, we agree. So why can't I write about what those human bodies are thinking, and maybe doing?"

He searched in the box, took out a sheet of the paper and various items . . . materials, charcoals . . . and spread them out on the little table under the window to examine them better. Since Frieda had washed the grime off the glass, the gloomy kitchen had an almost clean brightness, especially in the cold white snowlight.

"I must do a cartoon first."

"Like Leonardo!" Frieda arched her eyebrows.

"Indeed so Baroness . . . Leonardo, Lawrence, Leighton, we are all from the same school."

She thought of another little jibe, but decided not to.

The fire crackled and spat. Orazio pottered around, went out to the corridor, came back in with a basket of dried white cannellini beans, poured some into a terracotta jug, topped it with water, and placed it in the embers in a corner of the great hearth to slowly cook. Giovanni tramped in, stamping the snow off his feet and was immediately and dictatorially put to work by Orazio, chopping vegetables and whatever else to prepare a big cauldron of stew for the day. The pig's food had already been cooked in it—pig first. Giovanni took the cauldron outside and scoured it in the snow. Frieda started to chop some vegetables. Orazio told her to leave it to his brother, she was a guest, but she went on anyway, she had nothing else to do.

She finished her little chore and sat for a while watching the silent men at their tasks, then, of a sudden, she jumped to her feet and went to the door, threw it open, skipped down the step that Orazio had cleared, and out into the powdery muffled whiteness. A moment later there was a great liberatory shout. She scooped up a handful of snow, and rubbed it up and down her bare legs and arms, all the while giving out little shouts and cries, then she snapped some twigs from one of the trees that circled the clearing, and started softly switching her limbs and back till she felt her blood coursing with ice-hot energy. Revitalised by her Nordic snow cure, she came back into the kitchen and sat there simmering for a while in the concentrated male silence, till the dam could hold no longer, and she let out another great lioness roar. The red beard was not to be diverted, deep in a detail of his cartoon. Orazio bent down to fish a glowing brand from the fire to light his cheroot, only Giovanni stopped what he was doing and stared with open jaw till his brother aimed a chestnut at him.

"I am happy here," she announced after a while, getting up and looking over the artist's shoulder. He let her look.

"You'd be happy anywhere with me Baronessa."

"Really? Why?"

"Because you adore me . . . and because I take you to such freezing ice palaces," he said under his breath, glancing over at Orazio. "Orazio," he called across the room, "the Baroness is happy here, she says it reminds her of a German schloss." Orazio nodded. "Castello Cervi," Lorenzo continued. "Cervi means deer doesn't it, in the plural? We should make a coat of arms for you with a deer, or really a hart, if we want to be properly heraldic . . . Sir Horace Cervi, Bart. I like the sound of it . . . Here we are, guests of the noble baronet at his fine old country estate, Cervi Hall."

Giovanni looked round expectantly, hoping for more leonine roars, enjoying the talking, even if he understood nothing, but the room subsided again into silence. The Englishman finished his charcoal sketch, set it to one side, placed another sheet of paper down, fished out some oils, and squeezed a few colours onto a palette and a little turps. Frieda looked on glumly. Orazio rattled off something in dialect to Giovanni, who got to his feet, threw his cape round his shoulders and went quietly out. A few minutes later there was the muffled sound of wood being chopped across by the old buildings.

Lorenzo sat back and looked at the outline of his new picture, touching up little corners here and there. He had diluted the oils so that he could work fast. Frieda came over to look.

"Do you know," he said quietly to her, "I think hardship is good for us. We haven't had a quarrel since we've been here."

"If it was just a question of hardship Signor Lorenzo," she whispered back, patting him on the head, "we would never have had a quarrel in our lives."

He dabbed at her hand with his oily brush. "Only people who love each other quarrel."

"So what are you saying, that we don't love each other anymore? She pulled a tuft of his hair. "But I feel generous today . . . the Baroness feels generous . . . she loves you even if you are a misery."

"Me a misery? An' who's ter blame for that missis?" It was a question maybe he shouldn't have asked, especially with a Nottingham accent.

She was silent a minute.

"Go on lass, say what's on yer mind."

"Your mother . . ."

"What about her?"

"You know what about her. She got the most of you, and now there are only limited rations left for the poor Baroness."

He flushed. "German rations. If you will make war that's what happens."

There was a pause.

"Why are you so vicious sometimes? That wasn't called for." But she knew she had touched a nerve. Once, she had written a little skit about him and his mother, adapting it from his novel. It did not amuse him.

He took a deep breath, picked up a paintbrush and held it in the air. She watched him, unsure what his next move would be. He waved it back and forward a couple of times as if conducting, then started to make some sort of shapes with it in the air.

"From now on I'm changing your name. What does this say?"

She followed the tip of the brush. "That says Frieda."

"Try again." He repeated the airy cipher. "I should have thought of it before . . . not Frieda . . . Freuda." He beamed. He was a schoolboy again, happy with his playground joke. "You Germans . . . all that psychoanalysis . . . all that horrible Oedipus stuff . . ."

She snatched the paintbrush and rapped it on his head. "I'm just quoting you . . . Read your own book . . . and Freud is Austrian not German."

"Same thing . . . don't you think so Orazio?" he said. But there was a note in his voice, a note she knew.

Orazio looked over from where he was sitting by the hearth feigning invisibility. "I know not of what you talk," he said abstractedly.

"You are wise not to know." He turned to Frieda. "Next thing you'll be telling me that Jesus had an Oedipus complex . . . the Madonna and all that. Christ on the couch. No offence Orazio."

She gave a halfway little laugh, unsure. She grabbed his wrist nervously, pulled him up, and dragged him to the door. She opened it. An icy wind was whipping across the crust-white snow. She gripped his arm tight, as if she would thrust him out into the bleak landscape, into the glittering crystal dunes . . . thrust them both out.

"Wait till this afternoon. The wind will drop." Orazio called from the kitchen. "Now some snow has come it will settle again. It will be so. We will have some good days."

They came back in. Orazio bent to the hearth, picked up the steaming coffee pot and refilled their cups.

"Thank you Sir Horace. We rely on your knowledge." Lorenzo sipped his coffee. "Orazio, when shall we go up to the village of the woodpecker? I have given its address to half the world. The name Picinisco is now spread far and wide, from Munich to London to New York, even as we speak people are poring over their maps and spinning their globes and wondering how it is such a place had escaped them." He spun an imaginary globe on the table. "There will be post for me, and I in turn must send some. Do they deliver letters down here?"

"Giovanni says tomorrow will freeze. Sunday will be best, then you can meet your patron saint too."

Lorenzo looked at the old model. "My patron saint?"

"San Lorenzo, he is patron saint of the village." Orazio smiled bluffly.

"St. Lawrence . . . burned on the griddle. I am well named. The martyrdom of D. H. Lawrence." But behind the joking tone there were was an edge.

"Does the postman come this far Orazio?" Frieda turned the question back, she had heard the subtle inflection.

The old model shrugged and gave a weak grin. "The post is a bit . . . how shall I say . . . Italian."

"And is it a nice walk up to the village? Oh, and have you got any old boots we can borrow?"

"It is a bit steep, but we will go slowly. I have a good selection of garments . . . all the very finest . . . from Bond Street." He nodded to himself, longingly . . . "Bond Street."

Lorenzo was silent, chewing his lip. Frieda came and stood behind him. She put her hands on his shoulders and started to massage gently. He inclined his head to the side so that his face touched her slowly moving hand.

"Are we far enough away here . . ." he spoke softly, his voice strangely calm, too calm, his eyes half closed, ". . . far enough away from all those maniacs, from those police commissioners, from those jackanapes courts and all their vileness and all their vengefulness, all that filth that is inside them?"

Orazio looked over, perplexed.

"His book, Orazio, a beautiful book . . . It is called The Rainbow . . ."

"Frieda chose the title." Lorenzo patted the hand on his shoulder, turning his head to smile at her, but in his eyes there was bitterness. "I will tell Orazio . . . I will tell him if he wishes to listen." He looked down at the floor for a minute. "My novel . . . The Rainbow . . . they condemned it, they said it was obscene. No sex please, we are at war, it is unpatriotic, no sex ever, at least not in books. The funny thing is, there is no sex, not really, just men and women, their feelings, their private thoughts." He paused for a minute. "The Human body Orazio . . . You know about that."

He looked over at the old model, but his gaze was somehow unfocussed. "Was that the freedom we were fighting for, the burning of books? Burn, burn, burn . . . Burn everything . . . men, books, everything . . . blow their poor young bodies to pieces in those death-run trenches, but heaven forbid they should think about touch and feelings and warmth . . . and yes, pleasure, before the bullet pierces that flesh . . . congealed photos of wives and lovers squashed in the mud and blood under their poor mangled corpses." He shuddered. "God, let them live, let those bodies be the flesh and blood that they were made to be before you slaughter them." He hung his head. "Now they are the fallen, but they will rise again, or so they would have us believe, but I . . . I am just fallen, and they don't want me to rise again."

Outside, Giovanni's axe thudded. The fire crackled and spat. Frieda twisted little strands of her hair, then combed them out again with her fingers.

"Let's go for a walk anyway," she said softly, rubbing the nape of his neck.

"Am I offending you Orazio? Tell me if I am." Orazio shook his head slowly. "You see Orazio, I am not a man of war, and I let it be known, so with all that patriotism flying about, they wanted to finish me, discredit me and my book. But the obscenity was in them, in their minds, not in my book . . . and then there is my Frieda, she is German, so you can imagine . . . easy target . . . even as far away as Cornwall where we had moved to, still not far enough Orazio . . . and there were people there too, suspicious, mean, cunning people, they spied on us and then they said that it was us who were spying on them. That's how it works. They said we were sending signals to German u-boats off the Cornish coast, they came and arrested us, sent us away. Exiled in one's own country . . . My poor Frieda." His voice thickened. He took her hands and held them tight in his. "But then I am a born spy Orazio. Oh yes I am, Frieda can tell you." He gave a little false laugh, squeezed her hands and held them to his face. "I spy on wild flowers and birds and trees, but mostly I spy on thoughts and feelings. I am an outsider looking in, I am the face at the window, I am the watcher . . . and then I say . . . Look, this is you . . . not because I want to hurt them, but because that is what is. Damn it Orazio, I want them to live."

Orazio nodded again, slowly.

"Would that I could erase the world and start again. The body knows. It is the mind that fears. It fears the body and tries to impose its false craven reason on it. It wants control. It wants to send us all down a mine to live in the dark of ignorance. It is choking us. This is the battleground where all will be won or lost . . . the ancient sentient south of body and instinct against the new cerebral industrial north of murder and machines. We need a great ice age to come and wipe it all away, then start again."

"Snow-abstract annihilation," Frieda murmured.

"Who said that?" He turned and looked at her.

"You said it."

"Did I? Good, I must remember not to forget it. Orazio," he said, his tone coming round a little, "maybe we should settle here with you . . . make a community. We are looking for a place. What do you say? We have friends who want to join us. Would you like that Orazio . . . a little community?"

Orazio nodded uncertainly. He was getting used to these sudden changes of direction, sudden rises and falls and rises again.

"What do you think Frieda? . . . Rananim, right here, our little community . . . the Rananim of the Rejected Ones, a version of the Paris Refusés," he laughed, pleased with his little metaphor. "We could look for a place. What do you think?"

"Rananim! I do not know this word."

"Nor should you Orazio," Frieda took up the story, "it is a dream of ours to set up a community somewhere . . . artists, writers, like-minded people . . . to live separately, to live our own lives by our own rules, or lack of them. He has called it Rananim. It is a Hebrew name."

"A sort of Bloomsbury." Orazio said brightly, thinking he was getting the drift. "I went to those houses sometimes and I . . ."

A gale of laughter broke over the foreign couple. Orazio looked surprised for a second, then he joined in, happy that his words had had this effect but not sure why.

"Oh Orazio, Orazio . . ." Lorenzo spluttered, ". . . that sort of thing, but not quite with those people . . . well maybe one or two." Lorenzo wiped his brow. "Orazio, you must join us in our Rananim, you will be the joker."

Frieda sat down on the bench and warmed her hands against the fire. "Do you remember that lovely blue colour we painted the furniture at the cottage in Zennor when we first arrived," she asked, "don't you think it would go well here?" She looked around her a little despairingly. There was nothing of comfortable clutter, of carpets, settees, of sprawl, of half-read books and magazines, of just lying around—all that cosiness that the cottage at Zennor had offered, a couple of rooms looking away over the great ocean. But they had made it homely, nice old dressers they had bought for nothing at the market at St. Ives, and the piano, especially the piano, that she played whenever, in the quiet of spring evenings, singing songs, German songs, careless of who might hear, and they would entertain themselves—books, readings, little theatricals. Mornings, and the great expanse of ever-changing sea and sky, evenings, westerly into the setting sun . . . wandering out into the lonely remote night, the dark ocean heaving below, just themselves and the vastness of the universe. They had been happy there for a while, they had loved it that solitude.

"No more colours Frieda." Lorenzo put his head in his hands, his voice suddenly laced with bitterness again. "No more talk of Zennor. Anyway I like the furniture here."

Orazio gave a look of relief. The Englishman got up and paced restlessly up and down the small kitchen, turning and turning. Frieda watched — early hopes, a new place, a moment of wonder, The Promised Land — but always something waited, dark and malign. It came in the door with them, unseen, bided its time, sat quietly, till just as they were settling in and beginning to feel that this was the place, it would raise its head, and before they knew it they were on their way again, hopes dashed.

She watched him now as he paced and turned, a creature caged, pawing at the door. They would have to go out for a walk soon. In Cornwall he would be out and gone for hours, his long skinny legs eating the miles of coastal path, or lost in the empty Celtic interior, or crouched over small flowers that dug their roots in against the sea wind which ripped unshielded over the clifftops, and on he walked, breathing in the gorse, prickly yellow coconut-sweet gorse. And if he wasn't out walking, then he would be tending his little cliff-top garden, hoeing, weeding, clearing the ground, growing vegetables. It had kept them going, fed them, that and a bit of farm work nearby for which he was paid in produce, eggs, butter, and he made his own bread too. It was more than survival, it was riches. Yes, they could live well on little, and they did. They were settled, so they thought, at least while the war thundered on, but then, rolling half-heard off the battering sea wind—murmurs. What are they doing up there? Why are their curtains different colours? She is German . . . A ship was torpedoed out in the bay . . . They are signalling.

Lorenzo turned, saw the expression on her face, knew what she was thinking. He always knew, would always turn just at that moment and catch her. It was difficult to hide from him.

"Damn them and their empires, damn them and their wars, damn the politicians and patriots, damn the whole menagerie . . ."

"Don't." She reached a hand across to him. "We must finish with this now. Please Lorenzo . . ."

Orazio got up and wandered out to the front door. He opened it and stood there, looking out—perhaps whatever it was that was tormenting his guests would fly out too. Across the snow, Giovanni's axe thudded.

"Orazio," the Englishman called, "you will catch cold. Come back in, I need to talk to you."

The old model shuffled back in.

"My brother is making a good stack of wood out there," he said airily, hoping that the demon had indeed flown, but the Englishman hadn't quite finished.

"As you can see Orazio, I am in my gladiator mood. It comes on me." He sat down. His voice had returned to something like normal, a little self-mocking even. "Now, it says in your venerable book that the Samnites were the original gladiators, that it was a religious rite before the Romans made it into popular entertainment. So tell me, are you a gladiator, and if you are, then teach me to be one so that I can smite them with my gladius."

"Ha!" The old model nodded, but nothing else came.

"Orazio, you are admirably economical with words." A half smile finally found its way onto Lorenzo's face. "I, by necessity, am the opposite. Your body was your profession, my words are mine, but a body stays in one spot, whereas words have a tendency to fly all over the place."

Orazio stood there scratching his head. "Signor Lorenzo, if you like words, maybe you should go to the great Abbey of Monte Cassino before you leave, there are lots of words up there, Latin words . . . ancient manuscripts . . . but as for gladiators . . ."

Lorenzo leaned forward and put his head in his hands, rubbing his face vigorously as if trying to wake himself up.

"Latin words . . . but it is Latin words that are the problem. They have written our world. They have made us what we are . . . order, regulation, construction, subjunctive, and the verb at the end of the sentence . . . The verb at the end of the sentence . . . That is the problem. You see I want my verb to wander where it likes, to roam free. Out there the world is an architecture of Latin words. The Roman Empire still exists. We must smite it with our gladius Orazio. We gladiators must rise up and smite it."

Orazio swayed on his feet, looking around, trying to think of something to say.

"To the victors the spoils," Lorenzo had one last trumpet blast to make, "and the right to distort history. There is a line in the Livy about us Samnites, for I must consider myself one too, if that is alright with you. Do you want to hear it? It reads, 'nefarium latraggio Samnitium.' Roughly speaking I think it means—those Samnites are an evil thieving lot."

Lorenzo burst out laughing. Orazio nodded grimly.

"I thought you'd like it you odd bird. But you know, you have become too like a Roman, too long in London. Of course what Livy was saying was . . . We have done the world a service by overcoming those villainous Samnites . . . Rome, mistress of morality. Rome, the imposer of order, just like the Victorians.

"They have brigandage in the blood here," Orazio said, nodding ruefully and sighing.

"Then I love them for it Orazio, I love them. I am one with them. Brigands are a holy race, they have a holy duty. One day there will be a mighty uprising of brigands and I will be there amongst them. I will carry the banner, and we will clear away all the decay, all the vile putrid system, the politicians, the empires, the mine owners, their black souls, their black breath, their black money. We will make holy war. It will be Samnite revenge on Roman perfidy." He beamed devilishly at them. "The gladius awaits."

Chapter Ten

Orazio's forecast had been right. In the afternoon the wind dropped. The old model did indeed have some fine old garments with Bond Street labels, a chest full of clothes left over from his glory days, tweeds and woollens from country house parties and shoots that his wealthy hosts had afforded him, noble discards, good heavy walking boots, and there were shooting sticks and all sorts of crested paraphernalia, hip flasks, and at the bottom of a trunk even a twelve bore shotgun, which Lorenzo tucked under his arm and raised to his shoulder taking aim at imaginary snipe.

They plunged in, holding things up and trying them on, transforming themselves into odd eccentric characters, prancing around, starting up little theatrical dialogues, almost forgetting what they were supposed to be doing. Frieda dressed herself up in all the male attire, which suited her very well, and topped it off with a brightly coloured cloth scarf which she twisted turban-like around her head so that she looked like a hindoo rajah about to mount an elephant for a tiger hunt.

They paraded down the stairs and out into the winter landscape. It was a relief to leave the confine of the house, the cavernous kitchen, the fug of mental commotion, the smoke from the fire that stung their eyes, the clanging of the pig swill bucket which Lorenzo said reminded him of the bell for school assembly at the school in Croydon where he used to teach.

And so, finely accoutred, the two gentlemen set off for their constitutional. Orazio watched them as they stepped out through the deep snow—the English and their love of walking. Italians didn't go for walks, at least not around there, and certainly not the peasantry—a waste of energy. Breaking a living from the heavy earth was effort enough. Land was something to own, to work, to covet, to swindle for, not a country park for taking your pleasure, for admiring, for making botanical sketches in.

They had asked Orazio about the local flora, as they called it — what it was like in the spring — and he had scratched his head the way he did, and guided them somehow over the mountains and valleys, the high slopes, the melting snows, the fields of gentian . . .

"Gentian..!" Frieda had burst out at the mention, ". . . that is our flower." She clung now to any little sign that said they would be alright again, like their walk in the woods and the encounter with the magic beech tree. Now here was the little gentian glowing back at them.

"It means so much to me Orazio," she had whispered to the old model, "the gentian is he, you can see it in his eyes, that special blue which radiates. That is my Lorenzo. You have made me happy." Orazio nodded. Such a woman he had not expected.

They climbed a little way up the sheltering hillside, holding onto the skeletal branches of gnarled trees to pull themselves up the rocky white moraine, hearts thumping with the heavy effort of new snow, till they stood again on the edge of the woods, now lacework white. His chest was still not strong, would never be. She looped an arm through his.

"Not bad for a crock." He smiled, breathing deep the pure mountain air. They looked back down, screwing their eyes against the white glare. Under the new snow covering, the villa and the old stone casa colonica where Giovanni lived, looked like parts of the landscape, like jagged outcrops of living rock. A late low flash of solar energy shot silver-gold across the valley. Frieda tugged at his arm, eager to expend her pent up energy and climb further, but he pulled against her. He had a sudden desire to go down to the torrent.

They skirted back past the house, across the wooded meadow and down to the river bed. A misty luminescence hovered over the frothing waters, ice-crystal bushes and trees gave off a bluish glow in the fading light. Frieda stepped out onto the little dams of gravel and sand that banked up here and there, climbing up onto boulders, holding her arms aloft, commanding the waters, giving little yelps of high spirit. Lorenzo wandered further downstream, stopping to peer into the busy rills, crouching down, watching the eddying curves and geometries of stone and water, and like this they moved along the river bed, the villa now some way behind. But the humid cold soon got into their bones, and they turned off up a rocky embankment in the direction they hoped would lead them back towards the hamlet, tracts of stumbling stony path still just visible here and there where the snow had drifted. The going was a bit easier than the way they had come down, longer and gentler, and their sense of direction was right, for up ahead they could make out the backs of a line of old stone cottages, and beyond them, standing guard at the centre of the crossroad, the little chapel with its hatted bell tower.

They walked up to it, climbed the couple of steps and pushed at the wooden door. It was closed. Away across the white meadows, the villa stood sleepily on the brow of rising ground, a tail of smoke drifting above. There was still enough of a gloaming light to see by, so they set off to explore a bit further, taking the uphill path away from the hamlet. Wispy white breaths of mist floated spectrally over the valley depths. They walked steadily on, when there, high in the distance, the village itself came into view, sheer and precipitous, cleaving into the living rock like a lost citadel, behind it, a halo of moon rising.

It was too steep and icy and dark to go further now, but there it was, and he took it all in the way he did. Here then the place of the woodpecker god, here his band of youthful colonisers, his sacred ones, Oscan speaking, an Italy not yet tamed and hardly named, still its own, the crushing unity of Rome yet a long way distant—all this he could see.

On the way back down the hill path, a low glowing light appeared out of the darkness—an isolated little dwelling. An old woman in long black weeds and black woollen shawl limped out of a doorway to where a pile of wood was roughly stacked against the wall. She stood for a few seconds twisting her old body, preparing herself, clenching and unclenching her veiny hands, then, with unexpected agility, she bent, and with one sharp movement, hoisted up an armful of the heavy logs, her belly pushing forward and spine arching backward under the weight.

In the half dark, and thinking they were not seen, the night wanderers watched, but the old woman could feel their eyes on her back and turned to look. Frieda took a couple of quick steps towards her, stretching her arms out and making a lifting gesture— she would like to help. But the old lady just stared, then turned and swayed with her load to the door, disregarding. Frieda, undaunted, took a few more steps till she was almost by the door. The old lady started to say something in dialect, small black watery eyes moving up and down over this tall fair man-woman apparition, but she knew she wasn't understood, and gave a sort of shrug of resignation. Frieda took this as consent, skipped to the wood pile, scooped up another armful of logs, and followed the old lady into the house. A moment later she reappeared in the doorway and crooked a finger at Lorenzo who was still standing out on the path.

Inside was a simple rustic kitchen, like Orazio's. At the far end, a large open hearth was built into the corner of the room. The old lady was kneeling in front of it, positioning a new log into the smouldering glowing ash. She put the iron tube to her mouth and blew down it till a flame licked from the peeling bark. At a long wooden table, two children were sitting, a boy of eight or nine and a girl about a year or so older. They made no sign, as if the intruders were somehow invisible, just watched the old lady, then turned back to what they were doing, keeping their eyes lowered.

Here was silence. It hung in the air. It was here even before the strange couple had come in, an emptiness, something hollow, as if they were waiting for something, the answer to a question. Frieda made a girlish little dimpled smile at them, opening her eyes wide and wagging her head, trying to engage them, but there was no response, just the same lowered gaze, and quick furtive looks towards the back of the old lady still kneeling by the fire. Lorenzo, so good with children, knew instinctively that they were beyond his reach, that they were looking out on the world from another place, waiting to be called back. He felt helpless.

Finally, the old lady heaved herself to her feet, and without looking at the intruders, went across to a wooden sideboard, took out two little crystal glasses and put them on the table. She reached back in and brought out a bottle, half full with a dark liquid. The cork squeaked out. She poured the liqueur into the glasses, all the while the two little heads following her movements.

She handed the drinks to the strangers. "Ingilish," she said finally, her croaky voice scraping the foreign word out.

"Sì, inglesi," Frieda replied, leaving her nationality at the door so as not to complicate matters. The old lady sighed and shrugged her shoulders. The unexpected guests lifted their glasses and sipped the liqueur, a strong dark cherry brandy.

"Mmm." Frieda smiled with that kind enquiring smile. The old woman's face though was set, her mouth tight shut, her eyes screwed small with fading sight, pupils black and distant. A shuddering sigh shook her bony shoulders.

"Amici di Orazio," Frieda said.

"Ah." The old head gave a slow nod. "Orazio . . . Certo." She understood.

Frieda crouched down next to the children. On the table were some handmade toys, a little rocking cradle, an infant with a bonnet and coloured cotton blanket inside, and the boy had a rough carved wooden soldier with a rifle against its shoulder. Frieda reached over and rocked the toy cradle, trying to bring the little girl to her, but the child just kept her hands under the table and watched. Lorenzo felt a constriction in his throat.

The old lady unfolded a knobbly bent finger and pointed to the sky.

"Padre morto," she whispered, ". . . la guerra . . . gas." She tapped her fingers on her chest. "Mio figlio . . . Pazienza." She turned so the children wouldn't see and crossed herself.

Frieda though had heard. She put down the toys and stood up, holding her hands to her stomach.

"E la madre?" she asked softly, holding herself in.

The grandmother, with her old hands, made a mime of someone squeezing and wringing clothes, then pointed in the direction of the village.

"Lavora per il sacerdote . . . su in paese," she said.

The door closed silently behind them. They walked back up the hill in the dark.

Chapter Eleven

Lorenzo held up the sketch, then looked at the
wall, then back at the sketch, leaning his head from side to side,
dabbing his fingers at the mural to see if the earlier paint was
dry. He had chosen a section of plaster low down so he could
kneel or sit while painting. The outlines were there, maybe a little
adjustment.

He took the sketch over to his makeshift desk and sat down,
his thin shoulders hunched, his tongue between his lips, charcoal
in hand, concentrating. He held the picture up, blew off the black
dust and dropped it on the floor next to him. He wiped his hands
on a piece of cloth, then opened a notebook and poised his pen
over it.

Frieda had made up the fire. From the bed she watched him.
He could feel her eyes on him, knew what it was, he could hear
it in her breathing, in her silences, in her lack of movement. She
liked to do nothing, that was true, she liked to lounge, that was
also true, but happy lazy lounging had a different sound to it
— there was book lounging, eyes closed sensuous curled up
lounging, lounging oblivious to everyone and everything, clothes
lying where she had taken them off and dropped them lounging,
waiting for him to pick them up after her and fold them away,
playful thought lounging, lounging while he cooked the meal and
she did nothing, staring into heaven smoking a cigarette lounging,

and others. She had various lounging styles, but this wasn't one of them.

"I'm bored."

There it was. He smiled to himself, a grim affectionate hidden smile.

"Don't start my love." He shuffled his feet under the table and cleared his throat. "We are tranquil. You know how it sets me off. Find something to do."

She got up and moved about the room, something like a miserable ghost. She walked across to the window, back to the bed, over to the door and back again, up and down, picked up a book, dropped it, sighed, flopped down on the bed, closed her eyes and imagined herself in a house in a town far away, the noise of traffic outside.

She jumped back up and skipped across to the window.

"Oh look down there . . ." she said, her voice suddenly girlish excited. She rubbed a pane of glass with her sleeve, peered out and waved. ". . . Lieutenant Marbahr on his way from the barracks, and I'm sure he gave a look up here. Yes he did, he saw me."

She rapped at the window, waving with both hands, and mouthing words that only the phantom passerby could see. She smiled to herself, sighed, then gave a little pout. From somewhere behind her came a monitory clearing of the throat. She ignored it.

"Everyone is out and about, the streets are alive, and here I am locked away up here with you. I want to be down there. I want some company." Her voice whined childishly. "If you are too busy with your writing it is not fair that I have to stay in. I think I shall go to the kaffeehaus for a chocolate and a strudel. There are bound to be people I know there."

"Which kaffeehaus?"

"Why do you need to know?"

The man cleared his throat again, a bit louder this time, just the hint of irritation.

"Alright, the Café Stefanie. I might see that so wonderful clever woman there. She is so free."

"Why, are you not free?"

She hummed a little something to herself, a popular song she knew.

"And what is this so wonderful woman's name?"

"Franziska," she replied, all excited and girlish again, "she is an artist and a mystic. She writes for Jugend. You know, she said I should write something too and that she would get it published in the magazine. Wouldn't that be wonderful? Could you stand the competition?"

"And will this Lt. Marbahr be there too?" His voice had a soft innocent hint of menace.

"Karl? No. He will be at the Simplicissimus with all the other officers. The Stefanie is too tame for them." She hummed another few bars of the popular song. "So you don't mind?"

"Are you not expecting your sister and her husband?" he said with controlled disinterest.

"Oh Lorenz, what am I going to do with you? Your memory is so bad. That is tomorrow, and don't tell me at the last minute that you have an appointment with your publisher like you did last time."

"But I must work my dear, how else are we to pay for all your little fancies and your new outfits?" He turned to her and delivered a gently chiding look over an imaginary pair of glasses.

"I shall tell Hans to call me a carriage . . . And don't forget that this evening we are going to the theatre, and if you don't come, I'm sure Lt. Marbahr will accompany me."

"No. I forbid it," he said curtly. "A married woman in public with one of those young officers who think only of . . . only of . . ."

She burst out laughing, a strong throaty laugh that still carried a trace of her earlier nervousness. She came up behind him and threw her arms round his neck.

"You forbid," she said mockingly, "you forbid . . . like my father . . . you, a Prussian officer. I have married a Prussian officer. I suppose it was my fate . . ." and she burst out into a refrain from an old marching song she remembered from her childhood.

"Look," he said, tugging at her encircling arms and trying to make himself heard over the military parade, "now you've made me blot the paper. Now I can't read that word. What is that word?"

"It must have been the wrong word, that's why it's been blotted out. You see . . . I saved you." She resisted his tugging hands, tightening her embrace. "If we aren't going to the theatre tonight, then you must write me a play . . . you must write me a play by this evening."

"Prussians can't write plays, and I must advise you that from now on you will have to get used to doing without all your little bijoux and bits and pieces, for I am now officially a failed writer. Bankruptcy stares us in the face. They have drafted a special law, ad personam, so that no-one will buy my books . . . and so my dear . . ."

She squeezed her arms and hands round his face and mouth, smothering his words.

"Don't speak like this, I won't have it." She relaxed her hold a little. "And so what is this you are writing here?"

"This is what we will have to scrape by with from now on. My new profession, history books, and this is a little piece about those Samnite tribes of southern Italy, you remember, that time we went to stay with old Orazio. But I think I will have to publish under a different name to disguise myself. How about Laurentius?"

"Oh how clever! No-one will ever guess!"

"Yes, this is how it must be from now on. I'm finished with novels, stupid things anyway. No more dithyrambs from me. Dionysus has crept away nursing a hangover. Great Pan is dead. The old religion is no more."

Her hands slipped from his shoulders.

"Here beginneth the Lesson . . . And he heard the word, and from that time on he wrote only things pleasing to the Lord, and he became elevated among the righteous . . . Oh God!"

She went over and poked at the little fire in the corner of the bedroom, piled a few twigs on, and blew down the iron pipe.

"It's very effective this pipe thing they use. What did Orazio call it . . . a shooshatore or something? Onomatopoeic. Shoosha . . . Shoosha. Maybe I should put it in your ear and blow down it."

"Yes, do that my dear . . ." he nodded his head solemnly, ". . . Not I, but the wind that blows through me . . . !"

She gave a little squeal of laughter and recited another line from his poem: ". . . By the fine, fine wind that takes its course through the chaos of the world . . . That is you, that is us, taking our course through the chaos of the world. Clever my Lorenzo who turned my weapon against me."

She stared into the fire for a minute. He tapped his fingers on the desk.

"I'd like to give Orazio something. We cannot give him any money for our stay, there being none to give, but I would like to offer something."

She came back over and stood behind him, patting her hands up and down on his shoulders and squeezing him again.

"He is happy we are here, and you are redecorating the room with your mural. What more could he possibly want? And who knows . . ."

"Who knows what?"

She didn't answer.

"I have a theory," he said after a while, loosening her grip, "their impenetrable dialect, I think it is the very sound of these mountains, just like the music of their wild pipes. What do you think of that?"

She stood behind him and blew along the top of his head, making little furrows in his soft brownish hair.

"I am testing the boundaries of linguistic theory here," he said, straightening his hair. "You know the Oscan speakers wrote from right to left, like the Etruscans. Orazio said the British Museum has a bronze tablet with Oscan religious text on it."

She leant over his little desk, picked up his pen and tried to write a word backwards. "How did Leonardo manage to do it?"

"Next time we are in London I'd like to see that tablet," he continued.

"Next time?" She put down the pen. "Will there be a next time?" She was pensive for a minute, stroking his hair.

"Lorenzo?"

"Yes?"

"Do you remember our lovely Villa Igéa at Gargnano?"

"How could I not? Now that was in the mountains, but we could understand the Italian there pretty well."

"Yes, I don't mean that . . . I mean it was the happiest moment of my life, of both our lives. So much has happened since, to the world, to us, war between our peoples, war between us, wars with friends, wars, wars, wars. Do you think we will ever find peace?"

He looked at her through half-closed eyes, the ghost of a smile edging onto his face.

"Could we survive on peace? The Battle of Cornwall . . . trench warfare at its bloodiest, hand to hand combat. We should strike a commemorative medal for the survivors, all two of them." He pulled her to him. "Was it a glorious defeat or a bloody victory?"

"It was a victorious defeat."

"Quite."

"What a good idea . . . the medal I mean. I will design one, it will give me something to do, and we can have an award ceremony. I know I know, I can embroider it like one of those blazer badges you English are so fond of, and then I'll sow it on your jacket pocket and you can march up and down Pall Mall with the best of them . . . Good old Lawrence, they'll say, he's come round at last."

He grinned. "A two-headed phoenix with your head and mine rising from the flames."

She burst out laughing. He was so good at the absurd. She went over and jumped on the bed, and lay there, hands under her head, staring upwards.

Prussians and medals — her father had won a medal, he'd won the iron cross in the Franco-Prussian war, but the wound he had received had put an end to his military career. She always remembered though at the barracks in Metz when, on the Kaiser's birthday, the young officers had carried him on their shoulders in celebration of the action for which he had been decorated, and how astonished and proud she and her sisters had been . . . I don't mind who my daughters marry, her father used to say, as long as he isn't a Jew, an Englishman or a gambler. Whistle and it will come to you — her elder sister Else had married a Jewish professor, little Johanna had married a gambler, and she, Frieda, had married not one Englishman, but two. Two Englishmen! — How had that happened? Sometimes, over the past few years, when it seemed that things were falling apart, she would see her father wagging a finger at her and saying—I warned you, but you never listened . . .

"What . . . What is it? Where did you go?" Lorenzo asked after a while, still sitting at his little desk.

"Nothing."

"Nothing isn't a place."

He gave her a long concentrated look, but she didn't return it, just continued her upward gaze.

Two Englishmen. Sometimes she tormented herself with the idea that they were in fact two sides of the same coin, both from poor backgrounds, both with dominant mothers determined their sons should better themselves, both given opportunities to study, both linguists, both lovers of words, and both puritanical — because, for all they said about Lorenzo, and there was much now, especially after the obscenity trial — for all they said about him, he was a puritan, as much, if not more, than the good church-going Ernest.

Englishman number one—Ernest Weekley. Never talk to foreigners on walking holidays in the Black Forest. That's how she had met him. Ernest—professor, steady and stable, correct and upright, all work, church, family and respectability. Theirs was the perfect marriage, they never quarrelled, and she, wasn't she the most wonderful wife and mother to his children, she, who contributed to his success, who was most certainly happy, who beamed with it, bright and loving and motherly. Nothing could possibly disturb that serenity, it was ordained—just reward for his exemplary hardworking existence. The idea of betrayal was inconceivable.

Poor Ernest — a rock, a hymnal, a psalm, an echo — and he had honoured her, loved her in his way, a comfortable love, done by rote, without passion, when through that empty space one day, a fiery wraith had blown, a sickly, frail, penniless, nomadic young writer with piercing blue eyes, come to see his old tutor from Nottingham University, and those blue eyes had fallen on her.

It was all there in that first moment, like an awakening. She had known straight away, she had always known really, known without knowing that one day something would happen. While waiting for lunch they had chatted, the good hostess and the young visitor. Nothing more ordinary, social nicety. But during the meal she had become aware of his eyes on her, taking her all in, absorbing her, and she had felt her soul being drawn out of her.

Lunch over, he left. But straightway he wrote to her, completely open, declaring himself. A few days later he came again to the house. They went for a walk with the children, all nice and mannerly, and he played with the children by the riverside, even giving more attention to them than to her. And she watched him as he played with them, and as she watched, something grew inside her, irresistible, and she knew there and then that her old life was finished forever—that's all, simple and clear and devastating.

You are the most wonderful woman in all England, he had written to her. Maybe another woman, an English woman, might have rebuffed him, held on to what she had. But she wasn't an English woman. He wanted her with every fibre of his being, every fibre, and what he wrote, he wrote with his whole being, and when he made love, he made love with his whole being.

There was no escape, the choice must be made, he would brook no compromise, no lies, no arrangements, no half-lives, no deceits. She must tell her husband, she must tell him the truth. He was puritanical in this too.

A few months later, with the sum of £11 in his pocket, all his worldly wealth, they had taken the boat train together from Charing Cross to Dover, across to Ostend, and on to Metz—her hometown. It was done, almost. She sent her husband a message. She feared for his health and sanity, but if he survived, she knew that he would follow that terrible logic to the bitter end that men like him must—the children, he would take them from her.

She got up off the bed, came up behind him, put her hands under his arms and pulled him gently to his feet. He rose compliantly and allowed himself to be steered back over to the bed. She eased him down and climbed on next to him. They lay for a while just listening to the crack of the fire, her hand roaming carelessly over his arms and chest.

"Do you remember what you used to say before we ever came to Italy that first time . . . do you remember? . . . I feel one must go south, you would say."

Italy . . . He had heard its siren call, knew somehow that it held the antidote to the heavy slab-grey of England that he was finding so oppressive at that time, and it had the advantage of being far away from the turmoil that they would surely leave behind them—a broken marriage, incredulity, anger.

They crossed the Alps on foot, and there spread before them, the luminous world of the Italian lakes — a new life, completely poor but full of riches, a few pounds to live on, a little first floor apartment overlooking Lake Garda, almost at the water's edge, a shingled jetty below, the great mountains circling above, holding them in wonder. They lived frugally, bought their food from the local market, walked through the wood-columned terraces where the lemons were grown that brought wealth to the area, climbed the old mule tracks up through the half-cul-tivated half-wild hills, crossed deep ravines of churning mountain waters, stopped to rest at isolated inns for a restora-tive glass or two, like at San Gaudenzio — gaude, the Latin for rejoice — and always and wherever, deep below, cupped inside the snow-capped mountains like an immense sacred chalice, blessed and immune, the blue-violet sun-bright lake. But they weren't immune. Up there in their little lakeside paradise, the long tentacles of marital anger were reaching for them, and one morning, legal documents were served on them—divorce proceedings. The children! The ache would never leave her.

She turned her thoughts away, moved closer up against him, watching his profile, the points of his blue eyes. She loved his eyes, the way his lids came down over them, shy like a girl, then the way they might suddenly flare up in a fury, and she loved that too—afterwards. Now she looked, and she saw there another blue, soft and easy.

"The sea Lorenzo, the Mediterranean sea. Oh how I miss it. Remember in Fiascherino how the blueness did almost climb up into the cottage, dappling the white walls."

It was the year after Lake Garda, their second visit to Italy, but their first to the Mediterranean, a fisherman's cottage set among pines and scented fruit trees and gnarled olives, overlooking the Bay of Lerici on the Ligurian coast, three rooms and kitchen, simple like sea places are — live outside, eat outside, swim off the beach at the foot of the house, push out the little flat-bottomed boat. He loved to take the boat out through the surf, and she would watch from the shore, anxious — Shelley had drowned there, just up the coast. She didn't want it to become a graveyard for English writers.

"Mmm . . . Mmm . . ." she sighed languidly and lay back, her fingers rippling over his chest and navel — long afternoons soft with pleasure, salt-sweet beads of sweat on sensuous skin, the scent of citrus, the sun-glittering sea, the warm salt breeze, and in the evening, red-sailed fishing boats making their way in against the deep crimson-gold of the setting sun as it slipped below the horizon, and they, breath almost ceasing, drawn silent into the fading afterglow.

Italy, soft, passive, and pleasured, wresting them from the cold iron grip of the north, of England, corpse-grey England, industrial, machine crushed, black slag heaps, all gas and chemical and rock, inert, bloodless. Redemption lay, if redemption was the right word, in the return to the past, in the exaltation of the body, in the fearless penetration of the female mind-body labyrinth, not in the hope of slaying the minotaur but of being devoured by it, the freeing of the body from the curses and taboos that religion and respectability had laid on it, the drawing out of the nails from that poor Christ flesh. This was Italy, and this was she, and she took him by the hand and led him into forbidden places, sacred groves where a man might be torn to pieces, even a god. The mysteries of the female soul and body, wonderful pomegranate fruit of blood-red seeds, here in the sun-warm pagan earth of Italy—germination. For deep down, Italy was still a place of the body pagan—intuitive, pre-Christian, dark.

He would write, when he could, for even he was distracted. She would lay, hammock swinging, half inside half outside. He would stop, look up, puzzle for a moment, look at her, look into her, those folded-in intimacies, the female world that she had opened to him, secret female pathways, silent dialogue that was them, but not them.

But nothing was as lovely as those mornings, the first low rays of sun across the quiet waters, another day in centuries of days, body and soul one and warm and easeful, walking early through the light-shimmering olives, the small leaves swaying and flickering silver and dark and holy.

Salt-soft sea — and now it was she climbing into the little bright-coloured rowing boat, the tamp of her feet on the wooden boards, swaying slightly, seating herself, running the oars out, plashing and creaking, rowing gently across the bay to the Lerici side, the terracotta shoreline a gouache of colour, her eyes moist and unfocussed in the rippling reflections—draw in the oars and let the boat drift.

Sometimes they would paint together, and in the evening their neighbour Luigi would play his guitar, and they would sing English and German and Italian songs. Lorenzo loved her voice.

In that time before the war, he was so full of the certainty of himself—I am D. H. Lawrence from head to foot, that's everything, that's all . . . They can't get past me. They were the king and queen of Italy, cosseted and chivvied by their maid Elide. Yes they even had a maid, and the maid had a family, and all of them fussed after the two careless wandering souls, shopped at the market for them, watched over them, hurried after the distracted writer with a coat when he went out wandering in only his shirt on windy days. They knew gratitude.

"Zagara," she whispered blissfully to herself, "can you smell it, the scent of citrus? I can smell it, here, now. Oh my God, we must hurry to the sea. This place is too ecstatic, too icy and jagged. I need the soft Italy again, the Italy that caresses."

She brought her head up into the crook of his arm and looked at his profiled face, and she felt a swoon deep down, the warm salt perspiration of his body lapping through her.

"We will go there soon," he whispered.

But just as it had come, the vision went—winter has no scent. She was back in the cold bare room, dark corners grey with ghosts, smouldering ash struggling in the hearth. She shuddered and closed her eyes, trying to bring the images back, but what came was not the Mediterranean, instead it was the Cornish Atlantic swell, heavy, grey, and northern, rolling surf thundering into shingle bays, flying in hanging clouds of spray off the plunging cliffs, gulls wheeling and diving, riding the storm, just like her soul.

She got up from the bed, pulled a shawl from a chair, and walked over to the fire with that restless pace of hers that made her almost pounce in her movements, bare feet squeaking on the cold floor. He watched her, watched the soles of her feet, the round ball joints of her toes as she half crouched, half knelt in front of the hearth, snapping twigs with quick strong arms, bending further forward, blowing into the embers—and he noticed how the roundness of her body was like the roundness of her feet.

"Are you feeling tigerish?" He wanted her suddenly, wanted

her physicality, her strong limbs, the weight of her body pressing down on him. He liked it when she opposed him, when she fought. She was the only woman who could make him complete, and this by mixture of opposition and intimacy. She ringed him in like a stallion in a corral, he kicked and bucked, but he didn't want to win, not really.

He waited. She didn't answer. She stood up, swung the shawl around her shoulders, went over to the window and looked out.

"Can you see the sea?" he asked. But his voice fell on silence. Outside, the wind gave a sudden howling rush, rattling the tall balcony window, stopping the smoke rising in the chimney so that it backed a little into the bedroom.

"Err, it's like a colliery in here," he said, making a face and waving his hand at the invading smoke.

Frieda stared through the window, her eyes soft and watery, but not from the smoke.

Chapter Twelve

Up through the white woods, three figures treading silently, the one in front in a fine old Ulster overcoat and a deerstalker hat, close behind, a woman with a man's tweed jacket over her long skirt and a sort of turban round her head, and some way further back, a man with a red beard looking down at the snow as he went, stopping to pick up frosted leaves and iced nuts and berries, around his shoulders a black cape with half-finished embroidery on it.

It was the morning of the visit to the village. The man in the Ulster knew that the cape would cause comment when they arrived up there, but he cared less. Let them comment. He was enjoying his renewed sense of otherness. The company of his guests had broken a spell—their talk, their ideas, their playacting. He was making store of it all while he could. The man with the red beard was also making store of it all — the mysterious influence of the mountains, the hollowy old villa, the man up ahead, his tales, his old lived-in sad face, the once lissom body of a half-naked youth in classical pose. How many lives we live, how many layers we wear! This is where he likes to scavenge. He is a black crow hopping round a carcass in the white snow, pecking at the bloody entrails.

They were quite high now. A weak early sun threw thin tree shadows across the white woodland slopes, the faint muffled sound of a church bell floated from the valley depths, a startled bird fluttered up suddenly from the twiggy undergrowth.

The turbaned woman stopped and turned, a hand held over her eyes, scanning back down through the woods. She couldn't see him. Should she call out? No, he hates that — can't that woman leave me in peace just for once, leave me alone with my thoughts, always harrying me? Interfering woman. She caught sight of him. He was leaning against a tree, losing himself in the quiet calligraphy of the snow-blacked trunks. He emerged from his camouflage and gestured irritatedly to her to keep going, annoyed that she thought it necessary to stop for him.

They came out on a level path cut in the side of a low rocky mountainside, away below, a silver-bright sea of valleys and floating hills. Straggles of peasantry were making their way from outlying hamlets. Along the path on a corner was a little stone shrine with a rusty iron gate, inside, the usual chipped and faded statuette of a saint, eyes cast forlornly heavenwards, hands supplicating, a scatter of dead flowers at her feet.

They came to a crossroad with an iron crucifix, and over ahead, a little jutting promontory with what looked like a ruined chapel. The road from the valley curved sharply round a narrow bend to meet them, and on up towards the village.

Orazio turned and nodded to them: "We are arrived."

They walked up past a pink columned house which seemed quite new, then on through a narrow funnel of old stone buildings, past a shop with a sign over it — Sale e Tabacchi — and suddenly they were in the embrace of a crowded square, a simple stuccoed church facing onto it, archways leading off here and there, a long plain building with high up balconies, and behind and above, the round battlement walls of an old fortress. But the eye hardly saw all this, instead it turned away, drawn to the view of the great valley below.

Orazio straightened his old shoulders, pulled his hat down, and steered the two strangers through the milling market-goers to a doorway. It was the usual hostelry, a hubbub of men in conical hats and capes speaking their rapid guttural dialect, jibing at each other with that same friendly enmity as their murderous card game . . . *benevola malizia*, the Englishman thought to himself. It looked like a convention for brigands.

They edged through between the broad unyielding shoulders towards a corner where a brazier glowed. There was a free chair. Frieda sat herself down and set to drying out her legs and feet as best she could, lifting the hem of her long skirt, peeling down her red stockings, unconcerned. Orazio turned quickly and pushed his way through the throng, making gruff but friendly noises, exchanging comments, talking rapidly in dialect to one or other of the brigands so as to turn heads away from the heedless odalisque. He edged through to where the perennial old biddy was serving wine and other beverages on a table and heating coffee in a large battered pot. A few minutes later he was back carrying a tray with three coffees and three glasses of a bright yellow liqueur.

"Strega," he said in reply to their questioning look.

The two strangers sipped their coffee, then sniffed and sipped the liqueur. Orazio drank his coffee down in one, followed by the Strega, then left them to dry themselves out while he set off on errands.

The sulphuric brazier and fuggy interior drove Lorenzo back to the door to get some air, leaving Frieda to attend to her red stockings and stare down the dark-eyed glances. He hovered by the entrance, peering out at the busy piazza. It was another world, its own world — beautiful, ugly, harsh, cunning, threatening — all this he could see, and he understood how Orazio might not want to be part of it. He was just taking all this in, when a man, looking quite out of place in an overcoat and trilby hat, approached out of the crowd and ducked in through the doorway, almost bumping into him. The newcomer started to apologise in Italian, then stopped in mid-sentence and raised his hat. It was the man from the train.

"Well, well. So yus 'uv finally made it up to the big city," he said in his Tyneside accent.

Lorenzo, still in mid reverie, was lost for a moment, then recovered himself. "I am so glad to have run into you again." He waved a hand to catch Frieda's eye. She looked up from her toiletry.

The man lifted his hat to her. "I was wundering about yus both, after your little mishap. Still, we managed to see them off didn't we? And are yus coomfortable where you are?"

Lorenzo made a strange sort of uncertain face and cleared his throat. The man seemed to understand without words. "Aye, it takes a bit of gettin' used to round here . . . bit hard for us city folk." He smiled.

There was a little exchange of pleasantries, and the man offered to find them somewhere warmer up in the village. Lorenzo looked across at Frieda for a moment, then shook his head.

"We'll be leaving soon . . . off to Capri. And how about yourself, you said you had some business to take care of?"

"That's all done . . . a little piece of land to build a house on when I've got time. Yus'll 'ave walked past it on the way up maybe . . . in that big bend in the road where the crucifix is." He brushed the wet spray off his hat and coat. "Couple more days and I'll be off an'all . . . back to the missis and the bairns . . . too many Christmases without them already . . . the war ya know."

Lorenzo cleared his throat.

"Well I'm very glad we found you. We really wanted to thank you properly for that err . . . If it hadn't been for you at the station . . ."

"Please," the man raised his hand, "it was nowt. Glad I could help. I'm sorry ya 'ad to go through it."

Lorenzo signalled across to Frieda who was listening to the conversation, and pointed at the leather bag she had toted up with her. She opened it and took out a scroll of paper and brought it over.

"Nevertheless, we are in your debt." Lorenzo unrolled the

paper. "Look, I know it's a bit unusual, but I've painted this picture while I've been here and I thought I'd give it to you if I ran into you. I hope you can accept it. I couldn't think of anything else. I hope you don't mind naturalness." He held the picture open, then passed it to the man. "I've signed it here at the bottom, not that you'll find me in any gallery. I'm a writer not a painter." The man looked it up and down, nodding, and with a faint smile.

"Ya know, in me house in Newcastle, I've 'ad the ceiling of our front room painted by a lad who works for me. Classical scenes. My wife likes classical scenes." He examined the picture with an amused smile.

"Thank you . . . err . . ." he scrutinised the initials.

"D.H.L. The D is for David."

"Thank ya David . . . and if there's owt else I can do for yus . . ." But just as he was finishing the sentence, a woman came in. She stopped in the doorway, all pose and posture and exaggerated finery, more than enough to catch the eye in these parts, broad-rimmed hat, lace shawl, long dark embroidered satiny dress that she gathered in her hand to stop it trailing on the snow-wet ground, fluttering her eyelids, coquettish, like something from the music hall. It was an entrance, rehearsed. She stood, harvesting all the male glances. She stepped forward, stopping directly in between the two men as if they weren't there, looking about her with careless insouciance, glancing around as if she was searching for someone, bathing in the gaze of all the turned heads. Then, as if suddenly seeing them for the first time, she inclined her head to the man in the trilby, fluttered an acid sweet smile at him and floated on past and through the throng of men who parted silently to give her passage.

The man's face flushed, the veins in his neck swelled. He stood for a minute, the muscles of his jaws working. He forced a smile, thanked the couple again for the picture, lifted his hat, turned on his heel and was gone.

"What was all that about?" Frieda asked.

Lorenzo gave a shrug. "Don't know, but I think it might be he who has had his pocket picked this time."

"We still don't know his name. Go after him."

Lorenzo looked out through the door, then shook his head. Well dried now, and warmed by the yellow liqueur, they wandered out into the crowded square.

"Can't see any woodpeckers." Lorenzo looked up into the blue. Frieda smiled and took his arm. It was Sunday and a special Christmas market, an event not to be missed, and from the outlying hamlets high in the mountains or down in the valleys the peasantry had responded to the great meeting day. They came to hear mass, to see and be seen, young and not so young, they came to haggle, to buy and sell, the market stalls piled with clothes and materials, pots and produce, the men in their habitual costumes, the women, strong, in wide-sleeved blouses, shawls, long black pleated dresses and colourful scarves or headdresses.

An attrition of fierce bargaining was underway at one of the stalls, women poking and pulling at the piles of cloths and materials, laughing scornfully at the low quality and high prices, tossing them back in disgust, deriding — all calculated to grind down the beleaguered vendor — until, beaten into submission, he started wordlessly wrapping the piece of cloth with a shrug of resignation, while the victorious assailant nudged the other women, barely able to hide her greedy smile of victory. There was a mountain hardness here, a scornful cunning, especially the women, and always those brazen unyielding stares, nothing of compassion. Whatever happened in their church, out here the religion was another—better thy neighbour.

And while the women fought for cloth, the men stood around in little groups, talking, and it struck Lorenzo that this was where they lived really, in the open, under the sun, in the great square, all active thought, all here. Home was a place of passive silence, somewhere to eat and sleep.

Excited children ran up and down, tagging each other, or sliding on strips of flattened icy snow through groups of self-important old timers standing around gloriously in their buttoned ill-fitting suits—cast-offs from some relative abroad. An errant snowball thumped into one of them, dislodging his hat, showering white powder over his pin-striped dignity. He took a scything lunge with his walking stick at the fleeing culprit, followed by a litany of saint's names and Madonnas.

Orazio appeared again, walking towards them, a look of displeasure on his face. Trailing just behind him were a couple of young men in suits that were too smart—other London models or similar. They were on his shoulder, trying to take possession of him, jingling coins in their pockets, pleased with themselves, pleased they would be seen talking to the English couple, legitimising their new urban status, flaunting their London credentials. Orazio tried to detach himself. They started to speak in a sort of Italian-cockney, the latest slang expressions, verbally nudging the visitors. It was all part of the great culture of the piazza—see and be seen. Orazio reddened. Lorenzo didn't want it either. He turned away pointing at something to Frieda. The young men moved on.

"What can you do?" Orazio said with a shrug, "but look," he reached into his pocket, "letters for you. The Post Office is closed, but I got someone to check for me."

He handed them over. Lorenzo shuffled eagerly through them, scrutinised the handwriting of one or two, then held one up and gave it a big kiss.

"Frieda . . . a letter from Secker . . . my new and generous publisher." He flourished the letter in the air and sniffed at it. "Can I smell sovereigns? . . . Secker Frieda . . . I'll open it when we get back." He tucked the letter away. "Now show us more of your village good messenger, winged Mercury."

Nothing was better than receiving letters, especially ones with the promise of much needed financial relief.

From the piazza, a narrow road led steeply up behind the church. At the top was a sort of park overlooking a deep wooded ravine, white jagged mountains carving away into the distance. Here, at the high point of the village, the old fortress dominated.

"What is that Orazio?" Frieda asked.

Thankfully for Orazio, Lorenzo had already done his homework.

"Your inestimable history book says that it was built in the 11th century by the feudal overlord to defend the valley."

"Who were they defending against?" Frieda asked.

"Among others, the Saracens raiding along the coast. But you know what interests me so much Orazio is this Black Madonna of yours. It says there is a sanctuary to her in the mountains. Where is that from here?"

"Up there." Orazio pointed away towards some distant peaks.

"Is it far?" Lorenzo asked.

"Two or three hours on foot. I walked it as a child."

"Might then we walk it?" Lorenzo asked hopefully.

"In the middle of winter, with all the snow?" Orazio raised his eyebrows. "In the spring maybe, in the summer, or when her feast day falls in August, then hundreds of pilgrims come on foot and the village is full."

"What a pity. You see, it says it was originally a pagan sanctuary to the goddess Mefitis, a divinity to be found at crossroads and springs and in caves where magical vapours would rise up and bring on visions. Now I could do with some of that." He grinned one of his ruddy grins. "Your learned cleric was quite taken with her too, perhaps he was a closet pagan."

"You know more than I," Orazio said.

"Why is the Madonna black?" Frieda asked.

"I thought you'd ask that," Lorenzo continued, "Black Madonnas go to a very deep place in the human psyche, but the Roman Church doesn't like that idea, they just say it is centuries of incense burning. They should remember that God has only been Christian since Jesus converted him."

Just then the church bell started a furious clangour. Orazio crossed himself.

They wandered up the tree-lined slope to the foot of the great ashlar walls with their crenellated ramparts. A long tunnel entrance cut through the thick masonry into what had been a large square keep, now dwellings. An arch led down some steps to a narrow cobbled alleyway. At the foot of the steps there was a bar, and further along, a butcher, a bread-oven, and other suppliers. In a doorway a carpenter was at work in a little street-level basement, in another, a woman sat weaving a carpet in blue and yellow wool, occasional portals and viewpoints opened onto the valleys and mountains either side.

They walked further along until they came to a sort of largo with a vaguely baroque-style church facing onto it. Next to this, a much older square medieval watchtower had been converted into the campanile, the bell tower. A late churchgoer hurried up the steps through the mahogany doors, making a contrite sign of the cross as he entered. Hypnotic chants and litanies drifted out on the opiate-sweet incense. Lorenzo started to mutter something about visionary vapours and pagan goddesses but Orazio was saying something to him:

". . . San Lorenzo." The old model gestured at the door.

"Ah this is he . . . then pray for me." Lorenzo climbed the steps and pushed the door open a little to peer in, but soon backed out again. "I think I can smell burning coals . . . better make myself scarce."

Frieda took him by the arm and walked him away. Orazio led them back along the narrow street towards the great piazza, giving them the benefit of his knowledge as they went, and pointing things out, when suddenly he became aware that he was getting no response from behind him. He stopped and turned. Frieda was standing looking to the side. Lorenzo had disappeared.

A little way back was a sort of square tunnel arch with stone steps leading up to another narrow alley. Lorenzo was standing about halfway up, looking at something, a protrusion of living rock that seemed to grow from the steps as if it was seated there, leaning against the wall. He was running a hand over it, like a blind man feeling the features of a face. Frieda stood at the bottom of the steps watching. Orazio came up behind her.

"Look, look, can you not see her . . . can you not see the little maiden?" Lorenzo hands wandered slowly over the rough surface, over the uncut rock, and as he did so, a shape started to emerge, the lineaments of a face, long hair spilling over sad hunched shoulders, a little staring huddled figure, melancholy, alone, a waif, a beautiful lost child.

"What is she doing here? You are a cruel people to abandon her like this . . . neglected . . . unloved."

Orazio screwed his eyes, half in puzzlement and half trying to make out this hidden figure. It was something that had always been there, forever, unhewn, unnoticed, a piece of living rock, left there when the steps were cut how many centuries before, an oversight perhaps, nothing, just there, till now, till a man with other eyes had looked upon it.

Lorenzo crouched down. He leant close, as if to listen.

"Would you speak child? It is alright. You can trust me. I am like you, both of us outcasts. Tell me of yourself."

Frieda climbed the steps. She crouched down till she was face to face with the stone maiden. "What is your name lovely child . . . Du bist schön . . . Tell us your name. Orazio, what is her name?"

Orazio shrugged, bemused, unsure what sort of act this was, something serious or another one of their charades. But as he followed the wandering hands, he started to see her too.

"No name?" Frieda crouched still. "But look at her, how is that possible . . . such a lovely little creature . . . so sad and pretty."

Two townsfolk passed by. They looked curiously up the steps at the crouched figures. Orazio shuffled.

"Come Orazio," Lorenzo beckoned to him, "come and know her. She is the origin of this place. This is where you all come from. But see, she is fading. Soon she will fade away completely back into the rocks, and when that happens the village will start to die. Perhaps it is already dying. Come and touch her. Come and thank her before it is too late. She is your mother . . . child and mother. She is the little Madonna of the Steps."

Chapter Thirteen

FRIEDA STOOD IN FRONT OF THE BEDROOM WINDOW staring out at the white white world, whispering to herself: "Child of flesh . . . Child of stone . . ."

Lorenzo was sitting with his back to her at his desk table, reading his letters from the morning and already scribbling replies.

"What do you find so fascinating out there all the time?"

She said nothing. He went on reading, smiling at something, scribbling down an instant response, dashing off his thoughts, spontaneous, careless, living dialogues, the other person there before him. He poured himself out. This was his way.

"It's the children still isn't it," he said after a while, half with her and half still on his page, "the little ones the other evening, then Orazio's awful story about the trade in children, and now our lost waif from this morning?" He glanced over at her.

She let the words ride for a while.

"You know, I was thinking, we should find a sculptor for her . . . the little Madonna of the Steps . . . bring her back to life. What do you think Lorenz?" She looked over at him.

He laughed at something on one of the bits of paper.

"What did you say?" He looked up. "No, she needs no sculptor, she is alive enough for those with eyes to see."

There was silence again. He wriggled back and forward in his chair, conversing with the invisible correspondent — advice, money, annoyance, amusement, a sharp put down, a felicitous description — silent gestures and expressions shaping themselves to his changing flow of thought.

She turned away again . . .

"Whisper, whisper, whisper to yourself,

Only a reflection to hear you,

Window you have become my life . . ."

She stopped, a little gasp in her throat. If only she could have kept the children somehow and still been with him, or they could at least have come to stay with her sometimes, but they had been claimed by their father, the law on his side, she the betrayer — and he had shut her out, the mild educated professor, all church and consideration and kindliness, iron now in his determination, so that her very existence was being written out of their lives.

"Were you composing something just now . . .?" he said from his table, ". . . have you taken my place? That would be good, like a Greek tragedy . . . the gods take away his gifts and scatter them on the waters . . . a beautiful swan swims by . . . I want to hear it later."

The swan didn't reply, too wrapped in her thoughts, her own loss.

He sat back. "So tell me. Am I right? It's the children. It's set you off hasn't it!"

In their first years together he had been sympathetic, knew the great sacrifice she had made for him, understood her maternal feelings. But then things had changed, their relationship had become stormy and difficult, and his sympathy had evaporated. It wasn't enough that she had given the children up to be with him, no, now she must not even bring the subject up anymore. He wanted the all of her for himself. But as time went on, her sense of loss only grew stronger, and there would be terrible times when all she could do was think about them, and how to see them again, and wonder how they were growing, and if they missed her, and he, on hearing their names, would lose control. They had become rivals for her affection, and this he could not support. He could not bear that she was elsewhere than with him. She had to be his and only his. And yet he was so good with children, had indeed been good with hers when they first met, but seeing her continue to pine for them would send him into a fury of damnation.

She waited. He said nothing more. A faint glimmer of something like hope, but not yet quite that strong, travelled through her — perhaps they were far enough away from England for him to feel safe from their invisible presence. She took note of it, cautiously.

When they told Orazio about the visit — the old lady, the children, the sombre joyless pall that hung over the little house — he just shrugged. "Pazienza!" This word, the same one the old lady had used — it is fate, no use trying to fight it, one must just suffer — this is what that word meant.

"But at least they have their mother, that is a good thing," he added, trying to ease their concern.

"What do you mean?" Frieda's head spun round, her face white.

Orazio made a sort of cough, trying belatedly to muffle his words, remembering suddenly what Lorenzo had told him when they had been alone together, about how he and Frieda had met, about her previous marriage, the children she was hardly allowed to see anymore.

He coughed and cleared his throat. "It's the cigars," he said, tapping his chest, coughing again, hoping to escape, but Frieda's gaze held him. "Yes, I mean," he said, thinking quickly, "have you not heard of the Italian street children in London . . . no parents . . . no father and no mother . . . made to work like little slaves."

They looked at him.

He nodded slowly, pursing his lips. "Perhaps you do not know of this. I am older than you. It was in the time of our good Queen Victoria . . . Italian children roaming the streets of London, dressed in rags, with a little monkey, playing hurdy-gurdies or musical instruments they could hardly carry let alone play," he did one of his strange imitations, "and they would make such a din that people would pay them just to go away."

His guests listened, silent. He had deflected the earlier mistake, but now he could see they wanted him to explain.

"A terrible thing . . . their parents too poor to keep them, so they sold them to padroni. La tratta dei fanciulli it was called . . . the trade in children."

"Sold them?" Lorenzo looked up startled. "What do you mean sold? And who were these padroni? And how did they end up in London?"

"In Italy there is always a padrone . . ."

"Yes yes, I understand all that," Lorenzo interrupted, "but in this case what did it mean?"

Orazio cleared his throat again, he had got himself into something now.

"Where can I begin?"

"At the beginning."

He sighed, pushed his heavy grey hair back from his face. "This is what happened . . ." and he started to tell them: these padroni were men from here who had lived in England a while. They would come back, maybe once a year, and find boys and youths from the villages who wanted to leave, and there were many. The padrone would take them back with him and get them work and a place to live till they could find their own way, and that was fair. But there were others, not such good men, and they would find families of poor ignorant peasants, half-starved, with too many mouths to feed, and there were many of them too, and they would offer to help — I will borrow one of your children for a while, he will come with me to England, and I will keep him at my own expense, and he will earn a little money. Then in three years he will come back . . . or maybe five. The padrone would hand over a few coins, with the promise of a few more when the child was returned . . . oh, and a new suit of clothes for the little creature to come back with, all in the contract.

Lorenzo let it all sink in. "What contract?"

"They signed a contract, except of course the peasants couldn't read. But it made no difference in the end."

Lorenzo stared at the floor, then at Orazio. "And how old were the children?"

"Eight, nine, ten . . . A new suit of clothes for a lost childhood. Che miseria!"

Frieda was silent. Lorenzo spoke again.

"And were the contracts kept?"

"My word is my bond!" Orazio announced rhetorically, then shook his head. "No Signor Lorenzo, they were not kept. The children never came back . . . or hardly ever."

"That is indeed sad."

Frieda twirled her scarf, knotting it between her fingers.

Lorenzo saw, but he wanted to hear the rest of the story — the child would leave his little world and travel across Europe with his new padrone. On arrival he was put into a room with a dozen other little urchins like himself. They would be sent out onto the streets every day to earn coppers, and if they didn't earn enough they would get a hail of blows and no supper—this was their contract. But in London, people were taking notice . . . liberal reformers. It was in the newspapers. Campaigns were started to rescue the children, to have them sent back to their families, questions were even asked in the House of Commons, and also back in Rome, where the situation was seen as bringing shame on the new Kingdom of Italy. Consuls were asked to intervene . . .

"You seem to know a lot about it," Lorenzo said.

Orazio nodded.

"It mattered to you then."

He shook his head. "No, it did not matter . . ."

Lorenzo scrutinised the old model's face.

". . . perhaps they were lucky to escape," he went on, "yes perhaps they were lucky . . . blows and all. Blows were nothing new. One time, the Italian consul asked for my help. I knew him personally."

"What did you do?"

We walked the streets together, and when we found an Italian child he would try and ask him about his life and where he came from." Orazio made a gesture with his hands, turning his palms up. "Sometimes the child would talk, if you gave him sixpence or a shilling, but often he would take the coin and just run away. The consul made a list of names, some real, some not."

"And then?"

"And then?" Orazio shrugged.

A new suit of clothes for a lost childhood . . . Frieda listened, made herself endure it, but the words bit deep. She looked away into a private distance, saw her own children, happy and playing, then she saw the half-starved skinny little street children, begging and unloved, and somehow they were all the same, all just street children, all lost. Once, she had even wandered those same London streets hoping to come across hers — her husband had moved there from Nottingham — and suddenly there they were, her daughters, coming home from school, and they had looked at her as if she was a ghost.

She thought back to her own childhood . . . Christmas, coming downstairs to find the tree ablaze with candles and glass decorations and gifts. She and her sisters had started a tradition. During the year they would save some of their pocket money, and when Christmas came they bought presents for the children of the washerwoman who worked for them, and on Christmas eve, eight wan little creatures would be shepherded into the big house with their mother to receive their gifts.

Time for children—a nice middle-class consuetude. And she had been devoted to hers, she had had all the time in the world for them—a new suit of clothes for a lost childhood. Sometimes the pain was almost too much to bear, but she was alive, and in a strange terrible way, that pain made the aliveness of her new existence even more intense.

She left the men talking, wandered idly into the corridor, put on a coat, slipped out, and started to walk down the lane. It was dark. For a moment she thought of going back to see the two little children, just knock at the door, maybe the mother would be there this time, maybe she could be of help somehow, but the idea left her.

At the chapel she stopped. The other evening it had been closed. She climbed the steps and pushed at the door, and this time it opened—it had decided to give her sanctuary. There was no-one inside, no sound, just the sticky dry smell of burnt-down candles, one still alight, glowing in the half-dark. It was a simple bare little place, yellowing white-washed walls, three or four benches, a wooden altar with crucifix, and to one side, a statue of a Madonna and child, and underneath, an iron candle holder and iron box for coins. She had no money, but she took a candle anyway, lit it from the one still burning, and watched the little gold flame wave and search and flicker into life.

She stared into it, eyes blurring, then turned and looked slowly round, eyes still swimming, till they settled on the crucifix. She shut them tight and shook her head. She wanted life, not death. She was the life holder, he had said as much. Even when everything around them conspired to bring death, like the war, that great celebration of murder, it was she who held life for both of them. There had been a night in Cornwall when she had been by herself in the cottage, and the door had burst open on the wind, and from over the waters she thought she could hear the boom of the guns, and the cries of the dead and dying. The sentencing of his book had been another sort of death, and she had had to absorb that too, ward it off. There was a dark attraction around him which she must keep at bay. Then there was his chest. Sometimes it made him very ill. But he too had in him such life, death-defying life.

Would it be enough? Something gnawed at her, a fear that one day something would take him from her. It had always been there, even at the beginning, unaccountable, like the night they had arrived, the silver beautiful terrible moonlight flooding into the room, and she had woken up, and just for an instant he wasn't there. He had been infected by death, caught it somehow from the death of his mother, could never quite let go of it, this the paradox—he who had such a genius for life seemed to live in the shadow of death.

She looked up at the Madonna with its Christ child, one hand extended to the supplicant, painterly and perfect, not like the Bavarian statues he loved so much, peasant faces, coarse, hewn, a peasant soul you might meet on a mountain path, stopping to rest. Which Mary was she, she wondered, a painterly one or a peasant? Neither. She was another Mary altogether, the one that Jesus had cast seven demons out of, so that all she could do was follow him. Yes that was she—Leave everything and follow me, even your children. And she had obeyed, not to have done would have been a greater sin.

Her candle was alone now, the other one had guttered out. She cupped her hands round it. How exquisite—a little golden tear! Suddenly she was aware of something, a presence behind her. She hadn't heard anyone come in. She turned. A young woman was seated on the last bench by the door, her back against the wall, head lowered, shoulders hunched slightly, face half-hidden under long dark hair—this much Frieda could see in the candlelight. There was something familiar—the way she sat, her sad pretty face, hair falling over her shoulders. It reminded her of something but she couldn't think what.

Two women, a Madonna, a flame, a God child, silence. Moments passed. She walked the few steps back towards the door and stopped, her hand trembling with the desire to reach out, to touch the lonely shoulder. She pushed open the door and walked quietly out.

Chapter Fourteen

——◆——

ORAZIO SAT SMILING TO HIMSELF, SHAKING HIS HEAD, nodding, shaking it again — so many words, more words in a day than had been uttered in all the years the villa had been built, and enough now to last him a lifetime.

"What is that brings us together?" Lorenzo had asked him one morning. They were, as usual, seated in front of the fire. Frieda had stepped out somewhere. Orazio thought for a moment. The answer, the obvious one . . . Thornycroft, Rosalind, the network of acquaintances and connections, the circle of writers and artists which Orazio too had frequented in his shadowy way—all that, but not that. He knew not the obvious.

The Englishman poked at the embers as if he was writing something in them, then jabbed a sort of full stop into the pile of ash.

"There, I have sent some thoughts up the chimney." He chuckled to himself. "Come Sir Horace, something links us, something brings us together, it always does in these things . . . and with you dear Orazio, I feel it quite strongly. Come, what do you say..?"

Orazio rubbed his bristly jaw. "I . . . I am not . . ." but the sentence petered out.

The Englishman smiled, raised his eyebrows, fiddled with something in his pocket, leaned forward again to poke the fire, settled back, and fixed Orazio with a quizzical gaze.

"Yes?"

"Well . . . Well I suppose our mutual friend Rosalind . . . ." He stopped. He had fallen at the first and he knew it. The Englishman looked away, seeming to lose interest, his eyes glazing slightly, turning inwards the way they often would, heading off down avenues. He roused himself again.

"Come, you can do better than that caro Orazio. Throw me a line . . . without thinking, just throw it out there and let's see what happens, let's see what we can catch."

Orazio hummed a little behind his hand.

"Come . . . Throw . . . Cast. I saw a rod in your room and some flies in your trunk, so I know you can."

Orazio nodded. Nothing could be hidden from this spirit man — and he pictured himself, rod in hand by the Thames somewhere . . . an English summer's day, his line lying slack on the dark running waters, then a sudden jerk, a bite. How he would love to have been there at that moment, straw boater on his head, sandwiches and a flask of tea.

"Nice day isn't it?" Lorenzo peered over, a gleam in his eye. "You better hurry though . . . rain clouds in the offing, and the basket's still empty."

Orazio's hand reached slowly for the medal round his neck. He cleared his throat.

"Well now Signor David . . . talking of fish, you have not told me of your sojourn in Florence." The old model pursed his lips.

"Sojourn! Good word. But what's fish got to do with it?"

Orazio gave a sort of shrug.

The Englishman grinned. "Yes, well, let me see now. I can tell you first it was a relief to get there. Norman Douglas was . . ." He paused. "Do you know Douglas?" Orazio shook his head. "You'd like him, one of the anglo-florentines I suppose you'd say . . . anyway, as I was saying, I was very happy to arrive. Douglas had booked me a room in the same hotel with him. He was good company, very generous and amusing. I wrote you from there." Lorenzo chewed on his thoughts a moment. "There was also this fellow Magnus there, a sort of companion of Douglas's I suppose you'd say . . . a bit painful, but I even enjoyed his company too sometimes. You get all sorts drifting through Florence, all a bit decadent and outré, preening themselves, mostly awful sub-arty types, or boozers . . . the English trying to liberate themselves if you know what I mean, but for all that, congenial, at least for some of the time." He raised his eyebrows at Orazio to see how he was doing.

"Good." The old model nodded. "I think we are getting some-where," he said, settling into the English after dinner role he so relished. Lorenzo shot him an amused look. "And what about the city itself, the art, the museums, what did you see?"

"See? What didn't we see? We saw everything. Frieda joined me there from Germany and she is more insatiable than I . . . or maybe we are equal. You know it was three o'clock in the morning when she arrived and I took her straight out for a tour of the city in a carrozza."

"Hmm." Orazio thought for a minute. "And if you could pick just one thing from this everything that you saw, what would it be?"

Lorenzo smiled. "Orazio, you are steering me. You should have been a barrister, you are edging me towards an answer. But do you know the answer?"

Orazio gave him a sage inscrutable look.

"Ha . . . splendid!" Lorenzo grinned at his new adversary. "Now then. My favourite thing. I'll give you something . . . at the Bargello, Donatello . . . Donatello's David. Frieda liked Michelangelo's David best, it brought tears to her eyes, but if I want a David I think Donatello's is the one for me."

Orazio rose from his chair, bent forward, lit his cheroot from the fire and shuffled out of the kitchen. This, Lorenzo knew, always prefaced some new piece of knowledge or revelation. The stairs creaked up. A few moments later they creaked down again.

"Here." Orazio handed him a photo.

Lorenzo examined it.

"Is this you?"

Orazio nodded.

"Is it by Thornycroft?"

He nodded again. "The Mower. That is what it is called. You can see, I am holding a scythe. Does it remind you of anything?"

"I have never seen you in the bronze before." Lorenzo chuckled at his own joke, and looked closer at the photo. "My God yes," he nodded, "it's Donatello's David, only with trousers . . . same sort of contrapposto pose, same hat, except Donatello's has laurels in it if I remember, and you have a scythe instead of a sword. All you need is a foot on Goliath's severed head . . . Otherwise . . . Well well Orazio, you have made the case. We'll call it the case for the proposition. We are both Davids in our different ways."

Lorenzo examined the photo a while.

"Unfortunately, in my case, in this David's battle with Goliath," he said, pointing a finger at his chest, "Goliath won. The Philistines won. The British Establishment won. They slew me. How can that be Orazio? It goes against all mythological truth." Lorenzo held up the image in front of him, comparing it to the person of his host. "But as for you, it is different. I would say you have won."

Orazio peered at him. How had he won?

"Oh yes, don't look at me like that. You have won because you will live forever." He held up the photo, looking from model to bronze.

"A statue is not a living thing . . ."

"Not so Orazio, for every time someone looks at your likeness, life will flicker inside, you will live again, and just think, you will be eternally young."

Words and ideas popped like corks from champagne bottles, Lorenzo always pouring out more, trying a new vintage, and Orazio sipping unsteadily—now eternally young . . .

"Orazio, I am not sure about you. Do you love your land, your Italy, your patria, or do you hate the land you love?" Lorenzo asked another time. But before Orazio had even understood the question, Frieda replied for him.

"That is you," she said, "you hate England. You hate the land you love, and now you want to drag Orazio down with you. Leave the poor man alone, he is wasting away with all your questions."

Orazio gave a bashful smile and pinched his arms and chest. "Still a little flesh left."

"Love England, hate myself, hate England, love myself. I am just a poor confused writer. What can I do? Help me Baroness. Psychoanalyse my poor benighted soul."

She pursed her lips and looked at him. Psychoanalysis. This was a dangerous word.

"What, nothing doing in that direction?" He slanted a sly grin at her.

"If I do say something and you don't like it then you will say I am wrong, or that it is just a peculiar hokum invented by the Germans to get round all their sins. When you hear something you don't like it is always that."

"Alright, let me start again. Let me redirect the question. Can a German enjoy all these contradictions, all this love for his country which is really hate, or vice versa, or is this a special gift that only the English possess?"

She waited silently, struggling with all the conflicting emotions that had piled up inside her over the past years. It all sounded horribly familiar, jumbles of half thought-out ideas, words firing off and you didn't know where they would land, and the inevitable talk of England. England. Were they going to drag it around with them forever? She yearned for healing. She could sense something in him coiled and ready to pounce.

She picked up a plate off the table, fingering it as if examining the pattern, except it didn't have one, then she leant across and tapped it on his head, not very hard, but it was thin china, already cracked, and it broke easily.

"There," she said, "that's my psychoanalysis."

He picked a fragment of broken china out of his hair and peered at it, turning it over in his hand.

"Well, that is certainly one point of view. I however would come to another."

He reached for the pot of cold tea on the table, a shiny metal pot that looked as if it had come from a Lyons Corner House. He opened the lid, looked inside, closed the lid, stood up, and with slow deliberateness, baptised her lovely thick fairish hair with dregs of the yellow liquid, little trickles dripping off her springy curls, running down her cheeks, she immobile, accepting the response—at least this time.

He stopped pouring. They looked at each other, unsaid words passing between them. This had just been a gentle re-enactment, just a little pantomime really, and they both smirked a little, knowing what it had rehearsed — a no-holds-barred mutual assault with real intent, crockery flying, like so often at the cottage in Cornwall, the great breaking sea-lashed cliffs calling them to battle. But they had survived. They were battle-hardened now. Only the plate had made the ultimate sacrifice.

Then her face changed, suddenly, and her eyes widened dangerously. He flinched.

". . . And I don't love to hate or hate to love or whatever your twisted logic is, I just love my land and my people, my Germany . . . love them, just that, simple, straightforward. I don't need any analysis to know this."

"And I love them too," he whispered back, dabbing at her hair and face with his clean handkerchief.

She took him in her arms, her damp fair locks falling over both their faces, a tabernacle of mutual compassion.

"I will protect you," she whispered.

"I still fear a knock at the door."

"I know."

". . . And there will be the police and military come to evict us . . . You have three days to leave."

She placed her forehead against his.

"I am so sorry," he whispered, "I have put you so much in the way of harm. Forgive me."

She stroked his face and beard with her fingers, wiping little smears of tea away. "It isn't you. It is something that hovers around us."

He looked at her, almost a plea in his eyes.

"Look, we have come through," she whispered, ". . . your words, you wrote them, now we must act them. They must guide us."

"My Frieda," he stared heavenward, "you are the book of psalms, you are a benediction, you are creation."

She laughed, and shook her head with a sudden playful force, swinging it from side to side, sending out a spray of cold tea, and giving out her little lion roars at the same time.

"I am she . . . that is me . . . and this is a blessing of old cold tea."

He clapped at her little rhyme, and held out a hand as if feeling for the first drops of rain.

"What is this, the start of the second great flood? The world will sink under the waves, all except us up here on our mountain, and Orazio shall be Noah . . ."

"Oh yes, yes, I would love it." She stroked her damp hair down, then stroked his, and painted his eyebrows with her wet fingers. "Then we will start the world anew, Ich und du." She twisted little strands of her wet hair into plaits. "What shall we make the new official language . . . the new Hebrew?"

Orazio, the new Noah, looked on, named but unnoticed. After a while, the conversation floated off Mt. Ararat and back up the Thames . . .

"What do they think of us? Really. What do they think, not what they say, what they think?" Lorenzo looked into her eyes.

"I don't know, but if you mean those Bloomsbury creatures . . . too busy being witty to help the only true artist among them, it doesn't matter about them."

He shrugged. But he liked her words. At least one person in the world was on his side.

"I don't care about them either, it's the politicians I can't forgive . . . Lloyd George and all those other muckspouts. Versailles. They think the war is over, that war they so loved. Well maybe they will be happy to know it isn't, it is just suspended." He turned round to Orazio, suddenly remembering his presence. "Frieda can tell you . . . she can tell you what is happening in Germany. No, it is not over. They are sowing seeds, biblical seeds."

Frieda closed her eyes.

"We must heal this wound Lorenzo."

"Maybe I should learn forgiveness, but I cannot."

Orazio got up and shuffled about, clearing away plates and pots and mixing food for the pig.

"Orazio, you are a dear," Lorenzo said, coming back into the present, "you are a kind sensitive soul."

"If you say so." The old model shrugged.

"Apologies for the plate."

He shrugged again: "It was cracked anyway."

"Don't throw the pieces away, I will use them." Frieda said, gathering them up, and making a little pile on the table. "I will paint them with some of your paints. I will paint tears."

The Englishman cupped his face in his hands, rubbing his beard up and down. He stood up and walked over to the window, stared out vacantly, then turned back and sat down again.

"Orazio, I need your advice. Is it just me? What do you think? Why am I not patriotic . . . well not like others. You are a wise man, this I can see. Tell me what I am doing wrong."

Frieda raised her eyes to heaven. "Here we go again, round and round."

Lorenzo took no notice. "Do you love this new Italy? I love Italy, but it is different for me. Would I be patriotic if I were Italian? Is it just England that is the problem?"

Since he had arrived back, he had been struggling with this new Italy he had found. The old Italy, the Italy they had left on their last visit four years before — that Italy had still slumbered in its moss-covered marble classicism where shepherds guided their sheep through crumbling ruins. The war had come. Startled by events, she had been thrown violently from her bed, awoken

brutally from her secular slumber, suddenly aware of her naked-
ness, and like she had always done, had reached for another lover.
But this time, instead of the soft warm living flesh of old decadence, she had taken into her bed the cold steel of the new century,
turned ploughshares into weapons.

Instead of peace, their poet sang of war, instead of nature, their
new art was a paean to the machine age. This was the hymn of
D'Annunzio, the religion of Marinetti. A great cleansing must take
place, the sacred earth of the fatherland must be purified by the
sun-blood of its sun-people at the altar of industrial slaughter so
that a new race could emerge.

Orazio thought for a minute. "What is there to love? What is
there to be patriotic about? I am a forgotten man in a forgotten
land."

"You see," Lorenzo said, turning to Frieda.

"What do I see?" she said, shrugging. "And you keep saying
this is not Italy and then you ask the poor man if he loves Italy."

Lorenzo nodded sheepishly, acquiescing for once.

"It's all this being closed in, but you know what I mean . . .
the war here was about finishing off what the Risorgimento had
started . . . the re-unification of Italy, throwing out the old
imperial occupiers, the Austro-Hungarians, reclaiming the
sacred soil. 'Italia Irredenta,' wasn't that their cry? Now the man
from the train, our nameless saviour, he was a new Italian, he
was patriotic. He had returned from England to join the Italian
army. He told us about the conditions at the front, didn't he
Frieda . . . the fighting in the mountains . . . what he thought
about General Cadorna. Up there in Garda where we were
before the war, that was the border, the next town along was
an Austrian garrison town, Riva. Frieda was quite taken with
the Austrian soldiers in their uniforms, waltzing around." He
peered at her. She didn't respond. "Now it is Italian again, and
all the rest of that territory too . . . Trento, Bolzano, all the way
to Trieste. Are you not happy that you chased the Austrians
out Orazio?"

Orazio chewed on his cheroot. "Why? Did we win? Have they gone?"

Lorenzo burst out laughing. "Orazio mio caro, you are priceless. I think you would make a good journalist."

Orazio sat, solemn, muttering under his breath, but the Englishman wanted to hear.

"Say it out loud, I need to know."

"I said, what is Italy? We win and nothing changes. We could have lost, it is just the same. Here nothing changes."

"I think you have your answer," Frieda said.

Lorenzo tilted his head back, picking thoughtfully at the hairs of beard on his throat.

". . . And if we won," Orazio continued, "I don't know how we won. It is but two years ago that we believed it was all over. They had shot our fox."

Lorenzo spluttered with laughter.

"Orazio, what species are you? I wouldn't be surprised if we came down to breakfast tomorrow morning only to discover we are really in Berkshire . . . shot our fox indeed! I can just see the Italian generals galloping across the plains of the Veneto as if they were the shires . . . Tally-Ho . . . Where's that imperial fox Franz Josef?"

"Lorenzo!" Frieda interrupted sharply, "Orazio is being serious."

"Oh."

"It is alright Signor David . . . but it is hard to charge in the mountains, so instead, they turned the men into donkeys to carry the guns up to the top and the dead back down. At Caporetto, it was all over for us." Orazio looked around at them. "You have heard of Caporetto . . . The Austrians and Germans drove us back from the Dolomites right across the plains of the Veneto almost to Venice itself. It was all over, or so we thought, and you know what, we were happy, the men would come home. Italy? What is Italy? Patriotism? What is that? . . . a play thing of the rich, the educated . . . La borghesia."

The old model tapped his knife on the table.

"Old men and ghosts," he said after a while, "that is all that is left. We are a peasant nation, who will till the land now? Ghosts can't. Ask old Anna, the old grandmother, ask the two children, ask their mother. She is lucky, she washes clothes for the priest, and cooks. But who will plough their land? No, Signor Lorenzo, here there is nothing," he said wearily, "there is just today . . . there is no future. If you stay you will see."

No-one spoke. Orazio pushed a pile of vegetables across the table and started to cut at them, the blade of his knife clacking like a slow drumbeat on the wooden surface.

"Orazio my friend," Lorenzo said after a while, his voice soft now, "I am so sorry to trawl all this up. What can I say?" But what puzzled him, as it had done over the last few days, was why he had come back? If he felt like this—why?

"Carpe Diem Orazio. If there is just today, then you are well named. You are rich in that sense at least. Your namesake made a virtue out of it . . . the simple life."

The old model went on chopping. "O Signore!" he said after a while, defeat in his voice. How could he make them understand?

There was silence again, just the sound of knife on wood, clack, clack, clack.

"Wine, that is the answer." The Englishman ruffled his fine brown hair, and grinned hopefully round the room. "Horace was right about that too . . . Drink wine, live quietly. This was his way. Live quietly and there is plenty."

"Wine is for the good times." Frieda's voice trembled a little, in her eye a touch of moisture. Lorenzo looked up. She had been quiet all this while. He hadn't noticed.

"My father loved his wines, but the days of wine in Germany are gone, the world of my youth is gone, the young men I knew are gone. They were the harvest. There is nothing left."

Orazio looked from one to the other, wondering which direction the words would go next, racking his old brain for something to say that would bring them peace, all of them, him too. But it was Lorenzo who spoke:

"I will stay with my version, with Horace's version. But wine can be blood too, that is true. The war was a winepress of human suffering, the blood of the Christ, crushed and consecrated, and just like the Christ there will be a second coming." He took a deep breath . . . "Of death-producing wine, till treasure runs waste down their chalices." It was a line from one of his poems.

Orazio shuffled out into the corridor, and came back in with a dusty green bottle.

"Here then, let us drink our wine now while we still can, even if it is how you say Signor Lorenzo."

He wiped the dust off the bottle and drew the cork. For once it was a red wine. He poured out a glass each and splashed some into the pig's bucket just for good measure. They stared into the blood-deep liquid for a few moments.

"I am not good with words, and I have little to offer, but what I have, I offer you with all my heart." Orazio raised his glass. "Salute."

Lorenzo fingered his glass, turning it slowly in his hand, peering into the ruby liquid.

"You will get us drunk, drinking wine when we've hardly finished breakfast, teaching us all your Bloomsbury vices." He sipped and smiled and grimaced. "I am sorry Orazio. We talk too much. I talk too much. It is better to keep silent like you."

Orazio shook his head. "No Signor David, it is good for me. When you are gone there will be time for silence. I will remember our talking. It is good."

"We will come back. Frieda and I were just talking about how nice it would be . . ."

"No signore," Orazio interrupted, "no need to say these things. My life is this now. I will remember, and maybe sometimes you will remember too."

Chapter Fifteen

———•———

"I must send mail Orazio, to Capri, to Mr. Compton Mackenzie, just to remind him we are coming, after all it is five years since he invited us, and there has been a little matter of a world war in the meantime." Lorenzo was in cheerful mood this morning. "Did you remember your invitation to Rosalind when her letter arrived saying she was thinking of coming? That was before the war too, so she tells us . . . .Oh dear, and you got us instead." He made a little slanted smile from under his lowered lashes. "Poor Orazio. What a disappointment!"

"Will you be writing to Rosalind?"

"Yes, I think so, soon."

"Then tell her the truth Signor David. It is better so. Picinisco is not Pangbourne."

"No Samnites in Pangbourne." Frieda shook her head wanly.

"The poorer for it, but that is a good cue . . . a good cue." The blithe Englishman thumbed through some papers on the small table by the window.

"Seize the moment." He looked up and beamed around the room. "Yes indeed, I think it is time to hear the Liber Samnitium, the great epic, the alternative history of Italy, Lawrence versus Livy, the world according to the Samnites, dedicated to our noble host, fine wine-maker and man of melancholic wisdom. I hadn't really intended to but here we are . . . Carpe Diem."

Outside the door, the donkey brayed, and they could hear Giovanni parleying with it—his one true friend. The little man crept in, trying not to be seen, trying to read the mood. He settled himself on a stool in the corner near the hearth and took off his long conical hat, playing it through his fingers, watching from his cast-down eyes the movements of his brother — if there would be any signs, whether he would be despatched back to his own abode, not allowed to be present at the passage of higher things, and hoping that if he wasn't noticed he would be allowed to stay. Frieda gave him a smile. He glanced nervously at his brother.

"Hah," Lorenzo exclaimed with his newfound geniality, "Giovanni. Just in time. We have a full house. Ushers close the doors. Giovanni will love to hear a story I'm sure."

"My brother . . . hear a story? All he knows is mule talk." Orazio turned a darkly muttering gaze on his brother.

Lorenzo sorted the papers in his hand.

"Orazio, if you would be kind enough to give a little summary translation to Giovanni now and again when I pause, just a few words, not everything, you know how I'm sure."

Frieda clapped her hands.

"Can we join in? Can we make it a live performance?"

"No . . . Yes . . . I don't know."

Lorenzo motioned his audience to array themselves in front of him, while he sat with his back to the hearth. He held up his hand. Silence fell.

"Viteliu," he pronounced, his voice deep with Olympian gravitas. "Viteliu, the ancient Oscan word from which the name Italia comes. It means the Land of the Bulls."

He closed his eyes in reverential silence for a moment, then took a deep breath.

"We are the sons of the mountains, those great stones that bring us into being, that give us life. They are powerful and dangerous, but they cannot move. We move for them. We are their eyes and ears. This is the bargain. Sometimes they grow angry, even kill us, but it is through us that they know themselves, and I, Meddix of the tribe, high-priest and chieftain, must keep this world in balance. I am the messenger between heaven and earth.

"From the summit of Mount Acze to the farthest valleys, these are our lands, half the year rich pasture, the other half winter-wild and white. Nameless spirits wander these mountains, inhabit the groves and caverns, the woods and streams. Sometimes, by chance, on the darkest of nights, a faint piping sound might be heard, like the whistle of wind in the shaft of a cave, soft and distant at first, soft as new birth, then closer and shriller, not human, the voice of the wild things, of all those beings that hide and watch, that leave tracks in the snow, that sink their teeth deep, taste blood, predator and prey, lover and loved in mortal embrace.

"Every year in the spring, I go to the sacred grove to make sacrifice to the gods for the gift of these lands, first of all to the great god Mamers, he who brought us here, to Famel, goddess of the earth, Kerres, goddess of the harvest who has fed my people and flocks, Sancus, god of sowing, Feronia, goddess of the wild beasts, but more than any other to the great dark goddess Mefitis, queen of these mountains, and to whom I have a special devotion.

"My name is Mamerkis. I was born in the spring of that fateful year, and dedicated to the great god Mamers, in the month that bears his name . . ."

And so, pausing occasionally for Orazio to give a few grudging words in dialect to his brother, the bard told his story . . .

"Sixteen years had passed since the terrible time of sickness, of war, of hunger and death. The crops had failed, the livestock died of diseases, or were born deformed, the winter was hard, the summer brought drought, warfare had broken out with the city of the she-wolf to the west.

"Offerings were made to the gods, but nothing would appease them. There was just one sacrifice left, a rite which is performed only when dangers are extreme, when our very existence is in peril—Ver Sacrum, the rite of the Sacred Spring. It demands that every creature born the following spring must be sacrificed to

Mamers, the god of war, but also of agriculture and youth — all the new-born sheep and calves, every being, even the dogs and cats, and most sacred of all, the new-born children.

"But the children are not killed — although it is said that in times long ago even this took place sometimes — they are dedicated at birth to the god, they become his sacrati, his holy ones. But in the springtime when they reach their fifteenth year, they must leave their homes, their families, their villages, they must leave and never return. They are given into the hands of the god.

"That day has come. The sacrati gather. A fire has been lit. An ox has been slaughtered and his blood poured over the earth. Then, from behind the trees, arms outstretched, a priest appears, his body green, his face black, a headdress of red feathers. He circles around us, tapping a piece of wood the way the sacred bird taps with its beak on the trunk of the tree—the picus.

"We are blindfolded, led into the high mountains, and left there. Time passes. I hear the sound of wings quick in flight. We are being observed. Then I hear the rapid tapping of a beak on a nearby tree. I take off my blindfold. We are alone. I look around at my brother sacrati still wearing their blindfolds. I speak: 'The god is with us.' They are the first words of our new life.

"That is how we start, but then the strangeness comes over us and we enter into a state of being and a period of time that must have lasted several days, but when I try to remember it I cannot, and nor can any of my companions. It was like a waking dream, like the visions you get when you have a fever, but all gathered together in just one vision. We were in a blessed state, somewhere between two worlds. We belonged to the god for him to dispose of.

"When we awoke, we knew we had crossed a frontier into another world. It is so beautiful we cannot speak. We are new, the whole world is new, untouched — this was the sensation we all shared, as if we had been purified, reborn. On a high rock face, a bear watches our passage. It rears up, balancing on its hind legs, pawing the air, dancing from side to side, throwing its great head up and down, sniffing the air to see what sort of creatures we are. I stop, raise a hand to my eyes to see better, blinking against the white snow-bright light, and in that instant it is no longer a bear but a beautiful woman, young in figure and face but with the long white hair of an old woman. I rub my eyes and look again, but where she stood there is only jagged rock.

"The sacred bird dives down, a flash of green. We follow him till he disappears. We are standing on a good high place, a great fertile valley spread below. It is our new home. From now on it will be known as the Hill of the Picus."

The chronicler folded his papers, and looked about him with learned seriousness. "And that is how the village of Picinisco got its name."

Giovanni sat on the floor staring up.

"Why how have you discovered all this?" Orazio asked. "It is not only from that book I think."

"My husband has access to other knowledge Orazio, a universal knowledge." Frieda nodded sagely.

The old model looked at her uncertainly.

Chapter Sixteen

F RIEDA KNELT ON A PILLOW ON THE BEDROOM FLOOR,
poking a finger through a hole in a once lovely old petticoat her
mother had given her during her stay in Germany on the way
down—or really given back.

On the train from England, her luggage had been stolen. No
matter how poor they were — and they were always hardly more
than threadbare — something out there always wanted more.
They were always being robbed. She had arrived in Baden with
only what she stood up in. Her mother had dug out some of her
old clothes from years ago, kept in memory of the before, of the
good times, and among them, those of a young debutante waltzing
through the grand salons, all heads turning, even the Kaiser's.

She held them up, shook them out, examined them, held them
to her face, inhaled them, caressed them, whispered to herself—
names of places, names of people, German names — Aren't those
the von Richthofen girls! the Kaiser had asked his aide — and he
had commented on how pretty they were, especially little Johanna,
the youngest, she was the beauty. But Frieda had something more,
a life force, green eyes full of fire and play that would melt into
liquid gold and slay any young cadet foolish enough to look into
them, and she knew it.

She sighed—how many worlds had waltzed past and away since
then, how many lifetimes! Had it really existed?

Lorenzo lay on his back on the bed, hands under his head, musing to himself, ". . . a Greek tragedy, a unity of time and space. Here we are in the royal bedchamber, guests of the Tyrant of the Valleys . . . Orazio Rex!" He lifted his head to look over at her, expecting a response, but the young debutante was waltzing and gliding over the marble floor of the grand salon, an intoxicating mist of admiring glances following in her wake.

"And you my little maiden, down there on the floor, you can be the Greek priestess who crawls out on her hands and knees at the beginning of a play by Aeschylus." He glanced over again. "You know what, perhaps we should stage a City Dionysia here, a great drama contest." Still no response. "Very well, if that is your last word on the matter . . ." He brought his arms from behind his head and folded them on his chest. "You know, for once I think you are right. I shall give up the written word. From now on I am pre-literate. I am oral, a travelling bard. Yes I think I will abandon Euripides and become Homer. I will write nothing more down. We should return to those times don't you think . . . travelling minstrels, everything oral. What a different world it would be, and just think, no publishers, no reviewers, no magistrates' courts, no libel actions . . ."

He threw his arms in the air, happy with his solution.

"Do you think they enjoyed it, my little epic? I shall make Orazio commit it to memory so that it can be passed down through the generations."

He looked across again at the silent princess fiddling with her pile of ball gowns.

"Say something. What do you think?"

"About what?" she said distractedly, her fingers busy with her own Greek drama, nostalgic silk full of holes and memories—this one, she was sure, was the very petticoat she was wearing that night in Berlin at the Stadtschloss, and now here it was. If, on the night she had last taken it off, back in Uncle Oswald's house in Berlin in a delirium that only a young girl can know, the whole world at her feet, she and her sister telling each other about who they had danced with and who they had conquered — if she could have seen then that the next time she handled this soft silk, that that world, the Reich, the Kaiser, the grand balls, would no longer exist, and she would be kneeling on a cold bare floor in an icy little house in a remote mountain land forgotten by time, almost middle-aged, virtually penniless, her glorious petticoats now just a threadbare memory . . .

"Ugly, ugly, ugly, the world is ugly . . ." She smoothed the silk against her cheek, her mouth quivering, her voice a little girl's voice holding back tears. "No, it is not so," she sniffed, "the world is beautiful, whatever happens, it is beautiful."

She stroked the garments and folded them—with a little adjustment something might be done with them, some letting out. Maybe if she is nice to him he will help her. He is so good at that sort of thing. He is the hausfrau she has never been.

He watched her from the bed, her expressions, her little private whisperings and emotions.

"What did you say?" She perked up and looked over at him with a dimpled smile—one of his favourites.

"I was talking about my great woodpecker saga." He thought about it for a minute. "Are there such things as Roman sagas, or are they exclusive to the Nordic world?"

She smiled radiantly up at him. "Yes, I wanted to say, I haven't heard that voice before, that storytelling voice, not like that anyway."

"Are my novels not stories then?"

She made a thoughtful hum. "I don't know."

"Perhaps I am turning into an old country parson, pacing the country lanes, composing little novellas or local histories or making nature notes in between my sermons."

A disturbed expression flitted across her face.

"No church, please. I don't want any more churchgoing companions in my life."

But now it is he who is not really listening.

"No. I think I will leave it here when we go, on paper, just for Orazio. The question is, should I sign it?"

She shrugged, the thought of parsons and churches still bothering her, knocking her momentarily back into a starched righteous past of tea and gossip, of laundry on Tuesday, of shopping on Thursday, of Sunday on Sunday. Oh poverty of poverties—dresses with holes in, but such memories. He watched her flickering expressions, her telltale shadowy thoughts.

"Yes," he resumed, finally giving up on any meaningful response from her, "I will leave it. At worst he can light his cheroot with it. I don't suppose it will survive him anyway, a few old bits of paper in a box, and when he is gone, some brigand will come to clear his things, old Maria perhaps, eyes shining with vino, cackling away to herself, throwing things into the fire, papers with words, crumpled-up words, nonsense words, foreign words . . . and there they go, yellowing, smoking, crinkling into flames, rising up the chimney, out into the sky, flying away . . . 'Salute!' And down her old throat with a smack of her lips goes another beaker of Orazio's sulphuric white . . . But wait! Her cunning little peasant eyes narrow suddenly . . . Who will get the villa! She peers about her dizzily, eyes bulging . . . does she not deserve it for all the work she has done? Why doesn't she just move in . . . Giovanni is so simple . . . and all the new vines . . . the new vines!

"She creaks up the stairs, whispering something . . . a spell, eyes greedy with pleasure, sticking her tongue out at the distinguished men in the photos on the walls. She pushes open the bedroom door. Horror! She jumps back . . . crosses herself . . . a picture on the wall. Naked bodies, a man and a woman lying together . . .

"She stands there staring at it, bony hands on bony hips, nodding and gabbling . . . Men . . . Disgusting. So Orazio had a secret. She might have known it. For this he will surely be burning in hell now. With surprising strength she slides the wardrobe in front of the offending image. There. Now for the drawers . . . and what do we have here? Ha! She paws the silk ties, holds up the cufflinks, eyes bulging . . . fetch a nice few lire at the market all this stuff . . .

"They say in the village that once many years ago, an English writer came to stay . . . No, that is just a story poor old Orazio used to tell after a glass or two. It wasn't true."

Frieda gave a last sad look at her piteous pile of silken garments and pressed them back down into the case.

"You know what I miss, I miss lying on the floor." She rubbed her knees and screwed up her face. "Haven't they heard of carpets here?"

She sprang to her feet and tossed her main of straw-fair hair from side to side so that it fanned out—she is life, she can bring down any prey, she is a lioness. That is what her mother used to call her.

"Perhaps I should write a children's book," he says, half watching her, half thinking out loud, "that and the odd history book, like my European History. It might be the only way to earn a crust if things go on like this."

She looked at him, half debutante, half lioness — what is this man saying, lying there like a philosophising corpse? Something surged inside her.

"Not good enough. I don't want crusts, I want meat. I am a carnivore. I am starving. So if you can't bring me any game I'm going to eat you." She raised her hands and pawed at the air.

"I know," he said, coming up onto his elbow, "I could write a story about a little German girl with red stockings who lives in the woods. Her name is Frieda Freitag."

She jumped onto the bed and climbed on top of him, pummelling and squeezing at his thin ribs. They wrestle and turn, now one on top, now the other, till they are hot and breathless, but she is the victor, he the willing victim.

"That was a good battle," he was panting a little.

"I won."

"What does winning mean?"

"I am powerful. I am all-conquering. I have a red mane."

"A red mane?" He ruffled her hair. "You're not a lion. You have red stockings. You are an imp of the woods."

She closed her eyes. "Do you think there are witches here?"

her voice was soft and a little frightened, credulous, ". . . like the bear in your story, standing on the cliff, and then the boy looks a second time and she turns into a young old woman with long grey hair. I liked that. That was the best bit."

"She is real. She is out there, and she eats little German imps."

There was a squeal, and she mauled him again, and took little bites at his neck. He closed his eyes tight and let her have her way.

"Enough, I surrender. I am vanquished . . . Frieda vincit."

She sat above him. "Good that you have found out at last. I am an entire legion come to destroy you, you and your Samnite city, impose some Roman order round here."

". . . So the fateful day has finally come. I peer out from the ramparts, by my side the famous gladiator, Orazio the Stag, in full armour. Across the valley we see them advance, the legions, burning and laying waste all round, the Roman Eagle glinting in the sun.

"The famous gladiator lights his last cheroot. Just then a messenger arrives hot foot from far away Londinium with news from my publisher—Your book will be published. I look up to the sky—Oh ye great gods! They have answered my prayers, but with a twist of Olympian humour in the tail—I will be published posthumously, I will join the immortals, and the German imp will get all my royalties. Orazio and I embrace. We drink a final glass of his ghastly white wine and . . ."

She slumped down off him and rolled away laughing.

"Well that's one way of defeating the legions." He patted her quivering flesh. "You know the Romans came up over the pass, the same way we came when we arrived," he said, straightening his shirt and hair.

"What, on the bus?" she said between breaths.

He grinned at her, his eyes soft and boyish now under his long lashes. "No. It was full."

Her hand wandered gently over his arms and up to his face, her fingers playing on his mouth and beard.

"Lorenzo?"

"Yes?"

"Will you help me to mend my dresses?"

"I bet I could find where that lost city stood, Cominium. I am going to search for it. It will be there, even if there's nothing left. It will be visible to me."

"How?"

"Psychic powers . . . and the German imp can help me."

"What is this now, this Frieda Freitag? I didn't say you could go on with it. I will have to think about it." A little play of frown and smile tripped round her eyes. "So will you help me with the dresses?"

"Shall I tell you the story of Cominium? It was the Roman consul . . ."

She smothered his mouth with her hand.

"My dresses . . ."

He broke away, ". . . it was the Roman consul Carvilius Maximus . . ." She struggled to silence him again, but he held her hands off, ". . . the Roman army had wintered at a town called Interamna, by the Liri river, just over the hills there. Now it is spring, campaigning season, Carvilius brings his consular army up over the pass and bursts into the valley, destroying and burning as he comes . . ."

She struggles with him, trying to silence him. She gives up, and covers her ears.

". . . The city of Cominium is awaiting reinforcements, but it is cut off. The Romans surround it, the Samnite warriors are cut to pieces, the city destroyed. Carvilius takes so much booty that he erects a giant bronze statue to Jupiter on The Capitol Hill in Rome in thanksgiving for his victory."

He eased her hands from her ears. "You can come out now."

"My dresses, Roman consul, my dresses . . . And it is not true anyway, none of it . . . I won't let it happen . . . The Romans missed the bus, they were in the bar with Orazio and he got them all drunk. Orazio is the saviour of his people, he is the greatest

Samnite of all time, the city of Cominium still exists, and there is a bronze statue of him in the main square . . ."

"So he was a model even then," he chuckled delightedly at his own joke.

". . . a bronze statue," Frieda continued, "of a gladiator smoking a cheroot," she tickled his thin shaking ribs, "and all round here is an independent state where they still speak Oscan, and to celebrate Orazio's victory, every year a priest comes dressed as a woodpecker and flies around the statue." She folded her arms, determined and girlish: "I don't want them to be destroyed."

"Baroness," he said, coughing still with laughter, "you will be the death of me . . . Landlord, fill up the glasses of these stout legionaries, says the friendly gentleman with the deerstalker, smoking a cheroot . . . Yes sir. And what can I get the good consul? says the landlord . . . I'll take a chalice of your finest Vesuvian white, says the consul, taking off his helmet . . . And where are you heading with these brave lads consul?' says the man in the deerstalker . . . Into the next valley to deal with those thieving Samnites. What time's the next bus? . . . Plenty of time consul, not for another hour, says the stranger. Can I fill you up again? The Vesuvian is very good is it not? Same again all round Landlord . . .

". . . And this is the story of how Orazio the gladiator drank the legionaries under the counter . . . the Roman empire never existed, history stopped, hereabouts they still speak Oscan, Latin has vanished, in England they speak Celtic, the Vatican isn't there, Michelangelo had no ceilings to paint, the Renaissance never happened, there are no universities. Yes, I think I'll write that — the alternative history of Europe and the world — shouldn't take more than a couple of pages . . . Dear Reader, nothing happened."

They lay for a while, tangled in each other and in their new version of history.

"And what about us, did we happen?" she asked.

He pushed strands of damp fairish hair from her face.

"I will help you with the dresses, but we will have to wait till we can get the right threads."

She lay quietly in his arms making purring sounds.

"I have been doing some psychic investigating too," she said after a while. "I walked outside earlier and found just the perfect place under the snow."

"For my grave?"

She gave him a little slap.

"For your vegetables. Just think what we could grow here."

"We?" He laughed. "You've never dirtied those noble hands in your life. You don't know worms from spaghetti."

"I will learn . . . here in the Italian sun . . . not all those long English tuber things, long and grey and dull like the weather. Yuk," she grimaced, "Italian things . . . colourful, full of sun, tomatoes that taste red, greens that taste green, artichokes with those lovely purple flower heads. I love artichokes. It's worth it just for them."

"So, Red Stockings has decided. We are staying after all. That's good, then you can bury me in your vegetable patch and I will fertilise the earth and you can eat my essence."

"Ha . . . You . . . You would poison the soil, like quicklime or something . . . all your acidity . . ."

He struggled on top of her.

—·—

The day had almost gone. He sat quietly at his makeshift table. It reminded him of a card table. What hand would life deal him next?

Frieda lay on the bed, propped up on pillows reading in Italian, her lips moving silently. She had started learning the language back in Nottingham in that other life. Little did she know. Now she liked to think that it was a sign of things to come. But her Italian had become rusty after the years away, and there were a lot of words she didn't know. It was the novel Orazio had lent them about the mysterious young woman found unconscious by the roadside and taken in by the old writer and nursed back to health. They fall in love. Her name is Paola. But that is all she ever reveals about herself, and one morning he wakes to find her gone, swallowed up into the vast cosmic unknown, never to be seen again.

She put down the book and glanced across at the pensive man at his table. She started to sing softly to herself, a lovely German song . . . A stranger I came, a stranger I depart . . .

She got up from the bed, and wandered over to the window, peering out at the fading white emptiness. She breathed on the glass and started to write something, a message—if he read it before it faded, then he was meant to read it, if not, not.

Yesterday she had seen an eagle, just a speck high up in the sky. In the woods an owl hooted. She would like to see a wolf. She loved wolves. Orazio had told her a story about a wolf, that once, in his youth, he had been alone in the mountains. He was just lighting a candle in a little alcove cut into the rocks where the shepherds had put a statue of the Black Madonna, when he heard a growl behind him, and there not thirty feet away was a wolf baring its teeth at him. He was cornered. If he tried to run, the wolf would be on him. He said a prayer to the Madonna. Suddenly the wolf stopped growling and lay down, watching him. He summoned his courage and started to walk off. The wolf jumped to its feet and walked in front of him, turning its head to see if he was following—it was leading him somewhere. They came to a great old tree, a giant beech. This was the wolf's tree, it had its lair there. It started to dig with its paws, till just under the surface a large truffle appeared. It stopped digging and gave Orazio a look. It was a gift. Orazio took out the bread and meat he had brought with him and gave half to the wolf, and thus they sat, the two new friends, enjoying their dinner together.

Outside, the last glimmer of light was fading. She sang softly to herself, to the darkening whiteness landscape, to her heart: "Gute nacht . . ."

He put down his pen, closed his eyes and listened.

"Isn't that Schubert . . . the Winterreise?"

She carried on singing, her voice soft and deep. He turned to look at her. She sang another piece from the cycle . . . In the little house of a charcoal burner, I have found rest . . .

She stopped singing. There was a long silence.

"Lorenzo, I know it now. This is our Winterreise, our Winter's Journey . . ."

Chapter Seventeen

What would it be like, really, she asked herself, the early spring days, the melting snows, Lorenzo planting up his vegetables, hoeing his tidy little rows of salads, putting in sticks of beans and tomatoes, the artichoke experiment, and trying other things, cannellini beans perhaps, so popular here. He could learn how to yoke the giant white oxen, learn how to plough — slow, lumbering, timeless — the earth turning thick and black, his body turning strong and brown. And she, she would wander the woods, forage, gather acorns for the pig — they would have at least one — and in the evenings that lovely tiredness, the sweat of the day still not all washed off, twists of barley or hay in their hair, the song of a nightingale, the fragrance of orange blossom, a pale glowing early darkness.

Spring, translucent green groves of chestnut and oak, meadows of tall gold grass, yellow-tongued purple iris, liquorice-scented wild fennel — Orpheus's magic wand, Lorenzo had remembered from somewhere — the heavy-scented yellow broom rolling like clouds of summer mist over the hills and waysides, the white lilies of St. Anthony that bloom around his feast day in early June, and in the dark of woods, magenta cyclamen glowing sacramentally.

Lorenzo had asked, and Orazio had described it all as best he could, the writer's eyes glazing over like a lizard in sunlight, and Orazio had told them more, about the pencil-thin wild asparagus that grew in spiky bushes in the hedgerows — a favourite haunt of vipers — which they fried in omelettes.

"What, the vipers?" Lorenzo had chirped. It had taken a few seconds for Orazio to catch on.

There was a special mountain spinach too, called orapi, and of course herbs, like wild thyme, which the locals used to savour dishes of snails that they gathered in bucketfulls after a rainfall — ciamarruche in dialect — nothing at all like the Italian word for snails which was lumache.

They would learn about vines, plant a small vineyard, or buy an old one and graft new cuttings onto the rootstock. They would make their own wine, and it would be good wine, and they would design their own label for the bottles, all curls and florals and acanthus—she could just see it. Carpe Diem would be a good name. She would tell Lorenzo. He would surely like that.

If only he was better, right now, and they could see through this icy winter. In the spring sun he would be out among it all, on his knees, looking at the tiny new flowers — for this was his religion, his prayer, direct, no priest, no pallid morbid church sickness. And he would return with sheaves of flowers for her— long stemmed pink gladioli from the middle of the wheat fields, blue-gold iris. They would fill the house with them, everywhere, intoxicating.

Then they would have their pastimes and crafts, he his painting, and both of them the embroidery, and they would try new things, woodwork, sculpting perhaps, decorating wooden boxes—she had thought of carving trunks of trees into totem poles. Up at the village she had seen a woman sitting in her doorway with a large loom. There was a tradition of carpet-making in the valley, and each village had its own colours, here it was a combination of blue and yellow. Strange there were never any on the floors, they must sell them. And there were carpenters, skilled ones, cabinet makers, turners, sculptors, and other artisans. This, she was sure, was where their nobility lay. She would go and cut cane and reed, and they could make baskets, mats, containers, and perhaps a sort of fishing contraption, and they could try their luck in the fast running streams. There were plenty of trout in these waters, Orazio said, and even freshwater crabs.

They would get themselves their own little cart and donkey, and they would do something, they would carve and paint and decorate the cart with designs and motifs, give it its own soul, so that it came alive—and as they clipped jauntily along the highroad, all heads would turn. They would become known throughout the valley, and people would stop the foreigners and admire their artistry, and then other coloured wagons would start to appear, and a new tradition would be born, a new movement of craft people—colourful carters.

If only they had had something of their own hearth here, now, the delicious sense of isolation, the parsimony of winter. They wanted little Lorenzo and she, simplicity was its own abundance, two or three pieces of furniture, a handcrafted sideboard, simple, rustic. Somewhere they would find a piano, and the house would ring with English songs and German songs, and they would learn more Italian pieces to add to the Neapolitan songs they already knew. And they would sing long into the night, and Lorenzo would dance out through the door and into the woods, howl at the mountains, and the wolves would stop motionless in the snow, ears pricked.

They would put on little productions. He was so funny, such a brilliant mimic. He made her laugh like no-one else could. It would be like having guests without the trouble, and when guests did come, they would carouse the night away under great summer moons, all the world their own. And the visitors would marvel at this beautiful, awful, cruel, lyric of mountains and valleys, and they would stay, and before they knew it, their Rananim would be born—the dreamed of community, their communal dream.

And if Orazio raised his eyebrows they would have none of it. They had northern optimism. Orazio. Sometimes she caught him looking at her as if he would ask her something he couldn't quite formulate, like a ghost in Hades, a mute plea in his eyes—Orazio the crucified, Orazio the Dorian Gray figure, the brigand, the gladiator, the dandy, the model, the habitué of drawing rooms, of artists' studios, of Victorian London . . . And now..!

Upstairs on the landing there was a sort of empty space looking down over the stairs. Orazio had made it into another storage area for produce—as if there wasn't enough downstairs. Perhaps it was drier up here. Coming out of her bedroom one time she found him sitting there, working through a pile of corn, pulling off the sheaths. She watched for a minute, then sat herself on a sack in the midst of the jumble and joined in the ceremony. He shifted along, happy to have her company. She soon got in the rhythm, she liked the repetitiveness, a satisfying pile of stripped corn rising bright and golden in the gloomy corridor, glowing like a little sun. She leaned over and pretended to warm her hands against it, rubbing them together, then picked up a yellow corn and tossed it to Orazio, who caught it and threw it quickly away as if it burned his fingers.

Till this point they had sat in silence, but the shared playfulness set the old model off on his London anecdotes, Frieda secretly hoping for indiscretions, but he would always stop just at that point, never quite going as far as she would like, and she knew he knew things he wouldn't reveal. For all his acquired urbanity, deep down there was still a mountain innocence about him—the little peasant boy. When they finished, she took a basketful of corn and put it into her bedroom, golden and vibrant, and she was sure the room felt warmer for it.

In the afternoon, after the shared husking of the corn, he asked her if she would like to walk with him, and they went back to the little hostelry, the place owned by his sister and her husband. There was no particular reason for the visit, he just thought she would like to go somewhere. He could see her restlessness, and he hoped his americanised niece would be there so that the two young women could talk together. But she wasn't there, just the old parents.

At the sight of the fair foreign woman, the old couple jumped up in busy breathless welcome, running for plates and cups, telling Orazio off for not letting them know, only how he was supposed to have done that Frieda could not think. The inn was at the front of the house. The guests were ushered to a private room at the back — and suddenly they were in New York, a picture of Brooklyn Bridge on the wall, photos of Little Italy, a statuette of a Red Indian, cheap souvenir ceramics and the like on shelves and tables, gathered-in crimson drapes on the windows, even a carpet on the floor, much to Frieda's delight, and an electric candelabra dangling from the ceiling, though not connected to any power supply.

Martamaria, the sister, sputtered into her best Italian-American, a massacre of English vowels and local dialect, her gold earrings swaying with her bravura performance, but mostly incomprehensible to Frieda, while her husband, a little fat man in red braces, American style, smiled and nodded, and dropped in an occasional — "You bet" — just for good measure.

A table was quickly wiped, a cake made with rice and cheese presented on a dainty dish, a pot of tea, a bottle of white fizzy wine, Martamaria fussing and chattering, Orazio translating from Italo-Brooklynese into Edwardian English. Frieda responded by telling them a little about her and Lorenzo, and they nodded and grinned and cut more cake and poured more wine and understood little. But it didn't matter, it was the sound of it all, the appearance, even if there was no-one else there to see—a foreign guest, English as far as they could tell, and a lady. They were pleased with themselves, pleased that they knew how to be sociable, had manners, and in a foreign language too.

Cake finished, teapot empty, glasses of wine sipped and left, the conversation came to an awkward stop. Frieda stood up. She would go for a walk into the village, leaving Orazio to talk about beans and greens and wine and donkeys. She had mail to post for Lorenzo.

She walked down the road past a straggle of old stone cottages with blotchy green stained walls. Orazio told her later that it was from the copper-sulphate they used to spray the vines, but as she walked along the road it made her feel slightly sickly, and the shadowy mountain hills made everything cold and gloomy.

It wasn't much of a place this Villa Latina. It had had a different name till recently, till they had found Roman remains there and changed it. But in the old centre there was an unusually grand little baroque church with bell towers either side, quite unexpected.

She went inside. Over the high altar a blood-soaked Christ hung from the Cross, eyes rolling, the panoply of Catholic death all round, saints in satins and lace and cheap gemstones, doll-like, dead, dusty and airless inside their glass cases—but then they didn't need air in heaven, or in glass cases. High on their plinths they stood, in rigid forbearance of the old ladies kneeling beneath in their patched weeds and black shawls, muttering their toothless prayers, telling their worn-out rosary beads, sighing, supplicating, beseeching—Have pity.

But there wasn't much pity, just death. It hung there. It could come at any moment, come and steal them away in the night, just as it had taken the young men, taken their beauty, taken their bodies, now warm, now cold, now red, now white, ecstatic, visceral, horrible, sacrificial, feared and desired, loved and hated—dead saints in their airless glass cases.

Frieda leaned against a column, hands clammy and cold, face pale. She ran out.

Back at the inn there was a final flourish of American flummery, and then they started to walk back. She was still pale from the church but pretended it was just the cold down here. She tried to make conversation, saying how friendly the old couple had been, but it just set Orazio off on one of his censures — don't be misled, people were nice to her because she was a foreigner. They liked to put on a show, but if she stayed she would see how they really were. She protested—surely he couldn't include his own sister. But he only shrugged. She tried to bring him round — all small country places have an element of shunning outsiders, in Germany it is the same, in England too, but Orazio insisted that here it was different.

It was no good. She put a hand on his shoulder in silent conso-
lation, but felt him withdraw. She dropped her hand. Why couldn't
he find a woman here, or at least someone to come and clean for
him, just to have the scent of female softness around him, someone
like the young mother who cleaned for the priest, someone
presentable, not a Maria, not a drinker, someone young, yes young,
even if he was getting old? She gave a sideways glance at his
stubbly old cheeks. Why hadn't he married in England? He must
have had plenty of chances. An English woman would have come
here readily, she was sure, despite the hardships. It would appeal
to the romantic northern soul.

At the torrent, Orazio stepped on ahead. Halfway across he
turned to make sure she was still behind him, and as he turned
back she thought she saw something close round him, a sort of
mist, and the waters rushed up at her, whispering and hissing—
this is our world, you will never know it.

Chapter Eighteen

SOMETHING HAD HAPPENED TO GIOVANNI. SINCE THE telling of the saga of the woodpecker, he couldn't come near to the Englishman without staring at him, until Orazio had to bark something at him in dialect. He wanted to tell them, but he didn't have any words. His brother had caught the gist of it, but refused to listen further. So the little man hung around the house, redoubled his domestic efforts, cleaned, cooked, swept, followed his brother around, anticipated his every thought, dusted and cleaned after him, until Orazio had exploded, telling him to get out of the way, that he was like the shadow of death. But the little man persisted, and when he couldn't find anything more with which to busy himself, he would go and sit in the far room with the wine press, in the cold, as if he didn't even want to use up any of the precious kitchen warmth. In the end it had worked. Orazio capitulated. But he wasn't happy.

"My brother, he has got one of his mad ideas in his head. I advise you to ignore him, but he wants to take you to a special place he knows . . . a place of echoes." Orazio raised his eyebrows with hardly-contained exasperation. "La tomba del re, that is what he calls it, the tomb of the king. Who knows what he has found up there. I have never been, he would never invite me . . . and he says the woman you described with the long grey hair who turns into a bear, she really exists . . . Santa Madonna..!" He raised his eyes to heaven and threw his hands in the air, calling on his poor long-suffering mother and various saints to give him strength. "I don't know, you must decide if you shall go."

They decided. Orazio grumbled on like an old volcano, but the little man had taken them to his heart. They had entered a world he thought only he could see. Orazio would not allow that his brother had any understanding very much of anything, and that his accounts of kings and witches were just childish blather. The little mule-man lowered his head in submission, but across the way in his draughty little loft, he knew differently. He knew old things.

Orazio worried. He could see that the mind and will and curiosity of his guest were stronger than the fragile vessel that carried them, but he could see also how restive they both were in the snowbound house. He knew how they loved to be out walking — they would often talk about their long hikes, in England, in Bavaria, at Garda, but Lorenzo had been fitter then. Now he was still recovering from his chest problems earlier in the year. Orazio didn't want to go down in history as the man who had lost the famous writer—what would the London of his old friends and deeds have to say about that? He had muttered this to them, part jest, part serious, to which Lorenzo had replied that he would probably be knighted for services to the empire. But they were determined to go, and Orazio comforted himself with the thought that the energetic Frieda, who bounded and danced and frolicked around half naked, seemingly immune to ice and snow, that she would be strong enough for the both of them. As for Giovanni, the little man knew that this was the moment of his life.

The Englishman of words looked at the dark little man, and he saw shapes and thoughts struggling to express themselves, and the dark little man without words looked at the coalminer's son and saw whole worlds—elemental them both.

———

163

The sky was heavy, but it didn't snow. Orazio had been worried they would be caught in a blizzard and lose their way, get stranded. They wrapped themselves up, Lorenzo and Frieda in more of the country hats and scarves from Orazio's hoard, Giovanni in his sheepskins and cape, and off they set, three dark figures in a line treading across the white bleak landscape — an illustration from a children's adventure story, Frieda thought — occasional icy gusts making them lower their heads and hold onto their hats.

The little man walked ahead, hardly daring to look back in case they weren't there any more, then daring to look, and they were still there. He trudged on, finding the best path where the snow was harder and less deep, up through the woods the way they had set off on the Sunday to go to the village. But now they had been going some time and they hadn't come to the road, so at some point they must have struck off away from the village track.

They were traversing diagonally upwards, and the great cragged peak they could see from the valley was no longer visible. They were in the lee of the mountains. There might have been concern for Lorenzo, but he, for himself, had none, and was coping well, and once they got into a rhythm his breathing was easy. The little man stopped often, his brother had made him promise, and he was doing his best to remember and not let the excitement get the better of him.

Orazio had prepared for them a bag with food and drink, half a loaf of the good rough polenta bread, slices of his own prosciutto from last year's pig, cut thick the way they did here, a bit salt, and a bit chewy, a chunk of hard matured ricotta cheese, a couple of his large winter pears, a flask of his lip-staining red wine, and a good knife.

High on a jagged outcrop where teeth-like rocks jutted out over the abyss of valley below, they stopped. This was old country, secretive, watchful. The couple leaned against the pointed rocks and gazed down into the misty white valley, thick wooded mountains rising either side, not like the great open sweep of valley they knew. Lorenzo asked in slow Italian which way the village lay from here — he had wondered how they would communicate with the little man — they had never really heard him say anything, now they came to think of it. He threw back his cloak, stuck an arm up, pointed to the top of an adjacent peak, and made a gesture—up over the top and down the other side.

Frieda unwrapped the food. Giovanni had brought his own, a thick jellified pudding of some sort wrapped in a cloth, not unlike the mixture the pig got, in fact Frieda was convinced it was the same. Lorenzo cut thick slices of the crusty bread and chunks of the hard cheese, and they softened the mouthfuls with swigs of wine, sending an acidy warm shock into their systems, and they felt a surge of brigand energy course through them, dark and purple. Lorenzo, inspired, took the flask and dribbled a few drops of the wine into the virgin snow, writing their initials, an L and F overlapping. Frieda offered the flask of wine to their guide to help him wash down his pig's pap, but he shook his head shyly, reddening slightly, as if they had proposed something he would have to confess to the priest.

They took a last swig, poured a final libation into the snow, and packed the remains of food away. Giovanni waited, then pulled his conical hat firmly down onto his head, stepped away from the rocks and set off through the snow-thick woods of pine and beech, glittering sprays of crystal ice floating down on them. Here and there, large branches lay sheered by the weight of snow or gashed from a trunk and still half hanging, mountain mists drifted, white-black contours of wood and valley opened and closed around and below them. They climbed on, the little hunched man no longer turning to look back, until the woods started to thin out, and they emerged onto a sort of summit place strewn with boulders and low scrubby wind-bent trees like thin knuckled hands. From here, the valley was visible a good distance in both directions. A line of cut boulders, now much dislodged and toppled by earthquake and time, stood sheer to the edge of the little plateau. Lorenzo had seen an illustration of Samnite forts, the carved polygonal rocks, as opposed to the baked bricks of the Romans. It said a lot about the difference between the two cultures.

Giovanni clambered along and over the boulders with the surefootedness of a mountain goat, hanging from improvised grips, feeling along the cut blocks of stone, jumping from one to the other, brushing snow away to check the joints, below him a sheer drop. Lorenzo leaned against a sort of parapet peering down. A loose rock detached itself from near his foot, and he watched as it bounced and rolled down the steep slope, gathering speed, cracking against boulders, flying through the air until it disappeared into the drifting silent whiteness.

The little man had finished his inspection and was standing a few feet behind them. He looked up into the sky, shading his eyes, and pointed to a small black speck high above. They followed his arm, peering upwards at the circling raptor, a golden eagle. When they looked down again Giovanni was already walking away.

They trailed silently behind him, across the high plateau, through the bare skeletal shrubs and trees, the ground rising and dipping, until, after a few minutes, a rock face loomed out of the mist, craggy and gothic.

He stopped, his eyes flickering, half-closed. He walked on again, skirting round the base of the great cathedral rock. Where a tangle of vine and roots hung down, he stopped again. Behind the branches was a narrow hidden opening just wide enough for a man to push through, and without waiting, he started to ease himself in. Frieda, bundled up as she was, and with more of a natural girth than the others, looked at the narrow passageway with dismay. Lorenzo went in next, scraping himself along, she would go last so she could back herself out if she got stuck. She pulled her clothes tight around her, took a deep breath, and followed in and along, so tight in places she was tempted to call out, but after about half a minute she could see the other end, and she was through and into a great round arena of sheer rock open to the sky. It was like a little extinct caldera, about thirty or forty yards across. At its centre, as if it had heaved itself up through the ground, stood a great square boulder about five feet high, twined around with the roots of a gnarled old tree.

The little man stood with his back pressed against the cliff face, mouthing something to himself. The new initiates waited. Giovanni made no sign. They walked across to the altar-like boulder, amazed a little at how it sat there so central and square. Frieda leaned her hands on it and closed her eyes, Lorenzo circled round it, when suddenly, from behind them, the mute little mule-man who never said a word, took voice, sprang from the wall, leaped through the air, landed and leaped, leaped and landed, calling out as he flew, a language all his own, exclamations, cries, an alter voice, the voice of his soul, the walls of the caldera echoing to his words in a rhyme-like response. He came to a stop, fell to his knees, his face a sort of ecstasy.

Frieda needed no invitation. She moved away from the altar and started to circle round the arena, slowly at first, giving out little shouts of her own, then speeding up, skipping and dancing. The little mule-king jumped back up and set off again, twirling and leaping like a Cossack, cape flying, shouting his breathless liturgy, the walls echoing.

Lorenzo climbed up onto the rock, watching the two flying dervishes, till they came to a stop. He took a deep breath and called out: "My name is Lorenzo," and the walls replied . . . Lorenzo . . . Lorenzo. "Tell us your name," . . . your name . . . your name.

And now Frieda joined in: "Ich bin Frieda," and the echo came back . . . Frieda . . . Frieda, and they repeated their calls, till the names and the words kissed and crossed and collided . . . my . . . tell . . . ich . . . Frieda . . . bin . . . renzo . . . your . . . tell . . . bin . . . name, and it was no longer possible to tell which was echo and which not, and they became dizzy with it all, and the little man sat on the floor with his eyes closed.

Chapter Nineteen

"Why where have you been . . . so concerned was I . . ."

Orazio swayed slightly, kitchen implements grasped ominously in both hands. A thick bed of embers glowed in the hearth, and a disorder of pots and ingredients were spread across the table.

"It is night already. My brother, he has no sense . . . no sense. He has kept you out in this, and you with your chest." He glared ferociously round the room. "Giovanni, Giovanni," he shouted, but Giovanni had slipped away. "Come Signora Frieda, come Sir Lorenzo, warm thyselves."

He gestured towards the fire. It was obvious that a glass or two of something had slipped down, and his already modulated English had become even more Arts and Crafts, a distant echo of some Bohemian London soirée no doubt.

The explorers didn't need encouragement. They took off their coats, hung them on the chairs, and huddled against the fire, silently steaming, rubbing their hands.

Orazio shook his head.

"And pray, did you meet the fabled king?" He made a dismissive gesture with the kitchen knife. "Of course you did not. The mule has more sense . . . but see, I have prepared good pasta to warm you . . . and meat . . . and I have some wine. Agnese has brought it for you. Now where did I put it?" He looked around.

"Agnese?" Frieda asked, but she had already guessed, "the

mother of the two children? Oh I wish I had been here. You see Orazio . . ."

But Orazio didn't see, nor even hear, he had returned to his wine-fuddled preparations, screwing his bleary eyes, trying to remind himself what to do next. He bent unsteadily to the fire, poking the logs, sending out sparks and little flames, then straightened himself up, swaying slightly, balancing himself against the mantelpiece. A black pot hung in the hearth over the embers. He picked up a long wooden spoon and dipped it into the red sauce, gave it a stir, scooped a little out, blew on it, sipped it, and made an approving nod.

Lorenzo stared into the fire for a while, then turned round. "I declare that this is a place of magicians . . ."

Orazio squinted at him.

". . . and your brother has something of it."

Orazio's usually quiet old eyes suddenly flared.

"I will cut his throat." He brandished the red-stained wooden spoon. "Where is he this magic mule? Make him appear so I can kill him." He held the wooden spoon between his two hands as if he would snap it in two. "You are too nice with him . . . Nice English people. Who else would listen to his nonsense? Bah!" Then his tone suddenly softened, his voice quavering slightly: "I will miss you." He shook his head, gave a long sigh, cleared his throat and straightened his shoulders. "Now I must see to my cooking or we will never eat."

"Let me help," Frieda said. She looked around at the preparations, but couldn't see quite where to enter the fray.

Orazio reached slowly under a chair and brought up a large flask of wine that had already been well sampled, and placed it on the table. "Did I tell you that I had a visitor?" he slurred, then realised he had already told them.

Frieda tapped the top of the bottle. "If only we could do something for her. Let's drink some of her wine at least . . . wish her luck."

"I wish I knew some words in Oscan." Lorenzo was still

following through on his magic wizards theme. "I thought we heard some today up there, didn't we Frieda? It was either that or the distant echo of colliers on their way back from the pub. They like a bit of an echo." He chuckled, but he was talking to himself.

"I would so love to meet her," Frieda said, nodding wistfully.

The old cook looked from one to the other, struggling to follow it all. It was like a duet at the opera, but not on the same page. He picked up the bottle and looked at it suspiciously. "Why, it is open already," he said. "I have not drunk it . . . well just a little."

He wiped some glasses with his greasy cloth, held them up to a lamp to peer into them, then poured out some wine a little shakily.

"Drink Signor Lorenzo," he said, handing them the glasses, "and then you will surely speak Oscan."

He gave the cauldron another good stir, then turned and waved the wooden spoon around, muttering something to himself, little spots of red sauce dripping on the floor.

"Oh yes, and Agnese . . . she asks about England, about going there . . . and she talks too of Canada . . ."

"Tell her not England, not England. England is a place of bones." Lorenzo flushed, his blitheness of just a few moments before, suddenly evaporated. He was quiet for a minute, biting his lip. Frieda watched. She gave him a little shake of the head and narrowed her eyes—not now, leave it.

He sat down and leaned his elbows on his knees, staring forward. He drank some more wine . . . "But I fear it won't have my bones. No, I don't fear it, I rejoice in it. I want my bones bleached by the sun not buried in mud or blackened by their infernal coal. I would have my bones dried by the desert sun, hollowed out. Frieda, Frieda," he turned to her, his blue fierce eyes searching into her soft grey-green ones, "I tell you this now, before a witness. Bleach my bones. When I am gone, I want my bones to burn in the sun, I want them to whistle like flutes in the wind, smoothed by the sand, till they too become sand . . .

wind and sand and sun." He stared at her. "Don't let them take me back . . . If I am dying, don't let them touch me again with their vile hands."

He turned to Orazio. "Tell the young woman Orazio, tell Agnese, only people of blood can be free. England is not free, it is a corpse, white and bloodless. My ink is my blood, they want to drain me of it so that I become a corpse like them." He coughed, coughing up bits of England, but he would never cough it all up.

Frieda stared — wind and sun and sand — the burning bible of his mind, cursed and blessed, a force that would not be denied. She could not stop him. He was unstoppable. This she knew.

Orazio looked down at his hands, bloody with sauce, and started muttering again about murdering his brother. It was all his fault.

Lorenzo's chest gave a final shudder. "The sun . . . life. You cannot swindle life . . . like sex, you cannot swindle that either. That is why they fear it."

Orazio searched for words, but all he could think of was how much he missed that England which his English guest so much condemned, that England he had loved and left, given up for this barren hilltop of snow and rock.

There was a long silence. The logs in the fire caught suddenly and blazed up, fuelled by all the thoughts, all the regrets, frustrations, anger, injustice, loss.

Orazio cleared a space on the kitchen table and set down his sundry assortment of new and old chipped plates and the plain steel cutlery, hating what he saw, refusing Frieda's help. He served the short thick pasta, fished out the dripping shin of beef, and plonked it onto a wooden bread board in the middle of the table. They pulled up their chairs and sat down. A monastic silence descended. Orazio flushed deep from fire and flask, caught sight of his face in the glass of the bottle, and grimaced. He leaned forward to fill the wine glasses of his guests, unsteadily, till Frieda had to guide the neck of the bottle into them.

"I am a foolish man." He set the bottle down. "I curse my poor brother, but he is wiser than I. It is only fools who do not know that they are fools. That is why I curse him, because he is wiser than I." He held up his glass and stared into it. "Forgive me my poor house and my poor self and my poor hospitality."

They sat over their plates, eyes down, sipping the wine, the fire too had subsided into a pensive glow.

At last Lorenzo spoke, his voice calm again. "There is a parable in the Gospel . . . Mark I think . . . a poor woman gives her last coin to the temple, but in the sight of God it was worth infinitely more than the gift of the rich man." He downed his glass. "It is rather I who should apologise for being a poor guest Orazio. I wonder if there is a parable about the poor guest."

Orazio waved his hand dismissively, waved away the nice words. "Here we are cut off from the world, and so it should be. This is what we deserve. This is the Gospel of Orazio."

"And to that I would say . . . Amen, and let the world be cut off."

Orazio looked at the man who was talking to him. What was he saying? He held up his glass again and peered into it as if the answer lay inside, then looked around again. Who were these people? What they were doing sitting in his kitchen — a woman with fair hair that the light from the fire made shimmer, her eyes slanting like a tartar, now greyish now green now speckled with gold, and this man with the red beard who quoted the Gospel? Who were they? What were they? A visitation! It was all a blur. He shook his head. And who was he? Ah, that was the question, that was the one he had to find the answer to . . . and suddenly a strange smile crept over his saggy face.

"I am Pappus the old fool, I am Bucco the braggart, I am Maccus the glutton, and in time will I also become Dossenus the hunchback." He drawled out the names and patted an imaginary hunch on his back.

"What is this?" The red-bearded visitation was asking him something.

"What is what?"

". . . These characters, Pappus . . . Maccus . . ."

He peered blearily across at the questioner. "They are me, I am they . . ." Suddenly everything was becoming clear.

"I am a clown, and so if I am a clown then you must be a god." He smiled, pleased with his bibulous logic, and to put the stamp of approval on it, he poured himself another glass of wine and drank it down.

"Out of the darkness . . . light!" Lorenzo leaned forward, resting his elbows on the table. "But I think I would be more comfortable as a clown."

The old model thought for a while, then he sat himself up straight. The glass of wine had had the miraculous effect of briefly clearing his mind.

"Clowns are our true gods."

Frieda sat quietly, twirling little strands of her hair, still thinking of the woman Agnese. Lorenzo watched her for a minute. He wanted her to join in, but left to her thoughts.

"So tell me about these clown gods," he said.

"But Signor Lorenzo, you who see all things, surely you must see also them. They are all around you . . . foolish characters making foolish talk, and I am the chief fool."

"Orazio, if you are a fool, then you are a holy fool." Lorenzo leaned back in his chair, his hands behind his head. "But who are these characters, this Pappus and Maccus? They sound like some old tradition from medieval times or the Commedia dell'Arte . . . Arlecchino, Pantalone and all the rest of them. Am I right?"

"Medieval times!" Orazio poured himself another glass of wine. "Here it is still medieval times."

"Good, then I am in the right place."

"I have a book . . ."

"Another book!" Lorenzo threw his hands in the air, an amused expression on his face. "It's like the British Library reading room here."

But Orazio's moment of clarity was fading fast, and he started to sag, his eyes closing . . . "Pappus the old fool," he muttered to himself, his head dropping. He jolted back up for a second, opened his eyes wide, looked around, then sagged again, his old head sinking slowly down till it came to rest on the table.

The two candles guttered and spluttered and snuffed themselves out, the embers in the hearth threw long orange shadows over the walls. They sat for a while in the dark silence. A log cracked. The sleeping man muttered to himself, half raised his head, opened unseeing eyes, then subsided again.

"I feel so far from the world, like in some mythological land . . . the Ring of the Nibelung. Do you not feel it?" She shuddered a little.

Lorenzo said nothing, just sat.

"Speak. Say something." She rubbed her arms.

"We have brought a spirit back with us . . . from up there."

"Don't."

"He is here, he is curious, he is watching . . ."

"Don't. Are you serious? Don't . . . Is it a he?"

She felt cold suddenly, and rubbed her arms faster. "You know I always believe you. If it's just play then you can stop now."

"Or maybe it is the soul of one of those children who left here, never to return, at least not in physical form."

"That is not nice Lorenzo, not nice. I don't like this game."

"You know the Romans feared the magic here . . . these people of the mountains and their spirits. They thought they were wizards."

"What should we do?" she whispered, her voice almost child-like.

At that moment a dark shape filled the doorway. Frieda jumped up, knocking her chair over with a clatter. The dark shape stopped abruptly, the shadow of its conical hat stretching up the wall. He must have been there for some time, out in the stone cold of the corridor, waiting, knowing his brother would drink himself to sleep. But the keeper of hidden places who talked to echoes, existed only up there, down here he was the little mute man once more.

He took off his hat and played it through his fingers. Lorenzo asked him if he was hungry, if he wanted something to eat. He shook his head. He looked cautiously at his brother's slumped shape, then dug in his pocket, took something out, and held it in his palm for a minute. He put it on the table between them . . . a ring, gold, old, with a semi-precious stone.

Frieda's eyes opened wide. She glanced over at Lorenzo. "Oh my God . . . but I was just saying . . ."

The little man stood back and waited, wordless. Lorenzo picked it up. Frieda recovered herself and peered at the ring with him. He held it up to the firelight, and they could see an intaglio cut into the stone, a female figure, perhaps a deity.

The little man hovered, put his hat back on, and glanced at his prone brother. But Lorenzo had come to understand his mute language. He handed back the ring and stood up. The ring bearer turned and walked out through door. They followed. Outside, the ice-white night glittered cold and hard. They followed him across to the jumble of stone buildings. In the dark they could just hear the crump of heavy hooves and the low blowing of bovine breath as they climbed the stone steps on the side of the stable wall.

Giovanni pushed open the wooden door of his dwelling. A dim silver light filtered from a low window into the single room. He lit a candle on the stone ledge, knelt down at a corner fireplace, pushed some twigs in, and blew on the grey-red embers till they crackled into life. Against a wall there was a pile of skins and blankets that seemed to be the bed, not much furniture, a small table and one chair, an old stone basin, iron cooking pots by the fire, more skins spread on the stone floor.

Behind the door an old musket was propped against the wall. Giovanni saw the Englishman looking at it. He picked it up and held it to his shoulder, nodding his head—yes it worked. He pulled a block of wood out of a hole in the wall by the door, poked the musket through and pretended to take aim behind it. It went through at an angle so you could point it back down the stairs at anyone trying to come up—protection against the brigands that Orazio was always telling them about. But they too had mostly put aside their cut-throat ways and joined the great exodus, even they had starved enough, the last one, Orazio recounted, known as Fuoco, Fire, had been cornered and killed by the Carabinieri not ten years before, and they had brought his body back to the village and put it on display. But Giovanni kept his musket ready.

He put the firearm back down and stood for a moment or two uncertainly. The visitors waited, exchanging looks. The little man gathered his courage, picked up the candle, reached for a thick curtain that hung against the wall, and pulled it aside. Behind was an entrance into another smaller room with low slanting beams, empty but for a wooden chest. They followed him in, ducking their heads.

Giovanni stood holding the candle, momentarily lost again, then he nodded to himself, placed the candle in a little niche, pulled the chest away from the wall, knelt down, took a knife from his clothing and pushed the blade into the stonework. A brick eased out. There was a cavity behind. He reached inside, pulled out a rolled up bundle of heavy cloth tied with a leather thong, and laid it reverently on the chest. He undid the thong and unrolled it—copper and gold and bronze and amber glowed in the candle-light. He picked up a spiral copper coil, an armlet, and held it up to his arm, then he picked up some of the other pieces, a necklace of fine wound copper, a gold broach with a carnelian stone, a fibula in the shape of a bloodsucker. He reached into the cavity, brought out another cloth parcel, and rolled it out—the fragile remains of a copper belt, very wide, with a serpent buckle, a small terracotta figurine of Hercules, and the rusted remains of a long iron sword. He let them look for a minute, then he started to lay the treasures out on the long chest in a certain precise order. He lifted the candle up near the wall, and there, cut and drawn into a patch of grey plaster, was a copy of each piece, but with the outline of a skeleton running through them, just as he had uncovered it. He had drawn it all, like any good archeologist would have done.

Here was his king. He stood back and let them look and touch and compare. Where the skeleton was they did not ask, probably rotted, just an outline in the earth. But as if reading their thoughts, he pointed to the skeleton hand in the picture, it was holding a small stone, obviously of significance, more than all the silver and gold. He picked the stone up from the chest and held it to the picture, then he held it out for Lorenzo to take. It was oval, almost perfect, maybe a moonstone, and it had a natural pattern in it like an eye. The Englishman held it in his palm, closed his hand, closed his eyes, and waited—it seemed to want this of him. He blinked his eyes back open. Frieda was watching him intently. He handed the stone back, but the little tomb-keeper shook his head . . . it was a gift . . . for the priest of storytelling who had the power to see.

Chapter Twenty

CANDLES BURN ON A SIDE TABLE. ON THE HARD COLD
bedroom floor a jumble of painting materials. The artist is
kneeling, looking closely at his work, at little details, rubbing it
with an oily cloth here and there. On the bed, a woman is watching
him. She is his model and lover. She is pale and thin like him,
her skin smooth and cold. They have been ill. If things go on like
this, he jokes, they will both end up like the marble effigies in
the cathedral, side by side for eternity. But it will be an eternity
of pleasure, for the thinner they get, the more intense the lovemaking, and if they starved to death they would die in ecstasy.

He concentrates on a detail of the picture. The candles flicker
slightly. They are the last ones. He must finish the picture before
they burn down. He doesn't even have any more canvasses. He
must make a sale soon. He can't borrow any more money.

The woman on the bed picks up a mirror and looks into it.
Her eyes are sunken, but she knows customers who like this. She
selects a stick of liner from a box on the floor and starts to pencil
her eyes. The artist looks over — it is just work, a means of getting
some francs and some food and some materials. It was how they
met after all. He was poor then too, but she didn't mind, she liked
him, gave her services free, and in return he gave her more than
money, he gave her pleasure—something she thought she would
never feel again. The rest had followed. There had been a golden

period, his pictures had sold, they had money, she didn't need to go out onto the streets. But then his condition had come back again—his chest. For months she nursed him, but their money, the little they had put by, soon went. He was better now, but still weak.

She looked at her face in the mirror. They will be surprised to see her at the Folies. Maybe rich old Max will be there. If only she could eat something first.

The artist sat back on his heels and cast her a look.

"Your eyes are green, very very green. What is going on in there?"

"It is the Absinthe."

"It is the absence of it more like." He gave her a faint smile. He could read her little fantasy.

The fire in the hearth was low. His mural was coming along. She wondered what Orazio would think of it. She liked watching him paint, there was something almost meditative in his concentration, the way he held his breath, the slow brush strokes. He had put some blankets on the floor to kneel on.

"Mmm . . . oil paints . . . spirits . . . I love the smell." She took a deep breath in through her nose. "What is that little statue in the niche in the rocks?" She rolled over on the bed, peering more closely. "It looks like a little deity, like the intaglio on Giovanni's ring. But I like the picture. It is making me feel warmer just looking at it . . . the naked figures, the desert." She was going to ask if this was the place where bones were burned by the sun and hollowed by the sand, like flutes, but didn't.

"What place is it?" she asked.

He went on painting, silently.

"Bit Adam and Eveish though don't you think," she said, a little playful mockery in her voice, "and no fig leaves. Why is it always fig leaves that cover private parts, why not some other variety of leaf?"

"Privet," he muttered, "privet to cover the privates."

She gave a little squeal. He sat back, the better to view his work, then leaned forward and rubbed over something he didn't like with a cloth. She went on watching, the way a cat watches, eyes half closed, unfocussed, unreadable. Sometimes he was sure he could hear her purring from deep down in her belly. She pounced up suddenly and jumped to the edge of the bed, peering more closely at the picture.

"The male figure, it is you nay? But the woman kneeling in front of him, I don't think it is me." She screwed up her eyes. "Is it me or is it not? I feel it is not."

"It means nothing . . . just a picture to pass the time . . . She is universal woman."

"Of course it means something . . . and anyway there is no such thing as universal woman." She flopped back down on the bed, lying on her stomach, her bare legs kicking up behind. "Everything means something. She has an identity. There he lies, like the first man, like Michelangelo's Adam receiving the gift of life . . ."

"I think he has gone beyond that stage."

"Yes obviously, it is just his pose I mean, lying back like that . . . but . . . but . . . Can I make a suggestion? There should be a reptile on the ground nearby, not a snake, that would be too obvious, but a reptile, cold blooded, warming itself in the desert sun . . . the power of procreation, the power of the earth, sun and earth, a lizard, a beautiful lizard, all green-blue-yellow."

He looked pensively at his mural, wiping the end of a brush.

"How did you manage to live so long up there in Nottingham?" He held the brush up in front of his eye to measure a distance.

"I don't know. How does anything happen? Now I look back it is like a dream, repetitive, never ending, until one day a lizard-man slithered into the house, a strange little creature, a sun worshipper who had lost his way, he just appeared out of the blue . . ."

"Out of the green-yellow-blue . . ."

". . . a lovely lizard-man. It was impregnation at first sight." She liked her clever remark, thought he would take it up, but he said nothing, just dabbed at the mural with his brush. "Put a lizard in the picture . . . for me. Please put a lizard in, then I will feel that the woman could be me . . . Ich und Du."

"The Temptation of Frieda . . ." He went on daubing for a while. "Lizard . . . Lucertola in Italian." He repeated the word slowly, "Lu-cer-to-la . . . from the word luce, light . . . the light worshipper, the light being, the giver of light . . . like Lucifer, poor devil."

"Like you."

He coughed. "Cold floors are not good for lizards." He coughed again. A candle sputtered and went out. "See how easily the light is extinguished!"

"Don't speak like that," she said in a harsh whisper. "You have primal energy enough my painter man. What did Norman Douglas say about you? He said you have something of the elemental."

"And that is what I'm trying to avoid. I want to have something of the corporeal, not the elemental." He went on painting. "The Romans liked the lizard . . . thought of it as a friend, the symbol of divine wisdom and good fortune . . . the lizard that sleeps through winter. The Christians of course were more ambivalent . . . a distant cousin to the serpent, yet even for them it was a symbol of contemplation, a seeker of enlightenment, bathing itself in the rays of the sun, in the holy light of God."

She swung a leg off the bed and pressed it into his back, massaging with her heel up and down his spine. "This lizard is also a seeker, here she comes up your back, down your arm, onto your hand, onto your brush . . . and now she jumps . . . woooh . . . right across into the picture."

"Lizards don't jump, they scuttle."

"This one does, it has special powers . . . Please, a lizard," her voice was girlish and coaxing, "just for me. Paint a lizard all curved round on itself, then it would be male and female at the same time, lingam and yoni, androgynous."

He put his hands on his hips and made a face.

"Aya gorra piggle wi' ma picture missis?" he said in his Nottingham dialect. He liked to give her a dose sometimes, he knew it disturbed her, not the words so much as what it reminded her of. But she wasn't taking the bait this time. She placed her foot on his back again, massaging up and down with the ball and the heel.

"Try . . . Just for me. Piggle it just for me."

He mixed some blue and yellow paint on his palette and dabbed experimentally in a corner at the bottom of the picture, working it up for a few minutes, till a strange little creature with a curious expression started to appear, a beady blue eye fixing itself on the naked figures.

"Comme-ça?"

She watched him. He reminded her of a faun sometimes. He liked to paint bacchanals, and there he would be in the middle of them, naked and cavorting. Now, kneeling on the floor, he looked like one—curious, shy, startled.

"I want to stroke you."

He recognized that voice. He went on painting, holding himself silently against her, he knew it made her skittish when she thought he wasn't responding to her.

"Would you like to go east? Perhaps we should go east instead of west . . . forget about America." He sat back to admire his work. Suddenly she was on top of him. He dropped his brush and grabbed at the circling limbs. He had been half expecting it. They rolled around, all arms and legs and blankets, now one on top, now the other. Just then the sound of Orazio's voice carried from the foot of the stairs.

"You see, he can hear us." He disentangled himself, got up and went to the door. He opened it and shouted back down.

"Yes Orazio? What did you say?"

"I said the dinner will be ready soon. I await you."

He closed the door and shuffled back into the bedroom, mimicking the old model's slightly slouched ambling gait, running his fingers through imaginary long heavy locks and puffing at a cheroot.

"Soon the dinner will be ready," he drawled in the oddly refined diction of their host. "Would you take a glass of sherry first, Baroness?"

Frieda lay on the floor. "But you like him don't you?"

He tried to climb back down onto her but she rolled away, taking the blankets with her. He sat down by her side, his hands round his knees, then jumped back up and sat on the bed.

"But you do like him don't you?" she repeated.

"You know I do, and I think he is enjoying his role, part country squire, part majordomo, it makes him feel he is back in England. He should have a dinner gong at the foot of the stairs."

"Why did he come back, really? Never mind mountain spirits."

"Why never mind? You know what I think, people are shaped by their landscape, not pretty pictures, something much deeper. In a place like this it is very strong. It calls. Some respond, and for all his new-found sophistication, Orazio responded."

She got up off the floor and sat down next to him on the bed. "And where then is our landscape?

She hung her head a little. He watched her profile, the momentary uncertainty, struggle, descent, resurrection— that optimism that was the fountainhead at which they both drank. He turned her face to him. "Poor Frieda, what a hand the gambler dealt her . . . left her native Germany to become an English hausfrau. But there were more cards on the table. She drew one . . . Oh God! Another option, another choice . . . keep it or discard it. She kept it. She discarded the old one, and now she is no longer the English hausfrau. She has left England . . ."

"Has she . . . Has she really left England?"

He didn't answer.

"Now she is a hausfrau without a house, a houseless frau." She smiled and rubbed his back, rubbing in the caustic ointment of their existence. "And what are you?"

"Nothing. But two nothings make a something. Together we are something, more than something, we are complete and undivided, like your yogic lizard, and our land is no land, and exile is our home."

"I like being an exile."

"Rub some more."

"Cold-skinned lizard man."

He looked her fiercely in the eyes. "Will you be my fire, my sulphur?"

"And burn your cold scaly skin?"

"Yes."

"You are dark my Lorenzo."

"I was born into darkness my Frieda."

She watched him quietly.

"Come, burn my skin." He took her hand and closed it over his bare throat and chest.

"Now? But it's almost time for dinner."

"Is that denial?"

"Just for now."

"Damn dinner."

"But I'm hungry."

"So am I. It is you who are dark . . . penitential . . . Prussian.

"Sulphur man."

She dug her nails into the skin of his back. He screwed up his hands and face, waiting for her to go on, but her hand went limp.

"After dinner then." He squeezed the phrase out.

"With full military honours."

"Prussian!"

"Puritan!"

"Military honours then."

"And a band."

He got up from the edge of the bed and paced restlessly up and down the room till he had worked off some of the sulphur. He stopped in front of the mural.

"Marinetti was wrong, D'Annunzio too. They should have left Italy the way she was, not drag her into the twentieth century. She belongs in the past. That is her identity."

"Is that in your picture?"

"No, it just brought the thought into my mind."

"So it is there then."

"Alright, if you like." There was a hint of something in his voice—irritable, challenged, sulphur still smouldering.

"Is that fair, doesn't Italy have a right to a future?"

He shrugged. "What's wrong with living in the past? I would."

"So . . . Italy frozen forever in blocks of Carrara marble."

"Perfect, I couldn't have put it better myself . . . lovely smooth white marble that turns into classical limbs and torsos."

"And what about England, your England?"

"My England . . . Dirty black coal that coughs and burns living death."

"But that is your landscape. Don't you hear it calling to you, like Orazio is called by his?"

He flushed a little. He didn't like being trapped.

"Poor Frieda, she doesn't understand, she's not good at logic. If we lived in the past, there would be no mines to go down, no engines to drive . . ."

She blew out her cheeks. "Logic! Since when were you a logician? Can I never win an argument even when I am right? Carrara and coalmines . . . You are not a gentleman."

She rolled suddenly off the bed and crouched down in front of the picture.

"Oh God, I think I know who she is this universal woman of yours." She knelt closer, looking the figures up and down. "It's Rosalind. It is, isn't it!"

He flushed suddenly, his lips tightening.

"Rosalind . . . Rosalind Baynes?" He stared at the picture. "Don't be ridiculous."

"Aha, yes it is. Just look at your face. Your subconscious has revealed the truth, even if you won't."

"Ah, subconscious, that great chief magistrate before whom nothing can be hidden . . . Swear on the holy bible to tell the truth." He snorted with derision, but his face had whitened under his red beard. "And anyway, what truth?"

"That truth . . ." She stabbed a finger at the mural, her eyes cattish now, narrowing on their prey. ". . . You and the lovely Rosalind . . . lovely, lovely, lovely Rosalind, the object of your desire, crouching at your feet, hanging adoringly on your every word. That's how you would like it, isn't it! She wouldn't deny you would she, at least not in your private phantasy? I name this mural The Adoration of Lorenzo."

"Shut up . . . Shut up . . . you and your subconscious, your lubricious, pernicious, subconscious. Tell it to get back into its dirty little box . . . Absurd, all of it."

"Oh God. You don't even know it. That makes it even worse. It is her."

"I don't know it? I don't know it?" He looked down at the mural, swaying slightly, his chest starting to heave. "It's a naked woman, a naked woman, any naked woman."

She jumped up and stood in front of him, her face close to his, scrutinising him: "You," she said softly, "I knew it. You want her. Don't try and deny it. Does she want you? Noblesse oblige."

"How dare you! Shut up." He kicked a pot of paint across the floor. "Noblesse oblige! You should know about that Baroness . . . Noblesse oblige."

"Are you in love with her? I can leave if you want. I can move out." She spoke with an almost caressing softness now, her voice calm and reasonable.

He stared at her, mouth trembling, breath thin and short. "Subconscious . . . repressed sexual phantasy . . . Freud, Freud, Freud. You're all mad. That's why he could only discover it in Vienna. It's exclusive to the German peoples, repressed lunatics the lot of you."

"Ha, who are more repressed than the English?"

She dropped back onto the floor, rolling around and laughing and chanting: "Rosalind . . . Rosalind . . . Unrepress me Rosalind. Gentle little Rosalind, I need you, that horrible German woman doesn't understand me."

"Stop it. Stop it now." He clenched his fists, his jaw quivering.

"Why?" She looked up at him through wild dishevelled hair,

her arms spread out, tempting his anger with her helplessness. "Why?"

"Orazio will hear," he said feebly, his face white, then red, chest heaving.

"What a nice well-mannered little boy! Mother's boy!"

He froze.

She laughed. "And since when did you care what other people think? Anyway I can't stop, I am just a poor hysterical woman, and a foreigner too." She rolled around wantonly. "I am powerless. It is my hymen that speaks. I can't control it. It is too strong for me. Help me. Help me. O superior man. O superior English man." She rolled around even more, laughing and pouting and making seductive eyes at him. She stopped suddenly and sat up. "And that is why I never felt at ease in your England either . . . all that superiority . . . and you are part of it."

He breathed hard, chest heaving, little flecks of saliva in the corner of his tight shut lips.

"I am powerless before you. That's what you want isn't it . . ." She stared up at him.

He jumped down on top of her, pinning her, squeezing her wrists. She managed to pull them free, readying herself, arms braced against him, jaw tight. He stared down at her, his face thin with fury, his body rigid and taut, coiled, ready to strike, knuckles white. She waited for the blow, tensing herself. He held her with all his angry force, then, suddenly, his shoulders sagged, his arms loosened, his head dropped. He sat on top of her as if lifeless. She held her arms and hands stiffly up in case it was a trick. Seconds passed. She dropped her arms. He climbed slowly off her and knelt there for a minute, head bowed. He got up, walked a couple of unsteady paces and sank back down again onto his knees, eyes closed, head hanging.

She watched — uncontrollable anger she knew, blows she knew, terrible words she knew — Get out. Take your things and get out. Here, take half of my money, take it all, and he would run for his wallet and throw it at her. Take everything but get out. Go where you like, back to Weekley for all I care. Or a fight, a full physical fight, slapping and hitting, and she would fight back through her tears, like for like. All that. But this..?

She waited, watched, unsure. Was he acting? Maybe he was acting, and any moment he would jump up and dance round, or smirk at her from under his eyebrows and deliver a sermon, or maybe he was preparing himself to run at her again with renewed force and fury. They were not much her little accusations, her little ridicules, they were not much were they? She had said worse, much worse, and she didn't care about Rosalind anyway, not at all. Now, after all her vows to herself—the new beginning, the good intentions. She shouldn't have pushed him. Why did she do it? She bit her lip—defiant headstrong child, never tamed, uncontrollable, so always ready to rise up.

She watched. He started to crawl across to the mural on his hands and knees, feeling blindly around him for whatever came to hand, liquids, oils, pouring them onto rags, then slowly, wearily, he leaned forward, stared for a moment at the mural, then wiped a great smear across it, and then back again—he would wipe it out, he would wipe out his life, wipe out his whole existence.

She jumped up, pounced across the room, fell to the floor, wrapped herself round him, squeezed him tight to her. The rags dropped from his hand, his head dropped against her shoulder. He whispered something, something about coal dust and death and nothing mattering anymore, his words jumbled. Minutes passed, long silent minutes. She held him. She would protect him. She would hold him like this forever, an embrace of trodden love and pain—a Pietà.

The candles were going out one by one. It was getting cold, a thin silent creeping cold.

"Lorenzo," she whispered. She waited. He didn't move. "Lorenzo, the stars are out. They will heal us. Let us go outside. Wait and I will put clothes on you."

She got up. He stayed kneeling. She gathered odds of clothes and put them on him, lifted him silently to his feet. She guided him to the door — he let her — then down the creaking wooden stairs and across the dark hall corridor. Hens sheltering in a makeshift coop at the other end gave off a low sleepy warbling sound, Orazio, busy ordering plates and pans in the kitchen didn't hear them pass.

Outside, the night glowed spectral and still. She took a deep icy breath, scouring out the devils in her, in both of them.

"I felt some snowflakes on my face," she whispered, a little smile trying to break into her voice. She held out her palm. "Yes there. Oh lovely. They tingle. Put out your hand." But he didn't move. "Are you warm enough? We can walk down a little way, down to the chapel."

She took his arm and started to walk, down along the edge of the wooded hillside, the path all rock and snow and ice-crystal leaves. He let her guide him, not really caring. She stopped. She squeezed his arm and turned him round to face back up at the villa perched on its little tree-lined eminence—Orazio alone, Orazio in stone.

"Villa Villa on the hill . . ." she whispered, like a child's nursery rhyme. "You make up the next line." She pressed herself against him. He said nothing. "Shall I go on? I can't go on without you."

She moved her hand slowly up and down his back.

"I think I have a name for it," she said, trying to sound ordinary and conversational. "Do you want to hear it? I think it's good. Villa Janiculum. That is what I would call it, after the Roman god Janus, two front doors looking in opposite directions at the same time, two lives, past and future. Remember when we were on the Janiculum in Rome, overlooking the city, and we talked about just that. I will tell him. Maybe he can name it thus. What do you think? Should I tell him?" She thought for a minute. "Perhaps not."

She put her hand into his pocket and felt for his.

". . . And how many directions do we look in, you and me?" she asked after a while "A different one every month. Maybe that is the problem. No, it is not a problem. It is like you said . . . Our land is no land, and exile is our home."

They stood in the darkening whiteness, motionless, the glittering night sky arcing its immense wheel of time.

"Look up there," she pointed heavenward, "Orion. You see I recognise it. You have taught me."

Chapter Twenty-one

SHE WOKE. THE HOUSE WAS STRANGELY STILL, AS IF breathing quietly to itself. It wasn't the first time she had felt it. Not even the bagpipe players had come this morning. Her hand wandered behind her. The bed space next to her was empty and already cold. She hadn't heard him get up.

She creaked down the stairs, treading softly for some reason, not like her. In the kitchen the fire was burning but there was no-one there. She stood for a minute or two listening to the purring flames, staring vacantly. The sharp crack of a burning log shot sparks from the fire. It made her jump. She turned round. Orazio was standing in the doorway. She hadn't heard him come in. He was unusually silent, no bluff morning greeting of—I hope you slept well. Shall I make some tea? He shuffled forward and picked up a folded piece of paper from the table and handed it to her. She read it — *Your Ladyship. Gone out to set traps.* That was all. She flipped it over to look at the back. Nothing.

Orazio hadn't seen him go. He had come down as usual, expecting to be the first, had noticed Lorenzo's shoes on the floor where he had changed them for outdoor boots, and seen that one of the coats was missing from the hook. On the kitchen table was the remains of a hurried breakfast, the sheep's cheese still out, and next to it the note. She looked at it again, as if some other information might suddenly reveal itself—*Your Ladyship*. She felt a tightening in the pit of her stomach. Oh well, better let him walk it off.

She had hoped they had all been exorcised, the spirits of the night before, hoped that the lovemaking might have healed it all. Military honours had been performed, but not the way she had intended, and the band had been crashing and dissonant. It hadn't been kind love, it had been silent and remorseless—love between strangers. She had tried to bring him round, doing things she knew he liked, but it had just made him more brutish, more bent on domination, mechanical, grunting—Friday night, payday night, back from the pub. Get upstairs. Give us our due lass.

Yes there it was—you are not a gentleman, noblesse oblige, and all that about Rosalind. The Baroness always looks at me de haut en bas, he would tell his friends. But that was fine when he was fine and he wanted to mock, all just material, real but not real, although as far as she was concerned it was he who looked de haut en bas at her, treating her as if she didn't know anything, a poor lightheaded mooncalf.

But for all his natural genius, for all those gifts that set him apart, that lifted him out of any ordinary category of being, at least in her eyes, yes for all that, deep inside him residues burned, impossible to extinguish—his past, his father, his roots, the coalmines, Eastwood. Not that he denied any of it, he didn't, he owned it, he had told it all in his novel—this is me, the son of a coalminer who hardly knew letters and came home drunk. No, he didn't hide it. But he mixed in circles now, Lords and literati, he had become almost one of them, had drunk carelessly at the font of their noble admiration, and like the waters of Lethe, it made him forget.

It would have pleased his mother though this new elevation, if she had lived to see it, it was exactly what she had taught him, what she had wanted for him — escape from that horrible black brutish world to which his poor coal-smeared pit donkey of a father belonged, and for which he and his mother were too good. This was the narrative she had planted in him, and which he had grown up to accept as holy writ, for she, his mother, was book-learned, genteel, a class above, not very far above, but far enough.

Now, with time, the son was coming to regret the way they had all rejected him, this poor pitman of a father — home from the mine, off with his shirt, wash himself down in front of the fire, towel his white strong muscled back and arms, a beautiful man, fine and beautiful and handsome, physical beauty, supreme in its wonder and creation, more powerful than mind or learning, the power that had overcome his mother before class and respectability had whispered its insidious message in her ear. And he had been a man who would stand his ground, proud of what he was, never cowed, masculine, rich in his dialect, never bowing to the nicely words of his mother, a coalface man, like all the rest, born to it, almost illiterate, a poor uneducated pitman who lived by muscle and nerve and sinew.

But there was more, for underneath all that grime there was a man of soul and talent, gifted and sensitive. He could dance, and dance well, he used to teach it, and one time he had asked a certain educated young lady to dance with him, he just a poor pitman, supreme now in his art and beauty, all eyes on him, and she, the educated young lady, had accepted, flushed with pleasure to be singled out, just like any of the other girls. But she couldn't dance well, this young lady, so instead she had married him. And he made things, this pitman, things of iron, beautiful things. He could sing. Sometimes he sang in pubs, but he also sang with his children, or told them stories in his pit-talk dialect — about Taffy the pit 'oss what sneezed . . . an' the colliers would say, 'Ello Taff what'art sneezing for? Bin tae'in some snuff?' . . . and so they asked 'im if 'e wanted bit o' bacca? — and the story of the pit mouse that got in ya pocket an' ate your snap an' ran up your arm. Here was the father at his best, happy, not drinking, a maker, a craftsman, a teller of tales, and the son had listened, spellbound, and he had wondered at this man, at what he had in him, secretly— the collier who tramped off before dawn every morning, white and clean, and came back at night, black and grimy.

And now a thought came to him, this son, that perhaps it was from the deep dark underworld that his father had inhabited that his own gifts had come, from the depths, from the dark, from the deep, dug out by a poor black pitman, brought to the surface and bestowed on his ungrateful son — and when the world turned against him, this son, as it had, it was because he had turned against the bearer of those gifts, and against himself. No, the brute lovemaking of the night before had been a punishment, but not of her, not of Frieda, it had been a punishment of himself, and maybe also of his mother.

She looked at the note and looked at Orazio, and the kind old model allowed himself to place a hand on her arm, something he had never done before. In spite of herself she couldn't help but laugh for a second, a silly weak laugh — if the fugitive had happened to look through the window at that very moment and see them like this, Orazio's hand on her arm . . . ! But he wouldn't have minded, no not at all, he would have taken it all in the way he did—insatiable observer of human frailty, dark angel. No, he wouldn't have minded, it would have been the opening sequence of his next novel. Damn him.

The old model, innocent of his new role, moved off to make her some breakfast. She stood, absently, folding and unfolding the piece of paper. She thought for a minute of throwing on a coat and running out after him—she knew the paths he took, the places they had walked together. But which one would it be, any of them, or none? It would be none of them, of course not, not today, it was there in the enigmatic message—*Gone out to set traps*. Traps are set off the path, in the wild places. She looked out through the finger-smeared windowpane at the white world she had come to love and to fear a little. What would it be now?

—·—

He hurried on, long legs taking him he knew not where, a wayfarer, carried along, blown by the wind, unable to stop. And on he went, legs not his own, across the deep white rolling landscape, endless like the sea when you are swimming in it, on and on, his legs moving for him, just like they used to, no direction, the village on its cliff face no longer visible, and now he was in a white wooded place that was also dark somehow, as if the light was being devoured—at the end of winter there must be spring or there must be death. Was it he thinking these words or the woods? Oh for a moment's repose, oh to find a refuge . . . the words of the song ran through his mind, the song she had been singing the other evening—a charcoal burner's hut . . .

"Rejoice in the Lord, O ye righteous . . ." The 33rd psalm. He sang out the words in a pulpit voice and a vision of hymn numbers, and he was out of the woods and striding on again across the blasted whiteness.

"Ranenu Sadekim b'Adanoi . . ." it sounded better in the Hebrew, the way his Jewish friend chanted it, those words that had become the expression of his dream, the origin of his Rananim, the place that would be their home, but never quite was, and on they moved again, carrying gold, or was it myrrh? Here is a new place. And they would stop and look about them. But in a corner the dark god sat, and he would say—Not here. Not yet. Follow me. I will show you a better place. If you stop now you will be lost. You know it is so. Speak and I will speak through you. Speak in tongues—dark god, ancient and jealous of his chosen ones.

Suddenly the untamed energy that had propelled him along was gone. He sat down on a rock near a fast running stream, all twigs and ice and snow-buried roots. Further upstream through the trees there is something heavy and massive with high up windows, not a house. He can hear a slow rhythmic pulse like a great heartbeat thudding and thudding. He should go closer and look but his legs won't move, he is sliding down onto the freezing ground, his head against the rock, eyes closing, slipping away — and the heartbeat thuds and thuds and thuds, he can't feel the cold, he won't grow old, this is a place where stories are told.

———

Orazio poured tea. He had an endless brew on the go this morning, and he was telling her stories to while the time, all his old favourites—London, the artists he had sat for, Millais, Alma Tadema, and others. Frieda nodded absently, sipped, listened, half listened, drifted in and out, glanced at the window, tried to picture a man wandering the whiteness, where he might be, what thinking—there were no neighbours here to run to, no bus to town, none of the usual escape routes. What was the meaning? What sort of experiment was this? He liked experiments — Come, step onto this page a minute. You don't remember saying those words do you, but I do. Have a look, this is you. Was she out there in the snow with him now? Was he testing her? . . . Your Ladyship . . . not a gentleman . . . down a mine. He had never been down a mine in his life, but the mine was down inside him, coughing its black dust from the depth of his being.

Traps . . . Gamekeepers set traps. "Don't do this," she heard herself whisper.

The old model, in the middle of a story, looked at her curiously.

She stared out of the kitchen window not really seeing, hiding her face, her eyes blurring, her lips moving: "Be no other, my Lorenzo. Soar high above . . ."

She sipped her tea, suddenly aware that Orazio had stopped talking. She went up to her room, her lonely room, spare and lifeless now. She saw the mural and turned quickly away. She needed to do something. She dug out the copy of Norman Douglas's new book which he had given her in Florence. 'South Wind' it was called, a story about life on a siren isle—thinly disguised Capri. She lay on the bed, propped on pillows, closed her eyes, and held the book to her breast for a few moments — if she could only picture them both already there, then all would be well. It would bring him back, the sun always did.

"I hope it doesn't put you off," Douglas the old roué had said to her in German. She didn't know he could speak German, and he made her laugh, he was funnier in German than he was in English. He didn't go there anymore himself, but there would be

Germans there, and other nationalities too — Americans, Swedes, all sorts — it would dilute all that insufferable Englishness, and it would be like it used to be before the war.

Nepenthe — the ancient drug that caused you to forget suffering — this was the name of the mythical island where the South Wind blew. The book had already caused some fractiousness and pique in certain circles at the obvious caricatures of well-known denizens of the sybaritic isle. So Lorenzo wasn't the only sinner in this.

"Lorenzo . . ." She shut her eyes. She could already hear his name being whispered behind hands at gatherings, or called across the floor of a busy bar, or on a sunny narrow street, from a first floor balcony as they walked beneath, at a dinner with friends, wined and dined and making merry.

They are standing on the little terrazzo of their house, just he and she, staring out, wisps of white surf on the ridges of waves, blue sea, warm breeze . . .

"Lorenzo, it is such a lovely day, let's go for a walk up through the vineyards, up high, to that spot you like near Tiberius's villa . . . Look . . ." she points across the bay at little puffs of white in the clear blue sky, "Vesuvius is signalling approval."

She opened the book. She would read it, and when he came back she would tell him all about it. It would be amusing, she knew, and it would make him laugh. She wanted to hear him laugh. She puffed up her pillow and sank back, and soon the sirens came calling, and she was swimming naked in the blue grotto, sipping cool volcanic wine, looking out across the bay to Ischia, and slowly slowly her heart grew quiet.

She lay the book down, closed her eyes and turned on her side away from the wall, away from the mural with its accusatory gouge. Maybe it had all been for the good. It would purge them somehow, cleanse them, make them ready for their new island paradise. And this place? What of this place..?

She slipped away into a drowsy half-dream sleep. Sometime later she awoke, clammy and breathless — the dreams had not been of hedonist island retreats in sensuous blue seas, but of ice-fearful petrifying mountains. She felt the blood drain from her face — he couldn't, he wouldn't, life imitating art, the closing sequence of his last novel, Women in Love — Gerald Crich, the rich handsome mine-owner, rejected by the one person he realises he can't live without, his soul torn from him. He walks out of the mountain hotel where they are staying and up into a high place of rock and ice. There is a crucifix there. He lies down, closes his eyes, slips away—rejection, snow, rock, sleep, ice, death.

Oh God, is there a crucifix out there somewhere? She runs down the stairs. What time is it? How long has she been asleep? Orazio isn't there. Thank God. She doesn't want him to see her in a state. She throws on a heavy coat and whatever is to hand and runs outside and down the icy path, skating, sliding, nearly falling over, arms flying to keep herself upright, almost comical. It is mid-afternoon, she can tell by the light and the way the mist has settled in the valley bottom. She runs down the track, tripping on rocks, calling his name, as if he would be sitting there some-where, like a sprite.

She is down by the chapel . . . Which way? There are several ways. Damn crossroads, damn their existence. Which way! Oh God which way! She looks at the little place of cult, a choke in her throat . . . Say something. You saw him go by. Did you see him go by? Maybe he didn't come this way. She pushes at the door. It is closed. She has had her one permitted access, her one moment of sanctuary . . . Tell me. If I can't come in, give me a sign at least. But inside the chapel all is silent.

—·—

He opens his eyes. The soft round face of a young girl is looking down at him—gentle, concerned. She is saying something but he can't quite understand. How long has he been there?

"Signore . . . Signore . . ."

Her hand reaches down to his shoulder and rocks him gently. She smiles, her pale cheeks flushing slightly, strands of short black shiny hair falling across her face. She flicks them back. He moves his arms, touches his chest and legs, sits up a little, unfolds himself, then slowly pulls himself to his feet and brushes the snow from his coat and sleeves. The girl nods . . . That's right. She is a little mother except that she looks boyish. He is tall, with a red beard, just like the statue of the Sacred Heart in church—a wayside Jesus.

She peers up at him, the transparent pale skin of her cheeks glowing with cold. She has almond black eyes, lively and shining, short black hair, also shining, and she is wearing a thick green woollen sweater that looks much too big for her, tucked into a pair of old brown cord trousers tied at the waist with string.

He stands there. She stands there. She takes a couple of paces away, then turns and gestures him follow, and he does, without thinking. She walks with a strong quick step, boyish but not, keeping just in front of him, turning occasionally to smile and nod. They are heading away from the stream up a steep track, up a steep little hill, here and there old stone cottages, open farmyards with piles of logs and iron ploughs and implements, wood smoke hanging in the still grey air, a dog barking, but no people.

"Vieni signore." She says it gently, as if leading a child.

There is a rambling old pink-washed house at the high point of the hill, then the track veers off and disappears into woods and fields. She turns off the path and into the open farmyard, a threshing floor at the side, two large fig trees, and a cherry and other fruit trees at the back where the hill makes a little knoll. Against the pink walls of the house is a bare winter vine that would be a pergola for sitting under in the summer.

She stops in front of a door, turns and smiles, gives him another reassuring nod, then opens the door and leads him into a big old kitchen. In the hearth a large log asleep on a bed of embers wakes with the draft of cold air and sends up sparks. A little white dog, like a scotty dog, jumps perkily to its feet and runs round in quick excited circles at the sight of the stranger. It is a busy active room, hats left lying, jackets on the backs of chairs, on the table a thick piece of vine wood which someone has been carving. There are wooden armchairs, one or two pieces of furniture, rustic, but nicely made, a sideboard with oak-leaf decorations and glass doors and little special objects inside — souvenirs of Rome, the Vatican, holy pictures, mementoes, statuettes of saints, coloured liqueur bottles, little brass candlesticks, china coffee cups, a coloured photo of Vesuvius with a pall of smoke hanging over the Bay of Naples and Capri, with the date 1906.

He stands there looking around him. She is already busy, poking at the fire and moving things. She turns round, claps her hands up and down against each other to clean the wood dust off them, and purses her lips pensively. She points to herself and the chairs, counts out six fingers and raises them to him, then squeezes the bicep of her arm and makes a mannish face. He understands — she has six brothers, she is the youngest, the seventh, and the only girl. They are all out working somewhere about, including her parents, even in the snow, cutting wood, pruning, tending to animals, they are all out except one. She points to a framed photo on a shelf, a young man in military uniform, the black plumed hat of the Bersaglieri. There are flowers in front of it. She points to heaven and makes the sign of the cross. But there are no sighs, no pathetic eyes. She bustles around, sits him down at the big table, makes a sign that he should relax and warm himself, takes a bottle from the sideboard and a small thimble glass and pours something thick and dark.

"Noce," she says.

She smiles and rubs her tummy—walnut liqueur to warm him up. He doesn't speak. He could, he can speak Italian, but he doesn't want to, this is much better. She watches him sip, nodding with approval. There is a sink and draining board with pots and pans. She selects a big pot, goes out of the kitchen for a minute and comes back in with it full of greens and vegetables.

—·—

By the little chapel, bundled against the cold, a woman with wild yellow-brown hair stares out at the frozen empty landscape. She pulls her coat round her, her face suddenly set, and strides off with fast determined steps up the road, the one that leads uphill, the one they took the other evening, then just as suddenly she stops, turns, and walks slowly back.

She climbs the steps and slumps down, her face against the chapel doors. So this is it. On this step, on this day, in this ice and silence, unseen, unheard, unwanted—journey's end.

On the kitchen table there are a couple of iron files, some good wood-handled tools and the like. The wayfarer picks up the half-finished carving, turns it round appreciatively in his hands. It is of a man playing a flute, head thrown back, fingers flying, eyes half closed, tall hat, long hair, cape, sheepskin leggings. He can see the hands at work, strong peasant earth hands, gouging at it, holding it up, smoothing it, blowing the sawdust off. The girl looks over from where she is expertly and quickly cutting and chopping vegetables and dropping them into a small pot.

"Mio fratello," she says, "molto bravo," and she points to a couple of other little carvings on a shelf—a man with a fishing rod, a bear rearing up.

She hangs the pot over the fire and stirs it. Soon it is simmering. She holds up her hand to him, five digits. In five minutes it will be ready.

There is no-one about. There is never anyone about. Are they somehow invisible the locals? She had put it to Lorenzo that there was an enchantment on the place, but he just said it was her German imagination. It irritated her — he was allowed to fill the valleys and mountains with spirits and deities, but she was just an escapee from a Nordic fairytale.

Her eyes flashed . . . Well I'm not having it. No. Never. Not I . . . You and your games. She tossed her head defiantly, just like she would as a child when challenged, heedless of reproach, standing her ground — and hadn't they all loved her the more for it, especially her handsome old military father, the Baron. High spirits were the nursery of brave actions, she must get it from him, fine old Prussian stock.

She jumped to her feet, threw back her arms, and into the submissive silence let out a roar. The lioness was back, dangerous and glaring. She will not be cornered. It is she who will write the script from now on, not someone for her, not him certainly. If he wants the pleasure of suffering, then she will take it even further, she knows how to keep things going just the way he likes. Yes, she will take the initiative, she will be the one on top—and when he comes back he will find her gone. She will leave a note for him, and when he walks in, triumphant, expecting adoration and remorse, he will find Orazio, alone, looking glum, and the old model will hand him a note, and it will say—the note will say . . . She thought for a minute. It will say — I hope you caught something in your traps, as for me I am catching the bus. No that was absurd. It will say nothing, just Goodbye!

He will stare at it, turn it over and over, his arms will fall to his side. He will collapse into a chair . . . But when did she go Orazio? How did she go? Did she take the case? . . . And you let her? . . . What time is the bus? . . . the train? . . . What did she say? And Orazio will have that lugubrious expression on his old face, and he will shake his head and mutter to himself . . . Why how is it that such a thing has happened in my house?

And now it is he who will run out into the icy darkness, calling her name. He will run to the torrent, wade across, run to the inn, and they will say: Yes she was here, she got someone to take her to the village to get the bus. But it's too late to follow her now, the next bus is tomorrow.

Where has she gone, Rome, Naples, Germany?

A dimpled smile played at her lips—she will be the girl in the book, the mysterious Paola, swallowed up into the night, never to return.

He will wander back across the torrent, across the Styx, stepping in the icy waters, uncaring of his shoes and clothes, of the icy cold, and he will make his way here to the chapel and slump down on these same wooden steps, and somehow he will know that she had been there, that she had waited for him.

She ran a hand through her hair, ruffling her mane, piling it into new assertiveness. What is this nonsense he is trying to invent? I know all his games. He forgets, it is I who taught him most of them. He wants a new narrative. So be it. I will flatten him into one of the pages, then close it and squash him.

She laughs and bangs the chapel door with her hand and points mockingly at an imaginary figure — a sham, you are a sham, even your taking offence is a sham. You are like one of Orazio's street clowns . . . Pappus the old fool wasn't it? And I suppose you lay awake all last night planning it all. Revenge. It was such a lovely horrible scene that you didn't want it to finish—sulphur man. And you almost succeeded. Here am I, sitting on the cold chapel steps, contemplating finality. Go on, go ahead. I dare you to come back from the dead now. If you do, I will kill you anyway. So make your choice.

Then the roaring subsided. She sank back down onto the step. What if he's out there somewhere, huddled against a rock, freezing, slipping slowly away?

"Come back . . . Please come back."

She hugged her knees, her head resting against them. She will make things right. She will hold him close with all her strength. She will let him win, or think he has, it doesn't matter. She will let him believe that the man is always superior, like St. Paul, if that is what he wants. She will let him enjoy his little illusion.

203

The red-bearded wayside Jesus is dipping chunks of crusty bread into the hearty country broth of winter greens and beans topped with a delicious thick yellowish olive oil. The beans had been simmering in an earthenware pot in the embers of the fire when they came in. He finishes a second bowlful. She doesn't ask, just comes over and fills it again, just like she does for her brothers.

There is a jug of red wine on the table that she has filled from outside somewhere. He pours a glass. It glows in the firelight. It is good wine. She sits herself down on a stool by the fire and ruffles the fur of the little white dog. She rolls up the sleeves of her over-large sweater, a man's sweater, one of her brother's, her forearms are pear-white, her hands small and childish but dark with country work, the stain of plant and wood sap, short nails chipped and grained. She looks at them, then tucks them away, flushing slightly. She folds her arms on her knees and rocks back and forward. The little white tufty dog sits at her feet, neatly, looking over at the newcomer. It makes to come over to him, but then sits back down. She whispers to it. It hops to its feet and comes bobbing over with springy little steps and sits looking up at him. She nods — he likes you — and she smiles again, and the little dog trots back to her, message delivered.

A great sense of wellbeing is filling him. If he could, he would forget everything before this morning, his past, his whole life, his little bit of fame—all just pride, all just trouble. He wishes he could stay here, start again, a new identity, make things with his hands, like the brother, like his father.

She waits for him to finish at his leisure. Three bowls down. He sits back. There is silence awhile. Then she points to the floor and gestures with her arm outside, the way they had come.

"Antica," she says.

He understands. It means ancient, old. It is the name of the village—Antica, the Ancient Place. It is the best name for anywhere that he has ever heard. This is how it should be, small places that just grow out of the land, grow out of a past lost to memory. Here, the outside world doesn't exist. The Ancient Place. It is like the name of a psalmody, there should be music to it, a few verses in the style of Blake. It must have been ancient when it got its name, and back, and back, like the eternal olive tree, reproducing itself for millennia. Here time forgot to start.

She got up and came over to clear his plate away, raising her dark eyebrows playfully — would he like more — a little challenge behind her smile. He holds up his hand in surrender. She wags her head from side to side — you hardly eat anything, you should see my brothers when they come in. But she concedes. He is a skinny man, he has done his best. The little dog follows at her heels, hoping for a helping. In an instant, a glass of thick black coffee is in front of him. She goes to the sideboard and fetches out another bottle. Grappa. It is to kill the coffee, she says, and splashes some into the glass.

Across the valley, a woman picks herself up from the chapel steps and walks slowly back up the track to the lonely little villa. She won't go in, no, there is nothing to go in for. She hates the idea of the place, hates it, wishes they had never come. She stands huddled against the front door, the one they never use. A gust of wind whips a powdery funnel of snow into the air and drops it down again. She crooks herself closer into the recess of the door— but is it the door that opens into the past or into the future?

He has almost forgotten how he came to be there. If he gets up to go, where will he go? The girl is busy. Occasionally she looks over and just smiles. He isn't Italian, she can see that, but she hasn't asked him anything about himself.

How wonderful not to be asked who you are, what you do, not

to have to make up an identity—because they are all made up. It is so peaceful without words, without a self.

The woman is huddled against the door, staring out. It is she who will be found frozen and lifeless.

"If I die first, what will you write of me?" he would ask sometimes.

"Nothing, there is nothing to write," she would reply.

"I know what I would write of you," he would say.

"What?"

"I can't tell you. No-one should hear it, not even you. But what I can tell you is this. We have discovered the dragon's lair where all the riches of life are kept, and now and again the dragon roars and burns us."

This was her Lorenzo, something of the now and not the now, of the here and not the here, of the physical and not the physical.

Antica. In a kitchen in a house in a village that is very old, a little white dog stands at the feet of a girl in boy's trousers as she pours a second glass of grappa to kill a second cup of coffee for a man with a red beard and eyes the colour of mountain gentian.

It was all her fault . . . that terrible mad German woman with all her sex obsessions. We would have welcomed him back. We would have granted him absolution. An English writer should write in England. This is what happens if they go abroad. They die, they die to themselves, they die to us, and England dies in them. Give us back our son you ravenous she-wolf, give us back his remains. England wants him back, what is left of him.

She can hear it all now, ready to burst on her. She huddles closer against the door. They all hate me so, and now it will get worse. They wanted their little English writer to write little English novels that made them feel little English and righteous and sentimental, just so, with lots of thees and thous—proper literature. We are sailing happily over the sea, we don't want to know what lies in its depths. If you want to write, tell us of adventures, don't dredge up dirt. For all the social stuff and the odd tear we have Dickens, but that is far enough.

She reaches up and touches the initials above the door, O. C., trying to distract herself.

He died in Italy you know. That terrible woman drove him to it, and listen to this, he was hardly cold poor man, still lying there on the bed after they had found him and carried him back, and she just walked out of their bedroom across the corridor and into the next door room — that Italian who used to be a model, the man they were staying with, Orazio someone or other. She can't get enough of that peasant skin. They say she got a taste for it when they were up there in Garda while poor Lawrence's back was turned, she was still divorcing her first victim at the time. What a woman! She flits from one victim to the next like a crazed bloodsucker. She's gone quite native you know, you can't tell her from a peasant herself anymore, that's what they say, and she insisted on burying him there on a hillside under a pile of stones — a tomb worthy of his great soul, she said — not at all Christian though, and it has a slab of rock with words carved on it in some ancient language of those parts, some nonsense about him being claimed by the mountains, that the local gods had seen him and claimed him, that he was the reincarnation of some ancient seer of the peoples of those parts, Samnites or something . . . all that mystical mythical nonsense she was always blathering about and filling poor Lawrence's head with . . . receiving messages from the past. And now she holds pagan ceremonies around his tomb, around this pile of stones, and she gets dressed up as some sort of bird, a woodpecker I think they said, all green feathers and so on, flying around, swooping up and down, and she says she receives messages back from him. Poor man. Misguided of course, but it wasn't really his fault. He'll never find peace.

It's the Germans, they're all like that, all that Norse mythology and those sagas—quite stirs them all up you know. Look at poor old King Ludwig and his castles—a world of heroes. Trouble is, it is a ghost that always needs feeding, always lurking just under the surface. Wagner's another.

How did he die? — Don't know exactly, except that he went out for a walk one day and never came back. They found him curled up on an ice shelf up in the mountains. They say he did it on purpose, or that she somehow made him do it, drove him to it. There was a crucifix there, just like in that book of his. It's certainly made it a bestseller — Women in Love — fiction becoming fact and all that. One way to get publicity I suppose. She gets a tidy little income from it now. They never had a penny when he was alive. Poor old Lawrence! Can I pour you another whisky?

She kicked her heel hard against the door, then wished she hadn't. She didn't want Orazio to hear . . . Lorenzo, damn you, come back now or I will have to live in this moment forever. Don't do this to me. I don't want the money. Which way is this door facing?

Angry tears rose to her eyes . . . You self-righteous pig. I don't care if you don't come back. Go and set your traps, and I hope you catch a bear in one and it devours you. Did you catch me in your traps? Is that what you think? Well now I'm going to escape. I will happily deliver you back to your own kind, except they don't want you. Not really. You are trapped in your own trap. I will never submit to you. Damn you . . . Come back. Please come back. I don't mean it.

———

Why is it called Antica? — The grappa has loosened red-bearded Jesus's tongue, and he speaks Italian, good Italian. She smiles brightly—nothing like a bowl of her beans and a glass or two of wine to loosen a man's tongue. The scotty dog jerks to its feet. The stranger's funny voice has made him cock his ear. She strokes him. She gets up and goes to the cabinet and takes out a strip of rusty metal, the side of an ancient helmet, and hands it to him. He fingers it. Her father dug it up many years ago while ploughing.

She goes outside, and comes back in with another pile of vegetables and starts to cut them up and put them into a large cauldron. She pours more dried white beans into the ceramic container and puts it into the embers . . .

Dinner, she says, her brothers . . . they will come in hungry, and if the food isn't ready they will beat her. Then she smiles and shakes her head — No. Qui comando io — Here, I am in charge. And he can imagine her, bright, and at the centre, and vital, the last, the best, the girl.

He gets up to leave. She goes to the cabinet and takes out a holy picture and gives it to him — Santa Giusta, she says, the patron saint of the village, and also her name too. Giusta. He wants to give her something but he has nothing in his pockets. She shakes her head, and touches her heart—she will remember, that is thanks enough. Then she makes a comic worried face . . . You better go before my brothers come back. If they find you alone with me, either they will kill you or else you will have to marry me.

She walks him out and down the way they had come, past the fast-running stream where she had found him. It is called the Melfa, she says, after some ancient goddess. Up above, rising sheer against the white of the mountains, the village has reappeared. They come to a point where two paths cross. He doesn't recognise it. They stop. She points the way. He puts out a hand. She looks at it and slaps it away — Be off with you you silly boy. She stands and watches him till he is out of sight.

209

Orazio is grumbling around inside the house on the other side of the door, she can hear him fiddling with the lock He hardly ever comes out this way. Perhaps he heard her kick it. She makes ready. By the time he opens the bolts she can scamper away. He says something to himself and walks off into the store room, muttering still, against himself, against the world and the odd saint, but mostly against his brother. She thinks she hears her own name mentioned but not in the same tone. His steps come out of the store room and disappear back down the corridor.

She slides slowly down till she is sitting on her haunches. It is almost dark, just the glow of light from the snow. She pulls her skirt tight round her knees and rubs her clenched fists into her arms and thighs to warm them. From down the corridor she can hear Orazio singing an old music hall song. Maybe he has had a few nips, maybe that's what he was doing in the store room, digging out a bottle of some coloured liqueur.

She puts her head on her knees and starts to laugh and then cry a little. Just then she sees a figure making its way up across the lower meadow. The snow has drifted down there and he is sinking in knee deep with each step. She peers hard. It can't be him. If it was him he would use the path. She jumps up. The figure stops. She takes a couple of hesitant steps forward and screws her eyes. She runs forward and levers herself over the low wooden fence, and then she is brushing through the twiggy trees, plunging across the snowfield, trying to run, but it is too deep, her legs are heavy like in a dream, she is almost wading now, her heart bursting in her chest, her cheeks wet and red.

"Are you the postman?" She is standing in front of him, dizzy. She doesn't know why she has said it, except the song Orazio was singing was something about a postman.

"I thought you were the postman. Are you the postman? Please tell me you are not the postman."

"Postman? Yes I am the postman."

"Say it again."

He said it again. She threw herself onto him, and down they

both went, sinking into the deep drift, rolling over each other and down the slope, gathering snow as they went till they were entombed in it. She is trying to hit him but can't because their arms are snowbound, their clothes caked and sodden, their limbs tangled, and he is laughing and she is sobbing with fury.

"So you didn't miss me then!" he manages to get out.

She stuffs handfuls of snow into his mouth. "You have been drinking. I can smell it on your breath. Schnapps. Where did you get schnapps?"

He blows out the snow, coughs and spits, tries to turn his head away, tries to get words out between the icy mouthfuls.

"I call on the good Santa Giusta, protector of wayfarers, to come to my rescue."

"Schnapps schnapps schnapps," she cries into his face, and she frees an arm and hits out at his chest and arms, hitting and hitting, repeating the name of the awful crime, "schnapps schnapps schnapps . . . I will distill you, I will make you into spirit," and she squeezes his body with all her might, "I will schnapps you."

Inside the house, there is no sign of the music-hall performer, but there is a draught from the other end of the corridor—the music-hall performer had heard shouting and had gone out to investigate. It is the second time he has heard noises out there this evening. Nobody there. He shakes his head—so many strange goings-on today. He comes back down the corridor muttering to himself, and walks into the kitchen. He looks at them mystified for a moment, then shrugs and starts to sing the song about the postman again, whistling in the parts where he can't remember the words and helping them out of their sodden clothes. He piles the fire high till it is roaring and his guests are steaming, then he fills the kettle for tea.

Chapter Twenty-two

THE GREAT BLOODLETTING HAD SERVED ITS PURPOSE. HE was sitting at his table scribbling again, while she sat by the bed with the old cape spread out on it, concentrating on a corner of the patchwork of embroidery that was slowly becoming a tapestry.

"I feel like Hildegard of Bingen," she said after a while.

"The monastic life," he muttered absently.

"Is it the answer?" She drew up a long thread and tied it off.

"Why don't you go for a walk?"

At that moment a gust of wind whistled and whipped against the window, rattling the pane.

"That's why," she said. "What are you writing?"

On the table in front of him was the little coloured stone that Giovanni had pressed into his hand. He picked it up, rolled it in his palm and held it up to the light, squinting into it.

"This," he said.

She looked up from the embroidery.

"That?"

"A little epilogue . . . final payment, the mural and this."

"An artist paying for his dinner with a picture."

"Yes, I suppose that's right," he chuckled. "Which shall I be Frieda, painter or writer from now on?"

She got up and came and stood behind him.

"You are such a fool sometimes." She peered over his shoulder. "It's for Giovanni really isn't it!"

"Mostly. But there is a bit for Orazio too."

She read some lines quickly under her breath, running the tip of her finger along his neat small script.

"The echo . . . Oh yes, that is clever . . . the echo of the echo. But you must read it. The echo must be an audible echo, it must come to life. He will love it."

"My greatest admirer . . . someone who can't even read. Sums up beautifully where I am now."

He reached up to where her hand rested on his shoulder. "Then go and call them would you, they're probably just sitting in the kitchen glowering at each other. I will deliver it to my audience . . . like Dickens."

"Up here?" she said, surprised.

"Why not . . . change of venue . . . then we can make the official presentation of the mural to Orazio too . . . grand opening of the new cultural wing of the villa . . . fine arts and live performances . . . oh, and tell them to bring a chair each."

She walked towards the door.

"No, wait wait, we'll make it more ceremonial. There's a piece of old curtain in the cupboard, we can cover the picture with it, then we can have a proper unveiling."

A few minutes later came the sound of heavy steps on the stairs. They had left the door ajar, but Orazio stopped outside and knocked.

"Permesso?" He gave the formal request of entry.

"Avanti Savoia," Lorenzo replied, standing erect and ceremonious in the centre of the room. Orazio left his chair by the door and took a couple of steps in.

"Welcome Sir Horace, and thank you for agreeing to come at such short notice." Lorenzo gave a small deferential nod of his head. "We were wondering if Sir Horace would do us the honour of officially unveiling this humble offering from my wife and I, dedicated to your good and worthy self?"

Frieda came forward and ushered Orazio towards the wall where the piece of curtain had been hung over the mural, held in place by means of two leaning chairs. He stepped forward and lifted the curtain away. Lorenzo gave a little clap. The three dignitaries stood back and examined the work.

It was about four feet square, two naked figures in a desert setting, a man half reclining, a woman sitting on her haunches facing him, in a niche in the rock above them a statuette, a goddess figure, half in shadow, and on the ground watching, a curled lizard. He had reworked it the evening before. There was no trace of the attempted vandalism, and the female figure looked a little different too.

"Well?" Lorenzo asked after a suitable pause.

"It is very fine," Orazio pronounced. "You have put his lordship's materials to excellent use, better even than he himself."

"Orazio you are too kind. Do you think the V&A might like this as well?"

"Without a doubt."

"Were you one of the models for Leyton's murals in the V&A too . . . what were they called . . . The Arts of Industry? I refused to see them just because of the name.

"I have not such age," he said, rubbing his unshaven face. "I was still a child running around outside here when they were painted."

"Just think," Frieda said, "a little Orazio. I bet you were a pretty boy."

Orazio leaned forward, running his fingers lightly over the surface of the picture.

"Does it have a title?" he asked.

"You know something, it does not. Perhaps you could name it."

Orazio sighed. "I will not name it. It has been good your stay. It needs no name."

"You are wise Orazio, why do we have to name things? Let it speak for itself. What do you think Frieda?" They stood all three of them for several more moments regarding the picture, then Lorenzo looked round towards the door.

"What happened to Giovanni?"

"He won't come in here."

"Ah. Well, if Giovanni won't come in here then we will have to go out there."

Lorenzo wrapped himself up. It was draughty and even colder on the landing but he wouldn't hear of going down to the warm kitchen. They arranged themselves in front of the balcony windows. The wind had dropped. Giovanni hadn't brought a chair, he sat on the floor with his back pressed against the wall.

The storyteller settled himself with the sheaf of papers on his knee. He took out the little stone and held it up for Giovanni to see, and then he told the story, about a place in the mountains, a secret place where echoes were made, and of the guardian and keeper, the only person who knew of it, and how one day the guardian was sitting there dreaming when suddenly the echo spoke. From that day, the little guardian, who had never had a friend among humans, had something better, a living echo, and whenever he came to the place in the rocks, sometimes he would speak and echo would reply, but at other times he said nothing, and then echo would start to speak, would tell him things, tales of the mountains . . .

Orazio translated, Giovanni listened, his face twitching a little, eyes shining. Story over, Orazio nodded, and made to get up, but Lorenzo gestured him to sit down again.

"Not so fast Sir Horace, there is an echo for you too," and he started to tell another tale, about a young boy from the village of the Picus, and how he grew into a handsome young man. But the handsome young man grew restless. He had no love for the hard mountain life, and one day he set out to find his fortune in a far off city, in a far off land, a city of art and theatre and luxury, a Greek city by the sea. Here was everything he was searching for, so different to the world he had left behind.

". . . Now the Greeks have a fame all of their own, and it wasn't long before his good looks were noticed, and one day a sculptor asked him to pose for him. The young man became a famous model, renowned and rich and other things besides. He took on a new persona, became a Greek himself, adopted their ways, learnt Greek almost perfectly, and, with time, quite forgot about the mean mountain world from which he had come. Life was good to him, he had many noble friends whose hospitality he enjoyed. But one morning he woke up and looked in the mirror, and he saw there another, he saw the little boy he had once been, and the little boy smiled and beckoned, and the old model felt something move inside him, and one day he packed all his belongs, took his leave of the great city, and returned to the village of his birth. There he built himself a fine villa in the Greek style, and he learned the art of winemaking, and he settled down. Sometimes writers and artists from that other world would come and visit him, and he would sit sipping wine with them, reminiscing. Occasionally he missed the city, but in the end he lived out his life happily enough, cultivating his vines, watching the seasons, surrounded by his collection of pictures . . .

Orazio shook his head, a wry smile on his face.

"I will miss you Signor Lorenzo. You will leave me a different man." The Greek model got up again and made to go back downstairs.

"Wait. I beg forbearance of my audience for just one moment longer."

Orazio sat back down.

"I have a final message to deliver. It is from our friend Mamerkis, our beloved sacrato, founder of the village of the Picus. He has entrusted me with it, a warning from history. We must hear him out so that he may finally return to his own time and leave us to ours."

The storyteller held up the stone again. "Through this stone he can see us . . . here . . . now, and he bids us listen."

Lorenzo closed his eyes, took a deep breath, then opened them again.

"Soon after we made our home here, I, Mamerkis, set off alone

one day up into the mountains to find the source of the stream that runs into the valley. All day I climbed through hollows and groves, through narrow channels cut in the rock, the clear water swift and churning, till I was in a high mountain valley, and there, at the foot of an overgrown cliff face, I found the spring. I fell on my knees, dipping my arms in and out for the sheer pleasure of its coolness, scooping up handfuls to drink and pouring it over my head.

"A spring is a holy place, and I knew I must make an offering to the guardian spirit. But just as I was thinking this, in the water I saw the reflection of a woman's face. I looked up startled. She stared at me, her eyes flickering between sympathy and cruelty, her shape and features mutating between age and youth . . . no bear she, not this time.

"She raised her hand and beckoned me. I couldn't see a path, just steep rock, but somehow I followed her till we came to a hollow place covered with branches and long vines. It was the entrance to a cave. We passed through.

"After the bright daylight I could not see well, and when my eyes became accustomed, my guide was no longer visible. I walked on, deeper and deeper, till I realised that the light I was seeing by was not natural light any more, but a strange glow that came from the very walls of the cave. Suddenly, I found myself on the edge of a deep chasm, odorous white fumes drifting up, burning my mouth and my throat. I couldn't breathe. I felt a great dizziness. The chasm was going to swallow me. The cave walls started to throb, and just as I thought I was about to fall into the depths, she reappeared, floating in the yellow-white noxious vapours, terrible her appearance, her face now just a great empty blackness.

An indescribable energy filled the air, making my skin burn. Then, in the deep empty darkness of her face I saw myself, and there was a child with me, and he was holding my hand, then I was no longer there and the child was grown, he was a warrior, wearing armour, holding weapons, streaked with blood, and he was watching a scene of destruction and burning, a city, a valley, our valley. An old man lay at his feet, dying. He was like myself, but not myself. The scene dissolved, and I was looking into the empty features again, and out of the black void more pictures came — a time and place unrecognisable to me, men in clothes I have never seen before, men with strange helmets but no plumes or visors, and instead of swords they carried short hollow spears which spat fire. Great iron beasts with long straight beaks rolled across the earth breathing more fire, and wherever they pointed their beaks, the earth would burst into flame with the force of thunder. I saw the child again, wandering and lost, and I reached a hand out but he didn't see me.

"High on a hill there is a temple to an unknown god. It is thick with gold and statues, it is huge and white, and over the entrance is the word PAX. Inside there is a sacred bird like our Picus. I hear the sound of millions of bees in the sky. I look up. Enormous winged creatures are flying there, and from their bellies shiny iron eggs are falling, and where they hit the ground, fire erupts and walls fly in the air. There are cities like nothing I have seen before, and they are all burning, all burning. Now the child sees me. He is walking through the fire. He reaches a hand out to me, speaking in a language I do not understand, then there is a rush of flame, and I am the child, and I am looking at the man, looking at myself. We are one and the same.

"Much later I awoke. I was lying by the spring in the shade of the trees, my hand in the water. Over the years I have explored these mountains till I know every rock, but I have never found that cave again. But every year on that date in the summer, I climb the mountain and make offerings at the spring of the black goddess in whose terrible power I briefly found myself that day, she who stands between heaven and earth, between life and death, who knows the future . . . the goddess of the crossroads, Mefitis. When the times are good, the harvests are plenty, and the people are content, I remember those visions."

Frieda peeked through the bedroom door. She came back in. "Giovanni is still out there. I fear he may never rise again."

Lorenzo was looking at the mural. She came up behind him. "Come away. Let's lie on the bed."

She led him by the arm and pulled him down with her onto the pile of blankets.

"You don't think Orazio was offended do you, perhaps a bit too much innuendo . . . Herculaneum-on-Thames. I couldn't resist."

"He liked it. I could see. Perhaps he will cultivate his vines better now and be content."

"What say we go and visit Herculaneum on our travels south. We might even see a bust of Orazio."

"You are a funny man, full of wonderful nonsense."

He sighed, and just for once he nodded in agreement.

"There, I have done it . . . more pieces of paper to commit to the flames, more useless papyrus curling brown at the edges, catching light, old Maria grinning horribly, words going up in smoke, floating away into the valley mists, horrible foreign scrawly words, all that sacrilege . . . Burn, Burn . . . Poor old Orazio, he is surely lost . . . and down goes another glass of his finest red with a smack of her rubicund old lips."

"Rubicund . . ." she said, thoughtfully, "what a word. But how do you know she will survive him?"

"Ha," he made a sort of face, "they always do, timeless old creatures like her. You could come back in a hundred years and she would still be here, quaffing the vino and smacking her lips, or you could step back a few centuries, and there she'd be, sitting by the side of a tomb, grinning, nodding . . . another one crossed off. There's always one of her walking around."

"Or maybe the same one."

They lay for a while. She moved closer to him, running a snaky sensuous hand under his back and over his belly, taking little nips at him as she went.

"My little brindled adder," he whispered into her ear.

"Come and hibernate with me," she hissed, and they hibernated awhile, all arms and coiling limbs. This was how it could be. It was always best after a crisis.

They lay back, just breathing.

"What was all that Armageddon and visions and hellfire this morning?" she said languidly after a while, "all that war and exploding eggs, and a child walking through flames and destruction, and Pax over the entrance. Are you becoming a wizard too?"

He released his arms and rubbed his red beard.

"Yes, I don't know how that happened. I'd been reading about Monte Cassino, about how it had been destroyed several times over the centuries, first by the Lombards, then the Saracens, then by earthquake, and this destruction theme took hold, and I just imagined how it would be if it happened again. Above the entrance there is an inscription in great gold letters . . . PAX. Destroyed three times. How's that for PAX? Perhaps it's something to do with the site itself."

"What do you mean?"

"Don't raise your head or the devil will see you . . . and up there they raised their head and the devil saw. You know it was originally a temple to Apollo."

"You are beginning to sound like Madam Blavatsky."

He shrugged. "I don't know . . . There must be something there. Perhaps Apollo wants it back."

The brindled adder raised her head. "You better be careful putting Apollo and the devil in your stories, or they might see you too."

"Ha! Me? They have already seen me . . . They know about me . . . high on my hill, exposed to the world's gaze, inviting destruction." He chuckled. "But at least they wouldn't whine and get all cross and say . . . That was me in your book . . . and then sue me. They wouldn't set the courts on me and accuse me of obscenity, in fact they'd say . . . Spice it up old man, that'll never do. Did they have libel laws in ancient times? And anyway, what's wrong with a little caricature? A writer has to use something.

They do take on so all of them. I should be like H. G. Wells and cock a snoop at the lot of them. He can do what he likes . . . dozens of concubines. I just have the one." He narrowed his eyes and gave her a sideways look.

"Would you like dozens?" the adder hissed.

"What has happened to the famous English sense of humour, the self-mockery, and anyway you'd think they'd be pleased to be immortalised, another little fleur-de-lis on the escutcheon. They're all so fragile these days, so thin-skinned, all pride and self-importance . . . the English upper class . . . just so far and no further old boy, or else it's fetch the twelve bore and shoot the bounder. But I am a poacher who has turned his gun on them, and they don't like it, and I will again. I s'll show'em, I shall."

"Aha . . . the gamekeeper again . . . the gamekeeper turned poacher. What is brewing in there?" The brindled adder uncoiled a hand and tapped his head.

He grinned one of his mischievous grins.

"What are you doing with one such as me, Baroness? Have I got you on loan from some library of heraldic devices? Are you overdue? Will I be fined?"

"I will pay the fine for you." She stretched languidly, then huddled in close to him, making herself comfortable. She could feel one of his long rambles coming on.

"Is it because you're German . . ."

She nipped at his neck with her teeth.

"Ow." He rubbed the mark, and settled himself again. "Germany . . . Everything in Germany had Goethe in it once. Now it's gone from one pseudo-science to another, from Goethe to Freud. Don't look at me like that. The Greeks held the real truth. Myth. Myth and Psyche, that's the real truth. It's all there, everything you need to know. Look no further. All the rest is just pfui.

"Take our present location, Italy. It is Dante, it is opera. What need of science? I do so like Italy, even D'Annunzio. Do you remember when I used to read him aloud in the evenings in the cottage in Cornwall, those lovely round Italian words battling against the driving English rain on our Cornish clifftop. L'Innocente, that's what I was reading . . . pleasure, betrayal, infanticide . . . nothing immoral there then, just everyday happenings in Italy. You see, he's a foreigner, so they just laugh. But me, the merest hint of fingers on flesh and I am a pornographer.

"Integer vitae scelerisque purus . . . Upright in life and pure of sin. That is me . . . our friend Horace again. They though, those English condemners, they are sin up to their eyeballs, real sin, the sin of power. Oh God, I fear no-one will have the courage to publish me ever again in England. Perhaps I should write something here and see what happens, have it published here, in Italy. D'Annunzio writes what he likes and they love it. It is the English, they are the curse. The country blessed with the finest literature in the world, now censored into oblivion. You know they only used to come down on political stuff, Elizabeth and her enforcers, all the rest was fine.

"Peace be damned. War be damned. I just want to write. I am tired of scratching around in poverty. Still, we are come south, and that is good. South is the direction of life, as is west. We have left behind the Sodom of salt pillars and slag heaps. In the south women do women's work and men do men's. Thank God for the Mediterranean. Women must not be men. The Greeks knew that . . . They gave us a warning . . . Clytemnestra.

"What would have happened if England had lost the war? Remember that morning in Penzance market, the farmers going round saying . . . Defeat . . . Defeat. We are beaten . . . We are beaten. Remember?

"Worlds are crumbling, Bolshevism in Russia, riots in Germany, and here in Italy, D'Annunzio still. I think the Italians will do something, but they are too dramatic to get it right. They'll march around till they fall off a cliff. But I laud them for it. I want everything swept away. It isn't finished yet.

"I hate democracy, a world of muckspouts, everything reduced to the lowest, vulgar in the true sense. What good is that? No, I believe in an elect, not a world governed by the masses. The crowd is untruth. Who was it said that? Kierkegaard I think. Are your eyes closing little adder?"

The little adder stirred, coiled her arms round him, and hissed: "My bite is fatal. It cures all ills."

Chapter Twenty-three

FRIEDA SPUN AROUND THE ROOM IN A LITTLE SILENT DANCE the way she would sometimes, singing silently to herself. She stopped, rubbed her shoulders and arms, and made big round eyes to no-one in particular.

"I think I will play the piano." She flexed her fingers. "What piece would you like to hear?"

She sat down at the imaginary instrument and started to play, then to sing, but instead of her usual throatiness, her voice was thin. The man at the table let go his pen and put his hands to his face. She sang on, quietly, under her breath, in her private world. She came to a stop. Neither spoke. It was one of those silences where both are so aware of the other that it's hard to break it. His pen fell on the floor.

"Orazio was in that gloomy mood again this morning," he said after a while.

"Really?" Her voice was expressionless.

He leaned down and picked up the pen.

"Yes."

They sat there for a while facing in different directions, saying nothing. She took a long breath in, and exhaled.

"What did he say?"

"You know, the usual . . ."

"What usual?"

". . . I miss London I miss my gentlemen. I miss the pavements shining wet with rain. I am a fool . . . Orazio you are an old fool . . . that sort of thing."

"That sort of thing. I suppose we all have our that-sort-of-things." She hummed another little piece of a distant past song, then brought herself back. "And what did you say to him?"

"Also the usual . . . You are well away from London. Here it is another world. But there's no convincing him . . . No, Signor Lorenzo, that is just the snow. Here nothing is any good. I am no good. England is the only place . . . Oh god no, I say, England isn't a country, it's an industry, and out of its chimneys belches a darkness of hypocrisy such as to cover the sun. Italy is still a land untainted."

"And what did he say to that?"

"He used that phrase of his . . . I know not of what you speak."

She stood up and went over to the window. After the day of the gamekeeper, then the coming back together, the physical closeness, they were falling down again into a sort of ennui.

"Poor lost man." She tapped at the glass softly. "But I do understand."

He thought about it. "What do you understand?"

"I too feel lost. Right now that is what I feel."

He was silent for a minute.

"Do you mean that?" He gave a deep sigh. "Then if you are lost we both are, and then we all three are, then this a colony of the lost."

She walked over, got her cigarettes out of her bag, lit one, and went back to the window.

"That's right, light some incense."

He waited. She didn't respond.

"The Rananim of the Lost," he said, picking up his thread. "Could we not somehow turn lost into found?" He tapped his pen on his palm. "Send up more incense, make an offering, sit down at the organ and sing a psalm . . . I once was lost, but now am found . . ."

Her cigarette tip flared. For a minute or two she said nothing, just leaned against the window smoking.

"Here endeth the Lesson." She pulled the window open, blew the smoke out, tossed the half-smoked cigarette after it, and closed it again. "How you do like the sound of words," she said, sitting down at her piano chair in the middle of the room, "the sound of your own words. You should have been a psalmist. You are a psalmist."

"Then you tell me," he rapped his pen on the table, "you tell me in your words, in your words . . . what it is this lost thing, this state of being lost, then perhaps we can refine it, we can distill it, make a homeopathic medicine of it, and then we can take minute doses of it every day till we are cured."

She sat for a while thinking. A few minutes passed.

"Nothing coming?" he asked, a slight patronising tone in his voice.

"Patience . . . Impatient man." She cleared her throat. "Right, now I will tell you."

He pulled his chair with exaggerated deliberateness so that he was facing her, eyes large with expectation.

She commenced: "All my life I have spent in one place, a provincial town in the midlands. Nothing ever changed, day followed day, season followed season, the same streets, the same people, social certainty, small contentments . . . and it would have remained that way from cradle to grave. But inside me there was a craving. In a way I kept it hidden from myself. I dared not feed it with my thoughts. Then one day something happened. A man appeared. I don't know how else to put it. He was different, almost alien, another species, and certainly not of my social class."

"Am I not of your social class?"

"Did I say it was you?"

She paused for a minute to re-establish herself, and gave him a look.

"He is foreign . . ."

"I am foreign . . . to you."

She gave an exasperated sigh. "You ask for my words, then you want to hear yours. It's got to be you, always you, you can't resist."

He raised a hand in acquiescence. She composed herself once more.

"He is from the south, from Italy, his skin is somehow golden, his dark eyes too have something golden in them. He has a way of moving, slow and easy, his body is lithe and strong. He was giving a performance in a village hall with a troupe of travelling musicians, all foreigners, and he played the mandolin and the accordion, and he played well. I found myself watching him intently, not for the music, just something fascinated me.

"After the performance I stayed behind. The hall emptied. I looked at some posters but I wasn't really reading them, I was watching him out of the corner of my eye. Then, while he was putting his instruments in their cases I went over and talked to him, asked him where he was from. He looked at me. He didn't say anything, just looked with those yellowish eyes, and I felt something melt inside. And that was it.

"For a woman of my upbringing what I saw and felt was impossible. I tried to shut him out of my mind, but I couldn't. I had invited him in and I didn't want him to go. It was exhilarating. His way of being was different, his mind was different, impenetrable, somehow half-formed. I had no real understanding of him. And yet, and yet, I wanted him, oh how I wanted him, it was stronger than me. I cannot explain it. I was overwhelmed, nothing else mattered, I had gone out of myself and beyond, I had no more will of my own, I was carried along by powers out of my control, and it was wonderful . . . not to think, not to plan, just to abandon myself. I was responsible for nothing anymore. I was liberated. I was forfeit to this dark man and his dark will. I was completely lost."

Lorenzo stared. Down in the kitchen Orazio was jolted from his usual half-slumber in front of the fire by a bang and a shout from upstairs, followed by the sound of thumping feet dancing around the room. He half stood up, looked at the ceiling, then subsided again into his chair. He had heard this sort of tumult often enough behind the closed doors of London houses, but mostly country houses — English gentry in their school dormitories, high spirited, ragging. Seldom was it a scene where murder was taking place, the English were not operatic that way. He got up again and wandered out to the foot of the stairs, looking up. He could hear Lorenzo's voice, high-pitched, excited.

"That's it Effie. That's why we came here. My muse . . . my inspiration."

"Effie? Don't call me that . . . I hate it . . . that Englishness I don't like."

"It's a class thing." He whooped and danced. "Frieda Frieda . . . Oh my Frieda. I knew it was here." He whirled around the room in a sort of waltz, circling the captive muse. He came to a stop, catching his breath.

"Remember Alvina Houghton . . . Remember the novel I was working on up there in Garda at your much loved Villa Igéa . . . The Insurrection of Miss Houghton . . . ?"

"But that was before the war."

"Yes."

"I thought you had abandoned her."

"Abandoned . . . me? Never. No, she was just asleep, and now she has awoken. You have woken her, and praise be, she has broken free. She has finally done what she wanted to do, she has insurrected." He beamed at her. "Alvina Houghton is here, found and lost, lost and found, but here, of all places, here in this very house, here in all this snow and remoteness, and it is you who has brought her. I can hardly believe it. I hope she likes mountains."

He pulled her up and waltzed around the room, till he was out of breath and flopped down on the bed, dragging her with him.

"Phew."

"But where is the manuscript now?" she said, wiping little beads of sweat from his brow.

"My love, that is the only problem. It is where I left it before the war, with your sister Else in Bavaria. Why didn't we think to fetch it on your way down? No matter, she will have to forward it to Capri. You have unlocked it for me. I am going to rework it . . . a palimpsest. I will rethread the whole thing. How extraordinary, Alvina Houghton, here. Frieda, I am feeling washed anew, baptised in the River Jordan."

The bedroom door flew open and Lorenzo came running out.

"Orazio . . . Orazio."

He jumped down the stairs two at a time. The old model was still standing at the bottom, staring back up. Lorenzo stopped half way down on the little landing.

"Orazio. Oh there you are . . . Orazio, thank you."

"Don't mention it."

"Orazio, it has come to me, clear as an Italian sky . . . my Frieda showed me . . . and you too, you handsome old devil, you will be in it. I hope you don't mind. Oh Orazio, my dear fellow, what a splendid house you have."

The old model looked back up the stairs with benign but total incomprehension.

Lorenzo came back in from the landing and stood there looking at her with that deep blue gaze, and she felt a blood surge of pleasure down inside.

"Frieda . . ."

It was in her name, in the way he said it — single, entire, all — that she knew her life to be her life, and that all the turmoil, the love and hate, the grief and war, all that brokenness, that it was all worth it, and all the pain was taken up and made holy, all the guilt washed away, all the sins forgiven. Everything was predestined, she was with him for a reason.

A novel for which he had had high hopes, and which he had started back there before the war in that time in the Italian lakes when the sun shone on both their lives, but which he had never finished, here it was again, brought back to life, and he too and she too. It was confirmation. It was the new start.

"Alvina . . . Alvina Houghton, right here in these wild talismanic mountains, these wild pagan mountains and valleys, here in this old cold lovely awful villa, lost, loved, liberated. What a thing! I canna hardly believe it . . ." And so he ran on the way he did, repeating himself—excitement always made him repeat himself, and slip deeper into his old accent. That was where the boy discovering life still lived, and in his excitement he was back there.

"I have him before me now, your dark Italian with the yellow eyes. There is something about such as he that is fatal to the northern female soul, even Orazio has some of it. In essence they are all one." He gave her a mischievous smile. "I was right to be suspicious of you."

The dancing around and the agitation had made him flushed and short of breath. He took out a handkerchief and wiped his face.

"Take care Lorenzo." She came over to him and sat him down, took his handkerchief from him, dipped it in a jug of water, and dabbed his forehead.

"I can't remember much about her now," she said, pressing the cool cloth to his face, "in fact I don't think you really told me much even then. Remind me."

He had to recollect it himself — Alvina Houghton, daughter of a serially unsuccessful midlands businessman, leading the life of a young woman of her class, but not yet married. Something prevents her. There have been suitors, but she always withdraws at the last minute. There is something in her soul that marks her. But she is trapped in her midlands provincialism.

Her mother dies, and now she runs the house for her father. But his enterprises continue to founder one after another. Then he too dies, leaving her with little or nothing. It is now or never if she wants to make a life for herself, a life of her own finally. She moves to the nice city of Lancaster and trains as a nurse. The eye of a well-off doctor falls on her, middle-aged, impeccable, certain of himself and his opinions. Marriage is proposed. She is saved. A comfortable life beckons. Her new friends are pleased for her. She sleepwalks towards the happy event. But deep down that restless voice calls to her—this is not for you.

"And is that as far as she had got?"

He nods.

"And now?"

"And now? . . . I s'll tell thee an' now lass . . ."

She smiles. She knows where he's gone to look, but she wonders who will return with him. He gives a sigh back in time, back into the corners of his past. His face darkens a little—he too knows about refusing what's on offer. But nothing is so sacred that it can't be used, or at least adapted.

She watches the little flickers round his eyes, behind them a new narrative raging. "You can take your time."

"Nay lass, time isn't in it, in fact it's been there all the time . . . It's like this . . . The truth . . . It catches her. It won't let her go. It will punish her if she doesn't listen . . . She doesn't want this wonderful, respectable, death of a life . . ."

"And it will punish her if she does."

He looks at her a minute, wondering whether she knows already more than he.

"It is almost the day of her wedding. Outside her window one evening she hears a mandolin being played. How can that be—a serenade, the sound of a mandolin on a grey dark northern English evening? Then her mind suddenly jolts, a look of shock and disbelief on her face, but also something else. She knows who it is. He has come looking for her, announcing himself the only way he knows how, a travelling player who had worked once in her father's theatre, a mysterious sultry Italian, dark, brooding, alien to all she knows, a wanderer, like so many of his tribe, street-performers, hurdy-gurdy players, fortune-tellers, hokey-pokey sellers, not even working-class, not even English.

"The mandolin stops. She waits, suspended, unbelieving, a thousand thoughts fighting into her head, her heart beating. Then, from below the window, his voice . . . hardly daring to make itself heard, but knowing it must be heard, desperate, insistent . . . Alvina . . . Alvina. She goes downstairs and lets him in . . .

"How contemptible, running off with such a being, an immigrant Italian street musician, as low as you can get. She is lost for sure, her soul taken from her. Bitter words will follow her, and bitter missives. But she is free. They escape south together, to London, then on to Italy, out of reach, away . . . back to his mountain village to the house where his uncle lives . . ."

Frieda sat, letting it sink in, a distant expression in her eyes. "Does it not remind you of another flight south . . . out of reach?" She turned her gaze onto him.

He flashed a look back at her, a sort of smile that held something dark and inevitable in it. "We are damned Frieda, you and I, and I would not have it any other way."

———

Later, when he had written some hurried notes, they came downstairs to sit by the kitchen fire. The excitement had inflamed his airways and Frieda wanted him down in the extra warm. He coughed a little. She wrapped the half-decorated cape around him, and around the cape she wrapped herself, swaddling him, Orazio too fussed around him.

"Don't worry Pancrazio," he said, "I am quite alright."

Pancrazio! The old model looked at him. Did he really have a fever, was he becoming delirious. He piled the fire higher, worse than his brother, till it blazed and almost set the chimney alight, and now it was too hot to cook on and too hot to sit by. They pushed their chairs back.

"Here my friend . . ."

Orazio had fetched a bottle of some dark thick liquid, a local liqueur, and was warming some precariously in a little pan on the edge of the blaze, shielding his face against the inferno. He withdrew the scalding pan and poured a glass for each of them.

". . . Drink this. It is my remedy. I always take a little when in need."

"But I never felt better," said the fever victim, taking the warm glass and sniffing it.

"Mmm, that is good," Frieda said, sipping the hot dark liquid, and the fever victim sipped too, then drank it off in a gulp and held out his glass for a refill. After a couple more, he declared himself immune to anything the world could throw at him. He looked around the room slowly, his eyes screwed slightly, nodding to himself, whispering under his breath . . . "I think it is beautiful . . . They will come every day till Christmas now . . . I am glad there is a woman in my house . . . They are friendly to me . . . That is because you are a foreigner and they think you will not stay . . ."

Orazio busied himself with the fire, raking down the ash, catching odd phrases, bits of conversations he thought he recognised from their days here. Frieda sat with her eyes closed, leaning against the muttering man. He fell silent. A sort of spell descended on the room.

"Signor David," Orazio spoke very softly, as if he hardly dared wake his guest, "who is it who is speaking?"

"Ah," Lorenzo's gaze settled on the old model, "do you not recognise them? It is you . . . you and your nephew and his new English wife. They have come to stay, maybe even to live here. He has brought her home. Her name is Alvina. You will like her."

Orazio shifted uneasily. Maybe his brother was right, there was something of the sensitivo about this man. Around here there were people who could read the future—l'arte they called it. Having two names, two identities, this was not good. And what was this about a nephew? He couldn't remember telling him he had one. He would go and see the old lady he knew who could see into these things. He looked at his guest, then at the bottle, then at Frieda, wondering whether he'd done the right thing. Frieda returned the look, her green-grey eyes soft and pacific, reassuring.

After a while she spoke, her voice dreamlike too, almost as if she was talking to herself: "And what does Alvina have to say? Is she not a little stunned?"

Lorenzo's eyes narrowed again. "I don't know. You tell me."

She thought for a while. "A woman doesn't say. She listens to her inner voice, that's how she decides. It is on her skin if that is any help."

He put a hand on Frieda's bare arm, letting it rest there for a while, as if it might exude the hidden secret.

"Do you think she knows what is in store for her? Will she like it here?" Frieda asked.

"Do you?"

"Will she ever go back to England?"

"Will you?"

And suddenly she felt the inevitability of their destiny closing round them.

"What is his name? You haven't said."

"I don't know. She hasn't told me yet."

"Maybe she wants to keep it secret from the world . . . all hers, just hers."

He looked at her with watery eyes, lips compressed thoughtfully. It was at moments like these that she felt close to him, closer even than physical closeness, part of his very soul.

"Well whatever his name is, he is lucky to have such a generous uncle who used to be a model in London and has built himself a fine villa." The story-maker leaned over with an affectionate smile and patted the old model on the shoulder, and the old model reached for the bottle and topped them all up.

There it was. His mother had taught him well, need had taught him — throw nothing away, mend and reuse, and he did just that, be they clothes or shoes or people, even seemingly insignificant little details, all recorded by his unblinking unforgiving eye.

But how much trouble it had caused, accusation, recrimination, the loss of friends who had seen themselves caricatured on his pages, curious little corners of their souls laid bare. But she cared not if they were shunned, if backs were turned on them, in a way she even rejoiced in it, it drove other people away and drove them closer together—two savage spirits alone in the forest.

"What?" he said distractedly after a minute. She hadn't spoken. She wondered which dialogue he was listening to.

She glanced over at the old model who was fiddling with his shirt collar, muttering to himself. She smiled—he at least would not mind.

"I was just thinking, the uncle has a name, Pancrazio, here present, ask him what his nephew is called."

Orazio looked up, uneasy with his double identity, still a little bewildered. He wasn't even really clear whether this was another one of their games, a charade, or something else. He wouldn't ask.

Chapter Twenty-four

Orazio sat in the kitchen. The weather was closing in again. They hadn't come down to breakfast. He eased himself down on his haunches and lit his cheroot in the fire. The feverish spontaneous talking and imagining of the evening before had been a climax, they had found what they had come for, and that meant only one thing. Still, now at least he had sustenance to feed his poor old soul in the long winters ahead, however many or few he might have left.

He stood up. The letter that had announced their arrival was still on the mantelpiece, tucked away behind a little copper vessel with a brass handle his mother used to use to scoop water from a barrel with. He picked it up and looked inside. At the bottom there was an old coin and a long dead scorpion. He emptied it into the fire, the coin as well.

Life had come calling, had woken him from his slumber, and now it would depart again. He imagined himself sitting there sometime in the future, remembering their stay, telling an unknown visitor about it, if he ever had a visitor, which was unlikely, at least not one who would be interested. No, it would be a case of him sitting opposite himself, a jug of wine for company, spectral shapes flitting past, the sound of conversations, the antics and playacting, Frieda's laughter, the silences, the unpredictable moods, the storytelling — just like Lorenzo yesterday, which he had finally understood was not a charade — yes all this he would share with the phantom person on the other side of the wine jar.

"Pancrazio!" He smiled to himself and puffed at his cheroot. Was this how it worked then? Perhaps he should have been more careful with what he had told them over the days they had been here. No, it didn't matter. Let him put it all down on paper, a verbal picture of his poor old self, of his poor little grand little villa, of all they had seen, and just think, back there in London someone might pick up a copy of this new novel, someone who remembered him, and they would read it and say to themselves— Ha, that sounds just like old Orazio. He's still alive then, the old devil.

He sighed — this was no good, this life, sitting here night after night with just his brother creeping in and out. Outside, he heard the pig snorting and snuffling in the snow — Pasqualina, happy, intelligent, nuzzling up to him while he put out her food, cavorting with joy, but one day the slaughterer would come, and she would be hung up and sliced and rendered, and buckets would be filled with her blood, offal and intestines turned into sausages, her haunches into great hocks of prosciutto. It saddened him. He was fond of her. He had grown soft in England. When he was a little boy they had had an old farmyard mutt that always lay in the shade outside the door. It was a funny old thing with long floppy ears. He hadn't realised how fond of it he had been till it died. Then he had cried.

That was it! He would get a dog. Of course! Why hadn't he thought of it before, but a companion dog, a noble dog, not like the old mutt, or the great white Abruzzo sheepdogs they kept around here to keep the wolves at bay—he preferred the wolves.

A tame wolf! Now that would be something. He had seen a beautiful grey female in the woods a few days before, her fierce green eyes looking back at him with something that could become affection, he was sure. Yes, he would get a dog, a pedigree dog, like the ones in English country houses — the English and their dogs — a nice old dog curled up in front of the fire, that watched him, that flicked its ears attentively when he moved, that followed him out and about, or waited for him to come in, second in command ahead of Giovanni—and he started to think of names, good English names.

He got up, walked over to the window and peered at his opaque reflection, turning his head from side to side. A pretty boy, Frieda had said. Not anymore. Too late. How did this happen? No men were single around here unless they were like his brother, or had been widowed. Now, as old age beckoned, the weight of his decisions, or really his indecisions, were growing heavy on him. Hereabouts, children were the only guarantee of a dignified old age.

"Orazio, Orazio, look at me, I have no children, and I am not worried," Lorenzo had said when the subject had come up one time.

"But you are still young, and you have Frieda, you are married, and anyway it is different for you."

"Different for me?" Lorenzo's voice was somehow distant. "Yes, I suppose it is," and he coughed, and tapped his chest.

Orazio sat back down, his head in his hands. "No-one to blame but yourself," he whispered to himself. He looked down at his shoes, old London shoes from a good maker, now worn and scuffed, and he wondered if they still had his shoetree with his name on it. He reached down and took off one of them and made to throw it in the fire, then sighed and dropped it back on the floor. He would never have peace. He sat back resignedly in his chair. They were the same shoes he had worn that morning, the first triumphant return of the young man who had left here, hardly more than a boy. Things had gone well for him in London, modelling, and other little matters, he had coins in his pocket, a fob watch, wore a nice suit, and shoes.

Shoes — around here they marked you out, marked your passage from poor peasant to man of means, they meant you had moved on, stepped out of the leather-thonged cioce. When he had come up to the torrent on that first visit back, he had taken them off and hung them round his neck while he hopped across, the barefoot child again.

On the other side, he put them back on, climbed up the rocky slope, waded through the new tall meadow grasses, the scent of crushed herbs rising to meet him, childhood memories. And there it was, the jumble of old stone buildings, as if he'd just walked down the slope a few minutes before, so quiet, the murmur of bees in the mauve wisteria that twined against the walls of the house, the smell of farm animals, chickens pecking around the door. He trod softly so as not to make them cluck and scatter and give him away. He hadn't sent word that he was coming.

By the door under the big fig tree, he stopped. Inside the kitchen, his old mother, in her pale blue cotton over-apron, was busy making pasta, rolling out the fresh dough on the table, rolling and rolling, sprinkling flour, flipping it over, rolling again, her strong arms pressing down, that long rhythmic pushing motion. He crept up behind her and broke off a little piece of the fresh pasta, like he used to do as a boy — he liked to chew it all floury and yellow and soft — and just like then, she had slapped his hand away. She stopped rolling, her head dropped onto her breast, her shoulders shaking with furious emotion. She hardly dared look at him, but then she turned on him, and his fine suit paid the price in white flour, yellow egg stains and tears.

It was the year 1889. He settled in for a while, taking his ease, the young lord of the manor. While his mother busied, and Giovanni trundled in and out, he would sit under the great walnut tree, his hands behind his head, eyes half closed, or wander the brow of the little hill looking down over their small piece of land, and slowly, an idea started to grow in his mind. And one morning, sitting outside under the fig tree shelling peas, his mother watched her fine young son as he paced out a straight line, stopped, put a stick in the ground, turned at a right angle, paced out another equal distance, until he had measured out a good square of land next to the walnut tree.

Came Sunday — his mother killed a chicken, plucked it with

expert quickness, put it in the wood oven and went to Mass down in the little chapel. The young man put on his white shirt and waistcoat. Even if there was no-one to see him, he liked to dress, at least on Sunday. When his mother came back, they ate lunch under the fig tree, and then, sipping his coffee, the young gentleman felt in his waistcoat pocket, took out seven gold sovereigns and slid them across the table to his mother. There was no need to buy the land off her, it was worth very little, she would have given it to him. But still . . .

The foundations were laid, a silver English half-crown placed under the cornerstone for good luck, and his new villa started to rise from the hilltop. He couldn't really explain it to himself. He had no real need, he didn't even have a wife, and he probably wouldn't come back too often, although his mother was getting older.

But if you turn the earth, things grow, and one day — it was a fine day of early summer, waysides thick with sweet yellow broom — he was on his way to see the carpenter to choose the wood for his English-style staircase, probably chestnut, when his eye fell on a young girl who lived out in the countryside, one of those girls you never see, who live within the family circle. She had a quiet beauty about her, soft gentle eyes full of patience.

On 29th June, the feast of Saints Peter and Paul, they were married, down at the little chapel church of S. Maria di Costantinopoli at the foot of the hill. It looked like the young gentleman would be staying for longer than he had planned. The newlyweds moved into a couple of rooms upstairs in the old house while work continued on the villa.

A year passed, the villa was nearing completion, when, one morning he suddenly announced that he would be going back to London, just for a short while, just to make a bit more money so that they would be well enough off to live without relying on the land — at least this was what he told himself, and what he told her, his new wife. In his youthful certainty he knew that everything would go just as he planned, but now, all these years later, he realised that deep down he had had other ideas.

When it came time to leave, his mother had called him in. She looked at him quietly for a while, then closed her eyes and gave him a sort of blessing, calling on the Madonna to protect him — something she hadn't done the first time he had left — and she pressed a little gold Madonna medal into his hand to wear round his neck. She knew her son better than he knew himself.

With a forced casualness he asked why she was making such a fuss, but she just nodded slowly and pointed to heaven. He laughed — she was a fit healthy old lady with many years ahead of her, and anyway he would be back soon. Teresa, his new wife, made no protest at his decision to go. There were many women in her position, it wasn't unusual for the men to leave their wives behind while they sought their fortune abroad. She said nothing. He left.

A year passed, then two, then three, already a time span longer than he had promised, when, one morning, a letter had arrived, written in the fine florid cursive of the local priest. He knew what that meant, everyone knew what the letter from the priest meant— the angel of death.

He opened the letter, preparing himself for the worst, his heart sinking, the image of his mother before his eyes. But it wasn't what he expected. Teresa, his young wife, was dead of a fever, very quickly and suddenly.

He folded the letter. There was no point hurrying back for the funeral, out there the dead were buried the next day.

Why he had married her he wasn't sure, a sudden youthful infatuation perhaps, yes, in part, but also in a way to complete the image of himself as a man of means and respect in the village — old customs had a way of drawing you back in, even urbane young city dwellers who thought they had left all that behind.

He went and lit a candle in the Italian church in Clerkenwell — St.Peter's — on whose feast day they had been married. He sat there dutifully, remembering the day of the wedding, trying to feel grief, but none would come, at most just a sort of wistful fondness, but the worst thing was that he felt free.

He walked out of the dark church and into the fresh breezy London air. The world was his. He was quite well-off, handsome, and single once more, a fact that didn't go unnoticed in the streets of Clerkenwell. One or two Italian women put their eye on him, but he was having none of it, beyond some flirtatious dalliance here and there. He had purchase in fine houses, with real English society no less, and he had no intention of being dragged back into the crowded cacophony of Italian life.

There was work, and in between he would abandon himself to days of easy leisure, something like what the French called a flaneur. He had stayed in Paris more than once, quite a few of the young men from the village and the surrounding valleys had found work there as models, some had even opened art schools of their own. He might have been tempted to settle there once, but he considered himself English now.

But it wasn't long though before another letter in the priest's handwriting arrived. His mother's premonition had come true. There was no reason to go back now. Why he had ever bothered to build the villa he could not think. Perhaps he would try and sell it. He wouldn't get much for it, less than it had cost him so far—no-one had any money over there. He put it into a dark corner of his mind and forgot about it.

The years passed. No longer the sylph-like young model, he found himself with more time on his hands. Then something odd started to happen, he'd be walking across Soho Square perhaps, and out of nowhere he'd hear the voice of his long-dead mother calling him, the way she used to call him to come in to eat, he a little boy again, perched on a branch of the leafy fig tree that cast its welcome shade against the side of their old stone house, his legs dangling, his cheeks bulging with the sticky fruit which would surely have an effect later. Then, one day, he was looking at some photogravures that he had purchased from a French artist-photographer who had visited the area — pictures of the village and the valleys and the old fortress — and suddenly he could taste the figs, smell the wild fennel and mint, see the mountains . . .

Orazio woke from his reverie. Why was he thinking of all this now! He got up and poured himself a glass of Strega. But the thoughts wouldn't leave him, of his mother, of Teresa, yes mostly of Teresa. On long lonely winter nights he would wake sometimes from his doze in front of the fire and she'd be sitting there. One day he too would be a shadow, flitting eternally through these rooms, creaking endlessly up and down the wooden stairs, unable to leave. Perhaps she was she waiting for him there now, just on the other side, waiting for him to keep his promise.

Sometimes, when he was up in the village, he would look down at the cemetery below, at the stone square little death houses, the tall cypress trees waiting patiently, and he would see himself lying there on a shelf in the wall of the dead, unvisited, unloved, forgotten, while up in the piazza, people leaned against the same railing where he was then, chatting and joking, looking out across the valley. He feared death. On the feast of the dead at the beginning of November, when the red lamps burned in the camposanto, he hardly dared leave the fireplace to go to bed, he even let Giovanni stay late.

Upstairs all was quiet. He got up and stood with his back to the fire, but the cold wouldn't leave him.

Chapter Twenty-five

AFTER HIS BOUT OF LITERARY FEVER, AND ORAZIO'S strong patent cure-all medicine, Lorenzo slept fitfully. Dreams came — he was back in Eastwood, back in the streets of his childhood, looking hopefully at Parker's Picture Pavillion, waiting for his mother outside The Sun Commercial Hotel, running across Market Square, past Eastwood House, past London House, looking with dutiful disapproval at Henry Wyld's Wine and Spirits Emporium, the sanctimony of chapel sermons ringing in his ears. His mother was looking through the shop window of Jordan's the Drapers but keeping her purse pinched tight shut.

Frieda, half awake, listened to his muffle of incoherent dream words, young, breathless, giving, almost girlish, a frail little boy in short trousers running back from High Park Wood clutching a bunch of wild meadow flowers — These are for you mother — the view from his terraced house in Walker Street across the fields to Underwood, the distant church spire, Haggs Farm.

He woke with a jolt, the shadows of that other world fading into the milk grey morning light, the relief of present reality for once coming to his rescue.

"What are you thinking?" she asked after a while, her head crooked on her arm, watching his face in profile.

"I'm looking at the cracks in the ceiling."

"Look at me instead," she whispered.

He turned his head so that their faces almost touched.

"Not that close. Now I can't see you."

He turned his head back.

"What do you want to talk about?" he asked.

"Nothing. I just want to know you're there."

Outside the bedroom door there was the sound of feet shuffling and china clinking.

"Sounds like Orazio," he muttered.

"Go and have a look." He pulled the blanket up over his face. "Poor tired little boy. Alright I'll go."

She jumped out of bed, paced across the room and opened the door a crack. On the floor outside there was a tray with bread and cheese, and winter pears and tea. She carried the tray in and put it on the bed.

"Breakfast is served my lord."

"Is it that late? Bless him." He sat himself up.

She poured them both tea. They ate in silence, half seated on the bed, blankets bunched round them, Frieda making crumbs, Lorenzo sweeping them off with reproving looks.

She put the tray on the floor and curled up next to him.

"Poor Orazio, he didn't know quite what to make of all that last night. He got it though in the end . . . quite entered into the spirit of it. For once someone is happy to be in one of your novels." She thought for a minute. "I know, why don't we invite him to come with us? He would love Capri . . . Bloomsbury-on-sea. Poor Orazio."

"Poor Orazio . . . Poor Orazio," he mimicked. "What about poor Lorenzo?"

"Don't you like your role either?" She pinched his thin ribs.

"I don't know. What is my role?"

"God."

"Is it? Which one? The God of Abraham is a jealous God. No room for me there. And what is your role?"

"So what about it?"

"What?"

"Orazio . . . inviting him to Capri?"

"Hmm." He picked little bits of crumb from the bed clothes and dropped them onto the tray.

"Is that it . . . Hmm? Is that your answer . . . used up your quota of words last night and in your dreams? If you stayed here long enough that would be the sum of it. I can just see the pair of you, you and Orazio, sitting in front of the fire in the evenings, staring into space, just the occasional grunt. Even Giovanni would get up and leave out of sheer boredom."

She got out of bed and went to get her cigarettes.

"Not now."

"Not now! . . . Two words!"

She ran back over and jumped onto the bed so that they fell against each other.

"Woman!" He pushed her away. She wouldn't be pushed, and hung herself back on him. He roused himself and got on top of her.

"I . . ." she tried not very hard to struggle free.

"Shh." He put a hand over her mouth. She turned her face away and sputtered out some words.

"I, Frieda Lawrence von Richthofen . . ."

"Are you writing your last will and testament?" He forced his hand back over her mouth.

"Mmm . . . Mmm." She shook her head from side to side under his covering hand.

"And what is this von Richthofen? You, my lady, are completely and entirely, body and soul, a von Lawrence, wife of the scion of the great and ancient family of that name whose estates once covered half of the county of Nottingham, from the front door of No. 3 Walker Street, in the parish of Eastwood, down past the rose bush to the front gate. Testimony to this union is to be found in the registry office of the Borough of Kensington in the great capital city."

He let her go. She thought of saying something about noblesse oblige, but decided not to.

"Orazio thinks we talk too much," he said.

"No he doesn't. He likes it, he said so." She pulled the covers up around them. "Did your dreams answer any questions?"

"Was I dreaming? Did you hear me?"

"Were they about Alvina?"

He thought about it for a moment. "He is entering into her like smoke in the soul."

"What does that mean?"

He shrugged. "It means what it means."

"Has she told you his name yet?"

He shook his head. "He is here somewhere. I can feel it."

"What, physically?" There is no-one else here. You've seen everyone."

"Still, somehow, he is here." He turned on his side away from her.

"Well he better hurry up and make himself known. I hope she finds peace here that's all." She curved herself in behind him.

"I fear she won't."

"Oh my God, what have you in store for her?"

The breath of her words tickled the back of his neck. She put her free arm round him, running her hand over his belly and chest, then up over his eyes and forehead, feeling his thoughts.

"I think a gentle northern soul might not survive a place like this."

"Alvina?"

"Or you."

"You think I couldn't hold my own here!"

"Not without me to protect you."

"You to protect *me*! It is me who protects *you*."

"You would be hunted . . . brought down, like a gazelle brought down by a lion . . . the orgasm of surrender, the orgasm of death . . . the final consummation." He reached behind him and grabbed a handful of her thick mane.

"My hair Lorenzo," she disentangled his fingers, "it is already a mess beyond redemption."

She turned him round to face her, took his hand and rubbed it against her cheeks and lips, then closed her teeth around his fingers and bit hard. He yelped and pulled his hand away.

"There, that is what your gazelle would do," and she bit at his face and his nose. "Show me this consummation. Who is the lion here? Northern souls are fierce too."

And they struggled again in embraces, in a writhing of limbs, fighting for dominance, gaining it, losing it, tangling, and he would keep his eyes open the while, watching her expressions, and it would please him, her determination, her hair and softness and fierceness, and he would smile or snarl, but she didn't see it, for she would fight with her eyes closed, then suddenly open them, and seeing him watching her, gain furious new strength for his sacrilege—Diana the huntress. Then something came over him, and she felt it. She jerked her head away to look at him, to see who this stranger was. She wrapped herself round him again, ready for the game.

"I want to be devoured," her voice came up from deep inside her body, while he, a bird of prey, circled high above, but already in her entrails.

When it was over they lay back, just breathing.

"Two women for the price of one. Your lucky day." She squeezed him to her. "Did you expect her to be like that?"

"What happened to the lion?"

"That was the other me. But who was the other you?"

She gave a piercing little shriek and sat up abruptly.

"What?" he said, surprised.

"Nothing." She pulled at the knots in her hair.

"You are the strangest creature."

"I'm just a character in a book."

He turned on his side, watching her untangling her hair. "Six years we have been together."

"Seven."

"My God, is it seven? Then this is make or break year."

"Oh really? Well then do something, hug me, hard, here and

now, or I might just fly away with my nameless Italian lover and disappear into that other dimension of yours."

"No, no," he pulled her back down, squeezing her hard, "I should be too cold without you."

She let her body go limp in his embrace. "One day, in the distant future, someone will walk in and find us still here, you and me . . . Orazio . . . all of us, all of this, frozen in time, waiting to be released."

"Why released? I don't want to be released. Why can't we be like those figures in Etruscan tomb paintings, lying there feasting . . . a uxorious Etruscan Lucumo with his beautiful consort lying at his side, feasting at the table of life, feasting for eternity?"

"Are you uxorious?" She looked into his eyes.

"Are you eternal?"

"How do we know there isn't someone here watching us now?"

"We don't."

They subsided a while, the furies that had pursued them over these last years, that had savaged and clawed their souls almost to destruction, had let go, at least for the present. There had been something of the old ease in their coming together.

Frieda got up and threw on some clothes. She went over to the fire and poked hopefully at the cinders.

"What are you doing? Come back here next to me."

"Uxorious Lucumo you say, then the next minute you are unfaithful to me."

He watched her through narrowed eyes.

"It is my trade . . . the word is made flesh, the flesh is made word."

She laughed and wagged a finger at him.

"Come back here lass and I s'll tell thee a story."

She gave a quick look over at him.

"Aye . . . you know what it is."

She dropped the poker, scampered back over and dived under the covers. "Alvina..?"

". . . Alvina and her dark lover, her husband . . ."

"Her husband?"

"Yes, they were married in London, all very quick, just before they set off . . ."

"The same registry office as us?" She nipped his ribs.

He winced, then continued, ". . . south, to Italy. He will take her to his uncle's house who had been a model in London. They board the train, she, still not quite sure what has happened to her. They cross the warring seas of the English Channel, warring against her departure, at what she has done. But it is too late. She is gone, England sliding corpse-like and grey beneath the waves. They train to Paris, then on south, till, tired but exhilarated, there it is, the Italian border, the great classical landscapes spreading before them.

"She is in a daze, the light, the intense blue of the mountain sky, the sound of the language, the railway signs in Italian—all those little insignificant details that strangers notice when they first arrive in a foreign land. And the women on the train are friendly, they offer her bread and sausage and swigs of wine. It's like a narrative in a travel book . . . she will wake soon, and she will be back in grey midlands England, on the verge of a life that will bring her only to death.

"But it is strange for him too, her dark lover. It is as if he is seeing his country for the first time, through her eyes, and he is answering questions that the garrulous women in the carriage are asking about her in Italian.

"The uncle comes to meet them at the station, except he almost misses them because he was in the bar and he'd had a few . . ."

She was going to ask him if the pickpocket was there too, but held back for once.

"They climb on board the omnibus and head into the mountains, to the old uncle's little villa. For Alvina it is like a dream, by her side this dark beautiful man with yellow eyes who has broken down the barriers in her . . . and she feels like she has thrown herself from a high place into a nothing of air. She is stunned. She has gone through the tiredness. It is all so alien, but so wonderful, in the distance the wild flame-tipped mountains."

"Yes . . . Oh yes."

"They arrive in the little mountain town. She is leered at by the peasant women in their coloured head gear, strong and brazen and staring into her face. It is as if they have passed a frontier, gone beyond, out of the known world, into some place of rhyme and myth. She feels quite lost, but she doesn't care, she is alive, almost horribly so."

"Oh yes, I am this," she whispered, laying her head on his chest, "I am happy to be this. How do you write what is in my heart?"

"Now the last leg of the journey, a horse and cart, a crazed driver whipping down the hill, overhead a star-rich blackness, Alvina in a state of blissful exhaustion, a sort of horror and fascination and wonder, repulsed and attracted at the same time, and all the while her dark lover's eyes gleam yellow and inwards, as if another soul is emerging from him, his old soul, as if the brooding presence of the mountains is exerting some unseen power over him.

"She sees it, sees him change, but she won't let it bring her down, not now, not after all they have been through. — Are you not happy? Alvina asks. Are you not pleased you are coming home? — It is not my home, he replies."

Frieda gave an anguished little moan. "Stop now. Don't go any further. Let me arrive at least. Give me some hope."

Chapter Twenty-six

Orazio liked to lose himself in his London memories, and he liked Lorenzo's idea that a part of him was still there, that a fragment of his soul still flickered in those bronze likenesses of him, and that he could look out through those metalled eyes and see scenes and people, maybe even some he knew, and as they went about their London business they would glance up at him and remember. But then they would age and he wouldn't, and when all those he knew had passed, he would still be there, and he would still be there even when he himself had passed. But what about the present? It too was rushing past, and now another flying hour was about to chime its departure.

He crept up the stairs. The tray wasn't there. He came back down, poked the fire, then subsided into a chair. So, a dog, a fine pedigree dog. He drummed his fingers on the table and smiled to himself, remembering the drawing rooms and studies, the grand country houses, the spaniels and hounds and terriers, and how so often they resembled their master, or mistress. What sort of breed was he, he wondered? He would ask his guests. That would surely amuse them.

Just then there was a squall of clatters and bangs from upstairs, of chairs scraping on the floor, of running feet, of Frieda's deep throaty laughter, and then Lorenzo's voice, higher, almost boyish, giving one of his long sermons or telling one of his stories or jokes, maybe something even about their shabby host. The sound of them gone would be terrible, especially the sound of a female voice.

The bedroom door flew open and the bare running feet came jumping down the stairs.

"Orazio, Orazio, Orazio," Frieda's voice bounced down the stair ahead of her, "Orazio . . . Dove sei? Orazio, lord of all he surveys . . . Il Baronetto . . ."

She strode beaming into the kitchen. "Ah there you are."

He half got to his feet, the way he did when she came in by herself.

"Ach you are such a gentleman." She ran across and threw her arms round him. "It was so quiet down here we thought you might be out."

"I am just this minute returned from Leicester Square."

"Aha, a rendezvous. What is her name?"

He smiled, but inside he grimaced.

"We have had an idea, a marvellous idea. Guess what it is."

He looked at her blankly.

"We are going to make festive . . . have a party . . . What do you say?" She looked particularly attractive this morning, and all this enthusiasm made her glow.

"What a wonderful idea." But his face said otherwise.

"You don't sound convinced."

"Just the three of us?"

"And Giovanni."

"Yes of course," he said raising an eyebrow, "so four of us."

"Well not quite just four."

"How so?"

"Well, we thought it would be nice to ask Agnese and her children, and we can make some nice things to eat and some sweet things for the children . . ." She ran ahead of herself, breathlessly caught up in it all, heedless of Orazio's doubtful stare.

". . . Oh I wish I could make a Stollen cake, it is traditional at Christmas time in Germany. Oh that would be so good."

"And when will this take place?"

"Tonight."

"Tonight?" Orazio looked at her with amazement. "But I have no provisions for such a thing, nothing with which to . . ."

She didn't let him finish. "Didn't you say there was another Christmas market today?"

"Indeed, but it is already late. They finish by lunchtime."

"If we leave now we can be there by midday."

Orazio, usually slow and ponderous, found himself spinning in a whirlwind of hats and coats and preparations, carried away by the energetic Frieda, who was herself ready in a couple of minutes, wrapped in English tweed, her unruly fair hair tucked under the deerstalker hat. Lorenzo was staying behind. He had ideas he wanted to jot down, or so he said.

Frieda splashed ahead across the torrent, the old model trailing behind leading the donkey, which, for once, seemed quite happy with proceedings—Frieda had whispered in its ear before they left, something in German. Perhaps that was the secret. The icy waters too seemed to part for them, much less agitated than on other occasions, and they were soon at the inn. In the darkened interior, the caped hatted highwaymen were already at their cut-throat card play, red-faced and wine-stoked even at this early hour, flaring at each other, banging their fists down on the table and shouting their war cries — Settebello . . . Scopa — cries which signified winning tricks. Frieda repeated them to herself under her breath. She would find a use for them somewhere, perhaps next time she won an argument with Lorenzo. The brigands hardly gave them a glance.

Orazio hitched the ass to the cart and off they set at a brisk trot. On Frieda's orders he had sent Giovanni down to deliver the invitation to Agnese. But it wasn't long before he started with his usual litany . . . people here don't give parties . . . funerals are the gatherings they like best, then they feel good because misfortune has struck another, and not them.

Frieda screwed up her eyes, trying like this not to let his words pass into her. This morning she wanted another version, one that chimed with her good humour, and anyway it wasn't fair to include Agnese, a poor widow with children to support—and hadn't she brought that flask of wine, made an effort to be sociable?

Orazio grudgingly conceded. "Maybe you are right, but she won't come . . . and then there are the children . . . It is not proper."

She looked at him sideways. "They will come. I know they will come," she said under her breath, and she turned her head away so that his words were lost in the wind.

"Stubborn as the ass," she said to herself, and at that moment the beast gave a great swish of its tail, and she sat back and laughed behind her gloved hand.

Blasts of low rolling mist drifted across the flat white landscape, the road ahead barely visible. She closed her eyes for a while and let her body bounce and jog to the rhythm of the rolling cart. There was a sudden change of pace. She opened her eyes. They had left the valley and were climbing up to the village, the donkey, head lowered, labouring in its harness.

Orazio had been silent for a while, but it was a silence of words, she could feel it by the way he flicked the reins with an extra jerk, as if he was arguing with someone, flicking the words away, warding something off—semi-audible remarks meant to be heard as he walked by . . . Look there, that Orazio Cervi in company with that fair foreign woman, the one with the trusting open smile. What's he up to? They wouldn't like it. They wouldn't like that smile. They wouldn't like him being the recipient of it, as if he was somehow different to them. They knew who he was, they had heard all about him—and the poor foreign woman, so innocent and gullible, believing him something he wasn't. They knew. Oh yes. How had he lured her here? Even married couples hardly walk around in public together, and here is that Orazio, single for all these years, flaunting a fine figure of a woman, and foreign, and she, dressed in a man's hat and coat. He could hear the talk, see the malicious smiles . . .

"You must stay with me . . . stay by my side."

"But we were here a week ago . . . and I know my way round now."

"Yes, but you had Signor Lorenzo with you then."

Old mountain codes.

"Orazio, I love you dearly, but I have errands to run. I must look around on my own . . . and you'd be bored with me. No, it will be better if we separate. We will get things done faster."

He did not answer. The donkey strained up the hill. At the entrance to the village he came to an abrupt stop—not a step further. He cast a look over his shoulder, backing up slightly and nodding his head—they could get down.

Frieda stroked his sweating flanks and patted his head, and the donkey made big eyes at her.

"Schön," she whispered in his ear. He whisked his tail. "Have you a carrot for him Orazio?"

"If I find some I will buy one or two." The old model was still a little put out.

It was already past midday. Frieda had heard a misty church bell on the way. The general packing up had started, animals were being untethered and led away, carts loaded, men were arguing in loud voices, but already in the short time she had been here she had learnt that it was not anger, just volume. They weren't discussing the finer points of philosophy. No-one much looked at them. The great valley unconscious had accepted her, had taken in the presence of the foreigners. Orazio was worrying for nothing.

She stopped to look at some merchandise, materials for dresses and the like, and was immediately assailed by offers and entice-ments. Rolls of cloth were thrown open, thrust into her hands as if she had already bought them. The dialect was different.

"Napoletani," Orazio whispered with a note of warning.

They moved on, up past the fountain and through the arch, Orazio sticking close, then along the alleyway to the colonnaded square in front of the Baroque Church. She let him lead, stayed close behind, lulling him. Vendors called from their barrows, holding up oranges and tangerines, sun fruits from the south, Sorrento and Sicily, and they sliced them open and held them out to taste. There were piles of winter vegetables — all their own produce, they called out, all cut this morning — sacks of walnuts, chestnuts, selections of cheeses that weren't just the local pecorino, dried and salted fish, cured meats, salamis and great hocks of prosciutto.

She stopped to look at a stall, and the man sliced little slivers of cured ham and held them out on the end of his knife for her to try. She took a slice. Orazio tried to steer her away, saying not to waste her money, that he had his own prosciutto. But Frieda found his prosciutto salty, and he tended to cut it too thick. She nodded to the stallholder, and he set to with his big sharp knife.

"Orazio, you are so kind, but Lorenzo has given me orders to buy things for the party. Today you are our guest." She squeezed his arm. But the purchase had been noted, and as she wandered between the wooden stalls, other samples were sliced and offered. She particularly liked the savoury pie made with egg and specks of cured meat, good and dense and covered in crusty pastry.

"Pastone," Orazio said, "a traditional Christmas pie."

He was beginning to relax. He walked on ahead, she dawdled behind, making quite a stir with the eager sellers, accepting samples here and there, capturing little asides, remarks about her shape, her hat, the way she walked, nods and grins and jokes, and she let it all happen, she didn't mind, she played along with it—nothing wrong with being a woman.

Over near the wall of the church, almost hidden behind the stalls, a young girl was standing, eyes lowered, as if she didn't want to be seen. In front of her was a little tray of homemade pastries with fruit and jam fillings. Frieda saw her. She watched for a minute, something murmuring in her heart. The girl was pretty, long wavy dark hair, and she had taken care to look nice, too nice for the market.

Frieda made her way over. The girl looked up, startled, her cheeks reddening slightly, as if she was embarrassed at being discovered there, and a deep motherly tenderness welled up in Frieda's breast. She stood for a few seconds, then smiled her special dimpled smile and pointed to the little pastries, and the girl pronounced the names slowly for the foreign lady . . . albicocca . . . amarena . . . mirtillo.

Frieda repeated the names and indicated one of each. The girl wrapped them carefully. She lifted the little packets in the palm of her hand for the lady to take, and just for a few seconds their hands touched, and Frieda would have given anything to take them in hers, to hold them to her, to touch the sad young face. Their eyes met, dark brown ones and soft green ones—the lioness heart, so brave, but so easily torn open. How many times Lorenzo had seen it! She overpaid and hurried quickly away before the girl could count the money.

Orazio was standing at a stall, talking oranges, happily tasting juicy slices, wiping his fingers on his handkerchief, certain of her presence close by. Now was her chance. She slipped away down the alleyway, conversations tailing off as she approached and starting up again when she was past, eyes following her, but she was immune now. She walked quickly, occasionally glancing over her shoulder, until, not looking where she was going, there was a sudden impact, and she almost toppled backward as she bounced off the bulging aproned belly of a big peasant woman coming the other way, stout and fearless, a pleated scarf tied over her wiry grey hair.

"Scusi . . . Scusi . . ." Frieda recovered herself, breathlessly begging her pardon and making a sort of apologetic smile. But she had done little damage to the mountain woman, who straightened her scarf and lumbered on, nodding her head and muttering.

She hurried on through the arch and down the slope. Here in the open area of crossroad and fountain, carts were starting to trundle away. She was looking for one she had seen as they walked past earlier. It was still there. Standing behind it was a frail little man in a baggy suit, an old scuffed trilby hat on his head, a threadbare feather in the hatband, his stubbly face hollow and veiny. A burned down cigarette hung from his lip, the smoke rising heedlessly into his eyes. He puffed, coughed, ash fell, but his bony hands just went on carving and filing and gouging. He held up the little wooden figurine, blew the sawdust off, and started again.

Frieda stood a yard or two away and watched. He took no notice. She stepped up to the stall and gave him a little nod. He went on carving, coughing through the cigarette smoke.

There hadn't been anyone round his stall earlier, and it was the same now, as if it wasn't quite there, in its own world. She was happy not to be jostled or assailed. She leaned forward and peered at the wooden toys and figures lying on the brown oilcloth. The little man looked at her vaguely through watery eyes, put down his tools and stood back, puffing at his cigarette and fingering a metal watch chain that hung between the pockets of his thread-bare waistcoat.

Frieda pointed to one of the larger pieces on a little stand, a model boat about a foot long, an ocean liner with two funnels and a rudder and even a small iron propeller. He gave an imperceptible nod. She picked it up off its stand, examined it for a minute, then held it up and moved it through the air as if was on a wavy sea. He nodded—yes it would float. She put it to one side and fingered some of the other little pieces, a Garibaldi with a yellow beard and red shirt, a St. Anthony with infant Jesus, figures for the Christmas crib, a kneeling Madonna, Child in a manger, St. Joseph, angels, shepherds, lowing cows and a half-finished turbaned king, and there were other toys too. Frieda picked up a doll, but put it quickly down, a sudden ache inside. She took a deep breath and tried again. There was a nice little spinning top painted with fishes and birds, a waxed string round the narrow handle to whirl it. She picked this up, admiring the designs, then carefully put it next to the ship. The little man stood the while, thumbs in his shabby grey waistcoat pockets, puffing at his cigarette, impassive, as knotty and angular and ligneous as his little figurines.

She could have spoken, she knew a bit of Italian, but there was a sort of spell on it all which she didn't want to break, a sort of silent dialogue. She tapped the two toys with a finger and raised her hands to ask how much. The little hollow man looked at the pieces thoughtfully for a minute, then raised a few bony digits. To Frieda it seemed not very much. Orazio had said always to bargain, never to accept the first price, but she didn't want to bargain, why should she, she didn't want to grind him down, he looked half-starved already, and anyway, since their last visit before the war, everything was so much cheaper in Italy, the lira had devalued considerably.

She nodded. He looked down at his veined hands for a minute, turning them over and back again, as if they had a separate life, as if they too were part of the cast of wooden characters. He bent slowly down, reached under the stall, and lifted out some old pieces of cloth and string and started to wrap the purchases.

Frieda counted the coins out of her purse and placed them in two little piles next to Garibaldi. She made an attempt at a faint smile, but the sallow old face had just the one expression. He put the packets on the counter top. She waited for him to count the coins, but he didn't. He seemed hardly to have noticed them. She picked up the packets and turned to go when something caught her eye underneath a pile of paper. It was a box with a hinged lid, like a large cigar box, but bigger.

She put the packages down again, moved the paper aside and lifted the box up. It was lovely to the touch, warm from the earth, with the sensuous flowing vein of olive wood, the hinges in copper. She opened and closed the lid a couple of times, passing her fingers over the smooth striated surface. She held it out to him. He didn't move, just gazed. She put the box down and gestured with her hands—how much. Still he didn't move. She dug some coins from her purse and stretched out her palm for him to take some. He shrugged, his arms immobile by his side. She counted out some coins, looked at him, added a couple more, and placed them carefully next to Garibaldi's other booty.

Cigarette smoke drifted up. The little man stood, thumbs in waistcoat pockets, eyes glazed, almost absent. Frieda picked up the olive box and the toys and pushed them into the big leather satchel on her shoulder, a hunting bag for dead game from Orazio's chest. She had her woodcocks and her pheasants now.

She took a step back from the stall, stood for a few seconds, then gave him a little nod — a bit Prussian she thought, and she laughed to herself, but it just suited the moment, and then, as if a lever had been pressed, the little man's bony hand fumbled for the old feathered hat on his head and raised it jerkily and up and down. Frieda beamed, almost laughed, it reminded her of the little mechanical figure on the top of a musical box her father had bought her as a child one Christmas, which would lift its arm in clockwork salute to the tinkling sound of a Prussian march.

Happy — as happy and pleased as she had been since arriving — she wandered back through the emptying market, her mood carrying her benignly and aimlessly here and there. She found herself in front of the grimy little cavern-like bar, Grazia's place, and she noticed for the first time a faded sign over the door — The Post Restaurant it said — and this made her smile too, the idea of it having the sobriquet of restaurant. She hovered outside, the taste of burnt black coffee hanging in the cold air. A celebratory cup of the bitter elixir would go down well— complete the adventure. She stepped up to the entrance and peered into the sulphurous glowing interior. Dark faces peered back. Maybe she would wait for Orazio. But where was he? He hadn't come searching for her.

She wandered around, stopping to watch at a stall where some cages with rabbits and ducks were being loaded onto a cart. In her expansive mood, the impulse to buy a pair of ducks for Orazio's farmyard came on her, but she managed to quell it. Where would they swim, down on the torrent? She moved on, her encounter with the wooden man still playing in her mind—and she was already telling Lorenzo all about it.

The leather bag weighed satisfyingly on her shoulder. She

walked on through the groups of dispersing contadini with a sort of assurance now. They weren't that bad. Orazio exaggerated. Orazio's problem was Orazio. She sighed, a surge of generosity and friendliness rising up in her, and she looked about her, hoping perhaps to exchange a smile with one of them, maybe even say Buongiorno, and the thought came to her again—how would it be if they were to stay? When the snows melted it must be very beautiful. It was beautiful now.

At the edge of the market square she stopped and gazed. In the far distance the village of the woodpecker hovered above the mist. In a valley deep below, a man with a red beard crouched in front of the fire watching the little licks of blue and yellow flame.

The market was almost empty now. She glanced across in the direction of the little toymaker's stand, but he was no longer there, and her soft greenish eyes widened with half-remembered child-hood tales of magical elfin folk who made toys in caves. And when she got home, she would open her bag, and there would be one extra figure, a little wooden man with a hat and a feather, smoking a cigarette and carving a toy.

Where was Orazio? She wandered up the slope towards the arch, and was just about to pass through it when a wide barrow piled with sacks of vegetables came rumbling down in the oppo-site direction, an old man and old woman hanging on behind, trying to bring it to a halt. But it was gathering speed, getting away from them, and the old man's hat flew off as he ran, and he grabbed vainly at thin air, unable let go the wagon, and he cursed a stream of saints, and the old woman cursed him, and Frieda had to jump out of the way as the mad chariot rumbled past, till finally, some men sprang forward and hauled it to a halt.

From somewhere on the other side of the arch there was a yapping of little dogs, excited by all the commotion. Frieda walked through and glanced over. A few feet away by some stone steps, a man was crouching down on his heels stroking a little puppy. There was a cage with other puppies, sleepy-eyed little creatures all curled up round each other, one or two of the more lively ones bouncing up with their paws against the inside of the cage, still yapping and wanting to play. An old man was sitting on a low stool, poking his fingers into the cage, feeding in bits of dry bread, the puppies jumbling over each other, nipping at the fingers and the crusts.

Frieda stopped and watched. The crouching man took the puppy to his chest, stroking it and muttering to it. The little creature trembled and dabbed with its paw at the enclosing hands, its black wet muzzle nosing and sniffing, large eyes peering uncertainly at its new friend with a mixture of curiosity, hopefulness, and maybe already just a little love. Frieda walked over and stood looking down. The man became aware of her presence and glanced up at her with an expression she hadn't seen before.

"Isn't he beautiful!" he said. He came to his feet, still holding the little creature in his arms, stroking it all the while and looking into its face.

"He is a wolf, a great big wolf," he said, squeezing the little face, so that the animal yelped and pawed at his hand. "You are a terrible fierce wolf aren't you!" He raised the little creature high above his head. It whimpered with fear, and kicked its legs in the air till he brought it back down again.

"A wolf?" she said with just the hint of credulity. "No, he is a lovely orange colour, and white and soft, and look at his little tail," and she joined in the stroking, feeling its back and legs like someone who understood the canine race.

"What, not a wolf..?" Orazio held it up again, the little paws scrambling in fright. "So tell me the truth, are you a wolf or not?" He brought it down again into his arms. "No, he is not a wolf. He is a bracco."

"Bracco. I've never heard of a bracco," she said.

Orazio scratched at the furry soft stomach.

"Shall we tell her? Shall we? Shall we tell her what a bracco is?" He squeezed its little face again. "We will have fun together won't we! We will go hunting you and I, and we shall chase off the big wolves when they come prowling through the woods, and in the spring we shall catch hares, and I shall stew them, and you shall have half, and in the evenings we will smoke a pipe together, and you shall have a lovely basket to sleep in," and as he spoke, the old dog seller nodded long and sagely, understanding nothing but nodding anyway. Orazio dug in his pocket and handed over some money.

"But you haven't told me what breed a bracco is," Frieda said.

"Shall you tell her or shall I?" The puppy nestled in the crook of his arm. He held it near his ear, pretending to listen to it. "He says a bracco is an old Italian hunting dog."

On the way back in the cart, Orazio was almost happy. No, Orazio was happy. She had never seen him without something of that forlorn look on his face, even the donkey benefited from his change of mood, allowed to walk on at its own pace without the flicking reins, although it never did get the promised carrot.

They left the cart at the inn and made their way back along the road and down towards the torrent, Orazio talking all the while to the puppy in his arms. He put it on the cold ground and walked off, the little creature shivering and staring after him. Orazio stopped and turned.

"Why are you waiting? Lunch is getting cold," and the puppy came scampering after, and Orazio scooped him up again.

The donkey trotted on ahead and crossed the torrent with ease, looking back at the hopeless stragglers with nodding disapproval. But Orazio wanted more play, and he put the little animal down on a sandy bank in the middle of the torrent and jumped over to the next islet.

"Come along now Leighton," Orazio called from across the sea, his face all pretend sternness, "brave hunting dogs have to leap over big rivers."

The little creature whined, touched its paw at the edge of the fast freezing waters, and looked over helplessly at his unpredictable new companion.

Orazio put his hands on his hips. "Ah, I see, you don't speak English. Then you will have to learn. You will be the only English dog around here, apart from me." He jumped back over and scooped the puppy up, explaining the duties that would be expected of him.

In the kitchen all was quiet, just the hiss of a log in the fire. They dropped the foodstuffs on the table. Orazio picked up the pig's cauldron, poured some leftovers onto a plate, and put it on the floor for Lord Leighton.

Frieda went softly up the stairs and stood for a while staring out of the landing windows. There was a stillness over the house, as if quietness had been decreed and mustn't be disturbed. She wondered if he had gone out for a walk, but then she heard a cough and opened the door of the bedroom. The scribe was at his table, just as she had left him. He went on writing without looking up. She flopped down on the bed and lay there, arms outstretched, staring up at the ceiling.

"I will have to think about it," he said after a while, his head still in his papers. He finished scribbling and put his pen down.

"About what?" she asked sleepily.

"About what you are just about to ask me?"

"She sat up and stared across at him. "I forgot I was married to a wizard."

He waved a hand in acknowledgement.

"So could you . . . could you live here if it was springtime and sunny? Could you?"

He looked at her with a quizzical half smile.

"And where did all this come from? You, who have been saying you want to leave, that the mountains are all jagged and fearful and tearing at you, and that you can't wait to get to the sea."

She shrugged. "I think you could write here."

He stood up and stretched, then came and stood over the bed, looking down at her with a thoughtful stare.

"Your eyes are bright, sparkling. They look as if they have the sea in them already. Yes, I can hear the waves, I can see fishing boats with red sails."

"Not yet, not yet, not yet the sea."

He smiled. "I shall write that down." He leaned over and passed his hand over her hair and down over her eyes and face. "What 'ast 'er been doin' at market all this time? Gallivanting I should say! Can't let 'er out of my sight a minute . . . don't know who t'is 'ull come back."

She gave him a little frown.

"The market was wonderful . . . So could you stay?"

He sat back down again at his desk and scribbled the phrase . . . Not yet the sea.

"Well?" she said after a minute.

"Well? . . . No escaping the siren . . . Could I stay? Perhaps, but I fear it would reject us eventually."

"Not the house. The house is different don't you think."

"Maybe. But if Orazio's words are anything to go by . . ."

She jumped up from the bed.

"No, no, not that . . . I don't want to hear that anymore, not today, not ever, never more. Today is Frieda's day, and Frieda commands all negative thoughts to cease, and she commands that everyone must dress in their best gowns and uniforms, for today she is throwing a grand ball," and with that, she took the hand of an imaginary partner and danced away to the sound of The Blue Danube Waltz, a young debutante once more, whirling around the seated man, fluttering her eyelids at him with each pass. She stopped, bowed her head to her imaginary partner, then turned to the seated man and curtseyed to him.

"Does the Kaiser think I dance well?"

He twirled his moustaches. "You are ze von Richthofen girl are you not!" he said in his best German accent. She nodded demurely. "You danz very well my dear, and as a revard, the Kaiser vill let you zit on his knee."

He patted his lap. She gathered her imaginary ball gown and sat down.

"I understand my dear that you are a lover of the sea, so let me provide some waves for you." He made big lascivious eyes at her, and rocked his legs around so that she swayed about, and the young debutante wrapped her arms round the Kaiser's neck to stop herself from falling off, smiling flirtatiously.

"Now which sea is it you wish to go to my dear? I have a very nice Jutland one with charming Frisian Islands where I keep my yacht. Would you like to come aboard my yacht?" He puckered his lips and stroked her hair, ". . . Such a pretty little thing . . ."

"The Kaiser is too kind, but I must tell him that I am engaged to an Englishman."

"What . . . an Englishman! This is terrible. What is his name?

"Bert."

"I have a cousin called Bertie. I do not like him either. I might have to go to war over this."

"Like Helen of Troy."

The bellicose Kaiser laughed, and Helen of Troy gave him a peck on the cheek and swung herself off his knee.

"I will come on your boat, but in the meantime I would be honoured if the Kaiser would grace my grand ball this evening with his presence."

She patted him on the head, then went over to the bed, picked up the hunting bag and took out her purchases.

"What do you think? . . . For the children."

He nodded. "But did I hear yapping when you came in, like a small dog?"

"Ah yes, our first guest has arrived . . . Lord Leighton in person."

"Sorry, I thought you said Lord Leighton." He poked a finger in his ear. "He isn't carrying a cross is he . . . not about to tie poor old Orazio to it again?"

"He is the new member of the household. Orazio bought him in the market . . . there he was, clutching this little creature, talking to it. You should have seen him, quite another Orazio. I think our company has made him awaken to his loneliness. Now he will have someone to talk to when we are gone at least."

"And he has called it Lord Leighton?" Lorenzo laughed and

wheezed. "Oh that is too much . . . Now My Lord, if you want to earn your supper, you will have to stand on your hind legs while I paint you."

"No, I think the old hierarchy is still in place. His lordship is already in command. Orazio loves him."

"Does it resemble his lordship? Does it look like his photo on the stairs?"

"Identical."

She put the toys back in the bag and came and sat down again on his knee. He put his head on her shoulder, nuzzling into her, pretending to be a puppy, and she stroked his neck and tousled his hair.

"You know, I could see you from right across the other side of the valley," she said, caressing his neck still, "I could see many things from over there."

He sat quietly for a while, eyes half closed, letting her hand wander. "Oh yes, Giovanni came in when you had gone . . ."

"And..?"

"He was agitated . . ."

"Stop it. Tell me."

"Agnese will come."

Frieda made a little whoop and kissed him on the nose.

"At least I think that's what he said."

"You think?" she asked, suddenly alarmed.

"You know how difficult it is to understand him . . . but he was nodding a lot so I think it was a yes."

She gave his ear a little tweak. "That is for teasing me. And she will bring the children?"

"Yes, and the children."

"I knew they would come. Orazio said they wouldn't, but I knew, I knew, I knew," and she jumped up and started to dance around the room again with little whoops of victory.

"Frieda Victrix," he muttered, almost to himself. But she heard.

"I am she, I am she . . . Frieda Victrix . . ." and she gyrated away, singing out her new roundelay," . . . and I am Anna, and I am Ursula, and I am Gudrun, I am all the colours of the rainbow, and I am life . . ."

And the Will Brangwen in Lorenzo felt the passion for his Frieda Victrix, and he grabbed at her spinning waltzing shape and pulled her towards him and onto the bed, and for a while there was just the rustling of the corn sheaths in the mattress.

"Now I don't want to stop," she said through her hot breath. "You shouldn't have. I have to go down and help Orazio."

But he wouldn't let her go. She struggled with him, with herself, pulling away, surrendering again, pulling away.

"Don't worry about Orazio, Lord Leighton will take care of him," he whispered.

She jumped up and skipped out of the door, swaying dizzily, and laughing.

Chapter Twenty-seven

"Sant'Antonio . . . Sant'Antonio . . ."

The old model stood by the hearth stirring a big pot over the fire and muttering to himself, torn between the novelty of it all and an ancient resistance. Agnese had set foot in his house perhaps twice, once with her husband before the war, and now the second time when she had brought the wine the other evening.

Agnese, widowed, and still young. The villagers would know, they always got to know, nothing could be kept secret here, then they would talk, make up stories, tell versions of their own that sounded like the truth but weren't, then they would say — Ha! You see, you see what he is like. You know what they said about him in London, you've heard the stories haven't you . . . and he is such a grand signore . . . so far above us . . . and who knows what that English couple get up to!

He stirred the pot and looked over at Frieda as if she might make some sudden dispensation and call it all off, but an early glass or two of Strega calmed his nerves, and he rebuked himself — What should he care! He threw back his old shoulders and thought about what he would wear. He had just the thing.

Giovanni came in. Frieda made sure he understood he was a guest too. He looked at his brother for confirmation of this strange status, but Orazio just kept on with what he was doing. Later he sent him to Agnese's house to accompany her and the children back up the hill.

Lorenzo appeared. He hovered round the kitchen but didn't offer to help. Today was Frieda's day. So be it. He stood back and watched, enjoying the unusual experience of getting in her way, till one or two sharp looks soon convinced him that he best leave the field, and he sneaked outside into the glowing early darkness.

By the old walnut tree he stopped. It had a comfortable curve in it at just the right height to lean against, and sometimes he would stop and lean and listen. He leant against it now. A last solitary fruit was hanging from a branch just above his head. He hadn't noticed it before. He reached up and picked it, and as he did so he felt his eye being drawn back to the lighted kitchen window and the shadowy play of movement inside. He walked back over and peered in, watching the soundless ballet, the two figures moving about and around each other. And as he watched, the perspective changed, and another woman was going about her chores, a young English woman, but in her eyes there was a distance, and in her soul an emptiness, and in her belly a child . . .

He had been thinking of her earlier while the others were at the market, but he hadn't seen this—Alvina was with child. But all was not right. Where was he, the dark intense physical being who had spoken to a place inside her, who had brought her all the way from England to this remote mountain lair? Where was he, the father of the child? It wasn't that he was just outside of the room, no, he was not there, his soul was absent, it was written in her eyes. He was gone. She was alone with the old uncle. What could have brought this about?

The man at the window puzzled. He watched them as they went about their tasks, the young fairish English woman and the old uncle, lines of handsomeness still etched in his aging face, just each other for company now. They seemed not to want to look into the other's eyes, just kept themselves busy, hiding their thoughts, pretending all was well, or that all would be well, she with her English optimism and fortitude, and he, as best he could, making endless cups of tea, telling her stories and anecdotes about his time in London as a model, anything to keep them from talking about the one thing that was on both their minds. But it was there, even the man at the window could hear it, a permanent background dialogue that wouldn't go away.

What had happened? She had left that other life, given everything up, forfeited the certainty and dignity of a comfortable middle-class English existence, had come all this way to a place that was beyond, blindly, fearlessly, trustingly, and for what? It couldn't just finish like this. He wouldn't have gone back to England without her, she wasn't an Italian wife.

The man at the window stood back a minute, his mind wandering over the events of the last few days, looking for clues, listening to the talk, all they had discussed, of war and patriotism, of D'Annunzio and the new Italy. He put a finger on the glass and wrote something on it . . . Italia Irredenta. He had his ending—her dark man had been taken by the winds of war, called up, marched away, but not before he had sewn a seed in her.

Now all she could do was sit and wait, sip tea, listen to the old uncle's stories, hear in his voice the wistful longing for a past that would never return to him, while she, a child growing in her belly, wanting nothing of her past, but longing for a future that might now never come, her fate in the hands of the gods, those ancient gods that knew the right of human sacrifice. And if their gaze fell on her, if they decided to demand that ultimate sacrifice, what then! If one day she looked out the window to see the old postman trudging across the snow, that expression on his face that he had had to rehearse so many times now—the official communication. What then?

The man at the window turned away. In his hand he still held the lone walnut. He threw it across the snow into the silent darkness, and made a wish, that when the spring came it would take root.

He walked from the house to the foot of the escarpment and

started to climb, grasping at shrubs and roots to pull himself up through the snow, hands and face tingling, and soon he found himself quite high and almost lost in the circling silent crystal woods.

The climb had warmed him. He stood by an old thin oak and ran his hand up and down the rough bark. He scraped a seam of ice off a low branch and rubbed it into his beard and face and hair, then scraped off some more and put it in his mouth, letting it dissolve on his tongue. Overhead, a half-hidden moon lit through the clouds in a prism of glowing colour, and as he stood there, a strange sensation came over him, that he was somehow melting away, standing outside of himself. He didn't resist it, just let it envelop him. He wondered whether death was like this, a sort of awareness without thought. Then, close-by, he heard something move, deep heavy and slow, soft breath blowing. He kept quite still, willing it closer, and then there it was, there it was, great swept-back horns, magnificent, full of presence and owner-ship, lifting its head, scenting the air, black eyes widening—a mountain ibex.

At the very centre of a circle of trees, it stopped. It knew he was there, was curious of him, just as he was of it, a sort of mutual thrall. Its heavy breath billowed in the icy air, and he felt his own breath falling into the same deep rhythm. It stepped closer, a soft vapour rising off its powerful flanks, head raised, kingly, and just for an instant their eyes met, then it stepped away through the trees and was gone.

Chapter Twenty-eight

FRIEDA HAD TIED A THIN RED VELVETY RIBBON THROUGH her hair, and she was made up just a little. She was wearing a long white cotton shirt with a red and gold thread pattern round the neck, Indian, and over this a heavy necklace of dark carnelian she had had from her grandmother. He watched her through the window, the Christmas hostess sending out good will to all men, filling the room, holding centre stage, making exaggerated gestures, her eyes slanting in a permanent smile that made them even more Mongol, but he could see too the hidden displeasure that he wasn't there to help things on, that he had done his usual disappearing trick.

The two children, polished and neat and tidy, sat by the fire, watching, a little blue homespun wool jacket and knee-length breeches on the boy, the girl in a grey skirt with shoulder straps over a dark red blouse, their best. Agnese, the mother, stood behind them, hands on their shoulders, a grown version of her daughter and wearing the same outfit, the only difference being her blouse, olive green and buttoned to the neck with a little cameo brooch. Frieda had recognised her immediately—the young woman at the back of the chapel the other evening. Agnese too had recognised Frieda, had known who she was even in the chapel. It was obvious. They both knew the other knew but neither of them said. It was like a secret of the confessional.

Orazio hovered around the table. It was mostly laid already. Over the fire a big pot of polenta simmered. The old model had shaved, and was looking quite splendid in a blue velvet jacket, white shirt, and florid silk cravat—what company of high-spirited Bloomsbury revellers might drop in later, Lorenzo wondered? Only Giovanni was himself, furry half-jacket and skin leggings, seated on a low stool in a corner at the far end of the kitchen away from the privileged fire, allowing himself a minimum of space.

The absentee pushed the door open. All heads turned. Frieda came at him with a smiling rush, hands outstretched to the late arrival—the person of note she had almost given up on. He recognised the sequence, it was an entrance they had used in one of their impromptu theatricals back in London, a take-off of an Oscar Wilde play.

But there was an unforeseen prop this time, a trailing harvest of green leaves and berry-laden twigs that the late guest held in front of him, and that protected him from her welcoming assault, long strands of variegated ivy, branches of holly, a small juniper, mistletoe, and sundry other bits of evergreen that had caught his fancy up in the dark woods. Only a fine pair of antlers were missing from his head.

The children looked up, legs swinging under their chairs. They looked back over their shoulders to their mother, then back again at the apparition. The green man with the red beard bustled himself in, Frieda unravelling strands of his winter cornucopia, laying them on the table and floor, stringing lengths of ivy round her head and neck, and spinning round in a little dance.

The green man brushed himself down, then straightened himself up and cast large eyes around the room as if he was looking for someone in the throng, till they came to rest on the children, and he made a funny face and waved at them.

"We must decorate the room for our Christmas party," he announced. "Bambini," he called to the children, "Venite . . . Natale inglese. Orazio, you explain. You can be Santa. Tell them about the holly and the ivy and Christmas decorations. Frieda, let's put this little juniper plant into a pot. It can be the Christmas tree."

Frieda beamed — festive festooning — she knew he'd invent something. Clever man-of-the-woods—late arrival forgiven.

Orazio started to explain to the children, but he needn't have, they had already jumped from their chairs and were following Frieda around, trailing the greenery, hanging it here and there, plaiting the holly, twisting it around the iron candlestick in the middle of the table and so on, and she gave them more handfuls, and they were off again, looking across occasionally to their mother for approval, and then she too joined in. Giovanni was sent to find a pot for the little juniper. He came back with an iron bucket, and they wedged the plant in with bits of log.

Frieda ran upstairs, and came down a moment later with sheets of paper which she had been passing the time earlier daubing with colours and designs. She cut them into thin strips and hung them over the branches of the juniper, she cut out a star from a sheet of yellow-painted paper and placed it at the top of the tree.

Orazio stood, one hand in the pocket of his velvet jacket to just the right depth, his drawing-room pose, cravat nicely plumped, smiling benignly, the gracious host. Lorenzo held himself to one side. There were enough helpers. Then he caught a little movement he knew, Frieda, admiring her star, suddenly turned her face away for a few seconds, hand to her mouth, a little catch in her breath, then turned back again, smiling, but her eyes had moistened slightly.

It was the right moment, and with a great show he entered the fray, following them all around, peering at the handiwork, a little buffoonish, getting his hand caught in some strands of holly and calling for help so that the children were drawn to come and rescue him.

He picked up a chair, clunked it down noisily near the tree and climbed up onto it, bringing all the attention towards him, waving his arms around and wobbling slightly on purpose. He regained his balance, raised his arms to command silence and cleared his throat.

"Un inno di natale," he announced, "a Christmas carol." He closed his eyes for a moment, composed himself, and with his slightly high voice, started to sing . . .

"The holly and the ivy,
When they are both full grown,
Of all the trees that are in the wood,
The holly bears the crown . . ."

And he sang through the verses, and Frieda blew her nose, and rubbed the carol singer's legs up and down in grateful encouragement. She took some leftover strands of greenery, and as he sang, she draped them round his legs and feet, and the children watched it all in wonder, and it all felt so just right—a jolly English carol in such a place as this. Orazio gazed around and wondered that such a merry English time was being had in his old house. How he missed it all!

". . . Sweet singing of the choir."

The carol singer bowed. Frieda clapped, an exaggerated smile on her face, fighting it all back, and the others clapped too. Lorenzo bowed again, surveying all below, Jove-like, till his eyes fell on Giovanni. The little man was fiddling with the juniper tree, quite needlessly, it was well wedged in, but he needed something to do.

Lorenzo held his arms aloft.

"Sono il re . . . I am the king," he pronounced. There was something for everyone in Lorenzo's repertory. Giovanni's head twitched round. He stared up at the man-king, and he let himself stare, careless of his brother's displeasure.

The carol singer climbed down off his plinth, trailing bits of holly. It had had the effect he wanted, the children's faces were animated, and they were asking questions of their mother, fascinated by this bizarre world of foreign adults. Frieda had peeled some of the oranges and lemons from the market, and was slicing the skins into long strands and giving them to the children, who understood immediately, and went around twining them in among the greenery, while she cut other pieces into stars and pinned them onto the Christmas juniper.

She stood back to admire her work, and nodded to herself. She turned and signalled that they should all gather round the tree. Lorenzo had placed it on the little window table to give it some height. Agnese shepherded the children across. Only Giovanni was beyond recall, staring into the fire.

Frieda went round the room blowing out the candles, all except one, which she carried processionally over to the tree, shielding the little solitary flame with her hand. She stood there, eyes closed for a minute, the candle flickering. The children's eyes wandered from face to face. Then she started to sing in a thin pure voice, another voice, the voice of her childhood, of all those Christmases of long ago that glittered and glowed, silver and bright, innocent still of what was to come . . .

"Stille Nacht, heilige Nacht,
Alles schlaft, einsam wacht . . ."

The little orange flame guttered and dipped, the voice of the young girl floated, and Lorenzo knew that at that very moment, in that little place, forgotten by time, a sort of redemption was taking place, that the world that had turned against them with a will to destroy them, had been thrown back—he and his Frieda, somehow, impossibly. The blood that raged and loved and hated and brought forth new life, had carried all before it, triumphant, holy, burning, physical—a pure small voice and the light of a flickering candle.

He looked around him at the little circle of souls, children, widow, mountain man, model, the woman who sang. Hither they had come, he and his Frieda, not knowing quite why, and now they would go, not knowing quite where, but one thing he did know, she was the very essence of his being, the sound of his thoughts, and that without her there would be only the life of a wandering ghost.

". . . Jesus der Retter ist da."

The words floated away into the new holy silence. There was

no applause, just long sighs. They moved back around the room, quietly, Orazio ruffling the little boy's hair and telling a story about when he was little, of Christmases of old, and how the bears would come and knock at the door, and they would give them sweets, and the bears would sing, and then the wolves would howl in the mountains because they were laughing at the out-of-tune bears.

"It was beautiful, nay . . . my childhood, my Germany!" She was still holding the candle. She looked around for somewhere to put it, and wedged it in between strands of ivy.

He took her hands in his and looked fiercely into her eyes—his soul surging. She smiled, but her lips quivered. She looked away, trying to release herself from his gaze, from his hands, not because she wanted to but because she didn't.

"Stay with me." He squeezed her hands harder till they hurt, his voice a rasping whisper.

There was a sudden intake of breath, a constriction in her throat. "Don't make me weep, not here."

He looked down at the floor.

"Silent Night . . . Silent for me . . . Silent forever." He spoke softly. "You know, when I was in Florence waiting for you, I thought perhaps you might not come, might never come, that you might stay in Germany with your family . . . that you would decide that you had had enough. Then I would have been here by myself, alone, silent." He paused for a moment. "Stay . . . You will stay won't you."

"Will you?" she said, halfway between a smile and a sob.

There was a quietness in the room, the children played and whispered, Agnese busied herself around the table, Orazio leaned against the mantelpiece fingering a cheroot, the little man picked pieces of left over twigs and leaves off the floor and dropped them into the fire to watch the shooting flares of colour.

"Capri, it awaits." He held her hands in his, not letting her escape.

"Do they have lemons there?"

"Bitter lemons . . . the sort we thrive on . . . But you know, I think I like the mountains in a fearful sort of way."

"You should be a composer."

He smiled suddenly.

"Let us play a game."

"What game?"

"Not now . . . later . . . on a piece of paper . . . the yes or no game."

"And what is the question?"

". . . Will you stay? . . . Then we exchange the pieces of paper . . ." He blushed with a sort of boyishness.

She pulled her hands away.

"Why do you doubt me, or is it that you doubt yourself?"

He sighed and looked away, confused now himself. He hadn't meant it like that, he hadn't meant really anything. He didn't know why he had said it.

Take what you want from me, I am yours, he had said to her once. He poured himself into her the way he poured himself into his writing. His soul raged, it gave of itself the only way it knew how, entirely, sacramentally, and she received it into her. Without her, he was fire without air.

She rubbed the back of her hand over his eyes and face. "I know you don't doubt me . . . not really."

"It was in your voice, your singing . . . so beautiful, so much sorrow, so much loss . . . and I saw myself alone and without you, and it was unbearable . . . and if you hadn't come," he continued, "if I had been here by myself I think I would have died . . . died and been buried in a tomb of snow up there on the hillside, shovelled over by Giovanni, nothing to mark the place, just wind and silence and the passing of time."

Her hand jerked suddenly to her face. She covered her mouth and stared at him for a moment, then she started to laugh, her eyes shutting, shoulders shaking, and she couldn't stop, and then he started to laugh too, until they had let a good bit out of all the tension, and it subsided.

". . . But there was no need for you to be here by yourself," she said, when she had recovered herself, "if I had stayed in Germany you could have come here with Magnus. You and your friend Maurice, together, here. Imagine that!"

He laid his head on her shoulder, more little gusts of laughter rippling from his stomach, and she hugged him to her, and the children watched. Agnese's dark intelligent eyes turned away so as not to intrude, and by chance caught Orazio staring at her in a sort of dream. Startled, he looked away.

"My Friend! . . . Magnus! Oh the very thought . . . One thing is certain though, we wouldn't have been short of the olfactory if he had been here . . . all those silver-topped bottles of scents and essences and powders and pomades and I don't know what else that he must cover himself with . . . the puffed-up little pontiff . . . and he would have made me pay for a first class rail ticket for himself, like he did with the money I leant him in Florence, while I would have had to travel third class for lack of funds—his valet."

"Four seasons in one day, that is us, like the English weather." She stroked his hair, then played her fingers over it like raindrops.

"You know, when I was up in the woods this evening, something happened . . ."

But just then, the elegant host in his blue velvet jacket, cleared his throat, stepped forward, and gestured towards the table.

"Dinner is served . . . a tavola."

It was a sort of buffet, there was half a pastone — the Christmas pie made with egg and ham — the finely-sliced prosciutto, a chunk of parmesan, small artichokes and dried tomatoes in olive oil, the rough country bread. Agnese had brought an offering too, some dried fruits and a pie with ricotta cheese, and there were Frieda's pastries, the ones she had bought off the young girl in the market. But the centre piece was Orazio's polenta.

He had introduced Frieda to the secret art of polenta making — stir the coarse golden flour constantly, because if you didn't, it formed little lumps, and around here they called the lumps preti, priests, and you didn't want any priests in the house, or in the polenta. To go with it, he had made a wild boar sauce which had simmered away in a big cauldron over the fire, not the pig's cauldron of course, you couldn't cook a wild pig in the domestic pig's pot—it would know.

The blue velvet baronet tucked a towel into his shirt collar to protect it from splashes, scooped the steaming polenta out with a ladle and poured it onto the plates, a helping of the rich tomato sauce, a piece of wild boar, a spoonful or two of grated pecorino cheese . . . Of course the proper way to eat polenta, he explained, was to pour it onto long wooden boards in the middle of the table, one continuous layer about half an inch thick, a covering of sauce, smooth it over, and then everyone would sit down and eat whatever was in front of them, getting closer and closer to the person opposite, or else to your neighbour, depending on preference. This was the real polentata.

Lorenzo was all for trying instantly, but the host's blue velvet jacket with braid edges did not permit of such rustic behaviour. No, they would use the new plates they had bought at the market, it was probably the last time they'd be used, he said. When his guests were gone they would just sit on the shelf, gathering dust.

Frieda fingered the edge of her plate, revolving it slowly on the table. She wished she could do something for him. Still, for now he was happy. Giovanni was served last. Orazio passed him a plate, accompanied by a stern look, and the little man took himself off to the far corner, sat on a stool, watched the others and tried to copy them, blowing on the hot spoonful and sipping.

Orazio had dug into his reserve of white wine, the light, local, golden-white Maturano he kept for special occasions. Lorenzo did the honours and poured the glasses while the old model served. Finally, Orazio too settled at the table with his plate. He was just lifting his spoon to his mouth when he became aware of Frieda's eyes on him. He stopped in mid-air and looked back. She smiled, and made a gesture with her spoon as if to say how good it was, but she was thinking about something else. He nodded, and looked round at his guests with a feeling of well-being, almost of gratitude, as if his little villa had been built just for this, that it was finally a home, and just for a second, across the room he thought he saw another figure sitting quietly, his poor Teresa, and for once he had no fear, just an ache—she was still young and he was old.

He put down his spoon, took out his monogrammed hand-kerchief and blew his nose. He cleared his throat and raised his glass. "Buon natale a tutti . . . Happy Christmas to everyone."

"Buon natale . . . Auguri," came the responses around the table, and there was much clinking of glasses, and Frieda gave a greeting in German, and Lorenzo, not to be outdone, became Alfred Lord Tennyson, and delivered a few lines from one of his poems . . . "Ring out, wild bells, to the wild sky, The flying cloud, the frosty light . . ." It didn't matter that it was an in memoriam.

Orazio put his hands behind his head, leaned back in his chair and beamed, and the poet laureate delivered some more lines . . . "Ring, happy bells, across the snow . . . Ring in the Christ that is to be."

Orazio gave a gentle clap, his eyes welling a little. Frieda saw. How could they leave him! She would see him always like this now, she knew.

Orazio made to get up to clear the plates, but Frieda sprang to her feet, took them away, rinsed them, dried them and put them back on the table. They started on the other dishes, helping themselves, the children eager to get to the sweets.

When everything had been sampled, they sat back. Lorenzo jumped up and pounced on the children. They looked up star-tled—what now from the green red man who stood on chairs and said he was a king? He squatted down in front of them where they sat with their empty plates on their knees.

"Come ti chiami?" he asked the little boy. He had already been told, but he had thought of a game

"Diego, signore."

"E tu?" he said, turning to the girl.

"Mi chiamo Anastasia."

Lorenzo repeated the names slowly to himself, stroking his beard and making big round eyes — but how could this be, he asked, for if these were their names then they weren't really Italian. This caused a little outbreak of protest, and a playful to and fro of — sì, no, sì, no — till Lorenzo held up his hand . . . It is like this, he said to the little boy, Diego is a Spanish name, and therefore you must be a conquistador. And you, he said turning to the little girl, with a name like Anastasia, you must be Russian, and therefore almost certainly a princess. Now this was quite another matter. They looked at their mother to see if it was acceptable. Assent given, other games followed, and the boy-man crouched in front of the children, speaking odd phrases in Italian which he made up, nonsense phrases, and the children listened in wonder, and then he did the same in English, and the children had to repeat them, and soon they had entered into Lorenzo's world, kicking their legs under the chairs, waiting excitedly for the next nonsense phrase, smiling, even laughing a little.

He left them to play by themselves and came over and stood behind Frieda who was making a seated threesome with Orazio and Agnese. He leant forward and whispered in her ear . . . "and that is what war does to children." Frieda nodded, but without really taking it in, too busy with her own drawing room drama. She was sitting between them, making conversation. But she was brewing something, Lorenzo could see it, drawing her victims in, getting them to talk to each other—his little spider was sewing her web. Occasionally she let herself lean back, and the two innocents would continue talking, simple formal things to do with the land or recent harvests, but nevertheless. There was an age difference, this was true, but there were also two souls, alone, and children without a father.

"What are you up to?" he whispered, but she just smiled innocently back at him.

A little while later, when everything had been sampled a second time, and a few more glasses of the sparkling Maturano had slipped down, a silence descended on the room. "Angels flying by," Frieda whispered. She smiled at the children, repeating it in Italian and looking upwards, her eyes closing slightly, pretending to listen for heavenly wings. The children followed her eyes upwards, mouths open, straining to hear the wings.

Lorenzo roused himself again.

"Orazio, since when did gladiators wear blue velvet jackets?" he asked, then explained in Italian to the children that Orazio was really an ancient gladiator. The children looked at him, then at Orazio, wondering what was coming next.

"No no, I am Pappus the old fool," the velvet gladiator said, nodding his head and shrugging his shoulders. He didn't remember his performance of the other evening, but it was obviously something he told himself often, a self-castigation for the way he had ended up, a lifetime of errors as he perceived it, and his current state of decline. He made a foolish face at the children and repeated it in Italian: "Sono Pappus il vecchio sciocco." The children were getting used to the strange goings-on and asked their mother if this meant that he was a sort of ugly witch, like the one who brought presents on the Epiphany, La Befana.

Just then, there was a little frightened whining sound from outside in the stone corridor. The children stopped their questions and looked up enquiringly at their mother. There was another little whimper followed by a playful yap. Pappus, the foolish gladiator, got to his feet and left the room, coming back in a minute later with the puppy cradled in his arm, cooing and whispering into its face, the little creature all excitement, wagging its small soft body.

The children's eyes lit up. Orazio held the puppy in the air, then brought it down with a whoosh, and deposited the little animal at their feet. They jumped from their chairs and crouched down to stroke it, and the little creature wandered drunkenly round its new domain, the children scampering after, imitating the whines and yaps.

"Che bello! Che bello! Come si chiama?" they asked, excited, and Orazio told them its name, and the children knelt and hopped after it. "Leighton, Leighton . . . Vieni qua Leighton."

Orazio too bent over the puppy, strands of his long grey oiled hair falling forward over his face, and he added his hand to the children's hands, rolling the little animal over and tickling its tummy, while the little creature nipped at his fingers. Agnese watched silently. Giovanni, the while, had found his way to the fire, and was blowing down the iron tube, his eyes alight. Lorenzo sat perched on the edge of the table, a rare peacefulness on his face, returning Frieda's quiet gaze.

"Is it well?" he whispered to her.

"It is well," she replied.

"What are you doing later?"

"I don't know. I can't stay late. I have told my driver to come for me at eleven."

His fingers dug deep into the soft flesh of her shoulder. She let them dig.

"Do you think the world out there still exists?" she asked.

"No." He loosened his fingers and softly caressed the place of their crime, ". . . But if it does, it will have moved on without us, and when we appear again, if we ever appear again, it will not know us, it will not be the same, it will have forgotten us. That is the feeling I had when I was in the woods earlier, that I could just disappear . . . cancelled from history, from existence . . . never known. What is that?"

"Not even me . . . not even I would have known you?"

". . . And then I saw this magnificent beast with swept-back horns, and I thought I'd been visited by Great Pan himself." He paused, gathering the image back in front of him. "It meant something, I'm sure of it. It was a sign. Maybe it was my soul, my own very self. Maybe that is what I look like. What do you think?"

She reached her hand up and placed it over his.

"Giovanni knows. Perhaps you should ask him."

"Giovanni knows, but he can't tell. It's strange, but I feel like I want to be set adrift."

"With me or without me?"

She picked up the bottle and poured them a glass each of the white wine. It fizzed a little and settled. They drank it down in one. The bottle was empty. She got up and went outside to get another one where they had been left to cool. It was a relief to be out of the fuggy warm kitchen. She took a few steps over to the tree-circled little clearing, all silent, so silent. She hummed her carol to herself, and looked up at the tiny flashing points of light in the infinite ink-black heavens.

Across in the stable that was Giovanni's home, she could hear the sway of the white oxen in their stalls, softly lowing. She rubbed her bare arms, enjoying the icy tingle, shivering a little, and suddenly an inexplicable blissfulness welled up in her, a fullness, a sort of thankfulness, as if the universe in all its immensity was listening to her, just her, enfolding her in its embrace.

She dropped to her knees, salt-hot tears running down her cold cheeks and dripping into the ice-crusty snow. She knelt there, unaware of time, her knees going numb, her mind brimming, but somehow empty at the same time, her eyes wet, tears and sniffles and smiles.

She knelt. Time passed. The tear streaks on her cheeks started to freeze. A hand was on her shoulder.

"Did another angel fly by?"

She stayed kneeling. He rubbed her shoulders.

"I don't know . . . Perhaps it is you the angel. I can't see your face. Perhaps you have come to announce the good news, there is a stable over there after all." She held his arm and pulled herself up, lightheaded, leaning against him. She wiped her eyes and looked into his face.

"Well" he asked, "what do you see?"

"I see only a blaze of glory."

"You should be used to that by now."

She half laughed and half sniffled, and stroked his brow with her tear-wet fingers.

"Come, let's go back in, this heat and cold is not good for angels with bad chests . . . Come."

She steered him back to the door, picking the bottle of wine out of the snow on the way, and taking a last look back over her shoulder. Inside, the children were still playing with the puppy. Agnese hovered over them. Giovanni was prodding the fire. Orazio had lit his old cheroot and was watching the children, remembering the father, a quiet man who loved his garden and trees and gathering herbs with Agnese to make remedies and drinks. They knew the secrets of plants, not through study, just through natural sympathy, old ways—a man of the earth sent off to an industrial death.

Frieda stood in the doorway for a minute, then, the fresh red-cold energy surged through her and she swept into the room, her eyes still wet, but it didn't matter, it was the icy air, and she smiled her large smile. The moment was right.

She said something in German, half to herself, half to the room. She came up behind the children and brought them to their feet, then covered their faces with the palms of her hands to close their eyes, and gestured to Agnese to keep them like that. Then she strode from the room, ran up the stairs, came back down again a minute later, and placed three parcels on the table. The children's eyes were still dutifully closed. She took over from their mother, guided them to the table, and placed their hands on a parcel each.

They opened their eyes and looked over at their mother. She nodded. They started to unwrap the presents, for Anastasia, the decorated wooden spinning top and for Diego the model ocean liner. They were so just right, and Frieda smiled inwardly at the little notchy man with the cigarette in his mouth, and he raised his hat back to her.

From Anastasia's parcel another little packet had fallen out. Frieda nodded. She unwrapped the soft paper. It was a fine silk scarf in flowing greens and mauves that Frieda had bought in Munich long ago, art nouveau design, something that she loved, something which had seen many times and places with her. She wanted so much to give Agnese something but she couldn't really think how. Anastasia unfolded it and spread it out carefully, knowing it was something fine and expensive, unsure what to do with it.

Frieda looked at Lorenzo for inspiration, raising her eyebrows. He stepped forward and asked if he could take the scarf for a minute. He picked it up reverently, held it over his hands rather like a priest at Mass, and started to tell a story in Italian . . . This scarf had once belonged to a Russian princess, also called Anastasia, who just happened to be a cousin of Frieda's. It had been entrusted to them for safekeeping for a reason which they could not disclose, but when they found a certain beautiful young girl with the same name, Anastasia, they were to give it to her. It had special powers, the power to fulfil wishes. But there was a condition that went with it, the scarf must be kept by the new Anastasia's mother until the day before she was married—and with this he draped it over Agnese's arm.

Frieda turned quickly away and knelt down by the table. The wooden steamship stood majestically on its stand, Diego still looking at it in disbelief, hardly daring to touch it. Frieda reached out a hand, pointing out the features, portholes, funnels, propeller, encouraging him to join in, asking him what they were in Italian, till slowly he took possession of it.

The children played. Frieda watched. She was pleased. But much as she tried to stay here in the present, images of her own children kept swimming before her, and she wondered where they were, and what presents they would get this Christmas, and she prayed with all her heart that they would at least think of her, whatever their father might do or say to expunge her from their memories, that's all she asked—Christmas was a terrible time for her. She squeezed her hands tight together, holding herself in, till she felt an arm slide gently through hers and the quiet presence of Agnese by her side.

Lorenzo crouched down with Diego, looking at the ship . . . It will take you across the ocean to the new world, he said, patting the young sailor on the head, to Canada. Agnese gave a little start, her hand going to her breast. She hadn't thought Orazio would tell them about her dream of leaving, of taking the children, starting a new life somewhere, nor that they would be much interested. All that was left of her previous life was an inscription on the war memorial. But it had been his dream too, even before war broke out. Now, without him, it seemed an impossible dream, and she couldn't leave her old mother-in-law, but a dream was still a dream.

Lorenzo swivelled round and looked up at Agnese from where he was squatting. Frieda knew the look, could see the words forming, about to rush to the surface. She put a hand on his shoulder and gave a little shake of her head. He looked at her for a few seconds, then turned back to the ship. For once he had obeyed her.

Diego however was inspired. He would take command. He would be the captain of the ship but also of his family, the man of the house. He took his mother's hand—he would protect her, he would make those tearful sighs disappear. He was going to paint the name Canada on the side of the ship. He would take them there.

Frieda stood back, thoughts of her children subdued for the time being. How clever her Lorenzo, how just right his little narratives, bringing the gifts to life, the magic scarf, the ocean liner, how well they did things together, each sparking the imagination of the other, even if the Canada idea did conflict with her own one for Orazio. She felt happy with how it was all turning out, and a sudden rush of energy came over her, the sort of craziness that children sometimes get when they are excited, that makes them do funny little clownish things. She turned to Orazio and asked him for one of his stinking cheroots, and the old model handed her one, quite impassively. She bent down, fished a smoking brand from the fire and lit it, puffing away with gusto, flourishing it in the air. But the bitter smoke soon made her cough, and she held her throat dramatically, making big eyes, as if she was about to expire, then threw it back into the fire.

The children played. Anastasia had reclaimed the silk scarf and was twirling it around her neck like a grand lady, walking on tiptoe, arms and hands stretched elegantly before her, till she stepped accidentally on the paw of the scampering puppy. It gave a little yelp. She crouched down, caressing it, asking its forgiveness. Diego meanwhile was on the bridge of his liner dealing with a storm at sea, giving orders to his second in command, an old sea dog with long grey hair and a cheroot in his mouth who saluted obediently at each new order.

Giovanni had been shooed away from the fire and was sitting on his stool in the far corner behind the juniper Christmas tree, talking to someone only he could see, nodding, tangling and untangling his arms, playing with his conical hat.

There was still one unopened parcel on the table. Frieda picked it up, gave it to Lorenzo, and signalled with her eyes the little muttering figure in the corner. The man who told stories held the package regally before him, walked slowly over, and placed the gift on his knee. He didn't move, just stared back up at the storyteller. Frieda made little encouraging nods, but he just sat with his hands by his side, expressionless. The parcel didn't exist. He didn't have the mental vocabulary for gift, he couldn't see it, he had never had one, and he wondered what they wanted from him. Frieda tapped the packet. Nothing. She picked it up and started to take the wrapping off, and out came the lovely olivewood box. She passed her hand appreciatively over the wood, pointing to the flowing veins, then pressed it into his hands—a king must have something worthy to keep his jewels and treasures in.

Lorenzo took the small stone eye from his pocket and placed it reverently in the box—time to return it to its rightful owner. The little man stared, his hands resting on the casket, and there he sat with for the rest of the evening till his brother guided him gently back to his stable loft.

Orazio tipped a few chestnuts into the ash-covered embers, and Agnese crouched by the fire turning them and making sure they didn't burn. Frieda crouched down next to her in a sort of female covenant, raking and prodding, then, with true barrack room bravado, started to pick them out with her bare fingers. Agnese, horrified, protested, shaking her head, but Frieda was by now immune to pain.

Anastasia spun her top. It wandered away under the table stalked by Lord Leighton, who dabbed a curious paw at it, till it suddenly spun wildly away, and the puppy took fright and ran in the opposite direction.

Orazio disappeared out of the room. He reappeared a moment later with a mandolin crooked in his arm, a nice Neapolitan bowlback with mother-of-pearl butterflies on the soundboard.

"Orazio, what is this?" Lorenzo exclaimed.

The old model took off his velvet jacket, hung it behind the chair, sat down, crouched himself over the instrument and started to tune it by ear. Satisfied, he strummed a chord or two and looked up at his audience with a puckish grin.

"It has been a long time." He tried a few more notes.

"All the time we have been here and you have made no mention . . ." Lorenzo left his comment half said, sitting himself down the better to look at the instrument.

"It is a bit out of tune, but also am I a bit out of tune." He flexed his fingers, hoping they remembered their way, strummed another chord and a couple of vibratos, looked up at his audience, and started to play—a Neapolitan love song.

He finished with a little high note, rested the instrument on his knee and grinned around the room to wild applause and demands for more. He shrugged coyishly, took up the instrument, and this time started to sing in his gravelly old cheroot voice. And now Frieda and Lorenzo joined in too, Lorenzo's face reddening with pleasure — they had learnt all these Neapolitan songs years before in their little cottage in Fiascherino when their peasant neighbour used to come round and play them on his guitar in the evenings.

Requests were made, the old model played on, till his repertoire was finally exhausted and he brought the recital to an end with a flourish of high vibratos and a sheepish grin.

Diego lay in his mother's arms, eyes closing. Anastasia stroked the puppy on her lap, its eyes closing too. Agnese stood, lifting her sleeping son in her arms. Frieda insisted on accompanying them back home, taking on that male role that came naturally to her sometimes. Agnese protested that they could manage by themselves, but she was happy that Frieda was coming, and so was Frieda.

Chapter Twenty-nine

Fingers of silver light felt their way across the silent room, touching the softly sleeping eyelids, turning over thoughts, bringing dreams — a great mountain ibex, head high, full of power, infinite, momentary, eternal, horns swept back, ready to clash down all opponents . . .

The fingers moved stealthily on. The sleeping woman's breast rose and fell, eyelids flickering — she was kneeling naked in a windy desert plain of rocks and cactus and hollowed-out bones. She leaned forward to touch them, then they weren't bones anymore but a kite flying high in the sky, and she was holding the strings, trying to pull it back down to earth, but the more she pulled the more it soared, till it flew right away from her . . .

They woke late, a torpor of half remembered dreams mingling with pictures of the night before, and they would have indulged themselves longer if not for the sudden demoniacal wailing of pipes under their window—an irate mountain deity come to demand sacrifice.

Lorenzo buried his head in his pillow.

"Tell them to go away," he moaned.

"But I like it," said the female voice from under a drift of dishevelled fairish hair, "and so do you." She pulled the pillow away.

"No I don't, I hate it." He grabbed the pillow back.

"You love it really."

"I'm in pain."

The pipes stopped. They waited for another chorus. It didn't come. Lorenzo emerged from his pillow.

"Thank God." He breathed a sigh of relief. "How long have you been awake?"

"Just as it got light. But listen," she said, raising herself on her elbow and leaning over him so that her hair fell on his face, "you know what woke me . . . you won't believe it . . . something tapping at the window . . . tap tap tap, little rapid tappings, lots of them . . . tap tap tap."

He looked up at her, a suppressed smile playing round his lips.

"Shall I tell you?" she asked.

"Alright, tell me."

"It was a beautiful green woodpecker with a red head."

He pushed her hair aside to see what her face was saying.

"I swear it."

"A what?"

"A woodpecker . . . I was going to wake you. No really, it was . . . tap tap tap . . . very quickly . . . tap tap tap tap, and it was there at the window."

He put his head back under his pillow. "I will have to stop telling bedtime stories, they give little girls strange dreams . . ."

"No Lorenz, I swear it. I saw it with these eyes, with these waking eyes."

"So, the woodpecker god has come for us, is that what you are saying?" He emerged from his pillow, ". . . and I am coming for you." He pulled her face down to him.

"But you must believe me," she said, coming up for breath, "it was a woodpecker . . . just like you told."

"Oh my Frieda, I love you for your innocence. Such a beautiful child," and he took on his storytelling voice: ". . . My name is Mamerkis. I was born in the spring of that fateful year, and dedicated to the great god Mamers . . ."

"Giovanni thinks you are he."

". . . and anyway it's the middle of winter. There aren't any woodpeckers."

"Well then it was the Holy Ghost." She pouted, and turned her head petulantly away from him.

He gave a little chuckle.

"Any bird will do for the Baroness von Richthofen . . ."

"What do you mean?"

". . . anything that flies . . . birds, spirits, pilots . . . like your famous cousin. What did they call him . . . the Red Baron, and see what happened to him."

She pinched a few hairs of his beard and gave them an angry little tug.

"You shouldn't joke about the dead . . . and he was just a distant cousin . . . and anyway, a god in the form of a bird can come any time, even out of season, even in the middle of winter."

"Alright, I believe you." He sat up in bed, hugging his knees to him. "I had lots of dreams during the night too. One particular one. Do you want to hear it?

"What do you mean, too?"

"Do you want to hear it?"

"No."

"Why?"

"Because you said it in your sleep." She bit her lip.

"Did I? Then I won't bother telling you again."

They lay there a while, each waiting for the other to break the silence, to be the first to give in. She hated not knowing what he was going to say, but she wouldn't ask, not now.

Outside on the landing, the stairs creaked—Orazio on his way down to the kitchen. But this morning there were new sounds, little whimpers, and tiny paws scratching and sliding on the wooden stairs after him.

Frieda threw off the blankets. Lorenzo gave a quiet moan, grabbed them back and buried himself underneath. She swung her legs out from the warm rustling bed and paced barefoot across to the window for her ritual morning vision of the world and herself, peering into the drifting mist, making faces in the glass, a frown, an exaggerated smile, untangling her hair, grimacing.

"Is it springtime yet?" came the muffled voice from under the bedclothes. "Tell me when it is come and I shall get up."

She tapped the window, softly, muttering a malediction against the unbeliever. She turned back into the room and looked around for something to wear. It was impossible here, impossible to keep anything clean in the smoke-grimy kitchen, or up here. She had seen the women boiling up big tubs of water outside their houses, rubbing the clothes up and down on boards, squeezing them with their strong arms. Orazio wore the same clothes most of the time, the odd variation occasionally emerging from the pile on which he slept.

"I am sorry for my appearance," he would say, "but I have no woman."

Men could not do such things as wash their clothes for themselves, not here, unthinkable. Orazio would mutter something about old Maria coming and cooking up the cauldron outside when the snow went . . . When the snow went! Her Lorenzo would cause a revolution if they stayed—a man doing woman's work. He would be out there boiling away like a lobster.

They had managed to wash their bodies up here in the bedroom, a bucket of hot water in front of the fire, taking it in turns to scrub each other's backs, and Lorenzo would break into his Nottingham accent—just back from pit, scrub harder lass, and grunting a lot. Oh for Capri! Oh for the sea, warm blue water to plunge into.

She went downstairs in a pair of Lorenzo's cord trousers and a woollen cardigan. Orazio was on one knee in front of the fire, blowing down the iron pipe into a pile of twigs. He turned and looked up, taking in her male attire, a strangely sardonic smile passing over his old face. He would miss her. She would miss him. She was still curious about him.

The coffee pot simmered on earlier embers in the other corner of the big fireplace. He reached for it, stood up, poured her a cup, and went to spoon in some lumpy coagulated sugar from the encrusted glass bowl. She shook her head. He picked up the pan of boiled milk. She shook her head. This morning she wanted just pure black burning bitter liquid, she wanted to suffer a little, to shock herself into existence.

Orazio shuffled over to the cupboard and brought out the bottle of rum that had made an appearance the night before, and held the neck over her cup. She nodded—too good to resist. Wise wicked old Orazio. He splashed in a good measure, placed the bottle on the table, sat down, and gave a long sigh. He would often go into long sighing silences, they were a sort of wordless commentary on whatever he had on his mind and Frieda had become quite fluent at interpreting them.

"So, your last day," he said with another heavy sigh, his voice more croaky than usual after the night before.

She sipped her coffee.

"I loved the mandolin last night. I wish I had known before you could play. I love those Neapolitan songs," and she started to sing a few bars softly. He nodded his head, as if to say — yes, there are places, other places, not these lonely louring icy mountains, places where the sun shines and love songs float in the air.

"Come with us. Come to Capri." There, she had said it.

He didn't answer, just stared at the floor, like Giovanni when she had given him the box. Lorenzo was right, he was like a soul in Hades, sighing, remembering, longing—it had its own wistful beauty.

He looked over at her. She smiled, and settled in front of the fire, cradling the chipped cup in both hands, sipping the rum and coffee. The new wood wasn't catching well, and the smoke hung in the chimney, creeping back down into the room. She got up and moved away.

"It is the weather," he said, pointing upwards, "when it is like this the smoke won't rise. I apologise."

She came over to where he was sitting and put a hand on his shoulder. It made him sigh more—leaving was certain now.

". . . and after all the nice cleaning we have done. It is no use. You see." He looked around the kitchen, shaking his head, muttering to himself, and calling on Sant'Antonio, the patron saint of things lost.

She went over and peered out through the little barred window into the misty nothingness.

"Don't be sad," she said, her back to him, still staring through the window. "We had such a lovely party last night. That was the nicest gathering I have had for many months. It meant so much to Lorenzo and me. We lay awake talking about it half the night."

"Oh yes, just like an English soiree," he said, a cheerfully bitter self-mockery in his croaky old voice.

"And Agnese and the children. I think it meant so much to them. When we walked home she took my arm. She is lovely. Don't you think so Orazio?"

She turned and looked at him.

"Lorenzo says she is the reincarnation of the Madonna of the Steps. Do you remember . . . up in the village, the little stone waif sitting on the steps?"

He looked down and away. "The children . . . for them I pray. I hope your ship will indeed take them across the ocean, I hope it with all my heart. Yes, I will pray for it."

"And if it doesn't?"

"Then . . . Then . . . I don't know . . . Agnese without a man in the house . . ."

He had put a bucket of corn cobs by his feet. He started peeling them, throwing the sheaths into the fire, and the corn into the cauldron for the pig. She watched him for a while—corn, cut, cauldron, fire, corn, cut, cauldron, fire.

"Your wife, how long ago did she die?"

He had let the story out a little bit, not much, but now they were going she felt she could bring it up. He stopped peeling and looked over at her.

"Long enough . . . long long enough."

"Have you ever thought . . ." she hesitated, "have you ever thought about . . . ?"

"Ha . . ." he waved a corn cob in the air as if batting an insect away, ". . . she is dead, but she is not buried. I see her. She comes in dreams. I will never be free. I who wanted my freedom so much. It is fate. I made a promise to her. It is she who brought me back." He made a quick sign of the cross thinking Frieda wouldn't see, but she saw. She looked back out through the window, squinting into the billowing grey shroud of mist. She felt like running outside and yelling at it, fighting it, but it grew thicker, till almost nothing was visible.

Suddenly she jumped backwards with fright. Something had passed swiftly in front of the window, a black shadow. She spun round and looked at the old model, her eyes wide. Orazio looked back at her, puzzled.

"What?" he asked.

The front door creaked open. A gust of cold air blew in, and there in the kitchen entrance stood a beautiful fawn-like youth, pale delicate skin, long dark locks, lips slightly parted, soft yellowish-brown eyes peering back at her from under long lashes.

She stared, something warm and liquid moving deep inside her. He stared back, curious—a woodland creature strayed in by chance. Orazio, facing the fire, went on peeling, unaware. A soft murmuring of the half-asleep hens in the corridor made him look up from his labour. It all can't have taken more than a few seconds, but it seemed to Frieda to have lasted long minutes. The boy took a couple of steps into the room, loose-limbed, like a classical sculpture come to life, and all the while Frieda stared, and she felt an almost irresistible urge to reach out and touch him, to finger his curling black hair and soft, almost girlish skin.

Orazio dropped the corn and the knife with a clatter into the bucket, and came to his feet like a man drunk.

"Why . . . Why . . . Is it really you? How is it you are here? When did you come? . . . And without letting me know."

The youth turned his gaze slowly from the fair woman to the old model.

"Yesterday." His voice was hardly more than a whisper, as if he didn't really know how to use it.

Orazio stood for a few seconds, gathering himself. Then, with a sudden lurch, he came towards the boy in a sort of stagger and threw his arms round him, kissing his cheeks, patting his arms and shoulders, hugging him, kissing him.

"Let me see you. Let me look at you." He stepped back.

"Bello . . . Bellissimo . . . You are a man . . . You are a man now. When you left you were still a boy. Frieda, Frieda, look at him. Is he not the most beautiful..!" He reached over and pinched the boy's cheek in that Italian way. "Tell me about London, what you do, who you see, what you eat. Tell me everything . . . So beautiful . . . Bello figlio mio, just like I was, like your grandfather, he was handsome like you. It is so long since you last were here . . . How long is it? Oh I am so happy . . ." Words tumbled out. He put his hand on the boy's shoulder and turned him towards Frieda.

"This is my nephew. His name is Francesco, but we call him Ciccio. He is in London."

Orazio looked into the boy's face.

"Are you still in London or have you gone elsewhere?"

"London," the boy said, softly. He lowered his eyes. Words were not for him. Frieda watched, unable to take her eyes off him. She wondered briefly how he could be a nephew. Did the old model have other sisters? But it didn't really matter.

"Ah, but you will tell me . . . I will hear . . . I must have your news . . . no escaping." He pressed his hand to his heart, then he tapped his head as if he had forgotten something and gestured towards Frieda.

"This lady is my guest, she is . . ." He stopped, not sure how to introduce her. "Her name is Frieda. Her husband is upstairs. He is a writer. They are staying with me."

The boy's eyes flickered back over at her. There was a pause.

Orazio stood there nodding his head, then shaking it, then nodding it again, arms and shoulders rising and falling in disbelief.

"Still you carry the organetto," the uncle said, tapping a small wooden box-instrument that hung from the boy's shoulder, "still your best friend." The youth looked down at the floor, then raised his dark fluid eyes towards Frieda, and she felt herself flush.

"My boy!" Orazio exclaimed, and his eyes narrowed a little. "My boy . . . and have you perhaps news of another sort . . . la dolce compagnia . . . a beautiful young woman?"

The youth said nothing, just stood there, arms hanging limber by his side, and Frieda had the sensation that she was in the presence of another sort of being whose thoughts were hardly readable, hidden under the long lashes and faun-like eyes.

"So . . . But I will find out," Orazio said, wagging his finger, his face creasing into a smile. "You can keep nothing from me . . . I know . . . Yes you have . . . I can see it from here. Quanto è bella la gioventù!"

He nodded slowly, sighing his long sigh.

"Look at me. Is she English? Look into my eyes. She is English, I can tell. She is in love with you. She is pretty, a beautiful English girl . . . and educated," and the uncle probed and answered himself, and it seemed to be a game they both knew, old understandings.

"So when will I see her? Is she here with you? . . . Not here with you. Maybe you are right, this is not a place for English maidens."

The youth let his uncle ramble on until he felt the interrogation had finished, and then uttered his single word response:

"No."

Frieda was unclear which part of the Orazian preamble he was answering. It was all in the secret language that she had sensed at other times under the surface of this occult mountain people—a subtle movement, a hand gesture, an intake of breath, a downward glance, a hidden murmur deep inside.

The boy shifted his weight with an easy grace, and hoisted the strap of the organetto further up his shoulder, strong young arms straining at the sleeves of his dark jacket, and Frieda couldn't help thinking of the David, the Michelangelo David she had seen in Florence not three weeks before and which had brought tears to her eyes. He looked across at her with that yellowish look, and she felt her very marrow melting.

Orazio picked up a chair and placed it behind the boy.

"Why are we standing all of us? . . . Sit."

He nudged the chair so that it knocked the youth's legs from behind, and the boy lowered himself slowly onto it.

"Is he not a fine boy? . . . Bello figlio mio."

The uncle leaned over and squeezed the boy's shoulder.

"Would you have some coffee?"

The youth shook his head slowly. Orazio tapped his fingers, shaking his head still.

"Then shall you play something on the organetto . . . Shall you . . . for the lady? She will like to hear that I am sure."

The youth raised his eyes again and looked at her with an artless awareness, and Frieda felt the fine hairs of her bare arms tingle, as if a lighted match were being passed up and down them, and she imagined the effect he might have on pale fluttering northern hearts.

He unstrapped the little organetto and pushed his hands through the leather grips, fingers on the buttons, arcing the bellows. There was a sighing opening chord, then he played, all the while looking down and away, just a little shift of weight from side as he plied the instrument in and out. It sounded like something French. Halfway through the performance, Lorenzo came quietly into the room, an all-absorbing concentration on his face. There was a long final chord, and the boy lowered the instrument down onto his knee.

"Oh very fine," Orazio's voice croaked with emotion, "a real musician, not like his poor old uncle."

Lorenzo had seated himself on the stool in the corner where Giovanni liked to sit, a veil of invisibility on him. The boy looked at the old uncle, waiting for instruction.

"We will play another." Orazio thought for a minute. "What about la ballarella ciociara . . . yes la ballarella," and the youth struck into a lively dance tune, and Orazio clapped his hands and tapped his foot, and jiggled the unlit cheroot in his mouth in time to the music.

"Bravo Ciccio mio." He rapped his knuckles on the table with approval. "That is the ballarella. Did you like it?" Orazio looked at his guests, eyebrows raised, nodding and swaying still to the tempo. "Better than the bagpipes you are thinking." He chuckled. "Ciccio knows them all."

Lorenzo sat quietly, his head inclined thoughtfully. It should have surprised him but it never did. It was a law of attraction, a liminal place where realities met, the tangible and the imaginal, beings and events passing from one to the other. He knew he was here somewhere, the one whose name he didn't know, waiting to reveal himself—Alvina's beautiful dark man-being. No, he wasn't surprised, he knew himself the gatekeeper.

The writer watched from under lowered blue eyes, taking everything in, but the boy could feel the intensity of the hidden gaze, and he looked across at the newcomer, and it seemed to Lorenzo that in that look there was an implicit understanding, that he knew, that he recognised himself, that he gave his consent — and as if to seal the contract he opened out the organetto again and started to play, an English folksong, all the while holding the Englishman's steady gaze.

Orazio had gone quiet, aware of the silent exchanges, of Frieda's admiration, of Lorenzo's quiet concentration, and he sighed deeply, pleased at the impression the boy had made. He felt himself redeemed somehow, the boy's easy beauty evoking his own faded version, enhancing the narrative of his own past—this was he, the youthful Orazio. Good blood doesn't lie, that is what they said around here.

The youth finished playing and closed the little wooden instrument, buttoning the leather strap down. Lorenzo sat, unmoving, just the slightest nod of the head at the end of the piece. Orazio glanced over, wondering whether to introduce him, but he saw the writer's silent absorption, he knew his ways now, knew to leave him sometimes. Frieda meanwhile had decided she would try and make a little conversation, asking the youth about his life in England, just to hear a sentence, hear the sound of his voice, but nothing came, other than just a slight nod or a widening of the eyes, and a slow questioning turn of the head towards the uncle.

"Tell them," Orazio cajoled, but Ciccio just shrugged. "It is his nature," the old model nodded paternally, "he lets his music speak for him . . . Figlio mio . . . figlio mio." Orazio shook his head and muttered something to himself, a private inner dialogue. "He plays the mandolin too, much better than I, and he acts in musical dramas, sometimes sings a little or accompanies with his organetto. They like him very much, the audiences, especially the girls. Is it not so Ciccio? I have heard all about it. News travels."

The boy sat polishing the wood of his instrument with his hand. There was a moment's silence.

"How long shall you stay, Ciccio mio?"

"Une semaine," he replied softly in French.

"Seulement une semaine!" Orazio's face dropped. "Mais pourquoi?"

"Je vais a Paris."

"À L'Académie?"

The boy nodded.

"I am sorry." Orazio looked around the room. "He learnt French before he learnt English, he was saying he might go and work at the Académie . . . Oh but I forget. You speak French . . . Yes of course you do." He gave his head a little tap.

"Quelle Académie?" Lorenzo finally spoke. But again it was Orazio who replied.

"Paris was our first stop, the art capital, a good place for models, London came later. In Paris we learnt our trade. We were models for many artists, some now famous . . . Degas, Gauguin . . . many . . ."

"Gladiators turned models," Frieda said wistfully, "the decadence of time."

The boy looked over at her. She thought he might say something, but he just looked away again.

"But Ciccio mio, you are a musician not a model." The uncle frowned. "We must talk."

He shrugged. "Je veux voir Paris encore."

"And L'Académie . . .?" Lorenzo asked again.

Orazio turned his attention from the boy to his guest. "L'Académie Colarossi, signor Lorenzo. Filippo Colarossi was one of the first to follow the art road out of here . . . a model like me, but a bit before me. Then he became a sculptor and opened a school, an Académie, and it was a great success."

"How did he manage that . . . and in Paris?"

"Very simple. Women students." Orazio clapped his hands a couple of times in a sort of muffled applause. "Yes women students. For the first time in the great art city of the world, women students were admitted to the life drawing classes . . . nude male models and young female students. Mon Dieu! Quel horreur! It was a revolution." He shot an odd look at his nephew.

"A French revolution inspired by a vagrant Italian from a lost village on the edge of the wild Abruzzi." Lorenzo smiled. "Caro Orazio, why didn't you open an Académie in London? It could do with a revolution."

"I had not the talent . . . just looks . . . and now not even them." He put a hand to his face, running his fingers round his lined eyes and forehead, teasing out some of his long greying hair and sighing.

"You are still beautiful." Frieda reached a hand over and laid it on his arm.

"Zio," the boy said.

"What is it figlio mio?"

"I go now."

He rose to his feet and hitched the instrument over his shoulder. Orazio protested, trying to make him stay longer, but he would not. Uncle and nephew embraced, the old model's eyes clouding slightly, hugging and squeezing the youth.

"Come back anytime . . . Come back tomorrow . . . I have something for you."

———

Down at the torrent Giovanni bent to his task, heaving small boulders and rocks into the freezing waters. He had wandered a little downstream from the usual crossing point. The ice and snow of the past days had freeze-locked the mountains, reducing the flow of waters and opening up another fording place further down, much flatter and sandier. With a little skilful engineering it could become a temporary causeway, shallow enough for the donkey and cart to cross.

On the other side of the torrent the donkey stood patiently, hitched to the cart, flaring its nostrils, shaking and tossing its head in derision, till Giovanni unleashed a stream of lingua bestia at it. In the distance, just visible in the icy mist, a youthful figure with something strapped over his shoulder was picking his way across the water. Giovanni bent to his task once more, hands numb with cold, feet frozen, but he didn't care. He tossed rocks into the stream, damming up his new crossing-way, the waters welling up again, searching out paths through the sandy beds, through the sediment and stones. It might not last long, but it didn't have to, just long enough to get cart and donkey across. He would make it obey. He would be fierce with it. And tomorrow it would cross back again, this time with two passengers. He would carry them over, regally, not splashing around on foot in the freezing waters, and he would get them up onto the road somehow—he, Giovanni, knew how. It would be a crossing fit for a king. This would be his gift to them.

Taormina, Sicily.

Spring – Summer 1920

Fontana Vecchia, this the name of our new home, a curious old place with pretensions to be a villa, bricks scavenged from a Roman viaduct, small Roman columns flanking the entrance, gothic windows. But it has its charm, one being that it is cheap, only two thousand lire a year, and with the post-war exchange rate, well within my meagre budget. We love it. I have never felt so certain of a place. Already it brings good fortune — Women in Love is being published in America, Secker too is getting on in London. Finally things are moving.

On a height overlooking the sea our little temple place, surrounded by almond trees, in the spring the blossom something to behold, then falling and covering the ground like pink snow. There are carob trees and tall cypress, fruit trees, carpets of wild flowers, blue iris, deep blood cyclamen, narcissus and anemone, orchids, plumbago, roses, pink gladioli standing imperious and pale in the gold ripening peasant corn, rather like the foreign residents of Taormina, Americans and Swedes and such — not, I hasten to add, because the foreigners are lovely in any way, just that they stand out, tall and pink. Soon there is an abundance of apricots, nespoli, yellow peaches, dark cherries, almond boughs heavy with fruit, grapevines, and olives, always olives, quiet and silver-green, watching the centuries roll by, and away below, a shimmer of purple-blue—the sea, receiver of all our thoughts and emotions.

The house belongs to a cook who works at a hotel in Taormina, he and his wife our peasant landlords. Strange way round of things these days, a peasant renting to a Baroness — Russia in the ether — not really, just the age-old peasant way of thrift and gain. They live on the ground floor, while we are splendid above with our terraces. The rooms are big, noble, with thick walls that keep us cool. We feel quite grand. The sitting room we have painted green, blue the kitchenino. The furniture is basic, in an alcove a bust of Shakespeare and a clock, but we will buy more pieces if we stay.

The first days here could be cool, especially when the Scirocco blew, which is strange, considering it rises in the Sahara — grey mist billowing up the Straits of Messina — and I pile the big mantelled fireplace with pine logs and sit there writing.

There is a Capuchin church on the corner where an old stony road passes—the way into town. Peasants track up and down it, singing, or playing their reed pipes, like a classical frieze come to life, heading into the hills with their goats and sheep and asses, girls with bundles of corn on their heads, the original Siculi, here before the Greeks came, timeless, unhurried, watching the invaders come and go. And each time, just when the newcomers think they are the lords of the place, there on the horizon, more ships' sails, martial Rome, turbaned moor, chain-mailed Norman, and now other northern invaders armed with wallets and guide books who live in hotels, terrible to behold.

And up the hill the Siculi climb,
To pick the grapes, and make the wine,
And the glorious hosts they come and go,
Benedicamus Domino.

He tapped his fingers in time to his little rhyme. Through the window a straggle of wildfowl wavered north up the straits towards Messina.

. . . . I have got it all down now — Alvina, my fair English girl and her beautiful Ciccio. Finally I have a title—The Lost Girl. But

I hope I have not made her pay too high a price. Eight weeks it took me, just eight weeks, March to May — well eight weeks and eight years and a visit to a lost mountain world. Not long eh? She is so like me in a way, dead and rising again, anything but that other life. She knows it for me, lives it for me, but she carries the curse I cannot shake off. I can see it now. I must have infected her. I do hope it works. I have a friend reading it for me as I write. I await the verdict. I hope it isnt harm alone I have done them, she and her Ciccio — travelling player, dark man of underground passion but few words, the antidote to all that provincialism that would have smothered her. But I hope I havent been too cruel. I can be callous sometimes. I have a problem with resolving situations. I am pulled in different directions with equal force. I brought them all the way from England, and now he has gone off to war. But will he come back from that war? I have made him promise he will, but now it is out of my hands.

For all the long years she had to pass in that home place of hers, of mine — and which I feel I have made true — for all that, it is the last chapters I love most, there in those ice ecstatic mountains, the grand pagan twilights of the valleys with a sense of ancient gods who know the right of human sacrifice.

Here, by contrast, I feel like a lizard basking in the sun, and the writing comes so readily, I just flick out my tongue . . .

He shakes his pen . . . *except I have run out of ink . . . Sicily, ink dry . . .* He shakes his pen again, then puts it down and picks up a pencil . . . *and so letters will have to be lead based for now . . . And here we will stay, drinkers of sun, gazers of thoughts, charmers of time . . . And just for your delight, Frieda has become the goddess of pastry, the queen of scones. If we ever go back to England I will find her employ in a tea shop, or else we will open one ourselves, and it shall be called The Queen Bee*

Do come and see us sometime — we have room, and shade, and even a few shillings to spend . . .

He put his pencil down, a sticky-sweet aroma of pastry and cakes drifting up from the ground floor kitchen—the Queen Bee right on cue. Frieda learning cakery—surely it must be some sort of Sicilian spell.

She had buzzed down there one day, drawn in by the sugary sweetness, and now Gemma, the owner's wife, is teaching her the dark arts of pastry making, Sicilian style — and she will come up the stairs all proud and powdery, carrying a tray of treats, cannoli, cassata, but best of all, English Sicilian tea, cherries, scones made with polenta flour, clotted cream made with sheep's milk, jam made of figs. Oh the jam made of figs — soft, deep, dark, exotic, erotic — an English tea worthy of Aubrey Beardsley. Tea under a snow-capped volcano on the edge of Europe.

He gazes out over the bay . . . And what is that little vessel cutting a furrow across the wine-dark sea—the rhythmic plunge and pull of oars? Could it a Greek galley be? He raises a spyglass to his eye — Yes, Odysseus, it is he. And now the Ithacan shades his eyes and squints at the coast. Something glints on those far off cliffs. Is it foe? Is it some Trojan wanting revenge—a wooden horse bristling with spears? He looks again. No, it is a butter knife flashing in the sun. They row for shore—the irresistible aroma of English scones with lashings of butter, impossible to resist. The sirens are calling — Lash me to the mast. Too late!

How does one dress to receive Odysseus—the varsity blazer with rowing blue!

Signalling to foreign vessels again — the accusations that had got them into trouble once before — Frieda and her flapping curtains sending messages to German U-boats. She will try anything that she-devil—now it is scones. He smiles ruefully to himself, but at least he can smile.

And so the first weeks back in Italy — a few days in Turin, then on to Florence awhile, down to Rome, and then on into the wildness of the Abruzzi, to the noble little villa of the good seneschal of those parts, Orazio of the Cervi. We would spend the winter there—that was the plan at least. But we had to leave, too icy-mountainous, but not before we had been made a gift — such an unlikely place — and not before we had knighted the good seneschal—Sir Horace Cervi.

I am D. H. Lawrence, nothing can get past me—at least this what I tell myself. Now I am less sure. Frieda likes to quote me when times are hard. She has been quoting me a lot recently, I even heard her once in the night when she thought I was asleep, except she used her own name.

And so we left Orazio's and made our way to yet another English colony—Capri. Wherever we go it seems England clings on, impossible to shake off, like a virus. Poor Orazio was a terrible sufferer. He had picked it up while living in London. He suffered terrible bouts of it, like malaria, (I shall call it Anglaria—new medical term). Yes, even there in the land of wolves and bears, of mountain brigands, of wailing pipes and vengeful gods, even there, England sat in the corner sipping tea.

So Capri. Would it be here then our happy harbour, our place of places? At first it seemed possible, but a few weeks on Tiberius's ludic isle, and there was that urge again—and the needle started spinning. The Italians have a good word for it—scombussolato, uncompassed. Forget about True North, there is only one true point on the compass—True South. The south, head south, always south. But there wasn't much south left to head for. Europe was coming to an end. It would have to be soon. And then there it was right on the very edge, waiting for us—Fontana Vecchia, Taormina.

Here we are—Sicily, dawn old. Odd thing though, strangely homesick for Capri sometimes — sheer and sharp in the sea blueness, so beautiful, Naples, the Amalfi coast, afternoons with Compton at the Villa Solitaria, drinking, and singing English songs while Vesuvius fumes across the bay. Sorry he's not well. Wrote to him and told him to come down here for a spell.

Capri, so capturing, so restrictingly small, and not a little incestuous. Sicily is a continent compared, and here there is darkness. I feel I can breathe again, like letting your trousers out a notch after too much dinner, and I love the dark. I don't think I can work without it. I had forgotten. Capri seemed always alight, never asleep, like a laughter- tinkling cruise liner sailing through sin-filled seas, Captain Mackenzie at the helm, the passengers leaning over the rail watching the curling wake of wasted days flow by, but never realising that they weren't actually moving, too busy with the gossip, then down to dinner and the ballroom of never ending pleasures. Night games, cavorting in grottoes, blue-splashing and naked, Tiberius watching on. But it all gets rather tedious after a while, even the saucier stuff. And so onwards, and here we are.

—·—

"Sicily has been waiting for you since the days of Theocritus," Magnus told me. And for once he was right, the plumped-up little puck, pomaded, and popping up wherever I go. He is here, would you believe it? But for all his music-hall posing and posturing, he is still capable of insight. I should try and like him, but I can't.

But while on the subject of Monsieur Maurice Magnus, I must tell of my visit to the great Abbey of Monte Cassino. I had promised myself a visit there when I was at Orazio's, but couldn't get round to it.

From Capri, one morning, I took the dawn ferry back across to Naples, then the train to Cassino. High on its mountain top, the great ancient abbey, guardian of the world's secrets — and as I arrived, there he was to meet me, Magnus the Magnificent. From the backstreets of great cities, and the miasma of unpaid hotel bills, to luminous mountain-top monasteries — behold Maurice Magnus, angel of the hotel lobby and seeker of all-expenses-paid sanctuary.

"Do come, do come . . . Such peace up here." He had sent me letters. So I went. He had an in with the monks, prided himself on his connection, knew the guest master, Don Martino. He liked to think himself almost one of them, above earthly things, serene, untouchable, and he illuded himself that one day he too might don the habit, become privy to the world's secrets, hear confession, broker power, whisper great counsel, (for up there, emperors, kings, and popes pass through), dispense wine and wafer— Magnus il Magnifico, cowled and secretive and sinful to just the right degree.

He took me immediately to his friend Don Martino, the guest master, same age as me, tall, learned, multilingual, and they showed me down a long high-vaulted corridor to a stately stone-cold bedchamber. Then Magnus, already episcopal, escorted me learnedly round the columned cloister by Bramante, up the steps, through the thousand-year-old bronze doors from Constantinople, into the deep pietra dura dark of the great abbey church, whispered me down the steps of the crypt, the golden mosaic ceiling glittering in the silence — Magnus in splendour, who genuflected in all the right places and knew where the light switches were.

In the afternoon we wandered out over the hilltop, past the monastery gardens, through woods and over an old tumbledown convent, peasants minding their handful of sheep among the ruins. They were the old peasants, the hopeless ones who would never leave, and if you spoke to them they took off their hats and lowered their heads, as if you were a god they were not to behold.

I had meant to spend a week there, but after two days of the freezing bedchamber and Magnus's chatter, decided to leave. Back down the rocky path, Magnus scrambling along after me, pleading with me to stay. When safely away, I turned to look back, the great gold letters over the entrance portal—PAX.

The sea. Frieda is right. It is balm for us. From our Fontana Vecchia we gaze across the straights to the coast of Calabria that seems made of amethyst. On the other side of the house, rising up under heaven, the snow-covered peak of Etna, smoldering by day, then waking by night, shooting deep red fire into the blackness. England has not this.

A salutary amnesia is on me. That is what I need. Forget the English version of England, the English version of me, the English version of the world. Wake into new being.

There is a Greek theatre near here. We walk there sometimes, and Frieda — she is good at these things — gave me a new name, Lorenides, and it is true, I have enough material for a Greek tragedy now—my own.

In the garden there is a cave among the rocks. In the cave there is an ancient spring, the original fontana vecchia itself, welling up, up welling, bringing wellness. Also in the garden are the tumbledown relics of a little Greek temple. One morning as I wandered there I happened across a bearded man wearing a tunic, seated on a fallen stone, picking a thorn from his foot. I stood and watched for a while. He hadn't seen me. Then he glanced up

— Who was this strangely attired intruder in straw hat and striped pyjamas standing before him—a trousered Persian?

He jumped up — Has the Persian fleet arrived? Has great Darius landed? He shaded his eyes and squinted out to sea, the trousered intruder following his gaze, but when the intruder looked back, the tunicked Greek was no longer there. He had hurried away to give the alarm, to tell the tale in the agora. Maybe it was a message from the gods, the listeners say, or maybe it was the messenger-god himself, mischievous Mercury — Did his hat have little wings on it, or his feet? We should make sacrifice just in case.

Sicily, so old it is still at the beginning. Sicily, crumbling, invaded — Greeks, Romans, Moors, Normans — and still it is dawn, and still Empedocles is climbing the volcano, still standing at the top looking down into the crater, thinking about what he must do, launching himself into the depths, still flying through the air, still not reaching the bottom, two and a half millennia later.

Sicily, place of first places, dawn of the waking world. I too am waking. The first orange-gold of the morning sun touches my closed eye, feels its way in — and now I am up, breakfast on the terrace, toast and tea, butter and jam, linger and languor, soft mauve-blue sea whispering below.

Are we really here? When it is too hot we take our meals in the blue cool little kitchen. The garden is a larder, ever-renewing, a cornucopia, fruits of all kinds, vegetables. We could live here without going out. On special days, or Sundays, old Grazia — the owner's mother who shops for us — fires up the big wood stove and cooks turkey with potatoes and rosemary, or some other roast. We stroll into Taormina, a ten minute walk, past the women sitting in their doorways making lace and embroidery. Lunch sometimes at the Bristol Hotel—so good, and just a few lire. I have new sandals and shorts bought in Catania, and Frieda has had her teeth done. We walk, we eat. I am a tree, the sun on my leaf, and now the words that were frozen in northern constriction

are rising up in me like sap—that I should never go north again
I would care not.

Finally we have detached ourselves from England, well almost.
Here there are a few inglesi, but there is space enough not to be
with them out here in our Fontana.

———

Frieda at the window. She watches him going down into the
garden behind the house, picking tangerines. He stops, and
crouches down. Something has caught his eye—a blue iris.
Everything comes to life around him, jealous of his attention,
turning to listen — a prophet walking in their midst, this is what
she sees, he, unaware, innocent, lost in his world, a child in
wonder. Never had it felt so loved that little flower—or was it she
the blue iris?

There is a newborn goat of one of the contadini which he likes
to go and see. Walking back, he passes his hand through the
branches of yellow mimosa, snaps off a spray, plays it through his
fingers, brushes it over his face, over his hair, carries it back into
the house. It is for her.

———

"Oh you are so much better here."

He looks up from where he is writing, the scribe at his tablet.
He gazes quizzically over at her. She brushes flour off her hands
and wipes them down her loose cotton shirt. He is silent.

"So . . . words for novels, words for letters, words enough to
catch the wind and fly around the world . . . lots of words, but
none for me."

He smiles incredulously . . . "Fly around the world . . .
with the Italian postal service . . . Fly? Donkeys would fly
first."

She looks down over his shoulder. "Letters, letters . . ."

He covers his writings with his hand. She knocks it aside. ". . . Capri still, gossip still."

"Hark who speaks. It is she, the one who pronounces only Holy Scripture . . . every word a pearl of wisdom. Yea, verily, and I say unto you . . ."

She tweaks his ear, ". . . And this one to Katherine? Don't be mean to her. She is frail. She can't help being ill."

He jabs at her with his pencil but she spins away.

"Cats. That's what it was, a cattery . . . the Isle of Cattery . . . eyes in the rocks, paws hanging down . . ."

She makes a hissing sound. "You liked it too . . . chief cat among the pigeons . . ."

Fontana Vecchia,
Taormina,
7th May

Dear Rosalind,
My novel is done — primo.
I'm a free man from work — secondo.
Now what are you going to do this summer
It wont be so very hot here, this house is so
shady. But I do think we ought to meet some
where. How long are you staying at La Canovaia
Shall we meet in July — at La Canovaia,
or where Send plans.
My novel The Lost Girl is being typed
in Rome — going to cost *1000* Lire for typing
— horror . . . Secker says he is sending
Women in Love to print now, and The
Rainbow in early autumn, all being well . . .

Two big demijohns of good wine brought down from one of the villages on donkey-back by Carmelo, so good and so cheap—34 litres, one hundred lire.

The wind off Etna is blowing fair today. Here they say it brings separation, disruption. I think it auspicious. Let it blow — Etna, sparking red-orange into the night, drawing Sicily up from the wine-dark Mediterranean — Oh Apollo, what mortal could be sick or sorry here? But best be wary. Gods please themselves.

Today figs. I go down into the garden. Some fruit is low, but I ignore that. Who wants low-hanging fruit? Not I. I climb the tree, rustle around in the branches, the fruit comes away plump and easy into the palm of my hand, cool soft green fruit, eat some as I pick, peeling back the erogenous skin, red flesh splitting open, and I press it to my mouth and forget time—what is time when eating figs straight from the tree! And there are mulberry trees. I climb up to gather the big juicy berries. I am wearing just my swimming shorts, and the fruits squash against my body as I reach up, trickling thick and dark down my skin. Frieda says I look like a pierced Christ hanging there—deep red, purple, deep blood-red.

I come back in with my basket. Frieda is not there. I know where she has gone. The heat shimmers, eyes squint, everything blurs, rocks melt — she is down in her hidden place behind the cactus and prickly-pear, flimsy clothing lying on the ground beside her, body stretched out, offering herself. We are a threesome, the sun and Frieda and I. But I am not jealous of him, nor he of me. We share, and in the evening, red from his labours, he fades away crimson over the horizon, sated, feasted, gorged, fig, mulberry, wine, Frieda.

He is sitting writing. What is happening behind him? She is singing an incantation under her breath. He can hear bare feet on the tiled floor spinning in a sort of dance, arms flying. Is he about to be sucked under? Here between the rock of Scylla and the whirlpool of Charybdis, Odysseus approaching from one direction, he from the other, behind them both an epic of trials and denials, of false landfalls, they cross each other's bows. The Greek sails on, but the writer is sucked ever closer to his destruction. She dances on, then comes to a stop. He puts down his pen and waits.

"O great Zeus I have been spared, I have survived the whirl-pool."

He comes ashore. A beautiful witch is standing there, silent, statuesque, serene, holding a tray of scones with fig jam. She offers one to the seafarer. He eats it and is immediately enchanted. But before he sinks under her spell he just has time . . . "Oh enchant-ress, Is this the end of our Odyssey?"

Here we are . . . Eccoci qua. I think I will write a poem in Italian titled Eccoci qua.

I saw a picture in a shop in Taormina today, hidden away at

the back, forgotten. It was stretched on a frame, very nice, a grand old Sicilian palazzo overlooking the sea, nighttime, great yellow moon rising, tiny silhouette of a fishing boat below, the hills all lunar in the moonlight, almond in blossom. But it was the colours. Never seen them used like that. Can't get it out of my mind. It cost just a few lire. I think I might buy it. The shopkeeper said the artist was Hungarian — un po' matto, he said, a little mad, and that was in the colours, you could see it, but so brilliant. He said he had been sent by God, this artist, that the Sun was God, that he was the greatest painter of all time, greater even than Raphael. The shopkeeper felt sorry for him and bought the picture . . . many years ago now. Been there ever since. He said his name meant bones or something in Hungarian — the colours though, great silvers and pinks and greens and yellows, all next to each other so that they glowed. Maybe he really was sent by God.

—·—

Hope Italy doesn't go the way of Russia. It won't, but it will go off somehow, I'm sure, all those ex-combatants with nowhere to go, marching around with their tricolori, fascisti, cutthroats and what not . . . D'Annunzio's boys, the arditi with their daggers in their mouths. Italy is shaky, not here so much, but I read it in the papers . . . Milan, Rome. Saw a bit of it in Florence when we there . . . workers' marches . . . Talk of Italian financial collapse. That should do it. A land with volcanoes, the only one in Europe really. If it goes off, it will really go off. Etna is dreaming already, practising by night in case she is arrested by the carabinieri. As for the socialists, I don't care anymore. No, the bourgeois are my real enemy. That for me means England.

—·—

A lot of names with 'a' in them, Africa to the south, to the east the coast of Calabria, Aetna at the centre. I am becoming compass aware. That is good, it means I am at my centre. It quite thrills me the south, it is another Europe, not even Europe, or perhaps it is the north that is not Europe. Here Phoenicians still ply back and forth, fertilising land and sea . . . Asia is in the air. The north, what is the north! It blows off the Russian steppe. You never know though, if Italy really does go up, we might have to leave in a hurry, but not back to England, that is certain, not back there.

———

Fontana Vecchia, high in her almond grove over the sea. Fontana Vecchia . . . Fontana . . . Vecchia . . . lovely the words, like a first language, a sort of occidental Hebrew, but much more beautiful.

Odds and ends of English and Americans here, some Dutch, Swedes and the like, behaving like missionaries mostly . . . welfare of the benighted locals . . . while the benighted locals mutter against them and try and fleece them, nicely of course . . . a sort of tax for being here. Nothing wrong with that except when it happens to me. If you lord it you have to expect it. Italians always so ready to threaten law suits and the arrival of the gendarme if they feel word has been broken. But they have very stilted optic, they confuse hypothesis and project for contract, and run off and spend the lucre in their minds before its actually in their pockets, so when circumstances change and the idea does not arrive in port, they bristle with offence and outrage.

———

Sometimes we go for tea with the Duke of Bronté—known as Il Duca, descendent of Nelson. I am tempted to write something on him, perched up there in his palazzo on Etna. Aetna. The great naval hero was awarded the title Duke of Bronté for services to the King of Naples, which amounted to murdering some of his subjects for him, mostly Neapolitan nobility and such who had tried to overthrow the Bourbon King Ferdinand and install a republic, the ringleader, Admiral Caracciolo, hung from Nelson's yardarm. Meanwhile Il Duca pours tea on his terrace. Perhaps when Etna erupts, it will blow him back across the sea to Naples to face justice on behalf of his illustrious forebear.

—·—

Now it is summer, the wheat has been scythed, the heat is fierce, Taormina fans itself, indolence reigns. The locals lie immobile in the shade. The foreigners — gli stranieri — have mostly fled, and now the townsfolk, ever ready to grumble about them and accuse them when they are here, can't seem to function without them. They hate us and love us. We animate them.

A general torpor has descended. The Taorminesi have subsided like pythons after a feed, digesting in the shade. Everyone seeks shade. We stay mostly in the cool of our wonderful Fontana Vecchia looking out lazily through wafts of purple bougainvillea at the white shimmering mirage that is the sea and sky, or so they say. Why move? Why travel? I am drunk on sun and sea and light and night and fruit and Etna.

—·—

A little ritual of mine — I go down in pyjamas with my pitcher to the water trough under the carob tree by the wall in the garden. But today someone is there before me, claiming rightful precedence, a regal being, golden long, resting his diamond head on the bottom of the trough where the dripping tap has left a pool for him, his wide mouth cupping, his body arcing, slaking his thirst with soft unhurried elegant gulps. He becomes aware of me, looks up hazily, place and precedence his, tongue flickering, no hurry, and he arcs again, gums open, curving into the water, skimming over his own reflection—Narcissus making love to himself.

I should be frightened, his colour tells me to be, it warns

324

away. I wait, the sun waits, Etna waits. Up comes his head again, tongue flicking, lazily, looking royally around him, not concerned, taking his pleasure. He looks into the shallow pool, not to drink, but for a last look at himself, turns, loops back into the dark mystery of his subterranean palace. I pick up a log and hurl it at his disappearing tail which coils and whips with sudden swiftness back into his royal chamber . . . Why? Why did I do it? Ignoble being, ignoble human, and he a guest, a royal guest— the lord of life . . .

—·—

"Snake is you," Frieda says when I tell her. And she is right, the brindled one.

"Did I hear footsteps outside on the terrace?" I ask innocently.

"Oh god, not Magnus again. I'm not in," and she whips away snake-like into her royal chamber, into her blue grotto kitchen. It isn't he of course, I think he has gone away, but his name is enough—another log thrown.

—·—

I am worried. Sent MS of The Lost Girl to Rome to be typed, the only MS in existence. If it were lost..! — Italian Post so unreliable. Will make sacrifice to the god of the Italian Post Office—winged Mercury. Now that is funny.

—·—

Secker has agreed terms. Women in Love will be published, 1/= a copy for the first 2000, then 1/6 to 5000, then 2/= after. Fair wind off Etna. I was right. Fontana is indeed a well-full place. Truly she blesses us.

—·—

Our peasant landlord and his wife are going to leave us — off to Boston to work for two years. We will miss them, Frieda especially, and all the cake making, and just having them here below as we float above, terraced and turreted, royally regaled in imperial purple bougainvillea. I will profit by sending an MS of Lost Girl with them for the American publisher.

I think though it might be quite popular if the reading public can see themselves in it, like Arnold Bennett. But what to make of it? It depends which me is reading it, my centre is always shifting. I am so detached here that I am not sure which world I am in. Secker wanted to call it The Bitter Cherry, a play on Ciccio's surname which I have made Marasca. I stood my ground.

I am a little terrified for my Alvina though, left alone in those wild pagan mountains. But there was nothing else for it. We had to break away, she and I, whatever it cost, that or die to nothing, never really be, never know what lay beyond.

—·—

I love the sense of isolation that intense heat brings, cicadas filling the air with their zithering. In the garden giant marrows lie, huge melons, tomatoes. We can live without ever going to a shop, which is how it should be. Then at night, the sea is white and dark and lit yellow in the moon, like the painting by that Hungarian artist.

—·—

Down the stony path we scrape, down through orange and lemon groves with their great tanks of greenish water cut into rock ledges for irrigation. Peasants sit in the shade watching their sheep, or gathering fruit, quiet brown hands rustling in the leaves, tying, cutting, pruning. Terraces and gullies spiny with cactus and prickly pear. We scramble steeply down to the sea, sage and brush, tall wild fennel, aniseed scented, yellow asphodels and oxalis, and on we scramble till we reach the sea. We bathe. The water is warm.

I like it like that, but she, the Nordic nymph, says she would prefer mountain streams or something Baltic. I don't believe her. There is no-one else around. We take the sun a little, but I fear we might not come down here too often now, the climb back up in the heat is bursting.

———————

Time is no longer real, it is just a delirium of heat. The corn has been cut and they are treading it out with the asses, the earth rises in dry cloud-puffs, the ground is scratchy bare, the asses stamp and whisk their tails. Everything is withering to an autumn burnt yellow, just the leafy vines creep on greenly, distilling the sun's strength, giving us shade. The olives are their quiet eternal selves, unmoving, like the two soft-skinned plants with eyes lying motionless on the verandah, gazing out at the dazzled white horizon.

———————

Breakfast on the terrace.

"Last night I dreamed of the mountains, of snow, of wolves, of Orazio." She finished watering the geraniums and sat down. She looked at him across the table. A lilac dawn was rising over the opalescent sea, pale and beautiful. He stared out.

"What shall we make of him now? What did he make of us? What will become of him . . . Pappus the old fool? I miss him." And she pictured him, the old model, his acquired English soul with nothing to feed it, up there in that lost mountain world.

"Pass the butter over." He took a piece of toast.

"We are like two Victorian botanists, you and I, ever in search of new species, taking cuttings, sketching, writing up notes." She topped up his cup from the pot.

"You are in grand metaphor this morning." He spread the butter on his toast.

327

She sat back and ran her hands up and down her bare arms, picking here and there at the skin that had burnt and was peeling.

"You should be more careful down there on your little cactus patch." he said.

She shrugged, rubbed her arms vigorously, and threw back her hair. It had streaked and lightened in the sun. Her almond eyes wandered over him, that gaze that seemed to swim unfocussed, migrating with her thoughts. He finished a mouthful of toast and sipped his tea. There was a bowl of fruit on the table. He picked up a fig and held it up, looking at it, squeezing thoughtfully at the full skin, then put it down again.

"He is not alone anymore. He has Alvina for company, now and forever."

"Forever. What a frightening word." She shuddered.

He said nothing.

"We must send a card to him, tell him we have moved on from Capri. Can we send him a gift? I should like to send him a gift." She leaned forward and took a tangerine from the fruit bowl, balanced it on her palm, then rolled it across the table towards him.

"You think of something," he said, "a little view of Etna to keep him warm in the winter."

He put up a hand and stopped the tangerine from rolling over the table edge.

"By the way, I have started that painting I promised him before we left . . . Sir Horace in front of his Villa. Perhaps that will do. I have done a little mock up. I'll show it to you, only I can't tell if Orazio is the villa or the villa is Orazio, or which is forward or which is back, or which is past or which is future. That was you, you said that. Now I can't see it any other way . . . the Roman god Janus . . . do you remember, when we were outside under the stars that time . . . under Orion?"

She remembered.